PENGUIN BOOKS

If I Were You

Julia Llewellyn is the author of *The Love Trainer*. As Julia Llewellyn Smith, she writes regularly for the *Sunday Telegraph*, the *Sunday Times* and many other publications. Julia lives in London with her family.

D0229540

If I Were You

JULIA LLEWELLYN

PENGUIN BOOKS

For Sasha

PENGUIN BOOKS

Published by the Penguin Group
Penguin Books Ltd, 80 Strand, London WC2R ORL, England
Penguin Group (USA) Inc., 375 Hudson Street, New York, New York 10014, USA
Penguin Group (Canada), 90 Eglinton Avenue East, Suite 700, Toronto, Ontario, Canada M4P 2Y3
(a division of Pearson Penguin Canada Inc.)
Penguin Ireland, 25 St Stephen's Green, Dublin 2, Ireland
(a division of Penguin Books Ltd)
Penguin Group (Australia), 250 Camberwell Road,
Camberwell, Victoria 3124, Australia (a division of Pearson Australia Group Pty Ltd)
Penguin Books India Pvt Ltd, 11 Community Centre,
Panchsheel Park, New Delhi – 110 017, India
Penguin Group (NZ), cnr Airborne and Rosedale Roads, Albany,
Auckland 1310, New Zealand (a division of Pearson New Zealand Ltd)
Penguin Books (South Africa) (Pty) Ltd, 24 Sturdee Avenue,
Rosebank, Johannesburg 2196, South Africa

Penguin Books Ltd, Registered Offices: 80 Strand, London WC2R ORL, England

www.penguin.com

First published 2006
2

Copyright © Julia Llewellyn, 2006
All rights reserved

The moral right of the author has been asserted

Set in 12.5/14.75 pt Monotype Garamond
Typeset by Palimpsest Book Production Limited, Polmont, Stirlingshire
Printed in England by Clays Ltd, St Ives plc

ISBN-13: 978–0–141–01825–6
ISBN-10: 0–141–01825–9

With thanks again to Lizzy Kremer. At Penguin the hard-working and inspirational Louise Moore, Claire Bord, Clare Pollock and Rob Williams. As before, Victoria Macdonald, Kate Townsend, Ruth Davis, Sarah Smith and Frances Grey. Jana O'Brien – I'd never have finished this without you. And James Watkins.

I

Originally it was just Natasha and Sophie. They met at Betterton Ladies' College senior division when they were eleven and from the first day they were best friends. Both of them stood out in the class, Natasha because she was tall for her age and Sophie because she was from Newcastle and spoke with a weird sing-song accent that was quickly bullied out of her. By the time the bullies realized Sophie's stepdad was rich and she lived in a house with a swimming pool and tennis courts, it was too late. Only Natasha was invited to enjoy them.

Sophie's stepdad John had a son Sophie's age called Marcus. Initially, Sophie had little to do with him. Why would she want to associate with a boy who yelled things like 'he who smelt it, dealt it' and left muddy trails all around the house? Luckily, most of the time he was at his mum Nora's house, or away at prep school and then at Eton.

But then, Sophie and Natasha entered the world of puberty. They pored over the instructions on the Tampax pack. They studied the *Just 17* diagrams on how to apply eyeshadow. They giggled about lush George Michael and gorgeous Rupert Everett, oblivious to their idols' sexuality. (Natasha was even a little bit shaken when at the end of the decade she found out Freddie Mercury was not the marrying kind.)

Now when Marcus came back for the holidays, he was no longer an irritating irrelevance, but a boy from a major public school who knew other boys from major public schools and therefore had the ability to get them invited to parties attended by major public schoolboys, who – unlike Betterton boys with their bumfluff and acne – would look just like Rupert Everett or Nigel Havers in *Chariots of Fire*, wiping the salt spray off his lips as he ran along the beach, or Anthony Andrews in the TV adaptation of *Brideshead Revisited* (of course his character was gay too, but that bit somehow escaped them at the time).

Marcus, in turn, was thrilled to know two girls who knew other girls, whatever their background. Gradually, the three of them became friends: mixing advocaat and lemonade in his bedroom for sickly Snowballs to get them in the party mood, rolling spliffs, which they smoked under the apple tree at the back of the garden (Sophie and Marcus smoked a lot of cigarettes too, but Natasha had always refused – hadn't they taken in those pictures of diseased lungs on the walls of the biology labs?) and staying up all night watching videos of *Birdie* and *Midnight Express* and *Betty Blue*.

For a while, they became addicted to a game called If I Were You. Each of them would write their name and put it in a hat. Each then picked a name out. Someone thought of a question – something like 'If I were a colour, what colour would I be?' – and you had to answer it as you thought that other person would. Then the others guessed whom you'd been impersonating. For self-obsessed teenagers it was the perfect pastime – a brief insight into how other people saw you, which you could obsess about for hours as you lay on your bed picking at your spots.

'What kind of wedding would I have?' was one question Sophie came up with, as they sat in Marcus's room late one night, listening to the Cure and inhaling joss sticks.

Natasha had picked her own name. 'I wouldn't have a wedding,' she said firmly. 'I think marriage is an outdated institution. I'm going to live with a soulmate.'

Everyone giggled. Natasha was so obviously herself.

Marcus cleared his throat. 'I'm going to have a small wedding, just me and my bride – er, I mean my spouse – perhaps in Tuscany. Very private, very romantic, just the two of us and maybe the old lady who runs the trattoria in the square as witness.'

'Aaah,' the girls breathed. Marcus was obviously himself too – he loved Tuscany, where his dad owned a villa, tucked on a hillside near Pisa looking out over acres of undulating countryside. He was such a romantic, it was touching. Both were sure they'd meet a man of their own like that one day.

'Well, since it's completely obvious that Tash was Tash and Markie was Markie, then you might as well all know that I plan a huge wedding on midsummer's eve in Betterton church followed by a massive reception in the Betterton arboretum,' Sophie said. 'As many people as possible. A band. Loads of food. Everyone legless. And a photographer from *Tatler*.' And they all laughed at Sophie's irrepressibility.

Not that anyone was even remotely thinking about marriage yet. Sophie went out with a few of Marcus's friends, Marcus went out with a few of theirs and Natasha – well, Natasha wasn't really to public schoolboys' taste, what with her thick glasses and slightly intense air, but she eventually had her own romance with Steven, from next door, who went to the technical college in Guildford, so she wasn't a complete loser.

They were very happy times, until they were seventeen when Steven broke Natasha's heart and almost the same day Sophie's mum Rita announced that she and John were having a few problems and that she was going to go to her mother's in Exeter for Christmas – 'or however long it takes me to get my head together' – and Sophie was coming too.

Sophie couldn't believe it. Her mum had uprooted her from Newcastle and more or less insisted she embrace her new family. And she had done just that only to be instructed, at her mother's next whim, to forget all about them. She pleaded to stay at John's and at Betterton College, but Rita said she was her daughter and they had to be together. And very soon it had become clear Rita would never get back with John, after Jimmy, the barman at the Betterton pub who always refused to serve Sophie's gang, started visiting, every weekend and some week-nights as well.

Still, she'd kept in touch with long letters and phone calls (no email or texts then, impossible as it was to believe) and visits. When they all ended up in London after uni – or secretarial college in Sophie's case – they'd shared the house in Shepherd's Bush that John bought Marcus as a graduation present for several happy years.

Sophie was the first to break the trio, moving to her

boyfriend Charlie's place in Clapham. Then Natasha bought her own place, with the help of a lump sum from her parents. Then Sophie dumped Charlie for Andy and immediately moved in with him. For a couple of months she went completely off radar, preoccupied with her new romance. But more and more Andy started going abroad for work, and Sophie was back in their lives again.

And then a year ago, Marcus had met Lainey and fallen violently in love, and suddenly he was never around because he was always whisking her off on mini-breaks and staying in bed for whole weekends and doing the wedding list at the Conran Shop and so it was just Sophie and Natasha again.

2

Natasha Green looked at her Georg Jensen watch and felt a stab of anxiety. It was 3.53 p.m. on a Saturday in April and her minicab was crawling down Park Lane. A cold wind was blowing in through the driver's open window, but still she felt hot with panic. Marcus and Lainey's wedding started in seven minutes. Natasha was never late for anything. But she was going to miss this.

Her phone rang. Fumbling in her bag, she pulled it out. As she expected. *Sophie.*

'Soph, I'm on my way.'

'Where are you?' Sophie bellowed over jangling church bells.

'I'm coming,' Natasha promised. 'My flight got in late. I'm coming straight from the airport but the traffic's barely moving.'

'Oh, Tash.' Sophie sighed. 'I don't know what to do. You're not here. Nor's bloody Andy. Nor Mum. I'm trying to reserve a whole pew and Marcus's rellies are getting stroppy.'

'Well, there's nothing I can do.'

'Can't you get the tube or something?'

'Not really. I'm travelling with a huge great suitcase and a laptop.'

'Hang on a sec,' Sophie hissed. Her voice faded out slightly. 'Lavinia! How are you? Great, thanks! No, he's not here yet. He's working.' She came back in loud and clear. 'Tashie, sorry. I've got to go. I'll see you in a second.'

'I'm on my way. How's Marcus?'

But the line went dead.

Natasha sighed, looking down at her shoes. Black Bally pumps. Hardly wedding footwear, but what could she do? Her plane from Munich had been supposed to get in at 9 a.m., which would have given her hours to get home, have a long, hot bath, tart herself up and still have plenty of time to get to the church. But there had been 'technical problems' with the flight, which meant it had been delayed and delayed and then rerouted via Paris.

In the end she'd landed at Heathrow at 2.15 p.m. and by the time Natasha had left the airport it was nearly 3 p.m. and she had no time even to dash to the airport shops and buy herself something to replace her navy Jil Sander power suit that was ideal for a meeting with German TV executives, but not for a London wedding. Her wedding outfit, selected so carefully by Maeve, her personal shopper at Brown's, was hanging in the wardrobe back home. Why hadn't she taken it to Germany? She could go home and change, but then she would miss the ceremony and that was not an option. Natasha was furious with herself. She liked to control every aspect of her life. How could she have cocked up today so badly?

She pulled out her compact to check her face. Short, dyed blonde hair in a fluffy cut, a slightly hooked nose and pale skin. She blotted the oily shine with some powder, then filled in her full lips with her reddest Dior lipstick. She frowned at the result. Handsome was the best anyone could ever say about it; or striking, perhaps.

She stopped herself firmly. No one would be looking at her anyway. This was Marcus and Lainey's day.

Her phone rang again. Annoyed this time, she grabbed it. 'Sophie, I'm coming!'

'Who's Sophie?' said an amused voice. It was Dom, her deputy at Rollercoaster TV. Dom was her mate, of course, but there was an unwritten rule: they didn't call each other at weekends.

'What do you want?'

'Charming,' he laughed. 'I'm in the office and I need to get the file for the meeting with the Americans on Monday and I can't remember the password.'

'In the office on a Saturday? You sad, sad little man.'

'I know, but I have to go over it one more time. I've got a big night tonight so I want to reserve all tomorrow for my hangover.'

'Hang on a sec, I'll have to look it up.' Natasha jabbed at her Psion.

'So who's Sophie?' Dom asked idly.

'You know. My friend. The one you met in Jamie's that time.'

'Oh, her! The one who looks like Catherine Zeta-Jones.'

'That's the one,' Natasha said wearily. The car suddenly started moving forward at Zimmer-frame pace as opposed to tortoise. 'Dom, I have to go. The password's "superstar". See you Monday.'

'See you.' And he was gone.

As the car passed the Lanesborough and began driving down Knightsbridge, Natasha thought of what Dom had just said. Catherine Zeta-Jones. People often said that about Sophie. Before that, when CZJ was still a B-list television star, they had said Elizabeth Taylor — the younger version, obviously, with the violet eyes and raven-wing hair, rather than the bloated Betty-Ford version who wore kaftans and hung out with Michael Jackson.

'Who do I look like?' Natasha had made the mistake of asking once, over dinner, when she was about thirteen. Present were her, Mum, Dad, her sister Lesley, who was sixteen with a big bust, a perm and a boyfriend who'd left school already, and Sophie, who'd come round 'to do homework'.

'You're a *jolie laide*,' Lesley had said. 'Can I have some more, Mum?'

'What does *jolie laide* mean?' Sophie asked.

'It means pretty-ugly,' Lesley said smugly. 'Which you'd know if you were any good at French.'

'Don't be snide, Lesley,' Dad barked. And that was the end of that subject.

'What *does jolie laide* mean?' she had later asked Sophie's mum, Rita, who always had an answer for everything.

Rita had looked at her curiously. 'It means very attractive. Like, say . . .' Natasha could see her frowning as she searched for inspiration. 'Like Anjelica Houston. Gorgeous.'

'OK,' said Natasha. She spent a long time poring over pictures of Anjelica Houston after that. Gorgeous was not the word she'd use for someone with such a huge nose and ashen skin, even if she had been Jack Nicholson's lover for years. Anyway, in the end he left her for someone younger. And prettier, with a snub nose and tanned skin.

Of course, by now Natasha was used to living in

Sophie's shadow. She had come to terms with the fact that, no matter how many facials she had or designer clothes she bought, her friend would always be prettier than her, always have an adoring boyfriend on her arm. Natasha had to keep reminding herself that she wasn't exactly hard done by herself: she had a job as head of drama for the most successful independent TV company in Britain, which meant enough money to buy pretty much anything she wanted, an amazing flat in the centre of London and a hotline to the maître d' of each of the capital's best restaurants. With all that, who needed a man, who – unless you were as lovely as Sophie – would only sooner or later break your heart?

The car pulled up beside the church. Oh, thank God, there was Lainey, perfect in her long column of a wedding dress, keeping Marcus waiting as usual. Her father, who was surprisingly small, was holding an umbrella over her and looking flustered, while the three tiny bridesmaids giggled around her feet.

'Twenty quid exactly, darling.'

Natasha pulled a note and a couple of coins from her purse. 'Can I have a receipt?'

'No problem.' Slowly, the driver started writing on a little card. *Come on.* The group was turning in the direction of the church now. *Take your time, Lainey. Dawdle.*

There was a tap on the window. Natasha looked round. Waving through the glass was Sophie's mum.

'Rita!' she cried, taking the receipt and jumping out of the car. She hugged her tight, inhaling the familiar smell of Yves Saint-Laurent's Opium and Gauloises Blondes. 'You look glorious.'

She did. Rita's role model was Joan Collins and she religiously studied all her beauty books, imbibing huge quantities of avocado (fattening but so good for the skin), avoiding white pepper ('It's evil! Evil!'), smoking like a banshee (well, Joan looked great on it) and even obtaining a much younger husband. She drove Sophie up the wall but Natasha adored her, because, despite – or more likely because of – having had three husbands and a scandalous past, she always looked great and seemed to be having so much fun. Something, Natasha had written in her little black Smythson notebook, she really ought to have more of.

'Are you going to take your bags?' asked the cab driver.

'Oh, yes – sorry!' Natasha opened the boot and pulled out her grey Samsonite and matching laptop case.

'Darling,' said Rita, looking her up and down. 'This is a wedding, you know, not a conference.'

'I know. I've just got back from a meeting in Munich. Didn't have time to change.'

Rita laughed. 'Oh well. At least you'll stand out in the crowd.'

Natasha's mobile started to ring again. She glanced at it, then switched it off. 'Rita, that's your daughter. We'd better go in. She's saving us a seat.'

'I know. She's called me about eighteen times, the silly.'

Natasha suddenly got that wooden feeling on her neck that happens when someone is looking at you. She turned round. A stocky man about her age in a morning suit with a white streak in his black hair, like a badger, was watching them and smiling. Natasha recognized him instantly. Alastair Costello. Author of *The Silent D.*, one of the hottest novels of the past few years. Rising literary superstar. She'd always fancied him in photos, and in the flesh he didn't disappoint.

Flushing, she looked away.

'Come *on*,' she said to Rita.

'Coming, darling.' Rita blew a theatrical kiss at Lainey. 'Good luck, gorgeous. Break a leg.'

Rita had never actually been an actress; she'd gone to drama school but abandoned the stage to marry Sophie's father. Still, she'd never lost her taste for terms of endearment and odd superstitions.

'Heavens, I have cut it a bit fine,' she whispered as they entered the church. 'I just nipped into the hotel on the corner to buy some fags and there was old Milo Henderson. I hadn't seen him in years, so we just had a quick glass of champagne and I didn't realize where the time went. I *do* love coming up to London.'

'How's Jimmy?' Jimmy the former barman and Rita lived in a draughty cottage in Devon, where he restored pictures and she spent a lot of time watching daytime TV and driving into Totnes for coffee with her girlfriends. For obvious reasons, he hadn't been invited today.

'He's very well, thank you. Though I must say it's quite nice to have a day off from him. You can get cabin fever, stuck out together in the wilds.'

Natasha looked around and saw Sophie in the second row on the right, gesturing at them furiously. As usual, she looked devastating: in a blue silk dress, slit right up the side. Natasha glanced down at her suit, mortified.

'Come on,' Sophie hissed. 'Hurry up.'

'Hello, darling,' Rita said, kissing her. 'Don't you look

nice? You've always been so good at that English eccentric look.'

'Yeah, well, whatever. Mum, where have you *been*?' She turned to Natasha. 'Um, you look very smart.'

'Where's gorgeous Andy?' Rita asked, before Natasha could explain herself.

'Working.' Sophie scowled. 'As usual. I don't know who's worse – him or Tasha.'

'Is he? How boring. And on a Saturday. Does he never get time off?'

'He's doing something for the *Sunday Standard*.'

But Rita was on to her next object of enquiry, bending forward to scrutinize her former stepson, who was standing petrified at the front of the church. 'Oh, doesn't Marcus look handsome? Gosh, it must be . . . how long since I last saw him? Five years?'

'About that,' Natasha said.

'And is he still a banker?'

'Yup. Just like his dad. Dresden, Meissen, Scheldon. He's loaded.'

'Oh. How nice for Lainey. How was it they met, again?' Rita asked.

'In a club or something, I think. I'm not a hundred per cent sure. It's all been such a whirlwind.'

'Less than a year, isn't it?'

'That's right.' One day Marcus had been single, having been dumped by his last girlfriend for spending more time at his desk than with her, the next he had sent Natasha and Sophie an email saying: *I think I've met Miss Right*. Three months later he and Lainey were engaged and just nine months on here they were.

Still, Lainey was great: really, she was, quite unlike the identikit Sloanes Marcus usually went for. She was tall and skinny, blonde admittedly but with a short choppy style and a beaky nose actually not that unlike Natasha's. But while Natasha wondered every day if she was brave enough for plastic surgery, in Lainey's case, it just added to her already considerable character. She wore floppy ethnic trousers, vest tops, flip-flops and dowry-loads of silver jewellery from obscure boutiques, and before she met Marcus she'd been a dedicated clubber, spending every weekend away from the government offices where she somehow held down a job (although she never talked about it) dancing on podiums and swallowing vast quantities of chemicals.

At first sight, deep-voiced, dependable Marcus had seemed far too straight for her, but they had fallen so instantly and passionately in love that little lifestyle differences seemed irrelevant. Anyway, when you scratched Lainey's boho surface, she and Marcus weren't really so far apart: he was Eton, she was Cheltenham Ladies'; he was a banker, she was a civil servant; and no amount of pills and nicotine could dull her pink and white upper-middle-class complexion. And since the engagement, Lainey had made a big effort to tone things down, jacking in the class As, getting into t'ai chi, going mainly vegetarian and concentrating all her efforts into producing the wedding of the century. Initially unsure, Natasha was gradually warming to her, although they'd only met a handful of times, one of which was at Lainey's hen night in a club in King's Cross, which had to rank as Natasha's most hellish experience since her first month working for

Barney when he made her dress up as a chicken and hand out leaflets promoting the company's new quiz show.

Her thoughts were stopped short as her neck turned to wood again. She glanced over her shoulder. There was Alastair Costello – how come Lainey knew him? – staring at her intensely. Colour flooded her face as the organ struck up the Wedding March. Everyone stood up and looked around expectantly at Lainey, coming up the aisle on her father's arm. Marcus glanced over his shoulder and his frozen face melted away into a banana grin.

'Aaaah,' Rita sighed.

Quite unexpectedly, Natasha felt her eyes fill with tears. She glanced at Sophie who seemed similarly moved. They smiled at each other. Marcus, of course, was a grown man with a fabulous job and life, but to them he would always be their slightly bumbling surrogate brother.

'Doesn't he look cute?' Sophie whispered.

He did and the ceremony, even the potentially cringy Native American love incantation read by Lainey's dancer mate Taz, was very moving, although not so much so that Rita needed to sob theatrically throughout.

3

The reception was just five minutes' walk down the road, in a big Georgian townhouse behind Harrods made up of a maze of interconnecting rooms. As Natasha and Sophie walked through the door, a jazz band was playing and waitresses hovered with trays of champagne and cocktails. Lainey and Marcus stood on the landing halfway up the sweeping staircase, surrounded by effusive guests. Marcus's long-estranged parents John and Nora stood side by side, staring into space like strangers in a crowded lift; while Lainey's surprisingly Home Counties parents shook hands and made small talk.

'Wow,' said Sophie, looking around like a child in Harrods' Christmas grotto. 'How incredible is this?'

Natasha frowned. 'It's weird, isn't it? I mean it's not really very Marcus. Do you remember how he always said he wanted a tiny wedding in Tuscany, just him and his bride in the village square?'

'Lainey's way too much of the party girl to have ever gone for that,' Sophie said approvingly. Sophie had a bit of a crush on Lainey, second only to her passion for Nigella Lawson and Jools 'Mrs Jamie' Oliver: women who pottered round picturesque kitchens surrounded by equally photogenic children *and* were paid for it, even though their rich husbands made it unnecessary for them ever to earn a penny.

She tapped Rita, who was laughing uproariously with some elderly-looking guy, on the shoulder. 'Mum, got any fags?' She turned back to Natasha. 'I'm just going to have a quick smoke before Andy gets here and then we'll go and pay our respects.'

Rita handed her a cigarette without missing a flirting beat.

'Do you have a light, Mum?' Sophie said. 'Mum?' She turned to Natasha again. 'God, what is she like?'

But suddenly Alastair Costello was in front of them, flourishing a gold Zippo. Natasha's stomach lurched again. Not that he'd be interested in her: look at him, zoning straight in on Sophie.

'Thank you,' Sophie said, smiling sweetly. 'So rare to find another smoker these days.'

'Oh, I don't actually smoke,' the man said. He had a lovely Scottish accent, that spoke of glens and lochs and fine malts. 'I just like to be of assistance.' He held out his hand. 'Alastair Costello.'

'Hi,' she smiled, clearly not recognizing the name at all, just as a voice behind them said: 'S-Sophie.'

'Damn,' said Sophie, trying to hide the cigarette behind her back. A tall man was standing there. He had battered features, sallow skin and heavy-lidded eyes, all of which made up an oddly sexy whole. Andy. Sophie's boyfriend of nearly four years.

'So you made it,' she said coldly.

'S-Soph, I'm really sorry, it was a cock-up. I just couldn't leave this job.' He leaned forward to kiss her, but she ducked her head away, like Princess Diana when she presented Charles with the polo trophy.

'You bloody embarrassed me in the church.'

Alastair gave them an amused look, then turned to Natasha. 'Alastair Costello.'

'Natasha Green,' said Natasha, liking the feel of his smooth, warm hand.

'And what is your role here, Natasha Green?'

'I'm one of Marcus's oldest friends. And Sophie used to be his stepsister,' she added, gesticulating towards Sophie and Andy who were now arguing in low voices. She didn't know why she had to bring in Sophie, but men always wanted to know about her. 'And how about you?'

'Oh, I'm an old mate of Lainey's brother Geraint,' he said, nodding at a man with a pre-Raphaelite head of curls on the other side of the room. 'He lives in the States now, so I haven't seen him for years. Not really sure why I'm here. To make up the numbers, I guess.'

Normally when Natasha met someone she'd fancied from afar, she'd rather have pulled up her skirt and flashed her knickers than admit she knew their name. But Natasha knew a bit about writers, and she knew how to win their hearts.

'*The Silent D.* is my favourite book in years and years. I've given copies to all my friends.' Actually, that wasn't quite true: she'd found the book's tone a bit too flippant and heartless. It was very funny though. And anyway, who cared about a little white lie when it made Alastair grin so widely?

'You know I wrote *The Silent D.*? Wow. Makes it all worthwhile when you hear something like that.' He looked her up and down again. 'I like your outfit. It's – uh – very unusual.' He didn't sound bitchy, just gently teasing, as if she were an old friend.

Natasha flushed and then laughed too brightly. 'Oh God, I know I look a mess. I had to come straight from the airport. My plane was delayed. I was at a meeting in Munich yesterday.'

'In Munich? How glamorous.'

'It wasn't at all,' Natasha shook her head. 'Unless you think sitting in a boardroom from nine a.m. to ten p.m. with two twenty-minute meal breaks is glamorous.'

'What is it you do?' He sounded genuinely interested. She waved a dismissive hand in the air. 'I work in TV.'

'Really? Doing what?'

'I'm head of drama for Rollercoaster,' she said. It was hard to keep the bubble of pride out of her voice. Everyone knew Rollercoaster was the best.

'*Really?*' he said again, but just then Rita, who was still gabbling with the old boy, grabbed her.

'Darling, you'll know. Is it true Lainey is giving up her job?' she asked.

'Yes, she is.' Lainey had decided that the life of a servant of the realm was no longer for her.

'Excuse me,' mouthed Alastair Costello and disappeared into the crowd. Bollocks, bugger and damnation.

'And what's she going to be doing? Painting?' Rita persisted.

'Uh, yes,' Natasha said, her eyes still on Alastair's broad back.

'What are her paintings like?'

'I don't know. I've never actually seen any. But she's got to be pretty good to be doing it full time. She's going to have a studio in the new house.'

'I think it's marvellous.' Rita turned back to the buffet.

'Lainey and Marcus have bought a fabulous house in Notting Hill, apparently. Have you seen it yet, Natasha?'

'No, they only moved in last week,' she replied as a dinner-gong banged.

'Ladies and gentlemen,' bellowed Archie, Marcus's red-faced best man, 'please take your seats for dinner.'

'Dinner?' Rita said, glancing at her watch. 'But it's only half past five.'

'We're in wedding time,' Natasha said. 'You eat all your meals at weird hours and when you think it must be midnight you find out it's just gone eight.' That was her experience, in any case. Events like this could drag a bit when you were on your own.

They made their way up the stairs to the dining room, packed with tables with starched cloths and elaborate flower displays. Natasha was on the 'Ledbury Road' table. She checked the place cards: someone called Franklin Rivers was on her right side. No doubt Lainey's kind attempt at a fix-up. Why couldn't she have given her Alastair Costello? She glanced around the room for him, but he was nowhere to be seen. Instead her eye was caught by Sophie, two tables away, laughing with some curly-haired guy.

'H-hi.'

'Hi, Andy.' He was on her left side. Sophie had begged Lainey to put him next to 'someone he'd be comfortable with', since he was undeniably rubbish at small talk. 'How are you?'

'F-fine. How are you?' he said as the 'ironic' prawn cocktail starter was placed in front of him.

'Oh, you know.' She shrugged. 'Busy.' Natasha had a

degree from Oxford, but in Andy's presence her conversational levels were reduced to those of a five-year-old. 'What's up with you?'

'N-not much.' He glanced furtively at Sophie, but she was gazing raptly at the curly-haired man. He looked back at Natasha and lowered his voice. 'I'm off to Iraq next week, b-but Soph doesn't know that yet. She's going to kill me when I tell her.'

'Oh, right.' Natasha too glanced at Sophie. 'It'll be OK, Andy. It's your job. Sophie understands that.'

'Mmm.' When he frowned, he was more beautiful than ever. 'I don't know, Natasha. She keeps asking why I can't get a London-based job, like all her friends' boyfriends. But obviously I can't. Flying round the world is what I do. Still, it is difficult. I had to miss Clare's baby's christening last weekend and she was furious. Says she's sick of turning up everywhere on her own.'

I know the feeling, Natasha thought. But no one ever would know that about her. Natasha had gradually stopped ever discussing her private life, so much did she hate the pity in people's eyes at her perpetually single status.

'Andy,' Rita cried from her side of the table. 'Tell me what you're up to. When are you and Sophie going to come and see us in Devon?'

'Soon,' said Andy looking a little pained. Rita loved alternately to flirt with Andy or nag him about spending more time with Sophie. He never knew how to take it.

'Remember it's my daughter's birthday on Monday. I hope you've bought her something lovely. A girl needs cheering when she gets to thirty-two.'

Natasha was longing to hear his answer, but at that moment Franklin Rivers, who had slipped into his seat beside her, decided to start a conversation.

'So, uh, Natasha. How's it going? Franklin, by the way.' He was about half her height, with bulging insect eyes and an American accent. How flattering he should have been deemed a potential boyfriend. Still, she had to be polite.

'Nice to meet you, Franklin. Do excuse the outfit. I had to come straight from the airport in my business clothes. Must be early Alzheimer's.' She laughed brightly.

Franklin looked pained. 'My father died of Alzheimer's. It's a tragic disease.'

'Oh. Sorry.' Before Natasha could brain herself with the glass thing holding flowers in the middle of the table, she felt a hand on her shoulder. Lainey and Marcus, doing the rounds.

'Lainey! You look beautiful . . .' You could never say it too many times to a bride.

'Are you having a lovely time?' Lainey breathed in her husky sarf-London tones that belied years of expensive schooling.

Now was not the time for truth-telling. 'Amazing. And you're so gorgeous.' Natasha turned to Marcus, who was standing behind his new wife, his forehead shiny with sweat. 'Congratulations. How are you feeling about the speech?'

'Nervous as hell,' he said. His phone beeped inside his jacket pocket. He pulled it out and, frowning, read the message. 'Bugger,' he muttered. 'Sorry, Tash. Just a couple of problems with the office. Can you believe it? They never leave me alone, not even on my wedding day.'

'Come on,' Lainey said, tugging at his sleeve. 'We've nine tables to get through.' They moved on.

'Who do you normally fly with?' Franklin asked as the main course of salmon in miso sauce was placed in front of him. 'I find British Airways excellent, although it irritates me the way they serve the canapés after take-off. United on the other hand . . .'

Natasha could take no more. 'Excuse me,' she said, getting up and wiggling through the tables. The ladies' was downstairs. She spent as long in her cubicle as she could without people suspecting her of being bulimic, then brushed her hair out and reapplied lipstick. With any luck, by now Franklin would be boring Lainey's cousin on his other side.

She was coming up the stairs when she saw Alastair standing at the top. 'Having fun?' she said brightly, hoping he couldn't hear her heart banging.

'Yeah, it's great,' he said, unenthusiastically. 'Weddings always make me feel a bit sad, though.'

'Oh. Why?'

He shrugged. 'They just do. Anyway, Natasha Green, I was hoping I'd get a chance to see you again, because I'm going to have to rush away after the dinner. Friend's birthday bash. Shame because I'd love to have a good gossip with you about Rollercoaster. I've been a fan of the stuff you guys produce for ages.' Just then a tall woman in a long red dress snaked up to him and wrapped her arm around his waist.

'Ally, sweetie, I've been trying to grab you all day! How's Aurelia? Is she here?'

'Er, no, she's in LA this week.'

'Shame. Well, send her my love. I guess it'll be you two next. How long has it been? Six years?'

'Excuse me,' said Natasha hastily. She turned to Alastair. 'Listen, I'd love to have you writing for us. Do you have a card or something? We'll have lunch.'

'Er . . .' He fumbled in his pocket. 'No card. But here, this is my number.' He pulled the order of service out of his pocket and scribbled on it.

'Good,' she said briskly. 'I'll be in touch.'

She made her way back to the table where Franklin was sitting crumbling a bread roll, while Lainey's cousin ignored him. Alastair Costello had a girlfriend. Typical. But then a man like that would obviously be attached. That didn't mean she couldn't forge a valuable work link. Natasha was a pro.

As she sat down, a gong banged.

'Ladies and gentlemen,' shouted the by-now-pissed Archie. 'Prepare yourselves for the father of the bride.'

4

Sophie was furious with Andy for letting her down again, but she was also secretly relieved he'd missed the ceremony. Sophie had spent too many Saturdays standing next to him in churches, or register offices, or on lawns of country house hotels, hearing couples who'd known each other for half the time they had pledging their undying love.

The first wedding they'd attended together, she'd squeezed his hand during the soppy bits, but he'd simply yawned and stared into space, not embarrassed by her hints, just oblivious, apparently making no connection between the event taking place in front of them and their own situation. It was as if he was watching elephants rolling in hay at the zoo, rather than some ritual which *surely* any couple who had been together as long as they had ought to want to go through.

She was thinking this as she approached her table where a tall, curly-haired man with good teeth in a Paisley shirt and red velvet smoking jacket was sitting next to what she was pretty sure was her place. Suddenly the day brightened.

'Hi,' said Paisley, jumping to his feet and shaking her hand. 'I'm Elliot. And my luck's obviously in tonight.'

Sophie's eyes lit up. A harmless flirtation always gave her such a boost.

'Sophie.' She could just see Andy out of the corner of her eye at the table behind her talking earnestly to Tasha. She twisted in her chair, so his face disappeared from her line of sight. 'I'm Marcus's former stepsister. And since I've never seen you before, you must be a friend of Lainey's.'

He was, from Bristol Uni, and he started telling her about his job as the head of a small record label that had been bought five years ago by a multinational. Sophie was enthralled. All right, Elliot almost never finished work until midnight – since he was usually at a gig or schmoozing artists at the Oxo Tower – but hey, his bonus was double what she and Andy earned in a year and at least when he was away on business he was staying at the Four Seasons, Miami, unlike Andy who was usually dossing down on an army barracks floor in some war zone.

She laughed at Elliot's jokes, let him light her cigarette between courses, leaned forward and back when he did and totally ignored the old uncle to her right, but that was OK because he was laughing with some old aunt. As for the girl on Elliot's other side, well, she should have just made more of an effort.

Somehow, Sophie neglected to tell Elliot about Andy. But then he didn't ask. Anyway, Sophie always hated telling attractive men she had a boyfriend. What harm in keeping one's options a little open?

After the speeches, which consisted of all the old stories about the time Marcus had chundered into his grandmother's handbag and his slightly too intense passion for Lara Croft, Sophie sat back and lit another cigarette. 'Bit of a surprise, Lainey having such a traditional wedding, wasn't it?' she said, fluttering her eyelashes.

'It's typical Lainey,' Elliot said. 'She makes out she's so alternative but at heart she's as old-fashioned as they come. She hates work and now she's found her get-out-of-jail card in the form of a rich man to pay for her to mooch around Notting Hill all day.'

Taken aback by his bitchy tone, Sophie was rescued from a response by a bony hand resting on her shoulder. 'Sophieee! How's it going?' It was Maura, Archie's annoying wife whom he'd married when they were both about twelve.

'Good, thanks.' Sophie smiled without using her eyes. 'And you?'

'Oh, mad. You know, three kids. It isn't easy. They're with the nanny today, thank God. I had to bribe her with some Space NK bath oil to work on a Saturday.'

God, how Sophie wanted Maura's life, minus her huge arse. 'How's Andy?' she was saying. 'I saw him here somewhere.'

'He's fine.'

'Gosh, so you two *must* be married by now. It's been years, hasn't it?'

'Mmm.' Sophie tried to sound as bored as possible. 'We're not really into marriage.'

'Oh, I do understand. I mean, these days anything goes.' She patted Sophie gently on the shoulder, as if to say 'I see right through you.' 'But I can recommend marriage very highly, Sophie.'

'I'll bear that in mind.' *Now piss off, Maura, before I smash your face in.*

Maura smiled. 'I'm sure you'll be next. Keep me posted.'

Elliot watched the whole exchange, amused. 'So you're another marriage resister?' he asked.

If only you knew. I've been bloody desperate to get married for the past two years, but Andy's not having any of it. 'Yes,' she nodded. 'The whole idea makes me squirm. I hate the idea of losing my freedom. Being tied down.'

He grinned. 'I know exactly what you mean.'

Sophie was dying to get out of this minefield, but before she could get back to the far more enjoyable subject of Lainey, the lights dimmed.

'Ladies and gentlemen,' intoned Archie over a squealing microphone. 'Please gather round the dance floor for . . . the bride and groom.'

'Ooh.' Sophie jumped to her feet and darted across the room to the dance floor. The DJ had started playing 'The Way You Look Tonight' and Lainey was dragging Marcus awkwardly around the floor.

'Aaah,' Sophie sighed, then glanced at Elliot still sitting at the table. The girl from his other side had seized the moment and was flicking her hair madly at him. He was leaning forward and whispering in her ear. Suddenly Sophie hated herself for having flirted with him. He had probably found her pathetic.

The music changed to Little Eva's 'Locomotion'. With a whoop, some of the oldies shuffled on to the dance floor and started whirling around. Some younger couples followed. Sophie looked around the room for Andy, but she knew it was useless. He was far too shy to step out on the dance floor, let alone relax and be carried away by the rhythm. Sophie would just have to go for it herself. As usual.

So she danced and danced: to Deee-Lite, to Grand Master Flash and the Furious Five, to the Human League, the Jackson Five, Blondie and her personal favourite, Beyoncé. Sometimes she danced with whoever randomly crossed her path, but most of the time she was on her own. Occasionally, she ventured into the rave room, but the beat was too fast for her and Sophie hated dancing to songs without words. Out of the corner of her eye, she could see Andy still sitting at his table talking to a dull-looking guy with a side-parting. Natasha meanwhile was on a sofa pretending to be interested in Maura. It infuriated Sophie the way Tash never danced; she was far too frightened of losing face.

'What time is it?' Sophie yelled, collapsing beside her.

'Just after eleven.'

'God, is that all? I thought it must be about one.'

Minutes later Archie reclaimed the microphone. 'Ladies and gentlemen, prepare for the departure of the bride and groom.'

Everyone gathered at the bottom of the staircase. Sophie found herself standing next to her mother. Her mascara had run slightly but her hair was still immaculate. Joan would have been proud.

'Hasn't it been a gorgeous day, darling?' She was slurring, but only a bit. 'Where are they going on their honeymoon?'

'Tuscany.' Sophie glanced at her curiously to see how she reacted to this information. When Mum had been married to John, they'd had several fantastic holidays there. But not even a shred of regret passed over her face.

'How lovely for them.' She squeezed her arm conspiratorially. 'Perhaps you should move back a bit, darling. Lainey's going to throw the bouquet.'

'Mum!' Sophie glanced around furiously, checking no one had heard. She would love to catch the bouquet. Apart from anything else it would look gorgeous in the flat. But she couldn't face the nudgings and 'It'll be you next's that would inevitably follow.

'Here they come!' And suddenly, Lainey and Marcus were descending the staircase, hand in hand and incandescent with love. *Would Andy and I look so happy?* Sophie wondered. *But then we have been together nearly four years. Marcus and Lainey have only had a quarter of that. That glow always wears off.*

Now they were at the foot of the stairs. Lainey turned round to chuck her bouquet backwards over her head. 'One! Two! Three!' yelled the crowd. Sophie looked down as the roses and lilies flew through the air and landed squarely at the feet of Natasha.

'Tashie got them!' Rita exclaimed. 'How exciting. *Is* there a man in her life, darling?'

'Nope,' Sophie said shortly. 'Hasn't been for ages.' It annoyed her that Natasha was so clammed up about her single status; it was as if she no longer considered Sophie high-powered enough to confide in.

'Well, she's so busy with her career,' Rita clucked. 'She was telling me all about her new place earlier. Sounds divine.'

'It is,' Sophie agreed. Sophie had long been used to

feeling inferior to Natasha, with her brains and glamorous life, and the flat had been the last straw. She couldn't help comparing her and Andy's hovel in Harlesden and feeling hard done by. And if that didn't make her feel bad enough, she could dwell on Tash's job jetting round the world and meeting the stars, unlike Sophie whose day consisted of Harlesden, tube, office, tube, Harlesden.

'She's doing so well,' Rita continued. 'Just been in Munich apparently, and she's off to New York soon for a big meeting.'

'Is she?' Sophie said a little wearily.

'And she's looking so pretty, even if that suit is a bit of a cock-up. Poor Tashie. She has so little confidence in her appearance.'

'Do you think so?' Sophie was surprised. 'But Tash always looks amazing.' Before she could launch into how envious she was of her friend's army of beauticians and personal shoppers, an arm slipped round her waist.

'How are you doing?'

The warmth of Andy's body brought on a rare rush of affection. She kissed him on the cheek. 'Hi, sweetie. Have you had a nice time?'

'Great. Although I was thinking we should maybe make a move soon. It's still early enough for the tube.'

'Andy!' Sophie couldn't believe it. What was *wrong* with this man? It wasn't even midnight. The party could go on for hours. Though, when she looked around, she realized the DJ had stopped playing, people were collecting their coats (it was April and you still bloody needed them) from the cloakroom and the tablecloths, which had been so pristine and starched at the beginning of the night, were now grubby and greying. Still, she could see all Lainey's friends gearing up to move on. 'Tash,' she yelled as Natasha walked past them. 'How about a club?'

'Ah, no thanks, Soph. I've got a ton of work to do tomorrow. Got to prepare for New York.'

What was it with all these people and their work? Everyone took life so seriously. Mind you, Natasha had always been a bit of a goody-two-shoes. But this was *Marcus's wedding*, surely she could make an exception just this once?

'Come on,' Andy said, pulling at her arm. Sophie knew exactly what was coming next.

'Let's go out on a high,' she intoned as he opened his mouth.

Andy looked hurt. 'How did you know I was going to say that?'

'Because you always do.'

5

And so, ten minutes later, Sophie and Andy were sitting in a minicab on the way back to their flat in Harlesden. At least she had managed to avoid the tube, by stamping her foot and threatening to make a scene.

'D-d-did you have a good time?' Andy asked, reaching out and touching her knee.

'Great,' Sophie snapped, refusing to make eye contact.

'I did. A-and it's your birthday on Monday.'

'And why exactly is that a cause to celebrate?' Folding her arms, she turned away and stared out of the window. Bloody Andy. He just didn't get it at all.

She thought back to the first time she'd seen him, standing in the kitchen of Natasha's old flat in Finsbury Park, struggling to open a bottle of Dom Pérignon. As Sophie had walked into the room, he'd looked up and smiled, and she'd actually felt her groin twang. She'd never seen such an attractive man in all her life.

'Sophie,' Natasha said, 'this is Andy, the photographer I told you about.'

Had she? Probably. Natasha banged on so much about work, Sophie didn't really take it all in. 'Oh yes, I remember,' she smiled, graciously holding out her hand. 'How do you do?'

His hand touched hers. 'H-hi,' he said. 'Natasha hasn't

told me a thing about you.' *I can't think why*, he seemed to imply.

At dinner, she made sure she sat next to him, rudely ignored all Natasha's other friends and plied him with questions about his job. 'I-I don't really like photographing famous people,' he said. 'I like ordinary people who have experienced extraordinary things. They're my favourites. Recently, I did some pictures of a five-year-old girl who'd lost both her legs to meningitis. She was so funny and brave. I think she was my favourite ever. That's why I like war zones so much. The dignity of people who have nothing. It's so moving.' His stammer completely disappeared as he got into his subject.

'That's amazing,' Sophie muttered, gazing at him in the candlelight. She was sure he had loads of gossip about the supermodels and Kylie, but she'd get those off him later.

'It was lovely t-to meet you,' he said at the end of the evening. She knew he was going to ask for her number, but instead he just held out his hand and shook hers. Then he kissed Natasha. 'Th-thanks.'

'Who *is* he?' Sophie exclaimed when all the other guests had left. She had stayed on saying she'd help wonderful Natasha with the washing up. 'Does he have a girlfriend?'

'No,' Natasha said, bending over to put something in a cupboard. 'He says he doesn't have time for one. Always travelling.'

'Do you have his number?'

'Sophie! *You* have a boyfriend.'

'I know! I'm just asking.' Sophie had been going out with Charlie, a management consultant, for three years.

Once she had been in love with him but the flush had long disappeared and he was showing no sign of proposing. Secretly, Sophie had been scouting around for a replacement for several months. She grinned naughtily. 'I thought I might find him some work for the paper.'

'Bollocks, you might. You don't work on the picture desk.'

'Oh, give me his number. Please!'

With a show of exasperation, Natasha did.

She had never pursued in her life before, but with Andy she could tell she had no choice. It was hard work: he was always away on assignment, he was shy and – she now knew – his stammer meant he disliked picking up the phone. But she persisted and gradually his resistance was worn away. Four months after meeting him, she'd dumped Charlie and moved out of his pretty flat in Clapham into Andy's draughty conversion in Harlesden. She hated it there: there were no decent bars or restaurants within walking distance and the roof leaked and the walls were covered with Andy's dreary photos of refugees, but it didn't really matter because she knew that within a year they'd be married and have found a nice house in somewhere like Chiswick.

Or so she'd hoped, she thought bitterly as they pulled up now outside the old Victorian house, where they lived on the top floor. Nearly four years had passed and they were still living in this dump, and she was alone most of the time since Andy was always off taking pictures of war and disasters, with as much sign of a wedding as of Elvis's second coming. And now, if truth be told, Sophie wasn't even sure she wanted to marry Andy after all. His seriousness, his single-mindedness, his courage, the apparent glamour of his work, all of which had attracted her in those early days, were not necessarily qualities she wanted in a husband. Andy loved Sophie, but he was too far locked in his career (as well as being too broke) to provide her with the approval, attention and material possessions she craved.

Looking back, she acknowledged that a combination of fancying him rotten plus wanting to find a Charlie substitute had pushed her into a relationship which had never quite worked, but into which she had invested so much she couldn't just leave. Just like her Hobbs boots, which were a size too small but which she forced herself to wear, despite the agony, because they had been so bloody expensive.

'Christ, the gas *and* the phone bill,' Andy was sighing as he picked their post off the hall table, ignoring the mountains of leaflets for minicabs and delivery pizzas. 'Oh, but a few cards for you, Soph.'

'Oh goodie,' she exclaimed, examining the envelopes as she followed him up the stairs that reeked of cat pee.

'You can't open them until Monday,' Andy said, unlocking their front door. She followed him into the living room, with its little kitchenette in the corner.

'Why not? It'll cheer me up.' She ripped open the first. 'This one's from Mum.' A card of Marilyn Monroe blowing a kiss, which was how Rita imagined herself. 'To my darling Sophie, I can't believe I'm old enough to have a daughter of 32! Lots of love, Mummy and Jimmy. PS: Present's coming'.

'Yeah right,' Sophie sighed. As usual, the message was all about Mum and said little about her daughter.

She picked up a stiff white envelope. Inside was a card of a horse grazing in front of a country mansion. A cheque floated out. Sophie picked it up and studied it.

'"Pay Sophie Matthewson. One hundred pounds",' she read. It was from John, Marcus's dad. Oh no, she should have spoken more to him tonight, but he'd been surrounded by crowds of people congratulating him on his fine son. Being around John always made Sophie feel funny. After all, for five years of her life she'd been his daughter, or as good as. He'd picked her up from school discos when she was drunk on snakebites and told her off for getting her ears pierced without permission and now he was essentially a stranger again.

She showed the cheque to Andy. 'At least that should cover my mobile bill.'

'For the next couple of days anyway,' Andy said. She stuck her tongue out at him. Andy was always moaning about Sophie's extravagant use of the phone and had been appalled when he discovered how much she'd spent on votes during the last Simon Cowell talent contest. Once, she might have been secretly pleased to learn he'd been scanning her mobile bills but now she knew jealousy had nothing to do with it, he was just worried about money.

She opened the next envelope. A pink cat on a blue cushion. Sophie knew who it was from, but read it anyway. 'Dear Sophy, Happy Birthday, Love from Belinda and Daddy'.

'For fuck's sake,' she yelled. 'After all these years, the bitch is still pretending she doesn't know how to spell my name.' She ripped the card up and flung it on the floor.

'And why does Dad always get her to write it? Can't he send his own daughter a bloody card?'

Andy looked pained. 'Hey, hey, baby. It's OK. I'm sure your dad is thinking of you. And it's not Belinda's fault she can't spell.'

'If Dad's thinking of me, why doesn't he ever fucking ring me?'

Suddenly he turned on her, his sad dark eyes flashing with annoyance. 'Don't be such a spoilt madam. There are so many people in this world so much worse off than you. Why all the fuss over a birthday card?'

Sophie started to cry. She hated it when Andy got all self-righteous and angry with her. And she hated the fact he didn't grasp that tonight's fury was actually directed at him, that she had given up on Dad years ago when he'd married that poisonous witch.

'I'm sorry,' she sobbed. 'I'm just a bit over-tired.'

But he was kneeling before her, contrite. 'Oh, baby, I'm sorry. I shouldn't have yelled at you. Hey, hey. I'm tired too. Of course you're upset. Your dad's useless. But it's OK.'

It had been ages since they'd done it; nearly always one or the other of them was too tired, that was if Andy was there at all. But now they found themselves fiddling with zips, tugging at bits of underwear and ending up in a tangled heap on the sofa. Just like the good old days, Sophie thought as they lay there afterwards, both breathing heavily.

'That was nice,' he said in faint amazement.

'It was,' she smiled, much happier now.

'Still one more card to open,' he said.

'Oh, yes.' She reached out for the envelope lying on the coffee table.

'Oh. It's not a card. It's an invitation. To Josh and Lisa's engagement party.' *Josh and Lisa, who have been going out six months fewer than us.* Still, she kept her voice bright. 'It's a week on Thursday upstairs at the William the Fourth. Should be a laugh.'

'Oh. Right,' said Andy.

She knew that tone of voice. Twisting her head, she looked up at his face. '*Andy?*'

'I w-was going to tell you,' he mumbled.

'When are you going?'

'Tuesday morning,' he said sorrowfully. 'We'll do something nice for your birthday, I promise.'

'Andy, you only got back on Wednesday. For fuck's sake. Who are you going for?'

'*News Magazine.*'

'And why did you say yes? You promised, Andy. You promised no more trips until the autumn.'

'I know, but the money's fantastic, Soph. We really need it, if . . . if . . .'

'If what?' Despite her irritation, Sophie suddenly felt a little flicker of excitement. Maybe the proposal was coming now?

'If we're going to buy somewhere.'

Oh. Still, talking about buying a place was better than nothing. He is going to propose, Sophie decided. He just wants a little bit more money in the bank.

'We're so broke, Soph,' he was saying. 'And we need somewhere bigger if I'm going to have my own darkroom.'

39

Your own darkroom! How about the nursery and my walk-in wardrobe? 'How can we be broke when you're working all the time?'

'Soph, you know the money's crap. And y-you don't bring in very much.'

It was like dropping a firework in a furnace. Sophie jumped to her feet. 'What the fuck do you mean by that?'

Again, Andy looked contrite. Sophie was very touchy about her pathetic salary. She'd never taken work very seriously, because she'd always expected someone else to pick up the tab. He reached out for her, but she turned away.

'Baby, I'm sorry. I'm sorry. I know it's not your fault your job's badly paid. But it's just a fact. We don't have much money and I need to take every job that's offered me. Besides, going to scary places for months is what I *do*. It's me. You knew that when we got together.'

'Yes,' Sophie said bitterly. 'I did.' She turned away. 'I'm going to get ready for bed.'

As she brushed her teeth, she brooded on her situation. Almost thirty-two, unmarried, poor. How could this have happened to someone so golden, who had been promised so much? All through her childhood and early teens, people had exclaimed at Sophie's looks, saying she ought to be a model; the knowledge that such a glamorous and lucrative career lay ahead of her had prevented her from really trying at school. But when she was fifteen, she went to an agency, who told her that lovely as she was, at five foot six she simply wasn't tall enough. That dream shattered, she vaguely dabbled in the idea of acting, but when she auditioned for drama school they told her she had no talent at all.

She failed all her A levels – although Sophie blamed that less on herself than on Rita leaving John right in the middle of them – and ended up at secretarial school. There she'd fallen in love with Joel, who had his own car business, and spent four years with him, until it had fizzled out and she'd moved on to Carl, who was a teacher, and then Charlie. With each one, she'd fallen suddenly and violently in love, decided this would be it and devoted all her attention to being the best girlfriend possible, taking on menial jobs which left her energies fully intact for her home life.

People who had watched her flirting might find it hard to believe but Sophie had always been a monogamist, without even a one-night stand to her name. Nor had there really been any adventures: no backpacking round the world, no wild stories, no intrigue. When she'd heard some of Lainey's tales of hitching alone round Cuba or setting up a hair-beading business on an Australian beach, she felt half shocked, half jealous. But there was no time for any such escapades now, because they would delay her goal of marriage and babies, a goal which had already seen the thirty deadline come and go, and was now refixed on thirty-two.

She spat into the basin, then looking up smiled suddenly at her reflection in the mirror. Not too bad, she thought, casting a critical eye over the vibrant, dark woman in front of her. Recently – she didn't know why, probably because commuting took so much out of her and a posh gym was too expensive – she had started to get a bit heavy on the bust and hips and odd laughter lines (as they were so euphemistically called) were beginning to appear around her mouth. Sophie had always been used to being the prettiest girl in the gang, but lately – with Lainey on the scene and Natasha the recipient of the most expensive treatments money could buy – that position was in definite jeopardy. But tonight's sex had done more for her than any treatment. Her skin, which had seemed a bit grey recently, now bloomed; her lips were swollen to fullness; the lashes over her blue eyes were as thick and dark as tarantulas.

Happier, her mind moved on to Andy. He was a complicated, moody bugger but she did love him. She had to.

Lainey's advice had been to play the long game. 'Make no fuss; act like a perfect wife. In the end, he'll recognize what you have together.' Not that she could talk: Marcus had proposed to her in a fit of jealous passion after she'd gone on a forty-eight-hour bender with her friend Lisa. But Sophie had tried for years to prick Andy's jealousy, with about the same results you might get prodding a brontosaurus with a fork. Other friends said she should just issue him with an ultimatum, but the fear haunted her that if she did that he might simply agree that yes, he had wasted a lot of her time and perhaps they should both move on. And that prospect was too terrifying to contemplate.

She had no choice but to continue keeping her cool.

'Angel, you looked so handsome tonight,' she exclaimed, walking back into the bedroom. 'I was really proud of you.' But Andy was lying on his back, eyes shut and breathing rhythmically.

6

It was Monday afternoon and Natasha's cab was pulling up outside the Rollercoaster offices after a long morning out on location, watching filming of their latest romantic comedy series *Thrice*. Paolo, the maître d' of the posh Italian across the road, waved to her. It made her think of Marcus and Lainey in Tuscany. She pulled her phone from her pocket but then slipped it back in again. She couldn't disturb them on honeymoon.

Natasha would have loved a wedding post-mortem, but she also wanted to find out way, way more about Alastair Costello. How well did Lainey know him? How serious was his relationship? As soon as she got home could she please organize a dinner where Natasha happened to be placed next to him?

In their little glass office, guarded at the entrance by their assistant Emilia, Dom was munching on a goat's cheese baguette and reading *Media Guardian*.

'All right?' he said, glancing up. 'How was *Thrice?*'

'Not great. I'm really not sure about the dialogue. We're going to have to look at some of the rushes later and make a decision. How's it been going here?'

'Not too badly, actually . . .' Dom's mobile bleeped. 'Oh, hang on a second.' He picked it up, read the message and rolled his eyes theatrically. 'This woman is a nightmare,' he said. 'She just doesn't know when to stop.'

'Is this your future wife?' Natasha asked caustically.

Dom categorized women into two types: women to shag then dump, and future wives. Of course, as soon as he'd shagged the future wives they fell into the first category. That anyone wanted to shag him at all, given that he was gangly, jug-eared and had a face like a potato, was one of life's great mysteries, up there with the *Marie Celeste*. Yet all day his phone bleeped and his inbox pinged with messages from a stream of fantastically gorgeous girlfriends whom he treated appallingly and who usually ended up stalking him. One had even had to be issued a restraining order. Natasha had learned a lot from Dom about what men wanted from women, which seemed to be complete indifference. Asking them if they were free at the weekend was a bigger turn-off than confessing to genital warts. Natasha had recorded this in her Smythson notebook, for reference if she was ever foolish enough to have another relationship.

'The lawyer,' he replied now, frowning at his screen. 'Did I say she was a future wife?'

'I think so.'

'Hmm. Well, she's not. Way too eager and in any case, it can't go anywhere because her family are Hindus and they want her to have an arranged marriage. Anyway, I've got this nurse on the go as well. The lawyer's much classier – more beautiful too, but the nurse is way more dirty.'

'Do these women have names?' Natasha didn't know why she was asking. She'd stopped bothering to memorize Dom's girlfriends' names years ago, just like she'd stopped going out of her way to be friendly to them.

Why bother when their shelf life was shorter than that of a yoghurt carton?

'Of course they have names . . . Oh, hang on a sec.' His phone had bleeped again. He read the message and grinned. 'OK. Stalker alert.'

He was dying to show her. 'Let me see,' she sighed.

So how abt 2night?

'Dom! That's not stalking. That's a polite request to see you.'

He shrugged. 'Whatever. Anyway, I'm busy tonight. I have an urgent appointment with *Coronation Street*.'

The next message was from Mike, whoever he was. Nosily, she opened it.

I want u now, lick me, bite me, cum all over my face and tits.

'Dom! Who the hell is Mike?'

Scarlet, Dom snatched the phone away from her. 'That's not a bloke, that's the nurse!'

'A male nurse?' A big grin spread over Natasha's face. 'Dom, is there something you're not telling me?'

'No! She's a woman. Her name's Michelle. But I put her in my phone as Mike in case Sharmila was snooping.'

'But wouldn't it be worse if Sharmila thought you were getting texts like that from a male nurse called Mike?'

'Oh God. I hadn't thought of that.'

Natasha sighed. 'Dom, if you don't want Sharmila to read the nurse's texts, why don't you just delete them?'

'Yeah, I could, I guess.' Dom didn't look convinced. Natasha didn't press it. She knew he wanted to keep the texts because they made him feel like a stud, just like she kept every Valentine she'd ever received – all three of them, of which two were from Christian, the dweeb who lived downstairs from her in college and kept her awake at nights playing Motorhead. The third she suspected was from Marcus, to make up for the year they were house-sharing when he received eight cards from wannabe bankers' wives and Natasha got a summons for non-payment of the council tax.

'Delete them,' she repeated, swatting Dom over the head with the file.

'So how was the wedding?' he asked, holding out his hands to protect himself.

'Good. Oh,' she added, unable to resist a mention. 'And guess who I met? Alastair Costello.'

'What, *The Silent D.* guy?'

'Mmm.' She looked down, hoping he couldn't see her blushing. 'I'm going to take him out to lunch. Get him writing for us.'

The phone started ringing. 'Here he is now,' Dom said.

Despite herself, her pulse accelerated. She picked up the phone.

'Natasha Green?' she said huskily.

'Hello, angel, how are you?'

Mum. Natasha felt a stab of guilt. 'Hi, I'm sorry I haven't called. It's just been frantic today.'

'I know, darling,' Mum said apologetically. 'And I'm sorry to disturb you. I was just wondering how the wedding went?'

Having known Marcus since childhood, Mum had been a bit miffed not to be invited to the wedding. Natasha had had to explain at length about limited numbers, while the shameful truth niggled at the back of her mind that she'd positively discouraged Lainey from inviting her parents because they would stress her.

'It was great. Lovely. Lainey looked gorgeous.'

'Oh, I'm sure she did. I can't wait to see the pictures. And were there any nice people there?'

What she meant was men. Natasha's neck prickled in irritation. How come Rita was so interested in her career and Mum didn't give a toss about anything except her bringing home a nice barrister? Jane Austen was dead, for God's sake. The world had moved on, except at 22 Crossley Crescent, Betterton, Surrey. Other parents got divorced and other mothers were desperate housewives, but Natasha's parents still snuggled up to each other in front of the telly and her mum was gloriously fulfilled baking cakes, polishing floors and sitting on Women's Institute committees and hated the fact her younger daughter was missing out on such happiness.

'Lots of nice people,' she said firmly. 'It was a wonderful day. I'll tell you all about it when I see you.'

'And when will that be?' Mum pounced.

'Oh Mum, I don't know. Not next weekend, I'm going to New York. And the weekend after I may have to go to Zurich.'

'Have you been watching the tennis?' Mum asked, as usual not acknowledging her daughter's glamorous itinerary. 'That Martina Navratilova is amazing, eh? And she seems very happy in her private life too.'

'I'm not really into tennis.'

There were voices in the background. 'Oh. Lesley wants a word.'

Natasha's heart sank. Lesley, her sister, married to

boring Geoff and living with her two daughters just down the road from Mum. Natasha loved her, but sometimes it was hard to remember that.

'Hello,' Lesley said. As usual her tone was a mixture of superiority and aggrievedness. Lesley had never really got over her plainer, younger sister ending up living the glamorous London life. 'Fancy wedding, huh? Must have been fun.'

'It was, it—'

'What did you wear?'

'Um, actually I'd just got back from a meeting in Munich and there was no time to change, so I had to wear a work suit. I felt like a right idiot.' Natasha always played the humility card with Lesley.

It worked. 'You always were hopeless,' she snorted, sounding much happier. 'Well, nothing to report from here. Geoff's getting a raise at the end of the month. And we're off to Tenerife on Saturday.'

'That's brilliant,' Natasha gushed.

'Have you been there? We're staying in a five-star resort. Great kids' club. Mind you, that won't mean much to such a jet-setter.'

'Oh, it'll be gorgeous. Lucky you.'

'So any nice men at the wedding?'

'I just told Mum, no.'

'Hmmm. You need to get a move on, Tash. The girls are always asking when they're going to get a cousin.'

Natasha shut her eyes and squeezed her palms tightly. 'Listen, Les, I have to go. Send my love to Dad. Talk soon.'

She hung up, infuriated. *Breathe, breathe, Natasha. They*

don't mean to wind you up. But why couldn't they praise her for her success, rather than dwelling on her failure to find a man?

Gulping, as if she was about to dive from the highest board, she pulled the order of service sheet out of her bag and dialled Alastair Costello's number. It went straight to voicemail. 'Hi. I'll call you back,' said his peaty tones.

'Oh, hello,' she said. 'This is Natasha Green from Rollercoaster. We met on Saturday. So, just calling to see if you would be interested in meeting sometime to talk about doing some possible work for us. Yes. Work. So. Good. Lovely. Hope to speak to you soon.'

She left her number and hung up feeling as if she'd just run up Ben Nevis. Which was ridiculous. She made work calls every day. And everyone else called her back. Because Natasha Green was a powerful figure in the TV industry and people wanted her patronage. She just hoped Alastair wanted something more.

7

At mid-morning that same Monday, Sophie, the birthday girl, was sitting at her desk, absorbed in her third game of minesweeper (advanced level). On her desk sat a can of Diet Coke, three cards, a scented candle (from her office mates Caroline and Fay) and the latest edition of *OK!* She ought to hand it on to Yvette, her boss, but she was buggered if she'd do that before she'd read it. She needed some birthday treats. So far, they had been less than satisfactory. She'd opened her presents that morning: a scented candle from Mum, a scented candle from Andy's mum (the first time the old moose had deigned to acknowledge her birthday, so that was something) and a scented candle (well, actually a set of them and bloody nice Eau d'Hadrien ones but still . . .) from Natasha.

At least they'd made more of an effort than Andy, who'd left the house before she'd even properly woken up, with a kiss on her forehead and a promise that he'd have something for her by tonight. He'd bloody better, Sophie thought grimly, and not a plain navy scarf like last year. Deep down, of course, she was hoping for a ring.

'I think today it's going to be the salmon and rocket,' mused Caroline, who sat opposite her. 'Or the no-bread sandwich. That sounds healthy, doesn't it?'

'A "no-bread sandwich"?' snapped Yvette, who sat on the end terminal. 'Isn't that what they used to call salad?'

'Bollocks to all that healthy stuff,' squawked Fay, appearing behind her. Fay was twenty-five and looked like a member of a girl band with chestnut hair and a pierced belly that protruded slightly over the edge of her waistband. 'I'm going for a cigarette. Anyone care to join me?'

'Better not,' Caroline sighed. Caroline was always trying to give up. She was thirty-nine and had been an absolute babe in her day. Actually she still was gorgeous but she was now an anxious gorgeous, a nun to youth, with its rites of multivitamins, soya milk decaffs and pilates, which she hoped would extend her reign by an extra few months or even weeks. Despite her gorgeousness, Caroline had been single for seven years, since her third fiancé broke it off at the last minute. Why she hadn't been snapped up was a mystery. Sophie could only guess that Caroline was like a scratched CD, fine to look at but all jumpy when you played her.

'You know you want one,' shrugged Fay, who existed on a diet of Maccas and whisky. 'Birthday girl?'

'Oh, why not.' Sophie shrugged too. She always insisted she was a non-smoker – to be fair, she hadn't actually bought a packet of cigarettes for several years . . . well, months anyway. After all, she could always scrounge off Fay or anyone else who happened to be around. Sophie believed that scrounged cigarettes didn't count, just like food from other people's plates wasn't fattening. Besides, all the office gossip was formulated in the smoking room. It would be professional suicide not to make regular trips there.

'You smokers and your breaks,' moaned Yvette as they stood up. 'Do you know, I've worked out I should get an extra week's holiday a year to compensate for the time you spend in that nicotine-stained box.' She grabbed a ringing phone. 'Television,' she barked.

The editor of the *Daily Post*'s weekly television listings magazine, Yvette was famous for her grumpy demeanour and her clothes, which her staff had decided she must buy from some special website, since no shop in London, or indeed the world, could stock such horrors. Today she was wearing a sweatshirt covered in teddies, with little bows on each shoulder, and snake-green trousers designed to show off saddlebags to the best advantage.

Caroline was the writer; she did little blurbs on the must-see programmes and mini-interviews with B-list actors plugging their shows. Sophie was the PA, a job Natasha had obtained for her through her contacts, which involved spending most of the time on the phone to the BBC and Channel 4, calling in preview tapes. The rest of the time – when she wasn't reading *Heat*, *Hello!*, *Vogue* or *Tatler* – she was putting tapes in Jiffy bags to return to the BBC and Channel 4.

There were some perks: occasionally Sophie got tapes of *Kath and Kim* or *Desperate Housewives* a whole fortnight ahead of the rest of the world, but that was as exciting as it got. She'd hoped a job in a newspaper building would lead to something more glamorous one day, like a spot on the fashion desk, or the Saturday magazine, but in two years the only vacancies to come up had been in motoring and the computers pages. But it would happen. In time.

'Bollocks,' said Fay as they entered the smoking room. 'Where is he?' Fay, who actually worked for the health pages based at another bank of desks but for reasons lost in the mists of history sat with the TV crowd, had a complicated love life that involved a reflexologist, a Peruvian medical student and – somewhat predictably – a struggling rock musician. Then, last week, she had decided she also fancied Liam, the new number three on the foreign desk, and was therefore hoping to find him inhaling nicotine and flicking through the sports pages. Fay had worked her way through most men under thirty on the paper, discarding them like tissues when they started boring her. Sophie wished she could have filled her twenties with so much fun.

'He'll be in in a second if he knows what's good for him,' Sophie said, taking the proffered Marlboro Light.

'So what you up to this week?' Fay asked. 'Any more birthday surprises?'

'Dunno,' Sophie said sourly. 'Andy's bloody away again tomorrow. Though he's taking me out for dinner tonight. Oh, hi, Norris. How's it going?'

'Fine,' grunted Norris Wharton, the assistant deputy news editor who had just walked through the door: forty-eight, married, father of three and a smoking-room regular. He lit a Silk Cut Ultra Mild, inhaled and was immediately overcome by a violent coughing fit.

'Steady, Norris,' Fay laughed. 'You sure you should be doing this? You do know ciggies can damage your health.'

'Yes, I do know that,' Norris snapped. In fact his ten-a-day habit was playing havoc with his lungs, but his trips to the smoking room were the only way he could think of to wangle some minutes alone with the gorgeous Sophie Matthewson. Yet infuriatingly she never seemed to go anywhere without her annoying teenybopper friend.

53

Sophie's phone beeped. Norris's heart twanged with jealousy. Fay shot him an amused look. 'Who is it? What is it?' she exclaimed, as if no one had ever received a text before.

Sophie glanced casually at her phone. 'Oh, only Olly,' she said. She laughed as she looked out of the glass box. 'The fool. I can see him over there.' Sophie waved and smiled, holding one finger in the air. 'One . . . o' . . . clock,' she mouthed, then gave a thumbs up.

Olly Garcia-Mundoz was a columnist and feature writer, only twenty-six but one of the paper's rising stars. He had a first from Oxford, a PhD from Cambridge and he made regular appearances on *Question Time*. After chatting in the pub one night after work, he and Sophie had become mates.

'So you're not coming to Pret?' asked Fay.

Sophie laughed at her pissed-off tone. 'Fay, I come to Pret with you four days out of five. Today Olly is taking me out for my birthday lunch. Is that allowed? Now come on. Let's get back to our desks before Yvette calls the police.'

But Yvette barely noticed them return to their desks, involved as she was in her daily argument with her husband Brian.

'It's not my fault if there aren't any appointments, is it?' she was hissing. 'Well, you'll just have to be patient, won't you? . . . What do you expect me to do about it? . . . Oh, for Christ's sake, Brian, I have had enough. No really. I have had enough.'

She slammed the phone down. Fay and Sophie exchanged glances. A hang-up before lunch was relatively rare. It was usually around teatime, when Yvette experienced her sugar dip. Yvette was forty-three and had no children. Once she had confided to Sophie that Brian refused to contemplate the idea, saying he was saving any spare money he had for a hair transplant. Sometimes, Sophie wondered if Yvette wasn't terribly lonely and overcome with sympathy asked her to join their girls' lunches, but after an hour of having her ear chewed off about Brian and the management's inadequacies she always regretted it. She glanced at her watch: just coming up to half twelve. Could she drag Olly off half an hour early? He was usually pretty snowed under. Not that that ever stopped him being anything but cheerful and polite with everyone, to the point where even Yvette liked him.

The only thing wrong with Olly, in fact, was his looks. With an exotic surname like Garcia-Mundoz you might have imagined him to be swarthy and exotic-looking, like Benicio del Toro, whom Sophie fancied the pants off. But Olly had chubby chipmunk cheeks, pale skin, mousy brown hair and was a couple of stone overweight. If he was a girl you'd hint at him to do something with himself, Sophie reflected, get a few streaks put in, have his eyelashes tinted, a fake tan perhaps. But Olly was a man, and no doubt believed himself perfect.

'Oh, whatever. Whatever,' Yvette was saying. Caroline seemed actually to be dealing with a work call. Sophie sighed and clicked on her email. *To O. Garcia-Mundoz: When can we go? I'm starving.*

He pinged back instantly. *Whenever ur ready.*

Good old Olly. *Right now!* she typed in furiously. *Come and get me.*

She jumped up, snatched her bag and with a wave at Fay made her way through the rows of desks. She walked slowly in her stilettos – Sophie always wore heels, her legs were a feature – enjoying the fact that every pair of male eyes was turned on her.

She stood at the entrance to Olly's glass box. He was leaning back in his swivel chair, talking with a smile on his face to Keith Livingston, one of the executives. 'Well, keep me posted,' Keith was saying. Sophie waved behind his back. Olly sat up and straightened his tie.

'I will, Keith, I will. Now, if you wouldn't mind excusing me, I have a prior engagement with the lovely Miss Matthewson here. Taking her out for a birthday lunch.'

'Ah, Sophie, is it your birthday?' Keith said, spinning round. 'How old are we this time? Twenty-three?'

Sophie always felt a bit shy around Keith, ever since, bizarrely, she had had a dream that they were having passionate sex in a hot-air balloon. But today she decided a bit of banter couldn't hurt.

'No, your age, Keith,' she said, with a sly wink. 'Just thirty-two.'

'Ah, to be only thirty-two.' Keith sighed. 'Anyway, Oliver, we'll speak tomorrow. Enjoy your lunch.' He walked away.

'What do you have to keep Keith posted about?' Sophie asked Olly as they waited for the lift.

'Oh, politics,' said Olly with a faint smile. 'Tell you over lunch. Where shall we go?'

'The sushi place?'

Olly made a face. 'Sushi isn't real food, is it?'

Sophie pouted. 'Oh Olly, don't be such a fart. Think

of all those Japanese men who eat nothing but raw fish. They're all zillionaires.'

'Actually, the Japanese economy's in fairly dire straits,' Olly retorted as the lift arrived and they climbed in.

'Olly, please. Pleeease. It *is* my birthday.' She said the last in a baby voice.

Olly smiled. 'You're right. Sushi it is then. You can educate my palate.'

Sophie clapped her hands together in delight. 'Oh yum!' she exclaimed. She noticed Andrea Bussell, the deputy comment editor, who was sharing the lift with them, staring at her coldly. Sophie stared back. Bitch. Just because she was a secretary did that mean she wasn't allowed to be friendly with the writers? God, if it weren't for the likes of her, the *Daily Post* would cease to exist.

The drizzle of the last few days had gone and the skies were warmly blue. Sophie felt too hot under her coat and hung it round her arm.

'The first day of summer,' Olly said with a smile. 'Just for your birthday.'

The staff of Ikoko-San all recognized Sophie and nodded and bowed as she came in. 'Hello,' she smiled. 'Do you have tables outside?'

The manager looked at his watch. 'We do, but they're all reserved.'

'But we're here early,' Sophie wheedled. 'Surely you can fit us in? We'll be gone before the lunchtime rush.'

The manager smiled, unable as so many more before him to resist her winning ways. 'OK then.'

So she and Olly sat under a parasol, and she persuaded

him to order tempura ('No, you'll like it, the batter's all crunchy just like fish and chips') while she gorged herself on raw slivers of fish. Olly had a Kirin beer, then another one, and she had a birthday glass of wine.

'So how was your weekend?' Olly asked. 'Any pre-birthday celebrations?'

'No, not really. But it *was* my friend Marcus's wedding. Bit of an event.'

'Cool. I love weddings. Was there dancing?'

'Loads. It was really good fun.' Once again, Sophie thought wistfully about how she had been dragged away.

'I love dancing,' Olly said. His expression changed slightly. 'And has Andy given you your birthday present yet?'

Sophie shook her head. 'No. No. Tonight.' She wondered what it would be. She'd kicked up such a fuss after the scarf episode she knew that would never happen again, but she also knew better than to pay the ring fantasy too much attention.

'Right.' Something flickered at the back of Olly's tiny eyes. He fumbled inside his jacket pocket and took out a small parcel wrapped in blue paper. 'Actually, I hope you don't mind, but I got you a little something.'

Sophie shrieked, although she had been expecting it. Olly was very generous and constantly bought her little gifts: DVDs of films he'd talked about or books he'd enjoyed. Usually Sophie thanked him and put them straight in her present drawer to be recycled, but again it was the thought that counted.

She unwrapped the box. 'Oh my God, Olly. You shouldn't have.' And for once she meant it. Because there, sitting in tissue paper, was a chunky stainless-steel watch designed to slip round the wrist like a cuff.

His fat cheeks had turned scarlet. 'It's absolutely beautiful,' she gasped. 'But really. I . . . I actually don't think I can accept this.' Yet at the same time a counter-commentary was running in her brain. *Yes, you can. Wear it. And when Andy notices tell him who gave it to you. See if that doesn't give him the required kick up the arse.*

Olly smiled. 'Sophie, it's really sweet of you to be concerned. But look, I have loads of money and nothing to spend it on. Buying you presents gives me pleasure. You're a good friend.'

She stood up and, leaning forward, kissed him on the cheek. 'And you're a good friend too. Thank you *so* much.' She pulled off her old Casio and strapped on the new watch. 'Georg Jensen' read the tiny logo behind the dial. 'How did you know? I've always wanted one of these.'

'I remember,' he smiled. 'That night I met your friend Natasha? You were going on and on about how you wanted a watch like hers.'

'Yes, but . . . all the same.'

He put his hand up to silence her. 'Sophie, listen. I've just sold my book to the States. I'm getting an enormous amount of money for it, close to a million dollars. So I can afford a watch for a good friend.'

Close to a million dollars. Sophie was stunned. She knew Olly had been writing a book for ages, some political analysis of the British–US relationship. It sounded about as dull as instructions for a Stannah Stairlift. So how come so much money?

'That's brilliant, Olly. God, well done. When's the book

coming out again?' He'd told her but she kept forgetting.

'Not until the end of the year. But I can show you a draft if you'd like to read it.'

'Oh, would you? That would be great.' She could give it to Natasha, who actually enjoyed that kind of thing. 'So what are you going to spend the money on?'

'Well, I don't get it all up front – and I'll have to pay agents' fees and tax out of it and of course the dollar's very weak at the moment. But I have put in an offer on a house just down the road from here.'

'What? In Kensington?' That was where arms dealers and dukes lived. Not real people and especially not people from the *Post*, even though their offices were on the High Street. 'Wow, Olly, that's so grand.'

'You'll have to come and see it sometime,' he said, swallowing tempura. 'You know, Sophie, this food really isn't too bad.'

They finished their lunch in a leisurely fashion, keeping the rightful occupants of the table waiting for at least half an hour. 'But we'd booked,' Sophie heard a tall, whiny-voiced woman complain to the manager and smiled to herself.

They got back to the office at around half past two. Yvette was typing away furiously. Her nose looked very red. Fay too was tapping busily, but stopped. 'Good lunch?'

'Ve-ery nice.' Sophie smiled. 'Although now I'd kill for a post-prandial fag.'

Giggling, Fay jumped up. 'She'll only be two minutes, Yvette,' she promised, as they hurried off towards the smoking room. 'Caro, you come this time.'

'I told you,' Caroline said, looking up from *Elle*. 'I'm not smoking.' Then she saw Sophie's face. 'OK, but I'm not inhaling.'

As soon as the door was closed Sophie thrust her wrist under their noses. '*It's from Olly*,' she hissed. 'Isn't it beautiful?'

Fay gaped. 'From Olly? Bloody hell. That must have cost at least a grand. Shit, Sophie. The guy is seriously in love with you.'

Sophie flushed. 'No he's not! Don't be so silly.'

'Sophie, he is!' Caroline said. 'I've known it for ages. We're talking mad crush here. Stalkersville.'

'It's not like that! I told him I couldn't accept it but he said he had loads of money and no one to spend it on and that I was his good friend.'

Fay snorted. 'Good friend, my arse. Bet he goes home and tosses off over your picture every night.'

'Fay!'

Caroline sighed. 'It's not fair. You already have a boyfriend. How come you've got an admirer as well?'

'Life's tough,' Fay said unsympathetically. 'But, Soph, what do you feel about him?'

Sophie thought. 'He *is* my friend. He's funny and kind and he treats me well.'

'But you don't fancy him?'

She laughed. 'Of course I don't. Don't be silly. And even if I did, I'm going out with Andy.'

'Forget that.' Fay waved such considerations away like a pesky fly. 'But if you don't fancy him, you don't fancy him. Poor old Olly. Doomed to spend the rest of his life wallowing in unrequited love for you.'

'Oh, shut up!' Sophie snapped, studying the lighted tip of her cigarette.

'Well, there'll be plenty of other ladies queuing up for him. He's pretty eligible, you know. Especially now he's going to be made an executive.'

'What?'

'The youngest in the history of the *Daily Post*,' Fay said, enjoying her reaction.

'Oh. That must have been what he and Keith were talking about.' Sophie had forgotten to ask. 'He didn't say anything at lunch.'

'Modest too. He really is the perfect man,' Caroline sighed.

'Do *you* fancy him?' Sophie asked, beginning to feel guilty. Perhaps she should indulge in a bit of matchmaking.

But Caroline laughed. 'God, no, don't be silly.' She wasn't lying, her tone was more 'How dare you I'm not *that* bloody desperate'. Which was understandable. No one could fancy Olly.

Caroline's phone began to chime. 'Hello? Oh, hi, Yvette.' She pulled a face. 'Yes, fair enough.' She hung up. 'She's howling for us. Come on.'

'Sure,' Sophie said. 'After all, I have an urgent appointment with a copy of *Closer*!' And they hurried back to their desks giggling some more. For the rest of the afternoon, Sophie leafed through the magazine and browsed for shoes on the internet, but she was distracted by a thought growing at the back of her mind. *Olly is going to be an executive. He'll be editor one day. He's in love with me.* OK, she didn't fancy him. She was in love with Andy. But it never hurt to know that someone else wanted her.

8

Natasha had had a quiet afternoon, catching up on emails and working on budgets. But every time her phone rang her pulses thudded like someone slamming down all the keys on a grand piano. It was never Alastair.

'Who is it?' she asked Emilia as her line buzzed for the eighteenth time, trying to keep her voice in neutral.

'Someone called Andy.'

What on earth was *he* calling for? She picked up. 'Andy! Hi, how are you?'

'F-fine. I . . . Well, actually I was wondering if you could help me. I'm in Selfridges looking for something for Sophie's birthday. D-do you have any idea what I could get her?'

Natasha ignored the familiar pang of jealousy. 'Oh, I don't know, Andy. How about some perfume?'

Relief zinged down the phone line. 'Brilliant idea, Tasha. Why didn't I think of that?' There was a slight pause, then: 'What kind of perfume?'

'Well,' Natasha said very patiently. 'What do you think? What does Sophie keep on her dressing table?'

'Erm . . . It's sort of yellow.'

'Is it Clinique? Estée Lauder?' Natasha knew damn well what it was but she wanted to test him.

'Estée Lauder! Yeah, that's it.'

'No, Andy, it's Chanel. Allure. Chanel. Do you think you can remember that?'

'Allure. God, brilliant, Tash. Thanks. You're a mate.'

'Don't forget to get it wrapped. And buy her a card, too.'

'I won't. Tash, you've saved me. Again. Th-thank you.' He paused, then: 'Would you like to come out to dinner with us tonight?'

Oh, for God's sake. Most of the time Natasha thought Sophie was too hard on Andy but at times like this she definitely had a point. 'Andy, I really don't think that's a great idea. It's meant to be a romantic dinner *à deux*.'

'Oh, yeah. Right. S-see you then. When I get back from Iraq, we'll get together for a beer.'

A beer. Yes. That would be lovely, Andy. What a great idea.

Although he'd been with Sophie for years now, Natasha had never been able to forget the embarrassing fact that she had once been madly in love with Andy, a love he had never known a thing about. They'd met at the end of a cold March day five years ago when he had come to her office, a fledgling photographer just back from a spell in Africa. A friend of a friend had given him Natasha's number and he'd called her to ask if she could give him any advice on making British contacts. Because he sounded so nervous, she'd reluctantly agreed, pointing out that she dealt with moving pictures, not stills, but when he had walked into her office, she had felt his physical presence like a punch in the stomach. He was just her type, slightly used-looking and with an air of sadness about him.

'Extraordinary,' she had breathed, flicking through his portfolio. She wasn't referring to his work – which was excellent – but to the effect he was having on her breathing. She'd been hoping to get this meeting over as quickly as possible because she was meeting her friend Nikolai. Now she said: 'Listen. Why don't we go to the wine bar next door and discuss this a bit more?'

Andy had looked flustered. 'Oh, well, that would be great. But are you sure I wouldn't be keeping you?'

'Not at all,' she said firmly. 'So much nicer to chat there than in a sterile office.'

So they had had a drink and, after that, Natasha tried to put as much work his way as possible, introducing him to all her contacts in advertising and magazines. A few times, they had lunch, but they weren't great successes: he was awkward and she was stilted in a way she'd never have been with a purely work contact.

Still, she'd persisted: inviting him to parties which 'might help his career' and calling him with helpful tips. And gradually, he stopped seeming so bemused in her presence, began to laugh and tell jokes, and they discovered a shared passion for subtitled films and obscure Indian restaurants.

'I didn't figure you to be a poppadom and lager girl,' he'd said, looking at her appraisingly as they sat at a laden Formica table in the East End. 'The Ivy seemed much more like you.'

'God, what gave you that idea?' she'd laughed, trying not to think about the number of fat units in a poppadom. 'Horrible poncey place.'

The turning point came when *he* asked *her* to go to the

cinema. 'It's a Laotian film about a cow herder; I'd feel pretentious asking anyone but you,' he said. Natasha went around smiling for days.

Things got even better when Andy started getting lots of commissions from newspapers and magazines. He no longer needed to be nice to Natasha to get work, but he still called asking if she fancied a trip to a revival of an Ecuadorean cinema classic or a Pakistani place somewhere out near Heathrow.

She told none of her friends how she felt, for fear they'd laugh at *jolie-laide* Natasha hoping she stood a chance with this man who looked like one of the French stars who'd adorned her teenage walls. Of course, if this had been a movie, Andy would gradually have fallen for Natasha's inner beauty. But if this had been a movie, Natasha would have been played by someone like Julia Roberts with a token pair of glasses and perhaps an unflattering haircut, which, by the final scenes when she learned to make the best of herself, would have disappeared.

The difference was, Natasha thought sadly, she was already making the very best of herself. She went to the gym every day and ate virtually nothing (after every Indian she fasted for forty-eight hours), but she couldn't have her big bones transplanted. Or her misshapen nose, or her hands which looked like they belonged to a Hungarian weightlifter.

Still, she continued to allow herself to dream about Andy. The high point came after an evening with Sophie and Charlie, when the three of them watched the video of *When Harry Met Sally*.

'Do you think it's true?' she said at the end, trying to

66

sound casual. 'Men and women can't really be friends?'

'Of course they can't,' said Charlie. 'If you're spending time with a woman it's because you want to bang her.'

Natasha went home, her heart singing, and for a few days, her world twinkled and she could barely breathe from the weight of hope pressing on her chest. But then came her dinner party, when for some insane reason she'd invited Sophie (Charlie was away on business) and within days her best friend and her crush object were so busy falling for each other, no one noticed Natasha's heart breaking.

And just a few months down the line came another nail in the coffin when one night after a meal in a gastropub they all piled back to the house in Shepherd's Bush to smoke spliffs: Sophie, Andy, Natasha, Marcus and his girlfriend of the time, Sylvie, whom nobody liked, and a friend of Marcus's called Seamus. When everyone, except Natasha, was suitably stoned they decided to play that old favourite: If I Were You.

Giggling, they dreamed up various questions – 'What's my idea of a perfect night?' 'When did I lose my virginity?' – and everyone had to answer as if they were the person whose name they'd picked from the hat.

So far so jolly (although Marcus announcing that 'My most disgusting habit is I pee in the shower', before revealing he'd picked his own name, made Sophie and Natasha, who'd shared a shower with him for years, cry 'Eew!').

Then came the apparently most innocuous question of all. 'If I were a country what country would I be?'

'Bo-ring!' yelled Seamus. Since Sylvie had come up with it, Marcus kicked him sharply.

'OK, OK, we'll play it,' Seamus agreed. He dipped his hand in the baseball cap and smirked at the name he'd picked. 'So. If I were a country I'd be the US, because I'm rich but fundamentally brain dead.'

Sylvie looked at her piece of paper and smiled. 'I would be Brazil,' she said. 'Sensuous and exotic.'

Marcus read the name he'd picked and chortled. 'I'd be Nepal. Supplier of the finest grass on the planet.'

Sophie read her piece of paper. 'I'd be France,' she said. 'Serious and sophisticated.'

Natasha was sure that must be her. She took her slip. *Sophie*, she read. 'I'd be China, fascinating and full of un-realized potential.' Natasha wished Sophie would make more of her perfectly efficient brain, but had long learned nagging was counterproductive.

Andy frowned as he read his piece of paper.

'Oh, hurry up,' Sophie said.

He frowned again. 'I'd be Switzerland,' he said event-ually. 'Hard-working and efficient.'

And then it was time for the reveal.

'I was Marcus,' Seamus said with a chortle.

'What, rich and stupid?' growled Marcus, too mashed to really care. 'Fuck off. Well, Nepal was you but I wish I'd come up with something more insulting now.'

'I was myself,' said Sylvie complacently. 'Brazil.'

Sophie and Natasha caught each other's eyes and tried not to giggle.

'I was Sophie,' Natasha said.

'Oh, right,' Sophie said. 'Well, I was Andy.' She touched his arm and smiled. 'France, honey. Serious and sophisticated.'

'Well,' said Andy, jumping to his feet and reaching for a can of Stella. 'In that case, I was obviously Natasha.'

'What, Switzerland?' Sylvie asked. 'Efficient and . . . what was it? Boring?'

'No, not boring,' said Andy, glancing at his watch. 'Hard-working. Maybe we should call a cab now?'

Everyone continued chatting and laughing while Natasha sat there feeling as if she'd been slapped across the face. Switzerland. She had always thought of herself as somewhere like Italy, or maybe Ireland. Artistic and full of depth. But Andy associated her with the land of cuckoo clocks and banks, a land where, she'd read, there was a byelaw preventing men from peeing standing up after ten at night.

It was years ago but the insult still smarted, although of course she was well over Andy now. He and Sophie were clearly meant to be together, even if they didn't always seem that happy.

The intercom was buzzing again.

'Natasha, it's your friend, Sophie,' Emilia said.

Guiltily, Natasha picked up. 'Hey, hi, Soph. Happy birthday. I've been meaning to call you all day, but it's just been frantic.'

'Oh, that's OK,' Sophie sounded much more chilled than she usually was about such matters. 'Thanks for the candles. Anyway, listen, I just had lunch with Olly G-M and guess what he gave me?'

'Who's Olly G-M?'

'Oh, you know. You met him with me once after work. Glasses, mousy hair. Big bum.'

'Oh yeah.' Natasha did remember vaguely. He'd seemed

quite nice. Smitten by Sophie obviously, who was completely out of his league. She'd felt a burst of feeling towards him – one underdog to another.

'So guess what he gave me?'

'I dunno, Soph. A Prada bag?'

'No! Prada is *so* over.' Sophie devoured fashion magazines and couldn't understand how Natasha, with all the cash in the world to spend on designer outfits, could be so clueless. 'A Georg Jensen watch!'

Natasha felt another hot prickle of envy. No one *ever* gave her gifts like that. She'd bought herself the Georg Jensen as a congratulations present after she was promoted to head of drama.

Sophie mistook her silence for annoyance about something quite different. 'Tash? Don't worry, it's not exactly the same as yours. Now that *would* have been a disaster.'

'Oh, I wouldn't have minded that,' Natasha said truthfully. She tried to quash her jealousy. 'Wow, Soph! The guy is obviously hopelessly in love with you.'

'That's what Fay said. But he's not, he's just a good mate.'

'Good mate! Sophie, the guy wants to go out with you. No one buys expensive presents like that unless they're in love.'

'Well, even if he is, what can I do? He knows I'm going out with Andy.'

Natasha's intercom started buzzing. Could it be? Could it possibly be . . . ?

'Sophie, Sophie, I have to go. But listen, have a lovely evening with Andy. And let's go out soon. My treat.'

'Well, I'm free any time,' Sophie said. 'Andy's off to Baghdad tomorrow, the bastard.'

'I know,' Natasha said unthinkingly.

A slight pause and then: 'How do you know? Have you been talking to him?'

'No, no, of course not! I just . . . you know, it's been hotting up there, so it seemed like the natural place for Andy to go.' *Get off the line, Soph.*

'I guess so. Anyway, let's do something this weekend. A wake for my old age.'

'Oh,' Natasha said, glancing at her desktop diary. 'I'm off to New York this weekend.'

Did she imagine it or was there a slight coldness in her friend's tone. 'Fine. Anyway, you're busy. I'll let you go.'

'No. No. It's OK. Let's do something on Wednesday.'

'Well, if you're sure you can spare the time . . .'

'Of course I can. Love to. But now I've got to go. See you.' She hung up but the buzzing had stopped.

Buggeration, Natasha breathed. But then the buzzing started again.

'Who is it, Emilia?'

'It's Alastair Costello.'

It was him. It was him. 'Put him through.' She swallowed. 'Hello?'

'This is Alastair.' No Costello. No hesitant *you left a message, I'm returning your call.*

'Oh, hello,' she said, trying to sound as bored as possible. 'How are you?'

'Fine. So. I was hoping you'd call.'

'Well, I told you. I'm a great fan of your work. And I'd love to collaborate with you. So I think we should make a lunch date.' She glanced down at her diary.

'Although I'm quite busy right now. Off to New York and what have you. But I could do, say, Thursday?'

He laughed softly. 'I can't do this Thursday, Natasha Green. And then I'm away in Spain for a week. Writing. I could do the following Monday, though.'

Shit. She had a really important lunch with an Australian writer that day, who was only over for a week. Still, she could always shift it to dinner. Or a drink.

'That would work. Where would you like to go?'

'Do I get to choose?'

'Of course you do. Rollercoaster's treat.'

'Cool. Could we go to St John in St John Street? It's my favourite.'

'Of course we can. I'll see you there. On the day. One o'clock OK?'

'One's great,' he said. She hung up, hands shaking. Which was ridiculous. Because they were just having lunch. To talk about work. Like Natasha did every day. Still, maybe she should buy a new outfit for the occasion. She owed herself a treat for working so hard. And for bringing such a hot writer on to Rollercoaster's books.

9

After all the fun at work, Sophie's evening was a distinct let down.

She was out of work at 5.59 on the dot, home by 6.45, in the bath at seven and by 7.28 was arranged prettily on the sofa in her best new dress from Karen Millen, one arm back behind her head to display the Georg Jensen. What was on telly? Oh, goodie. A teeny music programme on E4. Andy had promised he'd be home by 7.30, but he'd be late and for once Sophie was glad. He couldn't understand why Sophie found watching boy bands gyrating round a stage entertaining and was appalled she knew each member's name.

He still wasn't back by eight. Oh well, *EastEnders* now. Andy got very stroppy about her watching that, claiming it was trash, which was totally unfair given he had never even sat through an episode. It was an especially dull one tonight though: all about Dot Cotton and the vicar. In any case, Sophie's enjoyment was marred by the fact that if Andy had just warned her he was running late she could have fitted in an hour in the pub with Fay. She never understood why her boyfriend, who was so anal about tidiness, could be so vague about timekeeping and positively evangelical about the joys of an unpredictable life. Mind you, she was obsessed with being a domestic goddess although orderliness was not her strong point.

Anyway. She picked up her mobile and bashed in a text. *Where fuck r u?*

Ten minutes later, she heard the roar of his motorbike outside.

'You could have replied to my text,' she said, eyes on some home-improvement show.

'I was on the bike. I'm sorry. I had to meet Orlando Bright's girlfriend. She had a package she wants me to deliver to him in Iraq.'

'Did she now?' Sophie said nastily. 'And she had to meet you on an evening when you had a date to take your girlfriend out to her birthday dinner?'

'Well, yes, she did actually. She's leaving for New York tonight.'

What was it with everyone and New York? Sophie had gone there with Charlie once on one of his business trips: they'd stayed at the Plaza and eaten at the oyster bar underneath Grand Central. Andy had never taken her away anywhere, apart from once to Switzerland where he'd hoped she would learn to share his passion for skiing. But she'd hated it from the first lesson and he got impatient trying to teach her to snowplough. He ended up spending all day on the black runs while she sat in their chilly two-star hotel room that didn't even have a TV. Then they'd rowed because Sophie hadn't bothered unpacking, which infuriated Andy who liked everything straight out of the case and on to hangers, while she couldn't see the point when it was only going to go back in the case again in a few days.

'Sorry,' he was saying now. 'I really am. Now, listen . . .' He bent down to fumble in his backpack. 'There's another reason I'm late, which is I bought you this . . .'

For a millisecond, Sophie's heart stopped. A gift-wrapped box. But no, it was too big to be a ring.

Andy was looking very pleased.

'Thanks, honey.' She ripped off the paper. A bottle of Allure. Well, better than the navy scarf, but not wildly original. Still, he had made an effort so she would too. 'Honey, well done. My favourite.'

'Yeah, Natasha said it was.'

'Natasha?'

Andy had the grace to look embarrassed. 'I didn't know what to get you, so I rang her.'

'Oh, bloody great. So this isn't a present from my boyfriend, it's from Natasha.'

Annoyance and confusion simultaneously crossed Andy's face. 'Well, I'm sorry, Soph, but I didn't know what to get you. Don't you like it?'

Sophie decided to let it go. Her birthday was spoiled enough as it was. 'It's lovely,' she conceded unenthusiastically. 'Thank you.' She kissed him on the lips.

'Now where would you like to go to dinner?'

There was a little pause. 'You mean you haven't booked?'

'Er, no. I thought you'd like to choose.'

Don't make a fuss. Enjoy your evening. It's the last one you'll have together for ages. 'The Glen,' she said firmly. The Glen was an expensive French restaurant in West Hampstead. Sophie had only been there once before with Natasha who had put the meal on her expenses and she had never forgotten the lovely, crisp white tablecloths and the baskets of petits fours they brought with the coffee.

75

There was a fraction of a pause, then Andy smiled. 'OK. The Glen it is. Shall we walk?'

'No. Let's drive, or go on the bike.'

'But then I can't drink.'

Sophie sighed, heavily. 'Well, let's get a taxi then.'

'Soph, we're not made of money. We'll get a taxi back.'

Sophie picked up the phone and dialled. 'Hello. I'd like a cab from twenty-six D Acacia Avenue to . . . What? Nothing. For an hour? Well, fuck off then.'

'How can you be so rude?' Andy gasped.

'I'd hung up by the time I said that,' Sophie said, ashamed by her outburst but determined not to show it. 'OK. We'll walk.'

She pulled on her new-last-week black leather jacket and waited for a response from Andy, but he looked straight through it as if it was just a jacket, rather than the thing that currently made his girlfriend's life worth living. Normally, she'd have pointed it out to him, but tonight she decided to save the big guns for the Georg Jensen.

It was about a mile to the restaurant and it should have been lovely in the gentle evening air, but Sophie, in her highest heels, could only feel her back aching and a blister forming on her left heel.

'Bit of exercise, do you good,' Andy said teasingly.

'I get plenty of exercise,' she said haughtily, aware she wasn't doing nearly as much as she used to.

'I was joking,' Andy said and she felt stricken. Where had her sense of humour gone?

As they pushed open the door of the Glen in some relief, they were hit by a wave of garlic and loud chatter.

'Two, please,' Sophie said to the sour-faced woman behind the desk.

'Have you booked?'

'No.'

The woman looked down at the diary. 'I'm sorry. We have nothing, then.'

'Nothing?' Sophie pouted. 'Can't you try to squeeze us in? We're going to spend lots of money and tip generously.'

But her charms, which had worked so neatly on the Japanese man at lunchtime, were as useless as Viagra on a castrato.

'Sorry, there's nothing I can do.' She turned and smiled at the elderly couple behind them. 'Mr and Mrs Connolly? How are you?'

The Lebanese next door was full too, as was the Chinese on the corner. Sophie refused to go Indian, because that was what Andy always wanted, so they ended up in the Thai, which was part of a nationwide franchise, where the microwave could be heard merrily pinging in the kitchen.

'Fucking great. We could be anywhere,' she said, her eyes blazing.

'We couldn't be in Thailand, I can assure you.' Andy was grinning, but she refused to be mollified. 'How about menu B? And shall we get the house red?'

The food was OK, but all in all the dinner was very frustrating. Sophie kept stretching her arm in the air and reaching out for his hand, in the hope he'd notice the watch, but he said nothing.

By the time he'd ordered lychees and she was having coffee, she decided to come right out with it. 'Do you like my new watch?' She thrust her wrist under his nose.

Andy was used to being asked to admire things and knew the correct response. 'Yeah, it's lovely,' he said, with a brief glance.

Sophie looked at him intently. 'Olly Garcia-Mundoz gave it to me.'

'Olly G-M?' Andy had covered a few stories with him. 'That was nice of him.'

Sophie wanted a bit more of a response than this. 'It's a Georg Jensen.'

'What's that?'

'For God's sake, Andy.' She put down her coffee cup and smiled at the man at the next table, whose head swivelled at the sound of her voice. 'You must have heard of Georg Jensen. It's like Gucci or Valentino or something.'

'Oh, right. Maybe I have.' He blinked. 'I d-didn't know you were friends with G-M.'

This was more like it. 'Yes, we're very friendly. He's such a nice guy. And doing so well. Fay says he's about to be made an executive. And he's got an American book deal for a million dollars.'

'Christ, and he's only twelve or something.'

Sophie didn't like being reminded how young Olly was. Though wasn't Chris Martin five years younger than Gwyneth? And what about Demi and Ashton whatshisface? No, younger men were positively hip right now. Not that hip was an adjective that could ever be applied to Olly. And not that she and Olly were a couple.

'Fay thinks he must really fancy me. But I don't think so. We're just good mates.'

'That's nice,' said Andy mildly. From the look on his

face, she could tell he was miles away, probably in Baghdad already.

It was hopeless. 'I thought I might go to the movies or something with him while you're away,' she tried as a last gasp.

'Oh, yeah. Why don't you? That'd be nice.' He turned to the waitress. 'Could we have the bill please?'

Time to try another strategy. 'Do you remember that first birthday of mine we spent together? When I got that rash and you had to call the doctor?' Sophie found herself doing this more and more with Andy, recalling past times in an effort to make them feel closer, so that onlookers would see her sparkling vivaciously, rather than sitting like an old couple lost for conversation.

'Vaguely,' he said. 'That's when I was doing that story about the children's home in Bermondsey, wasn't it?'

She gave up. 'How long are you going to be away for?'

'You know I don't know. Two weeks. Three at worst.'

That meant four. 'I'll miss you,' she said. It wasn't strictly true – Sophie used to miss him like crazy in the early days, when she'd also got a kick out of telling her friends he was in a war zone, but now what she felt was more like frustration when the car failed to start or the dishwasher broke down and he wasn't around to help her sort it out. Apart from that, she was so used to his long absences, she'd go for hours, even days, without giving him a thought.

He reached out and clasped her hand. 'I'll miss you too, babe. I'm sorry. I'll call you when I can.'

Three or four weeks. Sophie was beginning to reach some conclusions. She'd give Andy that long to come up with a ring. But in the meantime she was going to start the search for his replacement. Sophie sometimes thought she should be the one going to Iraq. When it came to secret missions she was unstoppable.

10

On Wednesday night, Sophie went over to Natasha's for her birthday outing. Natasha had told her there was no way she could make it home before eight, so Sophie, who as a matter of principle never left work a second after six, had to spend an hour and a half browsing the shops that were still open on Oxford Street and ended up spending money she didn't have on a beret, a top with a drawstring neckline (the following morning she realized that no bra on earth would work under it but she never summoned the energy to take it back) and a pair of sunglasses like ones she had seen Gwyneth wearing in *Grazia* to join the sixteen others knocking around her flat.

At five past eight, she rang on Natasha's buzzer.

'Sorry, sorry,' she heard her friend's voice behind her on the street. 'I ran from the office.' Natasha worked only two streets away on the other side of Charlotte Street and had no concept of the hell that was commuting. 'Come up,' she continued, jangling her keys. Sophie followed her up to the third floor of the converted Georgian house. She'd been to Natasha's scores of times but as she walked in she still felt her stomach clench with envy as she admired the perfect beige interior, set off by interesting artefacts from Natasha's extensive travels.

'I feel like I've walked into a style magazine,' she said as she always did.

'Oh, don't be silly,' Natasha said as she always did. Her mobile started to ring. 'Sorry, hang on a second. Hello? Oh, hi. Thanks for getting back to me. Yeah, no, I saw the rushes earlier. They're OK but it will need a lot more work.' She put her hand on the receiver. 'Sorry. I've just got to take this.'

'That's OK,' Sophie mouthed as Natasha climbed the spiral staircase to the mezzanine level, unlocked the door to her vast roof terrace and walked outside. It was a bit insulting the way she always did that, as if Sophie were an industrial spy. Oh well. There were never any magazines to read at Natasha's, so to entertain herself, she wandered into her friend's huge bedroom. When Natasha had bought the place there had been two bedrooms but, bizarrely, she had decided to knock down the wall between them and create a gigantic boudoir. Everyone had warned her it would do terrible things to the property's value but she'd been adamant it was what she wanted. Sophie was pretty sure it was so there was no spare room for that cow Lesley to come and stay. Or Helen, her cuddly apple-cheeked mum, whom Sophie had always wanted to be adopted by, but of whom Natasha always seemed embarrassed.

As usual, Natasha's big bed was made up, the duvet as smooth as a film star's brow. Why did she bother when no one was going to see it? There were fresh flowers in a vase on the window sill and not even a sock lay on the little chair in the corner. Natasha hung up all her clothes every night without fail and every six months had a clear-out of stuff she no longer wore. Not that there were too many of those items, as Natasha only bought classics:

black pencil skirts, well-cut trousers, cashmere sweaters, white shirts from Anne Fontaine – the sort of clothes magazines were always telling you were investment pieces, the sort Sophie got curry on in five minutes. On the bedside table sat a copy of *Silas Marner* by George Eliot, with a bookmark sticking out. Underneath was some book called *The Silent D.* by Alastair Costello, which Sophie remembered seeing posters for on the tube. Natasha always said she liked to have two books on the go – one a classic and one contemporary.

Was there anything about her friend that wasn't perfect? Naughtily, Sophie knelt down and peeked under the bed. Under hers and Andy's you would find nineteen copies of *Heat* and *Elle* purloined from the office, some hair curlers, thirty-three dusty shoes – most of which seemed to have lost their other half – and a few empty mugs. Andy was always moaning about how they needed to have a clear-out but Sophie's attitude was out of sight out of mind. As she suspected, Natasha's bleached-wood floor was dust free. Of course, Natasha had a cleaner, but all the same. The only thing stashed there was a pile of books. Probably more improving classics. Sophie picked one up. *Full Bodied! The Women's Guide to Enjoying Wine.* Sophie snorted. She didn't need a book to help her on that score. *French Women Don't Get Fat.* Ooh, Sophie had been longing to read this, but what was skinny Natasha doing with it? Perhaps she'd lend it to her? *How to be a Sex Goddess.* This looked interesting too. *The Love Trainer's Guide to Men.* Sophie had seen the author of this on *Richard & Judy* when she was bunking off work a few months ago. It had sounded as if it might be quite useful – or would have been if she'd read it before she met Andy.

'What are you doing?' Natasha said sharply behind her.

Sophie jumped up. 'Sorry! I dropped something and then I saw your books. I didn't know you had all these.'

Natasha snatched *The Love Trainer's Guide* away. 'Yeah, we're researching a comedy about someone who's addicted to self-help books.'

'Really? That sounds like a laugh.' Sophie was about to ask more when the door buzzed.

'That's probably Nikolai,' Natasha said. 'He said he might drop in after work. You don't mind, do you?'

'No, no, of course not,' Sophie said, as Natasha went to the entryphone and buzzed him up. Actually she did a bit. She liked Nikolai – he was so upbeat it was impossible not to, but this evening she'd been hoping to get Tash to herself. It had been so long since the two of them had had any decent one-on-one time. Sophie didn't like thinking too much about how things stood with Natasha. She was her oldest friend. Her best friend – or so she always claimed. But was she really? Once they used to tell each other everything, but over the past few years Natasha had become so secretive that as a result Sophie had started to clam up too. Friendships, she realized, had to be reciprocal. You couldn't pour your heart out without getting something back in return, otherwise you just felt like a blabbermouth. And now a vicious circle had developed, where they called each other friends but more and more treated each other as acquaintances. It made Sophie very sad; it also made her a little lonely. Of course she had other friends, like Fay and Caro, but they would never have her and Tash's shared history. But these days Natasha was too important for Sophie, her time filled with her job and other friends — friends like Nikolai, who was now bounding through the door.

'Hello, ladies, wonderful to see you.' Kisses on both cheeks. 'Sophie, my darling, looking gorgeous as usual.' He put his hands on both her shoulders and studied her. 'Love the heels.'

Sophie blushed. 'Thank you.' Nikolai was an actors' agent with all sorts of glamorous clients, and although he tended to patronize her she forgave him because he was also incredibly friendly and warm and (unlike some she could mention) full of funny stories about his disastrous love life. Sophie could always feel herself blossoming in his presence and wished they could hang out together alone, rather than with Natasha there as chaperone.

'God, I have had such a week,' he gabbled, heading to the stainless steel noticeboard by the fridge and peering at a couple of invitations. 'God, the BBC Two garden party. Are you going to go to that? I should but it'll be so bloody dull. And what about the Scissor Sisters launch? I mean, there'll be cute guys aplenty but for some reason they're having it in a bar in sodding *Harlesden*.'

'Oi,' said Sophie. 'I live in Harlesden, if you don't mind.'

'Oh, so you do, you poor love. Ah, well, nobody's perfect. So where are we going tonight? Nowhere too frantic, I hope. I've been having *such* a time of it. Ever since I joined Gaydar it's just been go go go. I had a date with this really cute Indian boy last night at Balans. Thick as shit, of course, but what a body. Anyway, I wanted a get-out clause so I told him I had to get up really early to catch a plane. But then we got pissed and started snogging and I kept saying, "I have to go, I have to go," but eventually we ended up back at mine and you know . . . but then I bloody had to stick to my story so at five the alarm goes off and I had to get up and shower and shave and kick him out saying my taxi was just coming. And then I couldn't bloody get back to sleep.'

'How tragic,' Natasha said dryly. 'Now, do we want a drink here or shall we just head out?' She clearly favoured the latter.

'Oh, just head out I think,' Nikolai said. With a barely perceptible wink at Sophie, he continued, 'So what do you think, Natasha? Maybe you should join some kind of online dating service. Tick tock, darling. Time's no longer on your side, you know.'

Sophie almost gasped. She'd been thinking the same thing for months but would never have dared come out with it. Not that Natasha looked thrilled by the question.

'Online dating is for losers,' she snapped brusquely, pulling on her slim-cut leather jacket. 'Anyway, I'm quite happy the way I am.'

'So you say, darling, so you say,' said Nikolai with another wink at Sophie. She had to suppress the urge to giggle. 'So where shall it be tonight?'

'I don't know.' Natasha yawned. 'I've been everywhere recently. I'm getting sick of eating out.'

Oh, darling, what a nightmare for you. 'I could cook for us all,' Sophie suggested. She had been so looking forward to a rare night out but then she did love cooking too – and Nikolai at least would enjoy her food, unlike Andy

86

who wolfed it down most of the time without comment and Natasha who would push it round and round her plate before claiming she'd had a huge meal at lunchtime and although it was delicious, thanks, she simply couldn't manage another mouthful.

'No, darling, no cooking! This is your little night on the tiles. Escape from Harlesden. We'll go to Fino.'

Ten minutes later they were sitting round a table in the buzzy basement tapas restaurant. Sophie looked around with excitement. 'There's Peter Andre,' she squawked.

'Oh, bless,' said Nikolai. 'It's so exciting for you, isn't it? Where is he, darling? Oh yes, rather sexy, I must say. I bet he's really gay.'

'You think everyone's gay,' said Natasha, sipping her spritzer. 'Anyway, who is he?'

Sophie and Nikolai looked at each other in horror. 'Darling, you must know who Peter is! You work in television.'

'Yes, but in drama. And he's probably some hideous reality star or something. You know that's not my bag.'

It was a bit of a joke that remote Amazonian tribes knew more about popular culture than Natasha. Sometimes Sophie wondered if her ignorance about the Beckhams' marriage and *Big Brother* was an affectation, but if so she was doing a damn good job of keeping it up.

'Natasha, Nikolai!' boomed a voice behind her shoulder. 'Hey, guys, how are you doing?'

It was a man with mousy hair and fine features. Nothing special to look at, but somehow oddly attractive. Sophie sat up straighter. Why had she started doing that every time she was introduced to a man under the age of a hundred?

'Gregor!' The others both jumped up and started gabbling away about viewing figures and advertising revenues. Sophie downed her glass of sherry and filled it up again, all the while smiling serenely and wondering if they'd forgotten she existed.

'God, we're so rude,' Natasha exclaimed. 'I'm so sorry. Gregor, this is my old friend Sophie.'

'Sophie, nice to meet you,' he said, holding out a hand and, as he clocked her, looking her up and down approvingly. 'Gregor Fry, head of public relations at Granada. And what do you do?'

It was the question Sophie loathed more than any other. 'Oh, I work for the *Daily Post*,' she said airily.

'Really? My favourite paper. Would I know your byline?'

If Natasha and Nikolai hadn't been there she probably would have lied. But too bad. 'Um, I work in an administrative capacity.' It was what she always said to this question. And Gregor's face suddenly went blank.

'Oh, right.' He turned towards the others. 'Guys, great to see you both. Let's do lunch soon, all three of us. I'll be in touch.' And he turned round and headed towards a table across the room.

'God, the rude bastard!' Nikolai exclaimed. 'Did you see the way he treated our Soph? Just because she couldn't do anything for him except be her gorgeous self. I don't know, it's at times like these I want to jack it all in and become a cowherd.'

'Yeah, right, I can just see you doing that,' Natasha

said. 'But he was rude.' She squeezed Sophie's arm. 'I never liked him anyway.' And Sophie felt comforted.

The meal was a lot of fun. Nikolai entertained them with stories about his dating adventures and Natasha told them funny stories about filming. Natasha was always more relaxed when she was with her gay friends, Sophie noted. Come to think of it, her and Marcus apart, did Natasha have any friends who weren't gay? There was lechy Dom in her office, but he was more a colleague. And no girlfriends that Sophie could think of. But Natasha wasn't very good at the girlie stuff: the confidences, the self-disparagement, the exchange of tips about different brands of face masks. Why were the two of them still friends? Was the only thing keeping them together nostalgia for their childhood? Did they have anything in common at all?

After the meal, which was a bit disappointing and astonishingly expensive, although Natasha picked up the tab without blinking, they went back to Natasha's for a *digestif*. 'Only the one, darling, I'm shattered,' Nikolai warned before swallowing two shot glasses of tequila in quick succession. 'Shall we have some music?' he asked, picking up Natasha's iPod, which was plugged into Bose speakers. He picked it up and began scrolling. 'Blah, blah, Beatles, Bob Dylan – darling, you do know we're in the noughties now, don't you? Shostakovich. Haven't you got anything a bit tasteless?' He paused. 'Oh, ho. Now this is a bit more like it.' He pressed play and the nerve-jangling sound of an electric guitar filled the room.

'Oh my God,' said Sophie, putting down her whisky glass. 'I haven't heard this in an age.'

A throaty woman's voice began to plead with them for their attention.

They jumped up and the three of them, even Natasha, began air guitaring to the strains of 'Fame' and stamping imaginary canes on the ground, while shouting about the price of fame and its toll in sweat.

'*Irene Cara's Greatest Hits*,' Nikolai gasped. 'By a very, very long way the greatest record ever made.'

'Whichever of us has a daughter first has to call her Irene,' shrieked Sophie. 'Do you remember, we agreed that, Tash?'

The opening strains of the next song began. 'Oh my God! "What a Feelin'". Do you remember? Alex . . .'

'The beautiful welder, who took her knickers off under the dinner table. And at the audition she slips and has to start again and by the end the nasty panel's all boogying along with her.' Natasha grinned at the memory, transported to those Betterton days curled up on the sofa watching the video while she and Sophie scoffed a whole tub of Wall's ice cream.

'Wahoo!' yelled Nikolai, turning a little pirouette. He grabbed Sophie and twirled her energetically round the room. He held out a hand to Natasha. 'Come on, baby, join in.'

But Natasha had sat back down on the sofa. 'You know I don't dance,' she said firmly.

'Tasha! Live a little, girl. Come on! Why can't you be more like Sophie, living for the moment instead of always worrying about appearances?'

'Sophie can dance,' Natasha said with a mysterious smile. 'I can't.'

'I *can't* dance,' Sophie protested. 'I just enjoy it.'

'And that's the difference between the two of you,' Nikolai yelled. Sophie realized he was drunk. 'Sophie enjoys herself. You don't.'

'I do enjoy myself,' Natasha said calmly. 'I just don't like dancing. So piss off, Nikolai.'

'Shall we find some other music?' Sophie asked, embarrassed. She hated confrontations between anyone. 'Oh, look, Duran Duran. Remember this one?' Simon Le Bon wailing filled the room.

'Ooh. "Is there something I should know?"' yelped Nikolai, instantly distracted.

He bounded round the room like a teenage kangaroo. Sophie giggled, then glanced at Natasha, who while smiling was stifling a yawn.

'I should be going,' she said hastily.

'Oh, let's all have another drink,' Nikolai shouted.

'No, Niko,' Natasha said. 'It's getting late. Time for everyone's bed.'

'Oh, you old misery guts,' he grumbled. 'I suppose you're right. Come on, Sophie darling. We can take the tube home together.'

'We should go out more often,' he said as they sat side by side on the Bakerloo Line. 'Show you the high life while Andy's away.'

'That'd be fun,' Sophie said over-eagerly. 'How about some time next week?'

But Nikolai's eyes glazed over. 'Yeah, maybe,' he said curtly. 'I'm a little busy next week. I'll call you if I have a window.' The tube slowed as it entered Maida Vale station. 'Oh, here I am, darling. Lovely to see you. Ta, ta.'

'Bye,' said Sophie, but he didn't turn round as he darted on to the platform. The doors shut and the train continued northwards, the better-heeled passengers getting off at each stop, until by Harlesden it was just Sophie, a hollow-eyed Asian-looking woman clearly returning from some kind of shift work and an old man clutching a beer bottle and smelling of urine.

Why hadn't Nikolai wanted to make a firm date with her? It was because she was boring, had a nothing job and lived in the sticks. If only she could be as confident and cool as Natasha. Why hadn't she worked harder at school and gone to university and got a better job? Then could she too be living in the West End and going out every night and spending money like it was water? Sophie asked herself these questions but she knew the answer, which was that as long as she could remember she'd wanted to get married, hold cosy dinner parties, have babies and create the perfect family life she'd never had. And she still would do that, everything would still come out all right. It had to. Because the alternative was too scary to contemplate.

11

The next couple of weeks passed unbelievably slowly for Sophie. Andy was in Iraq and their rare conversations were always unsatisfying. He talked about bombings and kidnappings; she talked about delays on the Bakerloo line and the winner of America's Next Top Model.

His day consisted of adrenalin and adventures. Hers were office, followed by home for a delicious little dinner experimenting with new ingredients from the Asian corner shop (Sophie loved cooking and profited from the time Andy was away to road-test all sorts of new recipes, which, she suspected, he never fully appreciated), a spot of telly and bed. Lights out sharply at eleven. Lying in bed, she thought about the 115-year-old woman who'd been the *London Tonight* 'and finally' item. She attributed her longevity to cycling and pickled onions. Compared to Sophie's, her life in the old folks' home sounded like the heyday of the Wild West.

Nikolai didn't call and she felt too shy to pursue him. She texted Natasha a few times but she was always too busy to come out. Twice she went out with Fay to All Bar One or the Chicago Rib Shack, where they knocked back a couple of bottles of the cheapest white wine over a plate of nachos, before stumbling on to the packed dance floor to dodge piles of vomit and have their bottoms groped by middle managers in Top Shop suits.

Usually Sophie would wait until Fay was about to cop off with someone, then sneak out on to the crowded central London streets more depressed than ever.

Then there were a couple of nights with Caroline at Soho House, which her friend had joined two years ago in order to meet more men. And she did meet them, starting with eye contact in the Long Bar, and usually ending up at theirs. But after that they never called, unless they were married or thought they were the Duke of Wellington.

'I don't know what's wrong with me,' Caroline wailed over dinner, as her eyes scanned the room for talent. 'Why can't I meet anyone? Do I smell? Tell me, truthfully. You would if I did, wouldn't you?'

'You don't smell,' Sophie said wearily.

'Surely Andy must know someone?' It was the nineteen-millionth time she'd asked this year. 'What about his friend Shacky? He's single, isn't he? Why don't you fix us up together?'

'I don't know,' Sophie said uneasily. Shacky had three children by three different women who, in any case, were all Asian babes, while Caroline was a statuesque blonde. 'I'm not sure you two are really right for each other.'

'*Why* not? You can never predict chemistry. When Andy gets back why don't we all go out as a foursome? You will ask him, won't you?' Caroline gestured to the waiter. 'A bottle of Chablis, please.'

'I will,' Sophie lied. 'Hey, weren't you on a fruit-juice diet?'

'Grapes are fruit, aren't they?' Caroline said defensively. 'Full of antioxidants. Though maybe we should get some

94

fags from the machine as well. Have you got any change?'

Nights out with Olly were far less demanding. Once they went to the cinema and afterwards to J. Sheeky's where they spotted Jordan having dinner with Simon Cowell. Another time she accompanied him to a grand party at the Garrick Club in Covent Garden, which was full of MPs. Olly introduced her to lots of them and she flirted happily.

'So you work for the *Post*? What do you write about?' one of them said, peering down her cleavage over his half-moon specs. 'Fashion? Beauty?'

'That kind of thing,' she said vaguely, not at all insulted.

She was sitting at her desk at work on a Monday afternoon giggling at the memory, when she was distracted by Fay, who, dressed in yesterday's clothes, was on the phone to one of her mates.

'So we start kissing and after a while we've got most of each other's clothes off, so we get into bed, then he goes down on me and it's very pleasant and then I think I ought to return the favour . . . Mmm-hmm . . . Yeah . . . So, anyway, I push him on to his back and I wiggle down there and put it in my mouth and I almost barf because the man has got a cheesy dick . . . Yeah, I know, disgusting. But you should have smelt it . . . No, the rest of him was clean . . . I know . . . No, really, it stank.'

'Fay!' roared Yvette, whose face had been growing redder and redder to match her culottes.

'Just a sec, Yvette,' Fay said. 'So I just stopped and he didn't say anything . . . I said: "Oh, I'm really tired," and we fell asleep.'

'Fay!'

'Anyway, I just called Shannon, because she used to go out with him and she said he definitely didn't use to have a hygiene problem . . . I just said: "See you," and by the time I'd got to work he'd texted me.' Just then her phone bleeped. 'Oh, maybe that's him again. Just a sec.'

'Fay! Stop this conversation at once. This is company time.'

Fay looked outraged. 'All right! Listen, Emma, I've got to go. Work needs me. But I'll call you later.' She hung up. 'Yvette, that was totally out of order.'

'You were broadcasting to the whole office,' Yvette snapped, staring angrily into her computer screen. 'And it's revolting. None of us wants to know these hideous personal details.'

'I do,' Sophie said.

'I wasn't telling *you*, I was telling my friend Emma.'

'At top volume,' Sophie giggled.

Fay's phone beeped again. She looked at her message, then screeched. 'God, he's asking if we can go out on Saturday!'

'Oh, yuck,' Sophie said. 'How will you blow him out?'

Fay looked at her puzzled. 'Oh, I'm going to go. Just no hanky-panky this time. Friends only.'

Sophie's enjoyment was spoilt by the phone ringing. She grabbed it. 'Good morning. *Daily Po-ost.*'

'Sophie?'

'Marcus! When did you get back?'

'At two this morning,' Marcus said. 'How are you, Sophie?'

'Oh, fine. You know. Boring. Andy's away. But how was the honeymoon?'

'Not bad. A bit rainy. I think we were there too early in the year. Anyway, listen, Lainey and I were wondering: are you free this evening? We were hoping you might be able to come to supper. We could show you the wedding pictures. You could even indulge us and watch the DVD. And more importantly you can see the new house.'

The new house, which had cost far more than a million. Marcus's bonus had covered the deposit, but he'd still had to take on a terrifying mortgage at a time when loads of people in his office were being made redundant. But Lainey had said that would never happen to clever Marcus and argued there was no point buying somewhere smaller, because they'd only have to move in a few years with the added expenses of stamp duty and removal men and builders. And Lainey was very persuasive.

'That'd be brilliant,' Sophie said now. 'I'll come straight after work.'

'Fantastic. Tash is coming too.'

Sophie's nose felt so out of joint it was time to go straight to casualty. So Tash who'd been too busy to hook up was willing to drop everything to go round to Marcus and Lainey's. And Marcus had called *her* first. Yet more proof that everyone preferred Natasha to her. But who could blame them when her friend's life was so much more exciting?

'Great,' she said a little more sulkily. 'I'll see you later, then.' The phone was ringing again. 'I have to go. Bye. *Daily Post*?'

'Is that the most beautiful secretary in London?'

She smiled. It was Julian, a freelance writer who used to do loads for them, until he bizarrely relocated from

London to Romania. It was a shame, because he and Sophie had always enjoyed a healthy flirtation, bantering down the phone to each other and over an occasional lunch, when he would pump her for office gossip and tell her how gorgeous she was. In different circumstances they would have had a fling, but there had never been a chance: she'd always been with Andy and he'd always been with Frankie, his childhood sweetheart who'd very unwillingly jacked in her job to accompany him to Bucharest.

'I'm the most beautiful secretary in Britain, if not the world, thank you very much,' she said.

'You're right, you're right. So how are you, beautiful one?'

'All the better for hearing your voice.'

They continued like this for a few minutes, and then Julian asked if he could speak to Yvette. 'They're filming some BBC drama out here, so I might actually be able to do a story for you,' he explained.

'Why don't you come home and then you could do stories for us all the time?'

'I like it out here. It's an adventure. And so cheap. Do you know how much rent I pay on my flat? You should come out and see it sometime, Sophie.' He always said that.

'Yeah, I'll have to see when Andy's got a free weekend.' She always said that.

'I don't want bloody Andy! I just want you.'

'I'm afraid that's impossible.' Sophie said primly. 'Anyway, what would your girlfriend say?'

There was a brief pause, then. 'Frankie? Oh. Didn't I mention? We've split up.'

'Oh. Oh, I'm sorry,' Sophie said insincerely.

'Don't be, it wasn't going anywhere. Anyway, listen, my battery's running low. Put me on to Yvette, sweetheart. But we'll speak soon, yeah?'

'Take care, Julian.' Sophie put down the phone re-invigorated. It was always the same repartee, but it always left her happier. Someone who liked her. Every little bit helped.

12

The evening with Sophie and Nikolai had left Natasha feeling strangely down. The fact that her two closest friends were able to have such a laugh together made her feel even more of a misfit than she usually did. When she was nine Natasha had missed two weeks of school with flu and when she got back she seemed behind on a load of important stuff, like how to do front crawl (she could never get the breathing right), the six times table and how to spell rhythm. Sometimes she felt the same was true of life. Was there a little rule book that had been distributed during that fortnight, but which she had never managed to get her hands on? Why did all the other people in her class know instinctively that the time to love Duran Duran had passed and you had to get into the Smiths? How come at university everyone but her knew the cool look was trainers, which before 1990 had been something reserved strictly for the sports field, while she was still in her penny loafers?

Why, fresh from her graduation ceremony, had she turned up for her interview at Rollercoaster in a boxy little grey Hobbs suit, carrying a briefcase, when everyone else in the office was in jeans, printed T-shirts and Doc Martens? Thank God, Barney had interpreted her look as eccentric rather than just clueless, and the two of them had hit it off. Natasha shuddered to think what might have been otherwise.

Sophie finding her copy of *The Love Trainer's Guide* hadn't helped either. Natasha had always been a great believer in books. As a child they had transported her to a world where a gang of children rounded up international criminals and Cinderella got the prince and now she still relied on her manuals that told her how to buy the best beauty products, how to dress correctly, how to decorate, how to have perfect manners, how to appreciate wine, how to stay in hip hotels, how never to put on a kilo, how to be great in bed. She kept them hidden under her bed and studied them earnestly at night time, writing down the key bits in her Smythson notebook. She hoped Sophie had swallowed her story about researching a drama, but she wasn't sure. She should have told the truth, that she'd been studying it for tips on for making her next relationship (should it ever happen) succeed, but she simply couldn't bring herself to admit that she felt in need of so much help, help with things that pretty, confident, optimistic Sophie mastered so effortlessly.

It was hard enough being around Sophie as it was. She loved her, she truly did, but in comparison with her friend she always felt so inadequate. If truth be told Natasha found her gay mates like Nikolai far easier to be with. It was an awful thing to admit but she felt none of the inferiority that tormented her around other women and none of the insecurity she felt around straight men. Gay men showered her with adoration in a way that was intoxicating: laughing at her jokes, calling her at all hours of the day and night, hugging and kissing her and making her feel as though they could, if only things were different, be her boyfriend – which, ridiculous as it was, was briefly reassuring for someone who was forever single.

But maybe all that was about to change. Over the next week Natasha was super-busy: going back and forwards to the studios, holding meetings about various scripts, arguing about casting, not to mention the New York trip (flying first class and staying at the Four Seasons) and a night in Zurich, but a little chunk of her mind was always on Alastair Costello and whether they'd actually have that lunch. She reread all his books and made a few notes, so she could flatter him with her encyclopaedic knowledge of his work, but when the day came she purposefully put on only her second-nicest suit and packed her gym kit so she could rush off for a workout as soon as she got the call or email telling her he was sorry he couldn't make it but he was just 'too busy'/ 'en route to Vegas to marry his girlfriend'/ 'had a better offer from Naomi Campbell'.

But the only person who did call was Marcus asking her to supper that night, so at quarter to one she went downstairs to get in the car she had ordered to take her to St John.

'Who's the lunch with?' asked Barney, as they crossed paths in the lobby. Barney lived in a mansion in Hampstead with Dane Flanders, who was half his age and had won *Pop Idol* two years ago. Sophie could never believe Natasha was actually on first-name terms with him.

'Alastair Costello,' Natasha said, chuffed she had an impressive name for him. 'You know, *The Silent D.* guy.'

'Good one, Natasha. Very hot. I'd love to get him on board.'

She asked the driver to drop her fifteen minutes away from St John to make sure she was late. When she walked in, Alastair was sitting at the table at the back of the white-walled, high-ceilinged room. He stood up as he saw her. He was wearing a clean blue T-shirt and chinos. Natasha's stomach clenched into a fist.

'Natasha. Great to see you.' He held out his hand. 'Thanks so much for finding the time for this.' Before she could open her mouth he continued, 'Please tell me you eat meat. Or at least you won't be offended by someone else really going for it. Because you know this place specializes in offal.'

Natasha took off her jacket. 'I eat meat.' Inasmuch as she ate anything, that was the truth.

'Thank God,' he said. 'I'm so tired of being looked at like a child molester whenever I order something that isn't tofu and lentils. That's the problem about being involved with someone who's vegetarian. Sometimes I think she's going to jump out of the coat cupboard in a place like this shouting: "No veal chops for him!" I'm not even allowed puddings any more. Way too much cholesterol, apparently, whatever that may be.'

Natasha smiled politely, while her mind churned over the implications of what he'd just said. Mentioning his girlfriend before she'd even looked at the menu. He might as well have said: 'I know you have fallen madly in love with me, like every woman I meet. But this is strictly work, so cool it.'

She wasn't going to dodge the issue. 'What does your girlfriend do?' Actually, she knew because she'd been mentioned in the cuttings, but no name or details had been given. 'I like to keep that side of my life private,' Alastair had been quoted as saying.

'She's an actress.' He raised an eyebrow. 'When they tell you actresses are temperamental, don't believe them. They're certifiable.'

That was Natasha's experience but she wasn't going to say so. If there was one thing life had taught her it was never to slag off someone else's family or partner. No matter how much they seemed to be encouraging you, it always backfired.

'Well, it's a tough job,' she said neutrally.

He laughed. 'If you think dressing up and pretending to be someone else is tough, then I suppose. Though I guess there is the insecurity question. It doesn't matter if she's just got the lead in a Hollywood movie, as far as she's concerned there's always someone younger, prettier, more talented and better connected scrabbling to push her off the ladder.'

'*Has* she just got the lead in a Hollywood movie?' She should ask her name, but she didn't want to in case he said something like Scarlett Johansson.

'Not yet.' He lowered his voice. 'But she's just had a meeting with Jan Kovak.' Jan Kovak was a young British director who'd taken the last Oscars by storm with a low-budget gangster movie. 'Could be tricky if she starts working with him. She'd want to move to Los Angeles, but I'm not exactly keen on uprooting myself to a town where no one's heard of Marcel Proust but everyone knows the exact calorie count of a stick of gum.' He laughed. So did Natasha even though she could have told him: 27 in bubble gum (10 if sugar free), 10 for chewing gum, 5 for Dentine. Didn't everyone know that?

The exotic-looking waitress was standing there, smiling. Natasha could see Alastair was the kind of person women all smiled at.

'Could we just have a minute?' she said. 'So what's her name?'

'Aurelia. Aurelia Farmer. Right now she's in a play. *Free Time*. Hasn't opened yet.'

'What, the one with Lara Barker?' Lara Barker was a big Hollywood star, now trying to raise her credibility with a month on the West End stage. The buzz around the play was huge. Emilia was meant to be sorting out tickets for her and Dom.

'That's the one. Aurelia's totally in awe of her. Keeps saying we must all have dinner, but I think if I want a dose of *Beverly Hills 90210* I can watch it on cable.'

'I'm surprised I haven't heard of her,' Natasha said. 'Aurelia, I mean. She sounds like one to watch.'

The waitress appeared again.

'I think we're ready now,' he said, ignoring her last remark. 'I'll have the brains. Extra spicy. And chips, please, lots of them.'

Natasha glanced at the menu. 'I'll have the chicken salad.'

Alastair looked at her archly over the menu. 'Er, excuse me?'

It was a test.

'Oh, all right,' she smirked. 'I'll have what he's having.'

'And a bottle of red?'

'Of course,' she said. He was the guest. Natasha never

drank at lunchtime, or any time really – way too many empty calories. But today, she was so nervous she found herself swilling it down.

'So tell me,' he said. 'How long have you been at Rollercoaster?'

'God, since I graduated,' Natasha said. 'I went there as a gopher and just worked my way up the ladder. Very boring.'

'Not boring. You're obviously doing brilliantly. Rollercoaster productions are what stops me from going out and smashing every television set in the land with a sledgehammer. You're the only people making stuff for people with IQs above cretin level.' He smiled at her, wrinkling his nose. Natasha suppressed an urge to reach out and touch it.

'But what about you?' she said hastily. 'How did the writing start? What were you doing before?' Of course she knew all this, because it was in the press cuttings too, but he didn't know that.

'Me? Oh, a bit of this, a bit of that. Been all over the place. I was in Madrid for a few years, bartending and stuff, just doing whatever it took to pay the bills. Writing at night. And the first book didn't do much but then *Showpiece* went stellar and then *The Magic Giant* and *The Silent D.* and . . . I've been very lucky.' He shrugged helplessly.

'Goodness, you deserve it all so much. You're such a fantastic writer.' The brains were put down in front of them. Natasha blenched and wondered how much she could slip in her napkin.

'"Goodness",' he said, imitating her slightly husky voice. 'What a sweet word to use.' She flushed and looked down. 'Hey, hey, I'm not being mean. I love it. Aurelia swears like a trooper. It's hardly feminine.' He took a mouthful of his brains. 'Wow, these are even more delicious than I remembered. You are going to love them.'

Over the main course, Alastair told her about his idea for a screenplay, which was about a man who was simply incapable of fidelity and his eventual comeuppance. From there they moved on to all sorts of things: movies, politics, where they lived: her central London ('You lucky thing,' he said enviously as everyone did) versus his Hackney ('I suppose I could afford to upgrade to somewhere smarter, but I like to keep it real – know what I mean?'). They talked about books, Natasha mentioning several of her favourites.

'God, a woman who actually knows about literature,' he exclaimed. He stopped himself. 'Sorry! Sorry! That sounds terribly sexist and it's not meant to. It's just Aurelia never reads anything except *Heat* and *OK!* to see if her friends are in it.'

'Doesn't she read your books?'

'Yeah, right,' he snorted.

The only dodgy moment came when Natasha mentioned a novel she adored by Nate Lindstrand, another hot young name. Alastair's lip curled as if she'd put a dog turd under it.

'Just don't get him. He plays to the gallery. All that bollocks about being half-Jamaican, half-Swedish. He went to public school, but everyone falls for him because he has dreads and wears a hoodie.'

'Oh, I mean what you know,' Natasha said treacherously, forgetting how she'd laughed uproariously over Lindstrand's last novel. 'I mean, I know what you mean.'

The staff mopped up around them as they lingered over coffee.

'It's nearly four,' Natasha yelped. 'I'm so sorry. I've kept you all this time.'

'Not at all,' he said.

She picked up the tab and they walked out on to St John Street.

'That was so much fun,' he said. 'To eat meat.'

'Well, we'll have to do it again,' Natasha said, slurring only slightly. 'And we'll have to think up some projects for you – I mean if you can possibly find the time . . .'

'I'll find the time for you.'

They stood awkwardly on the corner. He was going back to Hackney, she to the office.

'Well, goodbye,' he said, leaning forward and kissing her on both cheeks. 'And I hope we do it again. I mean, not just as a work thing. As a friend. It's great to find someone in the middle of this bullshit I can really talk to.'

'I'll be in touch,' Natasha said and – thanking the heavy traffic for disguising a mild burp – hailed a cab.

'How was Alastair Costello?' Dom asked as she reeled back into the office.

She glanced at him sharply. 'How did you know?'

'Barney told me. He's very excited about the thought of getting him on board.'

'It was good,' she said, slumping back in her chair. 'Very good.'

Dom gave her a knowing look. 'He's meant to be a total ladykiller.'

'Takes one to know one,' trilled Natasha.

'That's why he got such an amazing book deal, they say. Shagged everyone from his agent to Ella Lloyd.' Ella Lloyd was Alastair's very powerful editor.

'Really?' Natasha said. Somehow, the wine had anaesthetized her to what she was hearing. Dom watched her curiously. Along with the rest of the office, he speculated a lot about her love life. She never mentioned anyone. Sometimes Dom wondered if she wasn't a bit lonely, but then she was always busy. But before he could worry about her any more, his mobile bleeped a demanding message from Sharmila and Dom's mind moved on to the far more thorny question of how to put this relationship out of its misery.

13

After work, Sophie took the tube to Notting Hill and walked down Kensington Park Road trying to curb the envy that consumed her whenever she ventured into this part of the world. As soon as you got away from the scrum of people around the tube everything looked cleaner and fresher and more expensive than in the rest of London. Instead of Superdrug and KFC there were cute boutiques displaying kooky T-shirts and floaty dresses. Instead of Poundstretcher there were delis and organic greengrocers. Instead of harassed mums there were coltish girls in boho-chic talking loudly into their mobiles. Oh, what she'd give to live here. Did Lainey realize how lucky she was?

It got worse when she reached the house. It was huge: soft pink stucco with looming windows and wide front steps. Sophie rang the doorbell almost praying she'd got the wrong address. But no, here was Lainey, barefoot, in a blue smock belted at the waist over Paper Denim & Cloth jeans.

'Oh my God,' Sophie gasped as they embraced. 'You look fantastic. I missed you guys.'

'We missed you too,' Lainey said, hugging her. 'Come in.'

Sophie followed Lainey down into the basement kitchen, with its gleaming stainless steel units and walnut surfaces. 'Wow, Lainey. It's amazing.'

'It's not bad, is it? Apparently Stella McCartney has just bought the house two doors down.'

'It's a bloody palace,' Sophie said. The old house in Shepherd's Bush had been huge enough, but this was astonishing. 'God, you've got an Aga, you lucky cow. Lainey, this is the kitchen of my dreams.'

'You'll have to teach me how to use it,' Lainey said, smiling. Lainey was one of those weird people who genuinely didn't seem to be interested in food. If you asked her what she'd eaten at Pied à Terre or whatever restaurant Marcus had taken her to, she'd say: 'Oh, I don't know, some fish,' while Sophie could have told you every single ingredient in every single course.

'Laines, it's just perfect.' Sophie was genuinely thrilled for her, but it didn't stop her being gutted for herself. She looked around. Something was missing. Oh yes, that was it. 'Where's Marcus?'

'He's at work,' said Lainey, uncorking Sophie's bottle of Pinot Grigio (only £5.99, but you'd never guess from the classy-looking label).

'At work? On your first night back from honeymoon?'

'Well, that's his job. The financial markets never close.' There was a defensive note in her voice, which Sophie recognized. It was the same tone you heard in hers when she explained why Andy had been unable to make this garden party/dinner/birthday do.

'Men and their jobs. They're all the same.' Sophie looked around her, still woozy with envy. 'So . . . can I have a tour?'

'Sure,' Lainey said. 'Well, this is the kitchen.' She gestured towards the conservatory at the back. 'And there's my studio. Light just streams through. It's going to be so inspiring.' She walked back up the stairs into the hallway. 'This is the TV room and here at the front is the living room.'

Sophie felt hollow. Perhaps she should have married Marcus. But he was practically her brother and she felt about as much attraction to him as she did to a garden gnome. Wouldn't it be fabulous, though, to have a rich husband . . .

'Of course we still haven't finished decorating,' said Lainey, wrinkling her nose at the dull yellow hallway walls. 'That'll be my project for the next few months. Along with the painting of course.'

'Lucky you,' Sophie said with feeling, her attention turning to a huge pile of cardboard boxes in the corner. 'What are all those?'

'Oh,' said Lainey. 'Those are our wedding presents.'

Sophie was scandalized. 'You mean you haven't opened them yet?'

'Well, I only got up at noon. And then I had to call everyone. Let them know I'm back in town.'

'Oh Lainey! Haven't you even peeked?' Lainey shook her head. 'I don't know how you do it. Shall we have a look in one now?'

'No!' Lainey protested. 'We can't do that. I don't know, I think the whole wedding present thing is so silly. Marcus and I already have everything we need. But he insisted on it. Said people would be hurt if they couldn't give us something.'

'Well, you want your friends to know you care,' Sophie said, remembering the hassle and expense she'd incurred tracking down Marcus and Lainey's top-10 favourite movies on DVD.

'It's all such boring stuff,' Lainey continued. 'I wish you could do a wedding list for experiences. See the Pyramids at sunset. Trek to the heart of the Amazon. Talking of which, my friend Usha's just invited me to a huge rave in Uruguay later in the summer. I have to go.'

'But you've just got back from honeymoon.'

'So? It could be good for my art. I've never been to South America.'

Sophie smiled, then nodded back at the boxes. 'Come on,' she said coaxingly. 'Let's open one. Just one. I'm sure Marcus won't mind.'

Lainey sighed. 'Oh, all right then. But just one.' She picked up a box from the pile and ripped at the masking tape. Polystyrene padding flooded out. 'Oooh. What can it be?' She delved in and pulled out a beautiful cut-glass fruit bowl.

'That's gorgeous,' Sophie gasped. 'Who gave you that?'

Lainey glanced at the note. 'Helen and Gareth,' she said. 'Whoever they may be.'

'They're old friends of John's.' Again, Sophie nudged Lainey cheekily. 'Go on. Do just one more.'

'Oh, bloody hell, all right then.' Lainey opened another box and lifted out a smaller box displaying a picture of a candy-pink KitchenAid. 'What the hell's this?'

Sophie couldn't believe it. She'd been lusting after one of those for years. 'Lainey! It's this amazing kitchen mixer. Nigella swears by them. God, I'd kill for one. And look at the colour? Isn't it cute?'

'I guess,' Lainey said, frowning over the card. 'William and Rose. Nope. Dunno who they are either.'

With Sophie's encouragement, she went on to unwrap a new set of Le Creuset pans, an espresso machine, a cake slicer, a Shaker salt and pepper set and some bathroom scales that told you not only how much you weighed, but how much body fat you had, whether you were having a good or bad hair day and what your horoscope said.

'Just one more,' Sophie begged.

'For heaven's sake! No!' Lainey drained her wine glass. 'Anyway, I've just remembered, we've got a little birthday present for you. Sorry it's late, but we were unavoidably detained.'

'Thanks,' Sophie exclaimed. She examined the bag Lainey passed her. 'Santa Maria Novella.'

'We didn't have time to wrap it,' Lainey said as Sophie pulled out a scented candle.

'Oh, Lainey, it's beautiful,' she gushed, annoyed at her childish disappointment. Why couldn't they have got her a KitchenAid?

'So how's Natasha?' Lainey asked, rolling a herbal cigarette.

'Laines, I thought you'd given up!'

'Not the natural stuff. So. Natasha?'

'I'm not sure. She's never around to find out.'

'No boyfriend news?'

'Er, what do you think?'

Lainey grinned. Everyone knew Natasha never had a boyfriend, and even if she did, they'd be the last to know, so unwilling was she to discuss her private life. 'Well, it's not like she's lonely. She's out every night having a brilliant time. Jetting round the world. I think she has a great life, though I couldn't be doing with all that stress. I wish I could get her into t'ai chi.'

Just then the doorbell dringed. They both jumped guiltily. 'That'll be her now,' Lainey said. She ran into the hallway and flung open the door. 'Hello, gorgeous!'

'Sorry I'm so late,' Natasha said. 'I had to take this Australian writer for drinks at the Savoy.' She was looking prettier than she normally did, softer somehow. She kissed Sophie more warmly than she had for several months.

'Soph! How's it going? Sorry I've been so crap recently. It's just been mental.'

'That's OK,' Sophie lied.

'And how about you, Lainey?' Natasha asked as they followed her down to the kitchen. 'I want to hear everything about the honeymoon. Or have you two already been over it all?'

'No, she's told me nothing.'

'Nothing to tell,' said Lainey, whose back was turned to them as she delved in the fridge. 'The weather was shite and I must say I was surprised at how chintzy the house was. I'm going to suggest to John he gets my friend Cassa to redecorate. And it's a bit in the middle of nowhere. We checked out some of the clubs in Florence but the drive was a right bastard and of course one of us couldn't get wasted, so Marcus stayed sober, which was pretty boring for him.'

'Did you see the frescoes in Arezzo?' Natasha asked, eyes shining.

'No, no, never got round to that but we did make it to the Gucci outlet. God, it was amazing. I got two pairs of boots and a wallet. It's in an industrial estate in the middle of nowhere, but it was so worth it.' She frowned as she surveyed the inside of her cupboards. 'Oh shit, I thought I had some pasta sauce. I'm going to get Fresh and Wild to deliver twice a week.'

'Do you want me to cook, Laines?' Sophie volunteered hastily. Out of the corner of her eye, she saw Natasha nodding and grinning.

'Oh no, I'll be fine. Or we could order in.'

'Let me cook. You know I love it.'

So after a bit of snooping in the new blue Smeg fridge, Sophie knocked together a fantastic bowl of pasta, which they ate – or rather Sophie and Lainey did – while poring over six professionally arranged wedding albums.

'There's Mum looking shit-faced,' Sophie said wearily as Rita leered out of the frame, holding up a glass of champagne. 'So embarrassing.'

'It was great to meet her,' Lainey said. 'She seemed like a laugh. How is she?'

'Oh, all right. I'm not sure how well she and Jimmy are getting on. He's not very chatty when I call. And she's planning a girls' holiday in France. Always a bit of a dodgy sign. I reckon we'll be seeing husband number four before the decade is out.'

'Oh Soph, surely not,' Natasha exclaimed. 'She was so in love with Jimmy.'

'"Was" being the operative word. My mum can't do marriage. She has no sticking power. One blip and she's on to the next one. That's why I'm so patient with Andy.

He may be a pain in the arse, but who isn't at some point or another?'

'Mmm,' said Natasha, frowning, as she flicked through the pages. 'But sometimes don't you think people just aren't right for each other? They make mistakes and then they're too scared to stand up and say: "I got it wrong." Like . . .'

'Like who?' Sophie asked, interested. She looked at Natasha's untouched plate. 'Not hungry, love?' she said sarcastically.

'Sorry. I had the most enormous lunch.' Sophie and Lainey exchanged glances.

'Like who?' Lainey prompted.

'Oh, nothing.' Natasha flicked through some more pages. 'By the way, guess who lunch was with? Alastair Costello. From your wedding.'

'Alastair Costello?' Lainey wrinkled her nose. 'God, yeah, he's some friend of Geraint's. Gez wanted to catch up with him while he was back from the States, so I said he could come. I barely remember him.'

'Oh, right.' Natasha turned another page. 'I'd show you a picture of him, but I can't find one.'

Something in the studied casualness of her tone alerted Sophie. She looked up. She was right. Natasha *was* different tonight. Her eyes were sparklier, her mouth twitchier, her skin glowier. She was giving off excitement vibes. 'Tash, do you fancy this guy?'

'No!' She took a gulp of her wine. 'He's just really nice.'

'You do fancy him! I can tell.' Sophie gave a little war whoop and clapped her hands. 'Oh my God, Tash! How exciting. Tell us more.'

Natasha shrugged, both annoyed at being found out and relieved to get the chance to unburden herself. 'Nothing to tell. He's a writer. We've had lunch to talk about him possibly doing some scripts for us.'

'Wooh! So more, more. What does he look like?'

'Soph, he was at the wedding. You met him.' Sophie shrugged. 'OK, a bit like Richard Gere, but with a white streak in his hair.'

'How did I miss him? Anyway, sounds good. Age?'

'Ours. A couple of years older.'

'Perfect . . .' Sophie wiggled in her chair happily. 'Anything else we should know?'

'Um,' Lainey said. 'Isn't he engaged?'

There was a pause. 'Engaged? Natasha!'

'Oh, right,' Natasha said slowly. 'But it doesn't sound like it's going too well.'

'Hmm,' Sophie said. 'Sounds dodgy to me.'

'Why? I only had lunch with him.' Natasha folded her arms defensively.

'Tasha,' Sophie said gently, 'I really don't think you're going about this the right way. There have to be easier ways to find a boyfriend. If I were you, I'd try speed dating. It's supposed to be a real laugh. Caroline in my office did it and she said it was a hoot.'

'Sophie, I am *not* going to speed date.'

'How about internet dating?' Lainey tried. 'Everybody's doing it these days. I read an article about it. There's no stigma attached to it any more, you know. It's just like having your hair highlighted or wearing contact lenses and you do both of those.'

'Lainey, I am *not* going to internet date. I am happy the

way I am. Single. I don't need a man. Alastair is a work contact. And, as you said, he has a girlfriend.'

'Fiancée.'

'I don't know,' said Lainey. 'If you really like him, it might be worth going for. I mean, he's not married yet.'

Sophie looked at her, outraged. 'Laines! I can't believe it. Married men are out of bounds.' She turned back to Natasha. 'How about a blind date? Olly G-M's really nice and he's single.'

'What, the guy who gave you the Georg Jensen? I don't think so, Soph. I don't want your cast-offs.'

'What Georg Jensen?' Lainey enquired.

'Look.' Sophie stuck out her wrist. 'For my birthday. It's gorgeous, isn't it?'

Natasha flared. 'Soph, I don't know how you can lecture me about liking an engaged man when you're accepting gifts from lovestruck blokes. It's hardly fair on Andy, is it?'

'Why not? Olly's a good friend. And it's not like Andy and I are married.'

'You've been together four years. Way longer than Lainey and Marcus.'

'Yes, but Lainey and Marcus had the guts to stand up in front of the world and say they love each other. Until Andy and I do that, our situation is different.' Suddenly Sophie felt very sad. She had neither the glamour of being single nor the stability of a couple. She was sick of this in-between life.

'So who is this Olly bloke?' Lainey asked.

'Olly Garcia-Mundoz,' said Natasha. 'The rising star of

British journalism and politics. They're saying he's going to be the next but one Tory leader.'

Lainey clapped her hand to her mouth. 'Oh my God. I've never met him but I know exactly who he is. He's one of Woozle's oldest friends. They were at Charterhouse together. He's incredibly clever, isn't he?'

'I guess,' Sophie said.

'I didn't know you knew him.'

'Well, he works for the *Daily Post*, so go figure.'

'I suppose.' Lainey's brown eyes widened. 'Wow, Sophie, and he gave you that watch.'

'Yes.' Delighted as she was to have impressed Lainey, Sophie decided it was time for another topic of conversation. 'So I got an email from Antonia the other day. Baby due any second now. Bit of a shake-up.'

'Antonia was in our year at school,' Natasha explained to Lainey. 'She was the good-time party girl.'

'And then she got pregnant and was gutted,' Sophie continued, 'but she's sort of come round to the idea of a baby, though she says she'll kill herself if she doesn't leave the hospital in her pre-pregnancy jeans.'

'I don't know why she's making such a fuss,' Natasha said. 'She should have thought about all this before she decided to have a baby.'

'But she didn't mean to have a baby,' Sophie pointed out. 'It was an accident.'

'Bollocks. Does anyone really believe that story? Women don't get pregnant unless they really want to. There's no excuse for an unplanned pregnancy.'

'No, accidents definitely can happen,' Sophie said, turning pink. Actually, she agreed with Tash, but since her very own unplanned pregnancy was one of the tactics she was considering in the campaign to get a ring on her finger, there was no way she'd admit it.

She was rescued by the sound of the front door slamming.

'Duckie,' came Marcus's posh voice from the hallway. 'Duckie, are you there?'

'Er, yeah,' Lainey yelled, embarrassed by the use of what was obviously a private name. 'With Sophie and Natasha.'

'Oh,' Marcus said, stumbling into the room. His eyes were bloodshot, his shirt crumpled and he was very, very red in the face. 'Hi, ladies. Had a good evening?'

He looked terrible, Sophie thought. 'Yes, lovely, thanks.' She hugged him. 'Welcome home. Um, did you overdo the Italian sun?'

'I told him he should use my Sisley stuff but he refused,' Lainey said exasperatedly. 'And then he couldn't go outside for three days. Stayed indoors playing Nintendo.'

'Marcus! That is not how you behave on honeymoon.'

'I know. My wife made that very plain.' He slipped an arm round Lainey's waist. 'Sorry I'm a bit later than I said. The Dow Jones went into meltdown.'

'That's OK,' Lainey said. 'Just a shame you couldn't make it back in time to see your friends.'

Marcus's mobile rang. He pulled it out of his pocket and frowned. 'Fuck, it's Terry. Sorry, ducks, gotta take it. Hello? . . . Yeah, hi, mate, tell me . . .' With a mouthed 'sorry' he wandered out of the room.

Lainey shrugged. 'City boys.'

Sophie laughed, then glanced at her watch. 'Well, I should leave you newlyweds. I don't like getting the tube too late.'

'Can't you get a taxi?' Natasha asked.

Sophie looked at her in annoyance. 'No, I can't, Tash. Do you know what taxis cost? Or do you just claim them on expenses?'

'Well, I'm going to get one. I'll drop you at the station. Shame we haven't got to see Marcus though.'

Just then he stuck his head round the door. 'Sorry, girls, I'm going to have to get online and sort out this crisis in the San Francisco office.'

'You poor bastard,' Sophie sympathized, just as Natasha said, 'We were going anyway.'

'Sorry,' he said again, pulling a face. 'Such is a banker's glamorous existence.'

'Do you think Marcus is OK?' Natasha said when they were sitting in their minicab. They hadn't even been able to say goodbye to him properly, since he was hunched over his laptop in the TV room, shouting orders down a speakerphone.

'Marcus? Of course. He's just got back from honeymoon and he's living in the most fabulous house in the world.'

'I know. But he looked out of his mind with exhaustion. On only his first night back.'

'Second night,' Sophie corrected. 'And what do you expect? He's a trader. They take a lot of shit. But look at the rewards. Oh! Just here, please.' The taxi stopped outside the tube. She smiled at Natasha. 'Do you want any money?' She would have died of shock if her friend said yes, but it was only polite to offer.

'Oh no, don't be silly.' The friends kissed. 'Take care,' Natasha said.

'I will.' Sophie smiled again. 'Listen, sorry if I was a bit harsh earlier. But dodgy men aren't good for you. So just be careful, Tasha.'

'I will be.' Natasha smiled back. 'Don't worry.'

All the way home, Sophie felt disgruntled yet again by Natasha's secrecy. Once she had known every detail of Natasha's love life, but over the years her friend had seemed less and less willing to confide in her. And tonight she'd briefly opened up and Sophie had ruined everything by jumping down her throat too quickly.

And although she'd tried to brush Tash's comments off, Marcus's appearance had worried her too. He might look like a bulky, brain-dead Sloane but beneath his striped shirts beat a surprisingly sensitive heart, much as he tried to conceal it. He'd only gone into banking to try and make himself closer to his father, and he'd never really enjoyed it. Problem was he was bloody good at it and they kept offering him more money and more money was very, very nice . . . or Sophie guessed it was. If only she could find out.

Her mood was not improved when she got out of the tube at Harlesden to find that while she'd been underground she'd missed a call from Andy.

'Hi babe,' his message said. 'Hope you had a good day. Sorry to have missed you, but I've got good news. I'll be home a week today, should be getting the overnight flight out of Jordan. So look forward to seeing you then. Bye.'

'Oh,' Sophie breathed. At last, something to look forward to. She clipped up the road, past the grimy off licence, past the boutique that sold knock-off sleeveless tops and miniskirts, past the late-night Sudanese grocer with its uninviting pavement display of rotting potatoes and wrinkled root vegetables, past the hairdresser's that did perms for a tenner, over the hundreds of gherkins that horrified kids had discarded from their McDonald's, for the first time in days feeling happy. Andy was coming home. She'd go and meet him at the airport. And, finally, she was going to get an answer from him. She was sick of keeping her life on hold: she wanted to be like Lainey, tucked up in bed with the man she loved, who had promised in front of everyone to have and to hold her until death did them part.

14

'Sorry I got back so late, duckie,' said Marcus, climbing under the duvet next to his gorgeous naked wife. 'I meant to leave early, but there's so much to catch up on the first day back from a holiday.'

'That's OK,' Lainey yawned. 'We had a good time. I have to say, I never imagined myself being friends with people like Sophie and Natasha, but they're good girls. We had a laugh.'

He reached out to her and she snuggled in to him. 'Hello, sexy,' he muttered, cupping her buttocks in his hands.

'Hello,' she whispered back.

Twenty minutes later, they lay entwined and slightly more sweaty.

'Christ, I've got to get up in five hours,' Marcus muttered, looking at the ceiling, where the time was projected by his Oregon barometer clock. 'We're going to have to get into a routine, duckie. Start trying to go to bed a bit earlier.'

'But then I'd never see you,' Lainey whispered, stroking his face. 'Can't you just go into the office later?'

'Duckie, you know it doesn't work like that. If only.'

'Couldn't you work from home a bit more? Marie-Jeanne's husband does and they have a great time.' She stroked his thigh. 'Frequent sex breaks whenever he's the tiniest bit stressed. And then they rent a villa in the Alps for the whole ski season and he works from there. The wonders of broadband.'

Marcus sighed. 'Marie-Jeanne's husband is a hedge-fund manager. They have those luxuries.'

'Well, can't you be one of them?'

'I could try. But hedge funds are risky. You can make a fortune, but you can lose everything.'

'Sounds exciting to me,' she said, her soft breath on his cheek.

'I don't know,' Marcus said. He turned so he could just make out her spiky features in the street light creeping through the blinds. 'It's City stuff and just walking back into the office convinced me that I have to get out of the City. Do something more fulfilling with my life.'

'Cool,' Lainey yawned, her fingers pressing harder into his leg.

'But if I were to do something different, it might mean a change of lifestyle,' he continued, manfully ignoring the second stirring in his groin. 'I'm not sure we could make the payments on this house. How would you feel about that?'

'Babe,' muttered Lainey, who was now wiggling down the bed in a most exciting direction. 'I want you to do whatever makes you happy. Capeesh? That's all that matters.'

Marcus shut his eyes. He'd married the perfect woman. He opened them again and looked at the time on the ceiling: 1.17 a.m. And the alarm was going to go off at six. But he was hardly going to turn down more sex just to grab a few more minutes' sleep.

Yet afterwards, it wouldn't come anyway. Lainey snuffled gently beside him, as he lay there, worrying about the presentation he had to make to investors next week and the bill that had just arrived for the wedding flowers. How could forty grand possibly be right? He'd have to ask Lainey in the morning, but of course there was no way she'd be up before nine at the earliest.

His toes hit the end of the bed. Damn. Lainey had insisted on buying a sleigh bed, because it looked fantastic in the Lombok showroom, but it was just too short for his six-foot-three-inch body. He'd tried to point out this possible flaw when they'd placed the order but Lainey had told him he'd get used to it. He was sure she was right.

15

Like Sophie, Natasha went home irked. Why couldn't Sophie see how lucky she was with Andy? Why was she messing around with that poor Olly, who seemed so nice and obviously was smitten with her, when she had no intention of doing anything about it? And why was she giving her such a hard time about Alastair? Nothing was going on there; God, they had only had lunch, after which she'd spent all afternoon Googling Aurelia Farmer, who turned out to be a Charlize Theron lookalike but with bigger breasts. The whole internet dating thing had touched a nerve too. First Nikolai, now Lainey. Of course the thought had occasionally crossed her mind, but she'd instantly rejected it. As if she would do something as tacky as put her picture up on a website where the whole world could see it. Wasn't it humiliating enough being a thirty-something single career woman?

At work for the next few days, she felt restless. It was now Friday and she was trying to read a script, but was distracted by Dom, who was humming tunelessly as he tapped at his keyboard.

'Good night last night?' she asked.

'Not bad,' he said. 'I think I may have met my future wife.'

'Didn't you meet her the night before last? And the night before that?'

'Oh, ha, ha, ha. No, I think this one is different. I met her at a launch in Brixton. She's a viola player. Her name's India.'

'Right,' Natasha said, trying not to laugh. She'd got the picture, a Jemima Khan lookalike, probably one of Lainey's neighbours, who did a lot of yoga and had her aura cleansed regularly.

'I really think this could be it,' Dom said reflectively. 'I asked for her number and she wouldn't give it to me. So I got her email address off Mike. I'm composing something right now.'

'But she didn't want you to take her number . . .'

'That's just a game,' Dom said confidently. 'She's the type who likes to be pursued. She'll be pleased to hear from me really.'

'She'll probably report you to the police.'

'She's a rich girl,' Dom continued as if Natasha hadn't spoken. 'A bit spoilt, I think. So I'm going to play the slum card. Take her to a gig in a sweaty pub and then on to a greasy spoon.'

Dom always loved the early plotting stage. It was when the girls succumbed to his plans that he lost interest. The challenge was gone. Natasha had long taken note of this.

Just then her phone rang. Emilia was on holiday, so they were having to answer themselves. 'Natasha Green. Rollercoaster.'

'Ah. Natasha.'

Her heart jumped like a cricket in a box. 'Who is this?' she said, although she knew.

'It's Alastair.'

'Oh. Hi. How are you?'

'I'm fine. Very good. Listen, I'm in town and I wondered if you fancied another lunch. That is, if you're free, which a high-powered woman like you almost certainly isn't.'

Natasha had been planning to go to the gym, which is what she did religiously three lunch hours out of five. Well, she'd just have to go tonight instead. Should she make herself so available? She knew what Dom would say about someone who dropped everything to see him at the last moment. But no, this was work, so it didn't count.

'I dare say I can slip out for an hour or so.'

'Great. So I'll see you down in your lobby. In about fifteen?'

But it was more like forty-five minutes before reception rang to say he was waiting. At his suggestion, they went to a rather grimy steak house in Soho.

'So how's the writing going?' she asked, having copied his order of a rare steak and agreed they should share a bottle of red.

He shuddered theatrically. 'Let's just say it would be more fun undergoing open-heart surgery without anaesthetic.' He paused to carve off a corner of meat and plop it in his mouth. 'But hey, that's life. You've just got to get on with it.'

Natasha smiled politely. 'So have you seen *Clutch*?' she asked, referring to the *film du jour*.

'No, no. Not interested. Have you?'

'No, but I must. It's meant to be incredibly moving.'

It was the wrong thing to say. Alastair's face darkened slightly. 'That may be some people's opinion. The guy who wrote it's a complete charlatan. But he's in with the in crowd.'

Only because he's so talented everyone wants to know him, Natasha thought. But she said: 'Oh, I know. It's so unfair.'

'It is, isn't it?' he said, looking slightly happier. He took another bite, then added, 'Listen. Do you mind if we rush through this a bit?'

He hates me. He can't wait to leave. 'Not at all,' she said, starting to carve at the meat for which she had no appetite.

'Because . . .' He smiled. 'Don't laugh, but I was wondering if you'd come shopping with me. I mean, if you have the time. It's just I need a new shirt and I'm crap at doing that kind of thing on my own.' He lowered his voice and added, 'I hate shopping with Aurelia because she drags me in to all the poncey places on Bond Street and I'm more of a Gap man myself. So, if you wouldn't mind . . .'

'I wouldn't at all,' she said a little too quickly.

They walked up to Oxford Street and turned into Muji, where Alastair started rummaging through piles of identical blue shirts. 'Do you think the collar's too big on this one?' he said, holding up one which matched his eyes exactly.

'No,' Natasha said. 'I think it's perfect.'

'Thank God for that,' he said. 'I'll get it.' He glanced at his watch. 'Then let's get an ice cream from that place in Soho Square. Have you tried them? They're amazing. Aurelia won't ever let me have one. Goes on and on about how they're stuffed with E-numbers.'

Natasha was feeling like a foie gras goose, but she smiled gamely. 'Sounds delicious.'

'Oh, they are. They are.' He grinned at her. 'You are the last of a dying breed, you know. A girl who enjoys the good things in life. Not that you'd know to look at you. You must have a really high metabolism or something.'

Natasha's phone rang. She pulled it out of her pocket. Oh bollocks. Mum. She'd better answer. 'Hello, Mum. I'm very sorry but I'm with someone right now. Can I call you back?'

'Oh, no need, darling. I was just ringing to say have you come across that k. d. lang? Lesley played me one of her CDs last night. She's very good.'

'Really? Actually I'm not a huge fan. Listen, I really can't talk now. I'll call you tonight. Promise.'

'Who was that?' Alastair asked. They were standing at the cash desk now, waiting for his card to go through. Before she could answer, he nodded at a table covered in plastic folders. 'Do you like that box file? I think it's the kind of thing I need for my receipts. My accountant's always telling me off. Says I could save tens of thousands if only I were a little better organized.'

'Oh,' Natasha watched him sign his name with a squiggle, then glance at the cashier to see if he'd been recognized. But the young Japanese man's face was blank.

They headed out on to Oxford Street.

'So who was that?' Alastair asked again.

'My mum. Just ringing up to chat. You know, the way mums do.'

'Not really. My mum and I aren't close. My dad walked out when I was little. It's made her a little suffocating. She lives in Scotland and whenever I come to visit it's all:

"Can't you stay longer, Ally?" "Can you drive me to the shops, Ally?" I mean, I like her all right but we need to keep a distance.' He smiled to himself as they turned right into the grubby streets of Soho.

'I know what you mean,' Natasha said, although that wasn't really fair. She adored her parents even if she wasn't always the best daughter in the world. 'But don't you ever feel guilty?'

'No, why should I? My grandma wanted Mum to look after her in her old age, but she put her in a home. People do what they want to do and there's no point trying to stop them. That's the secret of life as far as I'm concerned.'

'And your dad?'

'He illustrates my point,' he said as they walked into the tiny gelateria. 'Mum stole him from another woman, thinking she could tame him. Make him settle down. Didn't work of course. I think there've been at least three others since her.'

'You think? You don't see him.'

'No. Why should I? He doesn't want to see me. Why put yourself through . . . all that emotion? Two strawberry cones, please.'

'And is it just you?'

'No, I've got a brother. Older than me. Not particularly close to him, either. His wife's a bit po-faced and he's got three bratty kids.'

They were sitting on a bench now, in the light drizzle. A *Big Issue* seller approached them. Alastair waved him away.

Natasha forced herself to ask the question that had

been bugging her since that day at St John. 'So when's your wedding?'

Alastair's eyes seemed to have lost their focus. He nodded at a Japanese couple. 'Look at those outfits. Always so chic. How do you think they do it?'

She smiled politely.

'When's my wedding?' Alastair said, almost to himself. 'I don't really know, you know. Sometime next year.' He looked at her full on. 'Do you think that's weird?'

Of course I bloody do. She shook her head. 'No. Not at all.'

'Don't you? Most people who are engaged know when they're getting married.'

'How long have you been together?'

'Nearly five years. We met through friends. And the first three years were amazing. But then, I don't know, things changed. Aurelia got into psychotherapy and I felt she was always analysing me.'

Natasha shrugged.

'She's not an easy person,' he continued. 'Bawls me out if I don't bring her regular flowers and breakfast in bed.' He laughed. 'Maybe I like that. Maybe I'm a masochist.'

'There must be something you like about each other,' she said. 'People don't stay together for no reason.'

'Oh, we love each other,' he said, as if that were obvious. 'But it's difficult. Often I feel we're more like brother and sister than lovers. But it's better to be together than apart. And then she wants children, although I've told her that simply isn't an option.' He turned to her and smiled. 'So what about you? Were you ever engaged?'

'No, no,' she said hastily. 'I'm not really into that kind of thing.'

'So what are you into?' he asked.

'Oh, just having fun. I'd hate to be tied down.' Time to change the subject. 'I saw Lainey the other evening.'

'Lainey?'

'Geraint's sister. You know, the wedding.'

'Oh yeah, of course. The wedding. Not my favourite social occasion right now. For obvious reasons.' He gave a little snort. 'Well, say hello, won't you? Not that Lainey would care. Geraint and I haven't been close since we were about twenty. Oh, sorry,' he said, as his phone suddenly blared out the Scissor Sisters. 'Hello? Oh, hi.' He pulled a face at Natasha. 'Yeah, no, I was pretty wasted. Amazed I could stand by the end of the evening.'

He chatted for about ten minutes as they walked back to the office. Natasha felt like a bit of a fool, strolling along beside him. She hated people who thought their phone was more important than you. But maybe it was a work call? Not that it sounded like it.

'Sorry,' he said again, finally hanging up as they arrived back at the Rollercoaster building. 'That was rude, I know. And I don't want you to think I'm rude. Because I really enjoyed today. In fact . . . I'd like to do it again sometime. Maybe if you didn't mind I could bring some of my new novel to show you? I'd really appreciate an intelligent woman's advice.'

'Yes, I'd like that.'

They stood on Rollercoaster's steps, looking at each other.

'See you,' Alastair said.

'See you,' she said. As she pushed open the glass doors she glanced back over her shoulder and saw him pulling his phone out of his pocket again. But she didn't care. She was an intelligent woman. And Alastair Costello wanted to see her again.

16

Like everything in her life, Natasha's Saturday ran to a strict routine. Up at eight, down to the gym for a two-hour workout and swim followed by a manicure, pedicure and facial in the salon. A gossipy dim-sum lunch with Nikolai. Afternoon spent reading the papers and then scripts. A salad supper, then often a DVD catching up on some piece of obscure world cinema which she could drop into conversation with Barney or whomever she needed to impress. She rarely went out – everyone knew Saturday nights were for Essex people – but instead had her one guaranteed early night of the week, tucked up by ten with the must-read novel of the month.

But today it just wasn't working like that. The alarm didn't go off and she woke at nine, leaving no time for the workout. Then Lowri, her usual beautician, was away, so she had to put up with a trainee who kept sniffing and moaning about her cold as she pawed at Natasha's face. When she got out there was a message from Nikolai saying he was blowing her out because he was in bed with a seventeen-year-old Mexican. So it was back home with the papers and a take-out sushi lunch, but just as she was unlocking her front door her mobile rang. An unfamiliar number.

'Hello?'

'Natasha?' That voice.

'Who's this?' she pretended not to know as her heart accelerated.

'It's Alastair. Listen. I hate to intrude, but you said you lived round here and I'm in the neighbourhood and I just wanted to ask you a cheeky favour.'

'Mmm-hmm,' she said, trying not to sound too happy.

'If I were to drop in with a few chapters of the new book, would you mind reading them? It's just . . . I'm really stuck and I need an intelligent opinion.'

'I will. But on one condition.'

He laughed. 'What's that?'

That you take me to bed and ravish me. 'That you grant Rollercoaster the TV rights?'

He laughed again. 'Tough woman.'

'And that you bring a bottle of cold white wine.'

'Oooh. I don't know about that. Would a warm one do?'

'Certainly not,' Natasha said.

'Then it'll be cold,' said Alastair. 'I know better than to disobey you.'

An hour later, she was sitting on the big blue sofa poring over his novel while he lay like a Persian cat on the rug by her feet, watching her intently.

'So what do you think?' he asked.

'I think it's great,' she said sincerely. 'Really, really funny.'

'Funny? Which bits?'

She gave a couple of examples. He nodded eagerly at the first but at the second a slight cloud passed over his face. 'That wasn't meant to be amusing.'

Immediately she backtracked. 'Well, not funny ha-ha.

More a sly wit, you know. But then your work's full of that.'

'You know,' Alastair said, pulling himself up on his elbow and looking into her eyes. 'I think you are the perfect woman.'

Natasha had that weird sensation you get when your train is standing on the platform and the train next door pulls out. But before she could think of anything sharp to say, he stood up and looked around appraisingly.

'This is quite a place you've got here.'

'Thanks.' She contemplated the airy living room. It was fabulous and so it should be, given the amount she'd spent on builders, interior decorators and designer furniture.

'Must have cost a fair amount. Rollercoaster obviously pay you well.'

'Not badly,' she said casually, wiping a small speck of dust off the side table with her sleeve.

The entryphone buzzed loudly.

'Hello, Mrs Popular,' he said. 'Is this one of your lovers?'

God, if only he knew the truth. 'Probably,' she smiled, jumping up and going to the handset. Almost certainly it was a pizza delivery for Stuart downstairs.

'Hello?'

'Angel?' crackled a voice.

'Mum!'

'Angel, you're in.' The voice grew fainter. 'She's in,' Natasha heard, followed by another voice saying, 'Good.'

'Mum, what are you doing here?'

'Oh angel, I hope you don't mind but Lesley and I were

139

in town doing some shopping for Paige's birthday and we thought we'd be in too much of a rush to see you, but we got it all done and dusted with an hour or two to kill before the train, so we thought we'll just try our angel. On the off chance. And you're in.'

'I'm in,' Natasha agreed.

'Well, can we come up? It's raining out here.'

'Of course.' Natasha buzzed them up, then turned to Alastair who was once again sprawled across the rug. 'That's my mum. And my sister. Popping in. Unannounced. So you may want to make yourself spare.'

'Why would I want to do that?' Alastair said, nonetheless hauling himself to his feet.

'Well, you know. You told me how you feel about families.'

He laughed. 'Yes, but I was talking about my family. I'm sure yours are charming. I'd love to meet them.'

'Well, you're just about to,' Natasha said grimly as banging started on her front door.

'Angel, angel!' Mum was standing there, beaming with excitement, laden down with carrier bags. Lesley stood behind her, the usual disapproving look on her face.

'Hello! Now isn't this a surprise.' Natasha was stiff and self-conscious as she kissed them, horribly aware of Alastair's presence.

'Oh angel, I hope you don't think we're intruding,' Mum said. The wily old bat. She'd planned it all along.

'Of course not. Come in. And, Mum, Lesley, meet Alastair Costello. He's a friend of mine.'

Mum and Lesley stopped dead in their tracks. Then they exchanged a look.

'How do you do?' Alastair said, reaching out a hand. 'Although there is no way you are old enough to be Natasha's mum.'

'Oh!' Mum's hand flew to her hair. 'Well, how very nice to meet you, Alastair. Natasha has kept you quiet.'

'Mum! He's just a friend,' Natasha cried before she could stop herself. But Alastair just laughed.

'Natasha and I were actually just enjoying a bottle of wine,' he said. 'Would either of you ladies like some?'

'A bottle of wine in the afternoon? My, we are living the fancy life,' Lesley hissed.

'Le—' Natasha began, but Alastair interrupted her before she had a chance.

'We are a bit, aren't we? But why not? Life's for living, I always say.'

'Hear, hear,' said Mum.

'Well, can we have a tour?' Lesley said. 'I've been dying to check out Buckingham Palace.'

'Of course,' said Natasha. 'I'd forgotten you hadn't been here before.'

'Never been invited,' Lesley snapped. She turned to Alastair. 'I've got two nippers and they keep me pretty busy. It's hard to get up to the City and see Miss Carrie Bradshaw here.'

'Two children? How lovely. What are their names?'

'Paige and Vienna. They're eight and six.'

'God, I bet they're gorgeous. Well, if they're anything like their mother.' Natasha glanced at him to see if he was laughing, but he seemed completely sincere.

Mum was fussing around in the kitchen. 'I'll make us all a cuppa, shall I, Tashie? Where are your mugs? You need a mug tree in here. Would you like one for your birthday?'

'Can't have too many mug trees,' Alastair said cheerily. Natasha glared at him. He smiled innocently at her.

So they did the tour, amidst much muttering from Lesley about how she'd love to buy all her furniture at the Conran Shop but the kids would ruin it and what was that canvas on the wall and did Natasha really call it art? Mum didn't think Natasha had a proper dining table and wondered if the one in the garage might do her, but all the while she kept looking at Natasha as if her lottery numbers had just come up.

'So do you have an arty job like Tashie or are you something sensible?' Lesley asked Alastair, when they were all sitting down.

'Oh no, totally Mickey Mouse. I'm a writer.'

'Yeah?' Lesley's eyebrows raised a fraction. 'Written anything I've heard of?'

'I very much doubt it.'

'Alastair wrote a huge bestseller called *The Silent D.*,' Natasha interrupted. 'It was one of the biggest hits of last year.'

Mum mumbled appreciatively. Lesley shook her head. 'Haven't come across that. I like thrillers myself. Martina Cole, she's great.'

'Really? I'll have to try her,' Alastair said, sounding as if she had just revealed the secret of eternal life.

'Um, if you're going to get the four-fifteen you should think about going,' Natasha said.

'Oh, we've got a while yet. Got any biscuits, Tashie? Or are you still a borderline anorexic?'

142

'Lesley,' Mum exclaimed. 'Come now.'

'So how's Dad?' Natasha tried.

'So well,' Mum gushed. 'Sends his little munchkin all his love.' She looked at Alastair. 'My husband and I have been together thirty-six years and we still love each other to bits.'

'Mum!' Natasha and Lesley groaned, for once united in embarrassment. Lesley looked at her watch. 'Tashie's right. We really should be going.'

'Do you want me to call you a cab?'

'A lift would be nice,' Lesley said acidly. 'But then I doubt we'd all be able to squeeze in the Porsche.'

'Not really.'

'A Porsche,' she sighed. 'That's life without kids for you. Still, they have their rewards, you know.'

Finally Natasha despatched them into a minicab. 'I'm so sorry about that,' she said to Alastair, who was back on the floor again. He smiled at her lazily.

'Why? It was great to meet them. They were funny.'

'Yeah, funny ha-ha. Not funny witty.'

'They were nice. I liked them, honestly.'

'Lesley can be a bit of a nightmare.'

'Oh, she's just jealous of you. As anyone would be who had such a beautiful sister.'

Natasha froze. He'd just called her beautiful. 'Oh, you old charmer, you,' she smiled. She hid her confusion by bending down to pick up the dirty wine glasses.

She felt his hand on her back.

'I'm not being charming,' he said. 'I mean it.' And as she turned round, he pulled her towards him. 'I've been wanting to do this ever since I met you,' he said.

'God,' said Natasha. 'How cheesy is that.' But her words were muffled, because Alastair was bending down to kiss her.

Their lips met for a moment, then Natasha pushed him back. 'Hang on,' she said. 'Wait. This is wrong. What about Aurelia?'

Alastair smiled. 'What about her?'

'Well, you're engaged to her. So you shouldn't be kissing me.'

Now, he laughed. 'Oh Natasha, you're so sweet.' He bent to kiss her again.

'No. Stop!' He frowned, annoyed. 'I can't do this. You're with someone else.'

'Natasha, Natasha. I don't really like talking about it. But since you ask, I'm actually not with Aurelia any more. We've split up. I've moved out. I'm sleeping on my friend Ant's sofa.'

Euphoria filled her chest like a bubble of air. But all she said was, 'Oh. Oh, right.'

'Although,' he said, leaning in for the third time, 'I was hoping I could maybe stay here tonight.' But before she could answer their lips met again.

17

On Monday, Sophie was up at six, bustling around their little living room getting it ready for Andy's homecoming. In the end, she'd decided not to pull a sickie, since she'd already had eleven this year, and had asked Yvette for a day's holiday. She placed some M&S croissants she'd bought yesterday in a basket on the table, added a pot of Bonne Maman jam, some butter on a china dish, a bowl of strawberries and poured two glasses of orange juice, which she left in the fridge. She put coffee in the bottom of the cafetière, so all that would be needed for a fresh cup was a quick boil of the kettle, and surveyed the results in satisfaction. Ever since she was a little girl, Sophie had loved creating domestic harmony. It didn't take a Sigmund Freud to work out why.

Time to drive to Heathrow to meet the plane, due in at seven-thirty. Annoyingly, it was a freak scorcher of a morning so she had to keep the windows down – Andy's Vauxhall Cavalier had been manufactured around the time of the first printing press and had no such luxury as air-conditioning – which meant by the time she reached the short-term car park, her carefully blow-dried hair was a mess. She hurried over to terminal four. The BA flight from Amman in Jordan was due in fifteen minutes, so she dashed into the loos, where she drowned herself in Allure, ran her fingers through her hair and pouted at herself. She was wearing a patterned red dress, which she thought gave her a gypsyish air.

'You look lovely, darling,' said the middle-aged Indian cleaner mopping the floor behind her.

Sophie whipped round and smiled. 'Do you think so? I hope so. I'm meeting my boyfriend. He's coming back from Iraq.'

'He'll be so happy to see you.' The woman smiled fondly. Young love was a wonderful thing.

'Oh, thank you.' Sophie's eyes pricked with tears. It was such a romantic thing, to pick your war-hero boyfriend up at the airport.

She stood at the arrivals gate, conscious of other people staring at her, wondering who the excited girl (Sophie still couldn't bring herself to think of herself as a woman) was. Eagerly, she scanned the string of arriving businessmen and -women dragging neat wheelie bags, returning holidaymakers with sunburnt noses pushing huge trolleys and looking disgruntled as they realized that London was just as hot as Greece.

A tall, dark man emerged and for a second Sophie's heart leapt but then he looked up and his face was nothing like Andy's. Where the hell was he? She called his mobile but it went straight to voicemail. The dozy idiot probably still had it switched off from the plane. All around her, people were embracing and exclaiming at how long it had been, how much children had grown. Sophie hopped up and down with impatience. Just then, her phone rang.

'Andy,' she gasped.

'Afraid not,' said a man's voice. Clipped, posh. 'Just wondering where you were.'

'Hi, Olly.' For some inexplicable reason, she felt a little guilty. 'I've got a day off today, actually.'

'Oh. Any reason?'

'Er – no, not really. Just catching up on stuff.'

Ding-dong went the tannoy. 'British Airways regrets . . .'

'Are you at the airport?' Olly said. He sounded put out.

'Um, yes. I am. I . . .' This was absurd. Why the hell was she lying to Olly? She wouldn't hesitate before telling Caroline or Fay what she was doing. 'I'm picking up Andy.'

'So he's back?'

'Yes, finally.'

'Great!' Olly said brightly. 'You must be relieved to have him back. Bugger for me, though.'

'Oh. Why?' Sophie was suddenly nervous. Was Olly about to declare his love to her?

'Just that I'd got a couple of tickets for *Free Time* tonight and I was hoping you'd be able to come with me.'

'Wow. How did you do that?' *Free Time* was *the* play of the moment. Sophie would have worn Marks & Spencer's crimplene for a year if she thought it could secure her a ticket.

'Oh, just contacts,' Olly said. 'Never mind. I'll just have to find someone else.'

'Can't you go another night?' she found herself saying.

Olly laughed. 'Now you really are asking too much of me. It's cool. My friend Zara would love to come. I'll see you, Sophie.'

'I'll be back at work tomorrow,' she said, hating the eagerness which had crept into her voice.

'Bye.'

'Bye.' Sophie stared at the phone, oddly discomfited.

She was so used to being Olly's number one girl, it unnerved her to think of some Zara waiting in the wings. Zara was a much cooler name than Sophie with its inevitable nickname Sofa, which is what Andy used to call her when they'd been getting on better.

'S-Soph,' said a voice behind her.

She whirled round. Andy standing there, unshaven, with deep violet patches below his eyes.

'Baby!' she exclaimed, throwing herself into his arms and kissing him hard on the mouth. 'Oh sweetie, are you all right?'

'Of course,' Andy said, bemused. He kissed her back. 'G-good to be home.'

'I've missed you so much.'

'Missed you too,' he said. Sophie's stomach rumbled like an approaching thunderstorm. 'Bloody hell,' he laughed. 'S-someone's hungry.'

'I didn't have any breakfast.' She smiled at him provocatively. 'I was waiting for you.'

They made their way out to the car park. Sophie would have liked them to have been strolling hand in hand, occasionally stopping to kiss one another, but instead she was pushing one huge trolley laden down with photographic equipment and he was pushing the other. It took an hour to load it all, and then an accident meant they had to sit for two hours in traffic on the M4.

In the end, they didn't get home until noon. The croissants sat limply in their basket, the flowers had wilted in the heat and the pat of butter had melted into a river of fat.

'It's all ruined!' Sophie wailed.

'No, it's not,' Andy panted, red in the face from four trips up the stairs lugging equipment. He looked at the bowl of strawberries encircled by buzzing flies and laughed. 'Well, maybe it's not in peak condition but that's my fault, not yours.'

'I wanted it to be perfect for you.'

'It is perfect. All of it.' He came up behind her and grabbed her round the waist. 'All of it.' His hand reached up under her dress, crawled up her thigh. Sophie wiggled happily. His fingers stopped. 'You're not wearing any knickers.'

'No,' she giggled.

He pushed her down on the sofa. She pulled him to her eagerly. But then his mobile rang.

'Ow. Sorry,' he groaned, staggering back from her. 'I'd better get this. Hello? Yes. Hi, Simon. Yeah, I've got the stuff. Do you want me to bring it in? This afternoon? Yeah, in an hour or so, would that suit?' He hung up. 'Sorry. Gotta drop this film off.'

'Now?'

'Yeah. Sorry.'

'But I've taken the day off for you. Can't you email the pictures?'

He grabbed a croissant from the basket and started ripping it with his fingers. 'No, I used film not digital. Better quality pictures. Sorry. We'll do something nice later.' He picked up the pile of post and flicked through it. 'Bills, bills, bills,' he sighed. 'Thanks for leaving me to deal with them.'

'My pleasure,' Sophie snapped. She couldn't *believe* this.

He opened an envelope. 'Oh, look, a wedding invitation.

Elinor and Felix.' He peered at the card. 'Not until November. Oh well. I won't be able to make it. Still, they won't miss me.'

'I'm sure they won't,' Sophie agreed acidly. Els had only been going out with Felix for *nine months*. It was absurd. 'Why won't you be able to make it? How can you know so far in advance?'

'I think I'll be in Iraq then.'

'Andy,' she said suddenly. 'Why can't we get married?'

He turned round and looked at her, as surprised as if she'd just asked if they could give all their money to a cats' home. 'Get married? W-w-what for?'

Sophie wanted to slap him. 'Because that's what people who are in love do.'

For a moment Andy froze. Then he shrugged and turned back to the post. 'No, I don't think so.'

Sophie couldn't believe this. She'd proposed and Andy had turned her down as casually as he might the idea of a trip to the cinema.

'Don't you think it would be fun?'

'It would be bloody expensive,' Andy said curtly. 'I just can't see the point. We could use that cash to buy a bigger place.'

'My dad would help out.'

'Yeah, I can just see Belinda agreeing to that.'

That was true. Sophie secretly worried about how they'd pay for her dream wedding in Betterton. Neither of them had any savings, her dad was married to a witch, her mum to a pauper and Andy's parents, while very pukka, didn't have a bean, having lost it all in the Lloyd's crash.

'Well, can't we just do it in a register office? Or on a beach somewhere. Just the two of us.' The thought of herself in a floaty white sarong somewhere on a clifftop was most pleasing. Or on white sands in the Caribbean. Sophie longed to go to the Caribbean. Lainey had been to Tobago twice and said it was paradise on earth.

'Soph,' said Andy, exasperated, 'it's not just that. I simply don't want to get married, all right? Now I'm going to have a shower.'

Sophie gazed after him, anger mixing with indignation. She'd finally done it, finally said what had been on her mind for so long and that was it. Door slammed. No discussion.

Time for Plan B. She'd been practising the line for a while, but her mouth still felt as if it was stuffed with crackers.

'I'm pregnant.'

She said it quietly, not believing she was actually going through with it.

Andy turned round in the doorway. 'What?'

'I'm pregnant.' This time she said it loudly.

Andy looked as if he had been hit in the stomach by a cricket ball.

'Oh, shit,' he said.

18

'Pregnant?' Natasha had absolutely no idea what to say. She and Sophie were sitting in her living room, curled up on the big blue sofa, both holding huge glasses of white wine, which Natasha had poured as soon as she got the call that her friend had split with Andy and was on her way round.

'Pregnant?' she repeated. What was the correct response? Congratulations or commiserations? Personally, she was shattered. She knew what this would mean. She'd seen it so many times before. Throughout the pregnancy she and Sophie would still see each other although each encounter would be less and less satisfying, with Sophie banging on about morning sickness and fluid retention and the nightmares of finding fashionable maternity wear, as if she were the first woman in the world ever to spawn. But the birth would mean the end of everything. Natasha would visit bearing the compulsory flowers and cute babygro, Sophie would tell her at length about her labour, while all the time focusing on the wailing thing at her breast, and Natasha would go home depressed at finding yet another friend appeared to have had a lobotomy along with her epidural.

But before she gritted her teeth to say: 'That's great

news,' the guilty smile that Natasha knew so well, from the years of Sophie borrowing her clothes and returning them reeking of fags and stale beer, appeared.

'Don't worry. I'm not really up the duff. It's a trick to let you know for sure how he feels about you. I got it from a book. And it works.'

'Soph! You lied to Andy!'

'So?' Sophie pulled a packet of cigarettes out of her pocket and lit one. 'I had to know where it was going. I love Andy but I want commitment.'

'Andy *is* committed to you. He's just worried he doesn't have the kind of stability for marriage and families and . . . all that.'

'Other people don't have that stability, but they still get on with it. They don't say: "Oh, shit."'

'Andy's probably just trying to get his head round all of this. Remember, he's a photographer. He's not good with words.'

'Tash, stop defending him. It's over. I'm boyfriendless. Homeless. Pregnant.'

'No, Soph, you're not pregnant.'

'Oh no,' Sophie said. 'Nor I am. I keep forgetting. Well, thank God for that at any rate.'

'I guess.'

'Are you all right?' Sophie asked, peering at her. 'You seem a bit . . . weird today.'

'Me? Yes, I'm fine.' Feeling her cheeks reddening, Natasha got up and started rearranging her Moroccan cushions, which seemed mysteriously to have moved themselves out of place.

'No, you're not. Something's going on. Tell me.'

'Soph, you have enough to worry about. It's no big deal, just a work thing.'

'No, it's not. You never get like this about work. Tell me. It'll distract me.'

She'd avoided discussing her love life for so long, it was like speaking Vietnamese. But her need to talk overwhelmed her.

'Well, you remember I told you about a guy called Alastair Costello?'

'Uh-oh. I think I know what's coming.'

'Well, he stayed the night here on Saturday. And it was . . .' She flushed again as she remembered. 'Wonderful. But then yesterday morning, he left. He didn't even want a cup of coffee. And since then I haven't heard from him.'

'This is the engaged guy, right?'

'He's not engaged any more! They've split up. He's sleeping on a friend's sofa.'

'Right,' Sophie said, trying to keep the scepticism out of her voice. 'Well, Tash, I wouldn't sweat it too much. It's only been a day. Guys love to torture you like this. I wouldn't start worrying until at least Wednesday.'

'Do you really think so?' Natasha's face brightened. Sophie felt a tug of affection for her. For Natasha to say anything about her love life meant she must have it really bad.

'Of course. And don't you even dream of calling him.'

'Really? But what if he's lost my number?'

'What, he's lost his mobile and he can't call you at Rollercoaster? I don't think so, honey. Or if that's the case, he's so stupid you really don't want him. What did he say when he left?'

'"See you."' Natasha shivered, remembering the delicious night, which had blurred into a blissful morning that had suddenly come to an end when Alastair had seen the clock and shouted: 'Oh Christ, I've got to go,' before disappearing into the shower, struggling into his clothes and dashing out of the front door, leaving her barefoot in her silk dressing gown to moon away the rest of Sunday and – more disastrously for her various projects – Monday.

'Tash, he'll call,' said Sophie with more conviction than she felt. 'And if he doesn't he's just not that into you.' She said the last line with an American accent, then laughed at Natasha's frown. 'It's from *Sex and the City*. How can you work in television and not know that?'

'Dom doesn't think much of girls who call him,' Natasha said reflectively.

'Dom? Oh, lechy Dom!' Sophie always enjoyed hearing stories about Dom and his harem. 'Well, there you go. I mean, not that I'm saying Alastair is a lech, but if he's just come out of an engagement . . .' Before she could expand her phone rang. She grabbed it. 'Oh my God, it's Andy! Hello? Hello?' She looked at Natasha in disgust. 'There's all this background noise. It sounds like he's on a train. Hello? Yeah, I can hear you. Just.' She listened, bit her lip and ducked her head. 'I'm OK,' she said, trying not to let her voice wobble. 'I'm staying at Tasha's.' Another pause, then: '*What?* So you could be away for days? When our relationship is on the rocks . . . Yes, I know how it is . . . Yes, you bloody know I do . . . OK. Well, we'll see about that.

'Christ!' She flung the phone across the room, then sat

down again. Her hands shook a little as she took a gulp of wine. 'A bomb's gone off in Paris. So he's had to go. Doesn't know when he'll be back.'

'Well, you know that's his job,' Natasha said cautiously.

'Yes, I bloody know! But that's at the root of our problems. He loves that job so much more than me. More than our unborn baby.'

'But there is no baby.' This situation was so confusing. It was rubbish of Andy to go off like that, but not so rubbish when you knew Sophie had lied to him.

'I know there's no baby.' Sophie lit another cigarette. 'God, this is a mess. Well, I'll just have to wait until he gets back. And in the meantime try and enjoy myself without him. I'm fed up with wasting time.'

Her phone rang again.

'Aha. Right. This will be him grovelling.' She fished it out from behind the cushions where it had landed. 'Not sure I'm going to answer, actually.' But then she looked at the caller display. 'Oh. It's not Andy. It's Olly. God, he's persistent. Hello? . . . Hi, Olly. Yeah, just having a chilled time . . . No, I'm not with Andy, actually I'm at my friend Tasha's. Remember her?' She smiled at Natasha. 'Olly says "Hi".'

'Say "Hi" back.'

'She says "Hi" too . . . Wednesday? Yeah, no, Wednesday I don't think I'm doing anything. Why, what were you thinking of? . . . *Free Time*! But I thought you'd been already . . . Oh, you had to cancel? Oh my God, Olly, that sounds amazing. I'd love to come. Thanks. Great. See you at work tomorrow then.' She hung up, smiling again. 'Olly's taking me to *Free Time* on Wednesday night.

You see! Life has to go on. I'm going to get out there and enjoy the single life.'

'Aurelia's in *Free Time*,' Natasha said softly.

'Who?'

'Aurelia Farmer. Alastair's ex. Really beautiful and talented too, apparently.'

'Even better. I can check her out. I bet if she's beautiful she can't act to save her life. Anyway, in the flesh she's probably not all that. It's when you actually see them you notice all the plastic surgery.' Sophie hesitated. 'Though perhaps now I'm single I should be thinking about some Botox. How much does it cost?'

'Sophie, you don't need Botox and you're not single. Andy's just gone away. When he gets back, you'll talk. You'll explain you told a silly lie and you'll sort it out.'

'I'm not going to tell him I lied! That would be hideous.' She stared at Natasha. 'Oh, come on, Tash. You can't seriously expect me to do that! You can't.'

Natasha shrugged. She knew that whatever she told Sophie to do, it would make no difference. Her friend was determined to bring things to a head and at this point Natasha couldn't blame her.

19

It was Wednesday night. Sophie was sitting in the darkened stalls of a West End theatre, bored out of her mind. Bored and guilty. She should be stimulated, moved, provoked by this innovative drama but all she could think was how much her seat was hurting her bum, how hot the room was, how the gin and tonic she'd had during the interval was luke-warm and cost a fiver and as for the programme . . . four pounds for a collection of bloody adverts. Of course Olly had paid for everything, but that wasn't the point.

Concentrate, she told herself. This is the hottest ticket in town. But the actors were always so offputting, shouting so people could hear them right up at the back. Apart from Lara Barker, who spoke so faintly you had to struggle to hear her. In fact, infuriatingly, the only good person in the whole production was Aurelia Farmer, whom Sophie was sure she recognized from *Emmerdale* or something. What the hell was she going to tell Tasha? Sophie searched in vain for a flaw, but all she could see was perfect porcelain skin, a halo of blonde curls, round blue eyes and a commanding presence that during her brief appearances brought the audience temporarily to life.

But even Aurelia wasn't enough to stop Sophie's mind darting around like a bird trapped behind a window. Nearly forty-eight hours had passed, Andy hadn't rung and she was far too proud to call him. She knew he was in Paris because she'd seen his photos in the paper, and that there were still investigations going on into the bomb that had killed twenty people, but she didn't understand why he couldn't have picked up the phone. Clearly her relationship was coming to an end. Sophie felt sad of course, but her overwhelming feeling was indignation that her game plan of marriage by thirty and a baby by thirty-one was so seriously out of whack. By the time she started again she'd have lost a disastrous amount of time: it would take a few months to find a new boyfriend, a year maybe before they could marry, another year before she'd get pregnant. Why hadn't she left Andy earlier? I'm a fool, she thought, clenching her fists in frustration. Then, glancing sideways she caught Olly's eye.

'Are you enjoying this?' he whispered.

She grinned. 'Not really.'

The woman in front of them whipped her head round and stared angrily.

'Shall we get out of here?'

'Shhh,' snapped the woman.

They were right in the middle of the row. And the tickets were forty quid each – Sophie had looked.

'Let's go,' she giggled.

Five minutes later they were on the street.

'I can't believe we did that.'

'Why not?' Olly shrugged. 'I don't believe in wasting time. If something's not working for you, then get out. Move on.'

Sophie looked at him with interest. 'That's exactly what I think.'

There was a moment's silence, while buses and cabs roared past them, tourists elbowed them and a beggar approached asking for change. Olly gave him a two-pound coin.

'Shall we get a drink?' Sophie said. 'Or a bite to eat?'

'Why not? Fancy the Groucho Club?'

'Ooh, yes.' Sophie had always wanted to go to the Groucho. Natasha seemed virtually to live in there; she said it was 'full of media wankers'. It sounded like Sophie's idea of heaven.

'It's such a nice night, we might as well walk,' Olly said. He looked at her anxiously. 'That is, if you don't mind.'

Thinking of her kitten heels, Sophie was about to protest, but she had a sudden idea that it might be important to be extra nice to Olly. 'Walking would be lovely. Er, it isn't far, is it?'

He laughed. 'It's about five minutes away. Just round the corner.'

So they walked up Wardour Street, down a short patch of Old Compton Street filled with laughing groups of gay men and on to Dean Street.

'I never knew it was just here,' said Sophie, enchanted by the discreet, unmarked door.

'Olly,' said a glamorous, tall black girl behind the desk. 'How are you?'

'Really well, Syrie.' He smiled as he signed himself in. 'This is my friend, Sophie.'

'Hi,' said Syrie, looking her up and down unenthusiastically.

The bar was packed with groups of laughing, red-faced men and exotically dressed women. Every head turned as they walked in, examined them and then, disappointed, turned back. There was nowhere to sit.

'Let's go through to the restaurant,' Olly said, frowning slightly.

But there were no tables there, either. 'Nothing before ten,' another annoyingly pretty girl informed them regretfully. Sophie knew not even to bother batting her eyelids and pleading.

'Damn.' Olly looked put out.

'There's loads of other places we could go,' Sophie said brightly. 'We *are* in Soho.'

'Yeah, I know, but . . .' He looked at her. 'Look, there's loads of nice food at my place. And wine. What do you think about going back there? It would just seem more relaxing somehow.'

Sophie felt a little bell tinkle at the back of her mind. Was he saying what she thought he was saying?

She shouldn't really go. She should plead tiredness and go back to Tasha's. But Tash had said she was going to be working late. Sophie didn't like the idea of going back to an empty house. She'd like to check out Olly's Kensington mansion. Anyway, she was hungry. Loads of nice food. It was a tempting offer.

But the offer wasn't just about food. Sophie knew that.

She felt slightly dizzy. 'Maybe we could watch a bit of telly,' she said slowly. 'Just chill out. Get that boring play out of our systems.'

'I've got cable.'

'Then what are we waiting for?'

*

161

Sophie couldn't believe Olly's house. It was just off Kensington High Street, a short walk from the office and Holland Park, in a Victorian terrace with a wide stone staircase leading up to the front door. Even bigger than Marcus and Lainey's.

'This is like something out of a Richard Curtis film,' she gasped. 'Nobody real lives in houses like this.'

'Well, I do,' Olly laughed. 'I had the money, so I thought why not spend it?'

Yet although she was impressed, the house also made her uneasy. Olly was twenty-six, so why was he living in the house of an elderly Saudi sheik? And inside it felt so bleak. The living room, which was about the size of the *Daily Post* office, contained only a sofa in a William Morris print, a state-of-the-art entertainment centre and a huge pile of surprisingly hip novels – the kind of stuff Natasha was always reading. But no photos. No knick-knacks. Nothing to tell you anything about who Olly really was. It certainly needed a feminine touch. Sophie wondered if he had ever had a girlfriend. Perhaps he was still a virgin.

She realized she'd always considered Olly a good friend, but in fact she knew very little about him. And now here she was, alone with him, in his house. He didn't *look* like an axe murderer but you never could tell.

'Do you have a family?' she asked nervously.

'Of course,' he laughed. 'Doesn't everyone? My parents live in the South of France. They retired there two years ago. And I've an older brother who's a geologist. He lives in Doncaster.' He walked over to the stereo. 'Music, madam?'

'I think so. What have you got?'

He fiddled with a few knobs and some astonishingly hip tune filled the room.

'What's this?' she asked. Sophie's musical knowledge extended as far as Kylie, Robbie and the complete works of Abba.

'They're called the Raybusters. Good, aren't they?'

'I guess. I didn't know you were a muso.'

Olly smiled. 'There are lots of things about me you don't know. Now, would you like something to eat?'

'Yes, I would. I'm starving.' She followed him into the kitchen. All Poggenpohl and again utterly characterless. But the fridge was filled with delectable pâtés, cheeses and salads in pretty china bowls. Olly spread them out over the mahogany dining table, while Sophie sat back in a hard chair and watched.

'And a bottle of champagne?' he said, waving it under her nose.

'When do you find time to shop for all this?' Sophie asked, puzzled. She was finding this display disconcerting. He couldn't keep all this stuff in his fridge just for himself. But surely it wasn't there for her? The thought made her a bit queasy and she suppressed it instantly.

'Oh, I just fit it in,' Olly said. 'It's important to live well, I think.'

'I thought only gay men lived like this,' Sophie said, popping an olive in her mouth. Then she saw Olly's face. 'I mean . . . I don't think you're gay.'

'Good,' laughed Olly. 'Because I'm most definitely not.'

There was a brief silence.

'I'll crack this open,' Olly said, picking up the bottle again. He filled their two glasses. 'Cheers.'

'Cheers.' They clinked. Then there was another silence as they both drank.

'So,' Olly said, not meeting her eye. 'How's it going with Andy?'

So they were talking about it. The hippopotamus in the middle of the cosy room that was their friendship, which so far both had managed not to mention. Sophie could feel every muscle tensing. 'Oh, you know, OK,' she said lightly.

'He's in Paris right now, isn't he? It can't be easy.'

'No.' She smiled. 'It's not easy.' She swallowed the champagne in one. She might as well start telling people. 'As a matter of fact . . .'

'Yes?' Olly said, looking at her intently.

She paused, then said in a rush, before she could change her mind, 'I think we're splitting up.'

'Oh.' Olly also took a gulp of champagne. 'How sad.'

'Yes.' She fidgeted. 'God, I'd love a cigarette.'

Olly jumped to his feet, like an obedient servant. 'Well, actually, I hope you don't mind but I took the liberty of buying some. Just in case you dropped by.' He opened a drawer. 'It is Marlboro Lights you smoke, isn't it?'

'Er, yes.' Now this *was* a little creepy, but then again, she could have a fag. She took a cigarette, lit one with matches also provided by Olly and tapped some ash into a saucer which he had shoved under her nose.

'I've got something else for you,' Olly said eagerly.

'Oh?' Sophie's heart lolloped. What might it be this time? A mink coat? A Ferrari?

'Yes.' He turned to the dresser and picked up a pile of

papers. 'It's a very early draft of my book. Because you said you'd like to read it.'

'I *did* and I *would*,' Sophie gushed unconvincingly, looking at the top sheet of paper. *The Politics of War*, she read. 'Thank you *so* much, Olly. That's fantastic.'

'My pleasure,' said Olly, going pink in the face. 'It's not completely finished yet, I'm still working on the final draft but you did say you'd like to read it and . . .'

There was a pause when they both sat there like actors who'd forgotten their lines.

'So you and Andy,' Olly said, clearing his throat. 'You *think* you're splitting up or you *have* split up?'

Sophie shrugged and took a heavy drag. 'I don't know. But it's looking bad. We want such different things.'

'What do *you* want?' Olly asked gently.

Sophie considered the question. 'A family. Security. I didn't have much of that when I was growing up.' God, she sounded like someone on *Oprah*. 'But Andy loves the unpredictability of his life. Not knowing where the next cheque's coming from. Not knowing if the next war zone he goes to will be his last. We're just too different.'

Olly was nodding sagely. 'That's tough,' he said.

The bells, the warning bells again. Sophie felt like Quasimodo. 'So what about you, Olly?' she said, her voice sounding forced and unnatural. 'Any excitement in your love life?'

Olly laughed a little ruefully. 'Mine? Oh no.'

Sophie suddenly wanted to hear it, to be reassured someone wanted her, that she wasn't going to end up old and alone, wandering round the supermarket with a basket containing one apple and a can of cat food and nursing an unrequited crush on the vicar.

'There must be someone you like?' she coaxed.

Olly looked away. He had a funny profile: that beaky nose hidden amongst fleshy cheeks. He would never, ever be handsome. Mentally, Sophie tried to redesign him: a diet, a bit of hair gel to give that prematurely receding mop some definition, better clothes. But no. It didn't work. It would be like trying to make over your grandfather.

'You know there is,' he said.

'No, I don't,' Sophie fibbed. 'Tell me. Who?'

'You know who.'

'No, I don't.'

The CD had stopped. There was no sound but the flickering of the fire.

Olly put down his glass. 'Sophie, you know I'm mad about you. Always have been. I think you're the most beautiful woman I've ever seen.'

Sophie put her fingers up to her face and peeked through them coyly. 'Oh no. I'm not.'

'You are.' He stood up. 'I know you were with Andy for a long time. I know you may need some time to get over it. But I'd like to think that one day, you might . . . consider me.'

It was so strangely old-fashioned, Sophie almost expected him to fall to one knee and kiss her hand and start talking about asking her father for permission. 'You're very sweet,' she muttered, half embarrassed, half touched.

He grinned. 'I hope I haven't made a total fool of myself.'

She stood up, feeling as if she were teetering on top of the school diving board. 'You're not a fool. Not at all.' She smiled too and then, screwing up her eyes, she bent over and kissed him on the lips.

20

Sophie had kissed enough men to know what a good kiss was. This was exceptionally terrible. At first Olly just pressed his lips limply against hers, then suddenly he stuck out his tongue and began licking her around the mouth like a cow with a newborn calf. She stepped back, holding out her arms to fend him off.

'Oh. Oh. Gosh. Olly.' Her mouth was covered in slobber. She wiped it with the back of her sleeve. 'Olly, I shouldn't have done that,' she said. 'I'm sorry. I'm . . . I'm just so confused about Andy at the moment. I mean, you're so sweet but . . .'

Olly's round face had gone very red. 'It's OK,' he said. 'I understand. I'm sorry. I took advantage of you.'

'Olly, you didn't! I kissed you. But it was a bad idea. I'm in a bit of a muddle. I'm sorry.'

He picked up the bottle of champagne, filled his glass and downed it in one. 'It's OK.'

Sophie smiled at him weakly. He looked at the floor. 'I've been keeping you up,' she said. 'It's late. I should get a cab.'

'Of course.' He walked across the room and picked up a phone. 'Yes, five Balfour Road. As soon as possible please . . . Yes. Going to Harlesden.'

'Er, the West End, actually,' Sophie said apologetically as he put down the phone. 'I'm staying with Natasha.'

She was waffling, but she needed to fill the silence.

Olly, back at the table now, picked up his glass but it was empty. 'The cab should be here any second. They never take long.'

'Olly, I *am* sorry,' Sophie said. 'But Andy and I are still trying to work things out. I . . . you know, if things were different, or maybe another time . . . but I have to get my head around it all.'

She didn't know why she was saying it, since she had no more intention of kissing Olly again than she did of learning to speak Azerbaijani. But it seemed the easiest way to leave things. After all, she was going to see him at work in the morning. At least he was smiling now, albeit ruefully.

'Sophie, I still think you're gorgeous. But I was wrong to say all that to you. You're in the middle of a break-up. You need time. Don't worry, I'm still your friend. You can always talk to me, you know.'

'You're so sweet,' she said, cringing as she realized it was the second time she'd said it. To her relief, a car honked outside. 'Well, that's me!' Christ, if she carried on talking such crap, Olly certainly wouldn't love her any more. And even though she would never want to snog him again, she didn't like that idea at all.

He got up and walked her to the door.

'You don't have to come downstairs,' she said hastily. 'I'll be OK.'

'Well.' He shifted nervously. 'All right, then.'

'All right.' She leaned forward to kiss him, just as he stepped back. She ended up brushing his left ear with her lips.

'See you tomorrow, Olly. Thanks for a lovely evening.'

'You're welcome,' he said wryly.

It was a quick cab journey back to Natasha's. Sophie prayed she wouldn't have gone to bed, but her door was shut and the lights were all off, with the torturous futon laid out in the living room.

She went into the bathroom, shut the door, sat on the loo and began to cry: acid tears that stung her eyes, then body-shaking sobs, louder and louder until she had to grab a towel and bite it to keep the noise down.

She cried for her and Andy, for the past they'd shared and the impossibility of a future. She cried for the end of her friendship with Olly, for the end of the harm-less ego-bolstering and spoiling that it brought her. She cried for her future self: having frantically to fill every Saturday night. Signing up for group activity holidays. Going to galleries and exhibitions to 'make the most of London' but with the secret hope of meeting someone. Getting all excited about parties and planning her outfit days in advance and then coming home disappointed and flat. Blowing out visits to elderly relations when a friend asked her round for Sunday lunch. All the stuff she'd witnessed Caroline doing and felt a cosy shudder of *schadenfreude*.

She got into bed where she hoped to cry herself to sleep, but it didn't work like that. At about 3 a.m., she got up, went to the bathroom and fumbling around found one of Natasha's sleeping pills, which her GP prescribed her for jetlag.

That did the trick.

*

Of course, she overslept. By the time she dragged herself out of bed, groggy and hungover, Natasha had left for work, although she'd left a sweet note saying she'd love to hang out tonight and hear everything.

At the office, she sat quietly behind her terminal with a litre bottle of Diet Coke and some Nurofen, leafing through the new edition of *Eve*. The sound of the page turning sliced through her head like a cheesewire through Camembert. Still, it was comforting to be reminded that while her own life had been undergoing an extreme makeover, the rest of the world crawled on untouched. Yvette was on the phone, her cheeks puffy with indignation as she snapped at Brian. Sophie marvelled at her orange blusher and pink creamy lipstick. Was it specially imported from the eighties?

'Yes, yes, but Sainsbury's closes at ten, doesn't it? . . . Well yes, of course that leaves us time to get there . . . Yes it does . . . Well, we can set the video . . . And I'll go to Robert Dyas in my lunch break . . . Oh, for heaven's sake, Brian . . . No, it was *your* turn to get the cat litter.'

'You all right?' Fay asked from her desk.

'Just tired.' Sophie felt a twinge in her womb and a spot tingle on her chin. Oh great, her bloody period. She'd have to get some Tampax from the machine. Could life get any better? She turned back to Fay. 'So what did you get up to last night?'

A furtive look passed over Fay's face. 'Not a lot.' Then she giggled.

'Fay! What did you do?'

She bent forwards. 'Remember Cheesy?'

'Yes. Oh my God, Fay. You didn't, did you?'

'Might have.'

'Fay! And how was it?'

Fay whispered into her ear. 'Like six-month-old Gorgonzola. Mixed with the oldest pair of socks. And a dead rat thrown in.'

'Yeeeurgh.' Sophie grabbed the bottle of Diet Coke and took a large swig. 'I so didn't need to know that.'

'You did. It's made your day.'

'But, Fay, you swore this wouldn't happen.'

'I know, I know. But a whole bunch of us ended up at a party in Leyton and it would have cost about a million pounds to get home and so we all stayed over and I had to share a bed with him.'

'You *had* to? What, someone put a gun to your head?'

'Well, no. But everyone else was paired off and there was only one room left and it didn't seem fair to let him sleep on the sofa.'

'Fay, it would have been totally fair. He's not your boyfriend. He's got a cheesy dick. And even if you did get into bed with him, you didn't have to do anything.'

'I know. But it kind of seemed rude not to.'

'Ruder to start doing the dirty with someone and then stop.' Sophie hesitated. 'You did stop, didn't you?'

'When I smelt it, yes. I couldn't have continued. I was practically gagging.'

'It's so weird. And you say the rest of him's clean?'

'The rest of him's fine. I can't understand it.'

'God, what a nightmare for him. Do you think anyone's ever going to get the courage up to tell him he has a cheesy dick?' There was silence as they pondered the

172

etiquette of the situation. 'I guess if you really liked him, you'd just get drunk and say it,' Sophie went on.

'But then *he* wouldn't like *me*. Anyway, how could I really like a man with a cheesy dick?'

'Well, you liked him enough to get into bed with him.'

'Only because I was tired and I thought I should give him a second chance. And I'm not a prick tease. Unlike *some* I could mention.'

'Hey!' Sophie flicked a rubber band at her face. 'What are you talking about?'

'I know you were out with Olly last night. He told me.'

'Did he?' Sophie's stomach flipped. What exactly had Olly said? 'So? We went to the theatre.'

'So I hear. And look at you this morning. Does your poor boyfriend know?'

'My poor boyfriend's in Paris,' Sophie snapped. 'As far as I know.'

'Anyway, it's my turn tonight.'

'Your turn?'

'To go out with Olly. He's got tickets for the premier of the new Jake Gyllenhaal film. How cool is that? There was an email when I got in asking if I fancied it.'

Sophie decided the best way to hide her indignation was to bluff it out. 'Ooh! He must lurve you.'

'Bollocks. He does not. You're the only girl he loves. Did you tell him you were busy or something?'

'No. And he doesn't love me,' Sophie said shortly. She turned back to the screen. A new email had popped up. *AWalters@photography.co.uk*. Mouth dry, she opened it. *Sophie, why are you ignoring my calls? Please get back to me. A x*

Ignoring his calls? What the hell was he talking about? Andy hadn't bloody called her. No one had, since . . .

Fuck. Since she went into the theatre last night and switched her phone off.

Heart banging, she reached in her bag, took it out and turned it on.

It rang immediately: 'You. Have. Five. New. Messages.' She listened with increasing happiness to Andy calling, first sounding a bit nervous and polite at around 7.30 p.m. – just the time she'd gone into the theatre; again an hour later; then again and again and again, until 2 a.m. – when she'd been lying in bed, sobbing her heart out. 'Sophie. I'm back in London. I need to see you. I . . . I've been thinking about the b-baby. We need to talk. But of course I'll be there for you.'

She looked up and saw Olly standing on the other side of the office, looking at her. He grinned and waved cheerfully, then turned his back and went into his office.

Who cared about him. Rapidly, Sophie jabbed Andy's number into her landline.

Voicemail.

'Andy,' she said softly, so the others couldn't hear. 'Andy. I wasn't ignoring you. My phone was off. But I can see you tonight. Back at the flat? Call me and let me know what time suits.'

She hung up, looking down to hide the big smile on her face. It was going to be all right, after all.

21

Andy was working all day, so she called and arranged to see him at eight.

'How are you feeling?' he asked her, his voice full of tender concern. 'Are you OK?'

'I'm fine,' Sophie said, guiltily. She should never have told that stupid lie – apart from anything now she didn't know if Andy really cared for her, or if he just felt bad about the imaginary baby. Oh, well: too late.

She couldn't decide how she should look. Gorgeous, but a bit pregnant too – not fat, obviously, but slightly pale and delicate. The lack of sleep helped and she had a fun half-hour in the loos covering her cheeks with powder and making her eyes up extra dark. She took the tube to Harlesden, closing her eyes faintly as it rocked along and tucking her hands protectively around her stomach, which she could practically feel growing tighter, rounder. It was so unfair she hadn't got into drama school.

Andy wasn't back yet, so she let herself in with her keys. The flat seemed oddly impersonal, like a hotel room rather than her home for years. Andy had clearly been having a tidy: her magazines were neatly stacked in the corner, her clothes picked up from the chair and hanging in the wardrobe, while all her jars and potions had been hidden away in the bathroom cabinet.

She looked at her watch in annoyance. Bloody late

again. She turned on the TV and started watching a quiz show. In the ad break, she opened a bottle of wine. Might as well have a glass while she waited.

By nine, she'd had two more, sent three unanswered texts and was debating whether to nip out to the corner shop for some fags, when she heard him coming through the door.

'B-baby, sorry I'm late. I got held up at the shoot.'

'You could have called me.' The old script, the lines remembered without a hitch.

'I k-know, but my mobile was almost out of gas. Sorry.'

The booze had her spoiling for a fight. 'Andy, I don't bloody get you. In the last day, you've alphabetized my CDs and colour-coded my knicker drawer, but you can't bloody charge your phone?'

'S-sorry.' He looked disapprovingly at the empty wine glass. 'You haven't been drinking, have you?'

'Why shouldn't I?' she snapped, then remembered. 'Only the one,' she said more softly. 'I was so stressed waiting for you.'

'Fair enough,' he said, also more softly. 'I think I'll have one too.' He walked over to the fridge, opened it and looked at the bottle of white. 'Sophie, you've drunk nearly all of it.'

'I haven't!' But he was holding it up: actually, there didn't seem to be much left. 'Well, I've had a bit, but . . . you were late.'

'And *you're* carrying our child.' He sounded harsh, but then he smiled. 'Soph. It's amazing news. I can't tell you how excited I am. I . . . I hope you don't mind but I've told Mum.'

Oh Jesus. Andy's mum made the Queen look like a dope-smoking rasta, she was so uptight. When they went to stay with her, they were still put in separate bedrooms. 'Andy, it's a bit early to be telling people. What did she say?'

'Well, she wasn't too happy about us not being married, but secretly she was quite pleased. Have you told yours?'

'Mine? Oh. No. Not yet. Like I said, it's a bit early.'

He walked over to her and put his arm around her. 'Soph. I'm sorry for the way I've been. I'm sorry for what I've said. I didn't think I was ready for a baby. But I've been talking to Shacky and he says there's no right time to have one and I guess he's right.'

'Does he indeed?' Sophie thought that if Shacky said the earth was flat, Andy'd probably start worrying about falling off the edge. Trust him, rather than Sophie herself, to be responsible for this conversion. 'Shacky's got three children by three different women.'

'Yeah, and he adores them all.' He kissed her on the cheek. 'Anyway, I'm really quite excited now. I've been thinking about names and everything. What do you reckon to Jemima for a girl and Cassius for a boy?'

'Cassius? God no! And not Jemima. I used to know a horrible Jemima.'

'Well, whatever. And listen, even though this flat's a bit small, I reckon we could cope for at least the first year. Or maybe we could think about moving to the country. I could commute and you'd have a lot more space. We could be near Mum's and then she could help out.'

Sophie felt like a knife-thrower's assistant, dodging an unceasing onslaught. Move to the country? Be near his mum? She'd rather run naked down Ken High Street.

And despite all these plans where was the wedding word? Or the love one, come to that?

'Well, there's no rush is there?' she said sweetly. 'We've got – uh – nine months to get ourselves sorted.'

'True,' he said and, bending over, he kissed her gently on the mouth. 'There's no rush,' he whispered then, stepping back, held her at arm's length. 'God, you look fantastic. Pregnancy suits you.'

They started to kiss again and Sophie, deprived of real physical contact for so long, felt something melt inside her as his hands ran over her breasts. Briefly she thought of the horrible kiss with Olly and squirmed. This was the real deal. Grabbing Andy's head, she pulled him close to her and slipped his hands under her shirt.

'Stop,' he said suddenly. 'Should we be doing this? In your condition?'

'I don't see why not.' She kissed him again and began tugging at his belt buckle. She was aching for him. It had been bloody weeks, after all.

'It might disturb the baby.'

'Oh, Andy. It won't. Come on. I want you.' She thrust her hands down the front of his boxer shorts. He groaned as she tugged at his trousers and sank to her knees in front of him.

'Oh yeah. Oh yeah.'

She looked up at him. His eyes were closed, his head back. It was great to have this power over him.

'Oooh. Oh my God. I . . . I . . .'

No. Quickly, she pulled away but it was too late.

'Aaah.' He had come. Come all over her face and down her pretty blue shirt.

She got back to her feet.

'Sorry. Sorry, babe.'

'It's OK,' she said grimly.

He was buttoning up his trousers, looking at her imploringly. 'I'm sorry. It *had* been a long time.'

She shrugged. A feeling of flatness came over her, like you got when you peeked at the end of a murder mystery. Why could she and Andy never quite get it right?'

'Oh b-baby, don't look so sad.' Stepping forward, he lifted her into his arms.

'Andy! What are you doing?'

'I'm going to make it up to you.' Stumbling only slightly under her weight, he carried her towards the bedroom. She shrieked in delight as he threw her on the bed and, leaning over her, shoved his hand up her skirt and tugged at her knickers. 'These are coming off.'

She shrieked again, throwing her hands behind her head as he rolled on top of her, his hands running up and down her thighs. This was more like it: what she had been longing for, for months now.

But then she remembered. 'Andy! Andy, stop!'

'W-what?'

It was too late. Andy sat up, confusion and shock etched on his face.

'Y-you've got your period.'

She would brazen it out. 'Andy, I was going to tell you. It came on this morning. I must have lost the baby.'

But he was standing up now, zipping up his flies. 'Why didn't you tell me?'

'I said . . . I was going to.'

But she'd always been a terrible liar. He leaned his arms

179

on her shoulders and looked straight into her eyes. 'Sophie, were you ever pregnant?'

'Of course.' Her voice was all wobbly and high. 'I said I was going—'

'I know you, Sophie. I know when you're lying. You never were. I can tell. You made it all up.'

'Andy, I didn't! I swear to God. I thought I was having our baby.'

'I thought this could be a turning point for us, Soph. I've thought for a while we were on the rocks. But you were lying to me.'

'OK!' she screamed. 'I was lying. But I had to know how you felt about me. I couldn't carry on the way things were.'

She'd never seen him look sexier. She remembered everything she'd ever loved about him.

'Get out, Sophie,' he said. 'It's over.'

22

The morning after she went to bed with Alastair, Natasha felt like Dorothy in *The Wizard of Oz* entering the Magic Kingdom and seeing her black and white world transformed into Technicolor. But now he'd vanished and she was back in the scrappy hamlet in Kansas, with nothing to look forward to ever again, except possibly the Christmas barn dance when (if she was lucky) she'd get a glass of watery punch and a chance to do-si-do with the farm hand. She knew she'd never hear from him again. She didn't deserve to. She'd been so dumb thinking she might deserve him in the first place.

She didn't understand how she could be so good at her job and so bad at relationships. But then it had always been that way. She'd been top of the class at school, but it had been years before she'd had a proper boyfriend. Sophie lost her virginity at fifteen to Harry Kaye, the best-looking guy at Betterton Boys', but Natasha had had to wait another two years to be deflowered by Steven from next door, in her bedroom under her Debenhams' duvet while Mum and Dad watched *The Two Ronnies* downstairs.

Still, at least she'd done what the magazines said you should and waited for someone she loved. Because she'd fallen for Steven passionately. In the six months they went out, they spent hours in each other's rooms under their

Che Guevara posters, listening to Joni Mitchell and the Sisters of Mercy, talking about injustices in the Third World, planning their round-the-world trip for after Natasha's graduation and trying out new sexual positions. She wore his copper ring on her engagement finger and laboriously copied out John Donne poems which she slipped through his letterbox.

But then at the beginning of her A-level year at school, Steven had gone off to Warwick University and although at first they wrote to each other once a week, phoned every other day and visited every second weekend, by the Christmas holidays she sensed a new distance in him. She'd saved all her spare cash to buy him an expensive pair of Ray Bans; he gave her a Massive Attack album. And although they spent New Year together, he returned to Coventry on January 2, saying he had work to do. His calls became more and more sporadic, visits home were cancelled because he had a party or a gig to go to and when Natasha suggested she visit him, a pained tone crept into his voice and he came up with all sorts of excuses. This was before the days of mobiles, so night after night she would sit in the living room, praying Mum and Dad wouldn't walk in, dialling and redialling his halls of residence, slamming the receiver down when another student picked up.

When she did speak to him she would plead and cry, and his voice would grow harder; and after four months he told her he couldn't handle this, that it had all got too heavy, that he was a student and he wanted to have fun. After that Natasha wept every night for six months. Luckily, heartbreak didn't make her give up on schoolwork;

in fact she embraced it as her only distraction from the pain and she won a place at Oxford, but even now, more than a decade later, she'd rather have kept Steven. Amanda, his mum, fed her just enough titbits about his life to make her determined to show him what he'd lost. When she'd learned Steven had gone into advertising, Natasha jacked in her plans of studying law, in favour of the more groovy option of TV. Steven had bought a flat in Bloomsbury, so Natasha bought a more expensive one in Fitzrovia. Steven was on seventy-five grand plus bonus, so Natasha slaved to get her basic package up to a hundred K. Steven went backpacking round Asia, so Natasha set off for South America. The only area where she couldn't beat him was the romantic side: Steven had plenty of girlfriends while Natasha remained almost perpetually single.

She briefly thought she'd sorted out that side of her life with Roberto, the half-Brazilian, half-Irish director of *Prizes*, her first miniseries for Rollercoaster. Their affair began promisingly with him pursuing her avidly, sending her flowers, chocolates and books of poetry, until finally she succumbed. But almost immediately she could feel his interest crumbling like a sandcastle at high tide. Even that first night when they lay coiled together between her sheets, a frantic voice inside her wailed: 'You're going to lose him! Watch out!'

In the next few weeks she watched herself morph from an ostensibly confident, glamorous young woman into a needy, paranoid obsessive. When she asked Roberto how he felt, he assured her he was as keen as ever, but she didn't believe him. When he said he wanted a night out with the boys, she told him she knew there was another woman; when he told her she was mad and went anyway, she spent all night calling his mobile, hanging up in shaky despair when it switched to voicemail. Soon, he told her he wasn't looking for a serious relationship and three weeks later, she found out he was seeing a make-up artist.

The pain wasn't as bad as with Steven, but it was still overwhelming. The mortifying knowledge that she was only an impostor, that she had to work so hard even to be presentable, that she deserved none of the happiness prettier friends, like Sophie, took for granted, returned worse than ever. It was around then she started her retreat from her oldest friend, too eaten up by envy of her looks and successful love life fully to relax in her presence.

She comforted herself with the fact that, unlike Sophie, she didn't actually crave marriage for marriage's sake. A career and friends were far more satisfying. The maternal urge hadn't kicked in yet, and if it did she could always adopt. Men were unnecessary, she decided, although of course, there were still the occasional lapses. Four to be precise: all of whom she'd gone out with for a few weeks; all of whom had quickly seen through her Audrey Hepburn persona to the Kathy Bates in *Misery* behind it, and dumped her. With the third and fourth ones, she'd actually precipitated the dumping by launching into bunny-boiler mode from day one, deciding that since they would soon find out the truth, she might as well pre-empt it.

The failed crush on Andy battered her confidence still more, although she still thanked God almost daily that by now she'd learned enough never to have hinted at her feelings for him. After that fiasco she'd decided just to give up, spending most of her spare time with her gay friends, friends who didn't care if she fancied them or not, who were always delighted to hear from her day or night.

Meanwhile, however, she brooded on where she'd gone wrong. She watched Dom treating them mean and keeping them keen. She studied books like *The Love Trainer's Guide to Men* that told her to keep her distance, be slightly offhand, to make it clear to any guy that she was busy, busy, busy and that he was lucky to have a piece of her. All right, so when she met Alastair she'd broken a few rules by ringing him first, but that didn't count because it was a work thing, and anyway he had a fiancée so she could tell herself there was no chance of romance. But then suddenly he'd been in her flat and he hadn't laughed at her family and he'd wanted her so badly it would have been rude to refuse. But by succumbing to him she'd blown it. Four days had passed now and he hadn't called.

On Thursday morning she went into work feeling like she'd swallowed a cannonball and no longer had the energy to drag it around with her.

'Wassup?' Dom asked as she came in. 'Big night out?'

'Not really. I was here till nine.'

'You're lucky. I've decided I'm never going to drink again.' He grinned smugly.

Thank God, he wanted to talk about himself. 'So, did you have your date with In-dee-ah?' She kept her tone as chirpy as possible.

'I did,' he said happily. 'Sweaty gig. Greasy spoon afterwards. She loved it. Always works. It's how Jefferson Hack got it on with Kate Moss: told her she smelled of wee.'

'But then Kate dumped him.'

'Yeah, well, he obviously lost his grip. Which will not happen to your uncle Dominic. Never fear.'

'Well, that's another weight off my mind, along with global warming and rising inner-city crime rates.' She turned on her computer.

'So easy,' he mused. 'I took her out, showed her a good time, got her drunk and then I put her in a taxi. Just a peck on the cheek. She can't understand it. She'll have lain in bed wondering why I didn't kiss her.'

'She'll just think you're gay.'

'No. She knows I'm not gay. She'll be wondering what she did wrong. Why I didn't fancy her.'

Just like me and Alastair, Natasha thought mournfully, just as he continued: 'Oh, by the way, Alastair Costello called a minute ago. Emilia tried to put him through to me, but he said he wanted to talk to you. How's all that going?'

'What do you mean?' Natasha asked, trying not to laugh as a great burden tumbled off her.

'Well, is he going to write anything for us?'

'I don't know. I'm working on it. I'll call him when I have a minute.'

She wouldn't call him, she wouldn't. All her books said she shouldn't, and Dom despised girls who called him straight back.

The phone rang thirty-two times that day. It was like someone was playing hopscotch on Natasha's nerves. Among the people she spoke to was Sophie, who told her Andy had been in touch and she was going round there after work, so she didn't see herself coming back to Natasha's tonight. Normally this would have infuriated her as she'd blown out drinks with someone important from Channel 5 to be around for her friend, but today it was the only piece of good news as it gave her an unexpected space to see Alastair. But by seven, he hadn't called.

Maybe I should *call him. It's only professional. After all, he called me. And we want to get him working for us.* She slapped down the thought as if it were a mosquito crawling up her arm.

It was 7.30 p.m.; he had her mobile number. Normally, faced with a rare hole in her diary Natasha would have started phone-bashing frantically in search of someone to plug her evening. But tonight she didn't fancy meeting a friend. Just in case. No. She'd go home. Empty again now Sophie had made things up with Andy. Miserably, she pulled on her jacket, packed her bag, walked down the stairs and stepped out on to Percy Street.

She saw him straight away, on the other side of the road standing under the awning of a Greek restaurant, but even though her heart banged in her ribcage like a butterfly, she continued walking steadily towards Charlotte Street.

'Natasha!'

Pretend you haven't heard.

'Natasha!'

This time turn round. 'Oh, hi, Alastair.' A vague smile. 'What are you doing round here?'

'Waiting for you, of course. Why didn't you return my call?'

'Your call? Oh. I meant to, but I was so busy today. Now, I'm sorry but I'm in a bit of a rush, so . . .'

Her words faltered. Alastair was laughing. 'Oh Natasha,' he said. 'You're pissed off with me. It's so sweet.'

'I'm not pissed off with you,' she said with a cool smile.

He laughed again. 'I'm sorry I haven't called. It's just been frantic the last couple of days, trying to get the opening chapter right. But I've been thinking about you. And then you didn't call me.'

'Sorry. I was going to tomorrow.' What did she say now? 'Listen, I have to go, Alastair. I'm meeting someone.'

'Oh, don't be like that. Can't we just have a drink? A quick one.'

She was standing in the middle of a see-saw trying to keep her balance. 'We . . . ell.'

'Just a quick one. Come on. Come on. I've been think-ing up some ideas for you. Don't you want to hear them?'

'Well, if it was a very quick drink.'

'It will be. Very quick.'

Three hours later, they were still sitting in a corner of the Fitzroy Tavern, with Natasha woozy on three pints and suppressed love.

'What about the friend you're meeting?' Alastair had asked halfway through pint number two.

'Oh, she texted me. Blew me out.'

He smiled. 'People can be so flaky.'

Perhaps she should have left after the first drink. But he seemed pleased to see her. He laughed at her jokes and told her funny stories in return and occasionally reached out and touched her face and every time he did Natasha felt a sort of swish inside her, like when she kicked off from the edge of the swimming pool.

'I'm sorry I didn't call you, you know, the morning after,' he said. 'But you could have called me, you know.'

'Oh, I was going to. I just didn't get around to it. Anyway, I'm not much of a one for the phone.' Even drunk, she knew what he wanted to hear.

'My kind of girl.'

By the time they stumbled out of the pub into the Indian next door, they were kissing occasionally. Over the curries and naan and rice, which Natasha pushed dreamily round her plate, they held hands and giggled.

'So where to next?' Alastair asked meaningfully.

'I have no idea,' she said coyly. 'Do you?'

'I thought maybe back to yours?'

Her heart started pounding like a tribal signal. 'That's very presumptuous of you,' she slurred, grinning. Just then a hush fell over the restaurant and she heard her phone ringing in her bag.

'Oh. A call!'

Alastair rolled his eyes. 'It'd better not be someone better looking than me.'

She put the phone to her ear. Voicemail. Clearly it had been ringing for a while, but she hadn't heard it.

'Tash, babe, it's me. Listen, I know I thought I'd be at Andy's tonight, but . . . he's found out and he's really angry. So I'm going back to yours if that's OK. Hope you won't be too late. Sorry if it puts you out.'

Bloody hell. Natasha's first chance of a relationship in years and Sophie'd gone and buggered it up. Not that she was to know, but then why had she been telling Andy such stupid lies in the first place?

Alastair was still smiling at her expectantly. 'So shall we get the bill?' he said. 'And then back to your place for a cup of Maxwell House?'

'Oh!' Natasha cried. 'Sorry, but you see it's not possible. Not tonight. You see, my friend Sophie's staying. She's had a bit of a drama and she's on my floor, so it might be a bit of a squeeze and . . .'

Alastair's eyes, which had been so smiley all night, were suddenly dead. 'I see,' he shrugged. 'Well, that's cool. Another time.'

'I wish we could. I've had such a lovely evening and . . .' She knew she was saying too much, but she couldn't stop herself.

He held up a hand to silence her. 'It's fine. We'll take a rain check.'

'I'm sure she'll be gone by the weekend.'

'I'm pretty busy then.' Having waved for the bill, he slapped thirty pounds on the table and stood up. 'It's no big deal. I'm tired tonight anyway.' He stood up and made his way towards the door. 'Oh look,' he said as she followed him on to the street. 'I'll get that taxi.'

'I . . .' But he was bending down, giving her a fraternal kiss on the cheek.

'See you, Natasha.'

'Oh, I . . .'

But he was climbing into the cab. Natasha stood there and watched it pull away. 'Bollocks,' she breathed as her mobile started ringing again. Saved. It was him, calling to apologize for his sudden moodiness, saying it was just he found her so ravishing he didn't want to let her go.

'Tashie? Where are you? Are you on your way home? Oh my God, it's been a nightmare with Andy . . .'

'I'm coming home,' Natasha said, trying to keep her voice calm, to not blame her friend who had no idea what she'd done. 'You can tell me all about it.'

She was opening her front door when it occurred to her. Why hadn't Alastair suggested they stay at his place? But he was sleeping on his friend's sofa too. That was never going to work. Natasha cursed the bad timing. Of course she'd tell Sophie she could stay as long as she liked but she secretly hoped that futon would skewer her back and the noise from the street would be too loud to stop her sleeping. Because the thought of letting this man slip out of her grasp was more than she could bear.

23

Fortunately, Sophie had come to her own conclusions. 'I feel terrible messing you around like this,' she gasped. 'I'll find somewhere new to stay in the morning.'

It was after midnight and again they were curled on Natasha's sofa, nursing cups of camomile tea. She'd told Natasha how Andy had found her out, how she'd begged, cajoled and pleaded to be forgiven, but he'd told her this was it, that the relationship he'd suspected was dying for several months now had to be put out of its misery.

In return, Natasha had told her how Alastair had waited for her, been lovely and then turned frosty when he heard Sophie was staying.

'I'll get out of your hair,' Sophie promised again.

'You don't have to do that,' Natasha said, feeling mean about her earlier thoughts. 'You can stay as long as you want.'

'No. I'm cramping your style. Though I think Alastair could have behaved a bit more gracefully.' She said the last bit gently.

'I guess. But we hadn't seen each other for four days.'

'But he'd disappeared without telling you.'

'He was working.' Natasha was looking huffy now. Then her eyes flickered. 'Oh God, you didn't tell me. How was *Free Time*?'

'What, the play or Aurelia?'

'Both.'

'The play was crap and she was nothing special.'

Natasha tried to conceal a smile, but persisted. 'What, to look at, or her performance? Because she got very good reviews.'

'Oh, I didn't think she was up to much.' Sophie groped to remember some imperfection. 'Her head's too big for her body,' she added triumphantly, then, alarmed by the hope in Natasha's eyes: 'But I still think it's not worth sweating it. At least, if I were you I'd just sit back. If Alastair wants you, he'll come. But I am really sorry if I ballsed things up for you tonight. I'll be out of here tomorrow. And then, I've told you, we'll have a blast. Think *Sex and the City*. We'll lead the high life for several series and then we'll settle down with Mr Big.'

Sophie was trying to keep cheerful, not to dwell on how appallingly she'd cocked up with Andy, but by mid-afternoon the next day her surge of confidence had waned. It hadn't been helped by *Single and Loving It*, which Caroline, the only work person she'd confided in, had given her.

'This is my Bible,' she'd said. 'Read this and you'll be sorted. Do you want me to organize your Soho House membership?'

As far as Sophie was concerned, you might as well give a depressed person a razor blade and a bumper pack of paracetamol. 'I can't be doing with this,' she moaned to Natasha down the phone. 'Listen. "Fifty reasons to love being single. Number one: you can eat ice cream in bed any time you want." I mean, why the fuck would I want to do that?'

'I can't imagine,' Natasha agreed.

'And listen to this. "You don't have to shave any more. You can turn into a yeti if you want." I mean, is this something I'm meant to be pleased about?'

'Yuck? Although who shaves? Everyone knows waxing is so much better.'

'And here's another one. "You can listen to Robbie 24/7." I mean is that any consolation for no sex ever again? And oh yuck. "You don't have to worry about sanitary towels not flushing away." Who *are* these animals? Are they saying that without men we'd all waddle around with hairy legs and blocked loos?'

Natasha laughed. Sophie suspected she wasn't really listening. Probably reading an email from someone more exciting, like Nikolai.

'Anyway,' she said to recapture her attention. 'You'll be pleased to know I'm making progress. I'm going to see three bedsits tomorrow. I found them in *Loot*. So by the end of the weekend I should be out of your hair.'

'You can stay as long as you like. You know that.' Natasha sounded as if she meant it. But Sophie knew she had to move on, before the fear of single living overwhelmed her.

So on Saturday Sophie went bedsit-hunting, clutching her Oyster card and the well-thumbed copy of *Loot*. Finding somewhere that was actually in Greater London and cost less than a hundred pounds a week was a bit like looking for a morris-dancing Greenlander. Places that fell into that category tended to be accompanied by ominous warnings like 'Christians preferred' or 'Strict vegans only'. But finally she'd narrowed down a shortlist of four, then, after one call was answered with an angry: 'Who wants that fucking scumbag?' three.

'I'm going to be a cool, single woman,' she told herself. 'Even if my room doesn't look much, I'm going to turn it into a haven with loads of bright pink cushions everywhere and I'll always have fresh flowers and I'll do all my shopping at farmers' markets and I'll light all my scented candles at last.' The final result would be just like Natasha's place, although hers might have to be a bit more shabby chic as she wasn't sure she had the discipline for all that minimalism.

The first place was in a tree-lined terrace in Brixton: neat little houses with brightly painted front doors and plenty of SUVs with Baby on Board stickers parked outside. Yes, this would do. Sophie could imagine living here. She was looking for number 43, towards the end of the street. She counted down the doors: 2, 7, 13, 19, 25. Then she saw it. The only house that looked like a crack den. Ragged curtains at the window, the grass in front several feet high, a rusting bicycle with no wheels lying across the footpath. All that was missing was a goat tethered to a chain and a toothless hillbilly playing the banjo.

A skinny woman with enough tattoos on her arm to fill the Tate Gallery opened the door. 'You wanna live here?' she asked dubiously. 'Well, it's up to you.'

They walked in. One not very big room, with a fridge and an electric ring in one corner and a saggy-looking bed in the other. An old pizza box lay in the middle of the floor, next to a half-used roll of loo paper.

'Bathroom,' said the woman, opening what looked like a cupboard in the corner and clicking on a light. A shower head over a dank-looking drain and a loo with no seat on it.

'It's lovely,' Sophie said. Well, it was quite near the tube and the market, which would be great for buying her organic vegetables and bread. And with a coat of paint . . .

Just then she heard a scuffling noise behind her. She looked over her shoulder. A rat had appeared from nowhere and was nibbling at the pizza box. Sophie screamed. The rat turned round, looked her in the eye, and then, languidly, as if he were going for an afternoon stroll, sloped off towards the fridge and squeezed under it.

'Oh, don't mind him,' said the woman. 'He's harmless.'

Sophie told her she'd be in touch.

The next bedsit, in Tooting, seemed fine, delightful even for only seventy-five pounds a week, until someone started banging on the side wall and shouting, 'Motherfucker! Spawn of Beelzebub. Go fuck yourself, devil woman.'

'That's old John. Must have forgotten to take his pills,' the landlady explained. 'He does sometimes. But he's harmless, really.'

So an 'I'll get back to you' there too, then.

The last place had described itself as a 'great location' and that it was, just along from Queen's Park tube in the land of delis and Starbucks. Sophie got there about five. A keen-looking girl in a pink and white T-shirt and pink skirt, clutching a book with a bookmark in the shape of a mouse, peered round the door. 'Sophie?'

'Yes.'

'Hiiiii! I'm Andrea. Come in.'

Andrea shared with Milly and Susannah, a fact not mentioned in *Loot*.

'I thought I was getting a bedsit.'

'Oh, well, no. This is officially a flatshare. But your room is very big.' Andrea gestured at the room. It was about the size of a hamster's coffin. 'Well, the living room's big anyway. And that's where we tend to spend most of our time.' She led her out into the living room. There was a Garfield poster on the wall saying 'I Hate Mondays'. Milly and Susannah were curled up on the sofa, hands curled around flowery mugs, watching a *Friends* rerun and laughing uproariously.

'Don't you love Joey?' said Milly.

'I just wish I was as pretty as Jennifer Aniston,' replied Susannah.

'Oh Suze. You *are.*'

Andrea smiled benevolently at them. 'We have a cleaning rota,' she said to Sophie. 'We each take on a week of doing the small jobs and then every Thursday night we all do a big job together, like cleaning the skirting boards. We order in a Chinese and we have *such a laugh.*'

'Right,' Sophie said a little faintly. She told Andrea she'd think about it. She was wearily walking back to the tube, preparing to call Marcus and ask if she could crash at his place when her phone rang. Oh no. The last person in the world she felt like talking to.

'Hi, Mum.' Tone breezy.

'Darling! What's this I hear?'

Oh God, why did she always have to be such a drama queen? 'What have you heard?'

'I called your flat. Andy answered. He said you'd moved out.'

'That's right,' Sophie said, trying very, very hard not to cry. 'I'm staying at Tashie's. Now, I have to go, Mum. I'm about to get on the tube and I'll lose my signal.'

'But this is terrible, darling! What happened?'

'We just decided it wasn't meant to be, Mum.'

'But you've been together so long. And Andy was so marvellous.'

For Christ's sake. Everyone knew that the only correct response to a break-up was 'I never liked him anyway', not least because your friends and family saying that guaranteed you would get back together again, have dozens of babies and go on to celebrate your diamond wedding anniversary.

'He wasn't right for me, Mum. Now I have to go.'

'Just one second, sweets. I was just calling to let you know I'll be in London a week today and I was wondering if we could all meet for lunch.'

'We all? I'm not with Andy any more, remember?'

'I know. Such a shame. Darling Andy. But no, no. There's a friend of mine I want you to meet.'

'A friend?' Oh, bloody hell. Sophie knew what this meant. 'So you won't be with Jimmy?'

Mum laughed, her best tinkly giggle. You'd never guess she'd been born in Nuneaton. 'No, darling. I won't be with Jimmy. Meet you at the Caprice at one. And wear something pretty, won't you?'

Sophie's call-waiting was bleeping: a number she didn't recognize. 'Fine, Mum. Now I really have to go.'

'Call me tomorrow for a proper chat.'

'Yes, yes, I will. I promise.' Click to the other line. 'Hello?'

'Sophie Matthewson,' said a voice that sounded a bit Cockney and vaguely familiar.

'Who's that?'

'It's your old mate, Julian.'

'Hello! What are you doing calling on a weekend? Bored with Bucharest?'

'You could say that. I'm off to London in the morning for a few days. Was wondering if we could hook up.'

'That'd be lovely.' You see! It was true. She'd been single for less than forty-eight hours and already sexy men she'd always lusted after were calling up and asking her on dates.

'Thursday? If your superhero boyfriend lets you out, that is.'

Great. So she could let him know. 'Actually I'm not with my superhero boyfriend any more.'

'Aren't you?' Julian sounded gratifyingly pleased. 'Well I never. I thought it was about to be wedding bells.'

'Ugh, no. What made you think that? Listen, Thursday's good. Give me a call on the day. We'll arrange when and where.'

She hung up, face glowing. And now her phone was winking with a little text envelope. Probably Andy begging her to come back. But she wouldn't. She'd embarked on a new, exciting dating life.

It was from Fay. *Have found flat for you. Sounds great. Call me 4 detaylz x*

Better and better. Sophie made her way down to the tube platform with a glow in her stomach. All she needed now was a pair of Manolos and her new career as Carrie Bradshaw could begin. She wondered if she could talk her bank manager into extending her overdraft. Cocktails were bloody expensive.

24

The flat Fay had found was occupied by Veronica, who was a friend of a friend of a friend, whom Fay had never actually met. 'But she sounds cool,' she told Sophie. 'She's Australian and they're always a laugh. She said her flatmate was deported last week and she's desperate for someone new. The rent's only fifty quid a week. And it's practically in zone one. Isn't that great?'

'Mmm.' After her flat-hunting experiences, Sophie was a little cautious. But when she phoned Veronica, she sounded really friendly and told her the flat was huge with a great kitchen. 'The rent's so low because the landlord thinks only one person is living here,' she explained. 'But he never comes round and if he does we'll just say you're my friend visiting from Kalgoorlie. So do you want to check it out?'

She went over that evening and liked what she saw. True, her room was small with a single bed and peeling paint and a view of some rubbish bins and a high brick wall, but there was a large, only slightly battered living room where Sophie was sure she'd spend most of her time and, best of all, it was a few yards from Mornington Crescent tube. And Veronica seemed great, chilled with great jeans which looked designer but which Veronica told her proudly were actually Asda. Sophie foresaw girlie conversations wearing face packs over Bellinis and tingled with excitement. Not that there'd be too many of those because

Veronica not only worked days as a hotel receptionist but also evenings in a bar. 'Trying to earn as much of your nice strong sterling as possible before I go back to Oz,' she explained. 'Great for you, though. Means I'm almost never here to get in your hair.'

Now it was Monday evening and Sophie was standing on the doorstep of the faded Victorian house in Camden Town, buzzing the top bell. Beside her stood Natasha, three suitcases jammed with clothes and a couple of Poundstretcher bags. High above her a window opened and a cropped red head looked out. 'Hey, Soph! I'll chuck the keys down.'

The keys, held together by a dirty piece of string, flew through the air and landed beside Sophie and Natasha in the gutter. It took them about five minutes to work out which one went in the three different locks. They entered the hall.

'It's darker than I remember,' Sophie said. The carpet was dirtier and more worn too, but hey, she wasn't going to be sleeping here.

Veronica was slumped in a flowery armchair in dirty combats and a sweatshirt watching TV. 'Howya, Soph!' she drawled, not taking her eyes off the screen. She nodded at Natasha. 'Hey.' Then her eyes rested on their gear. 'So, what's with all the stuff you've got?'

'This is only like a quarter of it.' The rest still sat forlornly in the wardrobe in Harlesden. Sophie hadn't had enough suitcase space to squeeze it all in. She and Natasha had gone over to the flat yesterday when she'd ascertained Andy would be out and packed up. It had been sad, but not tear-jerkingly so, at least not when Marianne downstairs had put on her bhangra CD at wall-shaking volume. No more zone three, Sophie told herself. Time to move on.

'Cool,' Veronica said. 'I can't wait to check out all your gear.' She reached out and fingered Sophie's green silk Paul & Joe top, which was her pride and joy. 'Love this.'

'Thanks.' Sophie took a step back.

'My old flatmate and I were always borrowing each other's clothes.'

'Oh, right.' Sophie looked again at the grubby sweatshirt.

'So . . . I was just doing the maths,' Veronica said, falling back in the chair. 'Might as well get it over with straight away. You owe me a month's rent in advance, obviously. Then there's the TV licence.'

'The TV licence?'

'Yeah.' Veronica pulled a scrap of paper from her bag. 'I just had to renew it today. So that'll be half of a hundred and twenty-one pounds, which is . . .' She shut her eyes as if she were calculating pi to the eighty-ninth decimal place. '. . . sixty-five pounds.'

'Actually, I think it's sixty pounds fifty,' Natasha said hesitantly.

'Yeah, whatever.' Veronica waved a casual hand in the air. 'What's in there?' she asked, pointing at the Pound-stretcher bags.

'Food,' Sophie said proudly. 'A few treats. I thought I'd make us a moving-in dinner.' She bent over and took out a couple of artichokes and peppers, then the two tuna steaks she'd been lucky enough to find in the fish section. It was so exciting having someone new to cook for.

'Oh, right,' Veronica said, eyeing the bags like they were a dangerous dog. 'Nice of you. But . . .'

'But what?'

'Well, I had some stew I made yesterday which kind of needs using up. Do you think your stuff would keep?'

A stab of disappointment. 'Oh. Oh yes. Of course it would.' Sophie smiled brightly. 'The fish can always be frozen.'

'Ah, yeah. I forgot to tell ya. The freezer doesn't work. I tried to get it fixed, but the quotes were so ridiculous and of course I don't want the landlord involved in case he finds out about you.'

'Oh. OK. Well, it'll be fine until tomorrow.'

'I need to explain the food rota here,' Veronica said. 'I hate all that "This is my shelf and this is yours" crap. So studenty. So what we do here is you just buy whatever you think you need, keep the receipt, chuck it in that pot on top of the fridge and then once a month we split the difference. Got it?'

'Yup.' Bollocks. She hadn't picked up the receipt at Poundstretcher, but then the first shop couldn't count. 'Sounds very sensible.'

'I'll put the food on now,' Veronica said, going to the fridge and taking out a chipped bowl of what looked exactly like the diarrhoea Sophie had got on holiday in Turkey with Charlie.

'There's a great market just up the road,' Veronica said over her shoulder. 'If you go at the end of the day you can find some real bargains.'

'Oh, great.' Sophie remembered her shopping in markets fantasy. It was all coming true. She remembered something else. 'Can I do a wash tonight?'

'Course you can. Though the machine won't start until

after midnight. Electricity's so much cheaper then, so I put it on a timer.'

'Let's see your bedroom,' Natasha said. Sophie led her in there, they shut the door and looked at each other with trepidation.

'Are you sure you'll be OK here?' Natasha asked. 'I promise you, you can stay at mine.'

'Babe, I'll be fine.'

They hugged.

'Now don't get all soppy on me. Betterton girls are made of stronger stuff than this.'

'I know,' Tash said, but she sounded a bit choked. Sophie bit her lip hard. There were to be no tears. This was the start of a whole new adventure. At the same time, though, she felt affection for Natasha flare up inside her like a match. After so long growing further and further apart, in the last few days their friendship had got firmly back on track.

'Grub's up!' Veronica yelled.

The stew tasted a little bit like diarrhoea too. Sophie tried to put this to the back of her mind, but she only managed about a quarter. The cutlery she noticed all bore a tiny Vermont Gardens Hotel crest.

'Don't you like it? I'll have yours if you don't want it.' Veronica grabbed her plate and scraped off the murky brown gloop. 'You know, there's a great market stall on Wednesdays where they do like cans of stuff that are only a little bit past their sell-by dates. I used some luncheon meat from there for this. You can save so much if you just think.' She sat back and burped. 'So what are your plans for tonight?'

'Oh. Just unpacking, I guess. Early night. Then tomorrow I was thinking of joining a gym. Do you know where the nearest one is to here?'

Veronica wrinkled her nose. 'No idea. Whadda you want a gym for, Soph? Walking's free, isn't it? Or use some cans for weights.'

'Yes, that's a point,' Sophie muttered faintly.

Veronica, it transpired, was going out to the Cock and Bottle where she worked. 'It's my night off, but they give me free drinks there,' she explained, pulling on a frayed cord jacket. 'Fancy coming?'

Sophie could think of nothing she would like less than sitting in a noisy pub surrounded by people yelling and Veronica dodging her round.

'No. No. Like I said, I've got a lot to sort out.'

As soon as the door clicked shut, Sophie sat on her suitcase and bawled. Why was she here? Why wasn't she settling into her house in Fulham with a Farrow and Ball paint chart? To calm herself down she went into the bathroom and splashed her face with cold water. She dabbed her face guiltily on Veronica's towel. It was rough and scratchy. Something was monogrammed in the corner in blue squiggly letters. Vermont Gardens Hotel. On the edge of the bath she noticed a plastic pot of Nivea body lotion hacked open by scissors so every last drop could be scraped out.

'It's cool,' she told herself firmly. 'It's cool. It's just different from what you're used to. You've got a date on Thursday. Focus on that. A whole new life lies ahead of you.'

Just then she heard her phone bleep in the other room.

'There you go. That'll probably be Julian.' Was talking to yourself the first sign of madness? Oh well, fuck it.

But the text was from Olly. *Hope u OK. Wondering if you fancy a ball at my old Oxford college on June 11. Should be fun. O x*

An Oxford ball! Sophie loved the sound of that. Her in a long black dress like Scarlett O'Hara at the top of a winding staircase. But then Olly wasn't exactly Clark Gable – more like Shrek. And if she went to a ball with Olly, he'd expect a snog again. Or if he didn't he was a serious masochist.

She decided to call Marcus for advice. He had always been her key to the male mindset. But Lainey picked up. 'Hello! It's Sophie!'

'Hi,' she said flatly.

'Are you OK? You sound pissed off.'

'I am. Marcus is kicking up a stink about me going to Uruguay.'

'Uruguay? Oh yes, for the rave.'

'Yeah. He can't take the time off work and I said, "Fine, it's not your scene anyway," but he's saying he feels uneasy about me going alone. Which is bollocks. So I'm booking my ticket tomorrow, but I could do without the stress. Anyway, how about you, Sophie? Have you moved yet?'

'Yup, I've just unpacked and it's great,' Sophie lied. 'And, listen. Olly G-M has invited me to a ball in Oxford. Do you think I should go?'

'An Oxford ball?' Lainey squawked. 'Oh my God, what a laugh. I went to a couple when I was at Bristol and they were excellent. You have to go, you absolutely have to.'

It was what Sophie wanted to hear. 'But you don't think I'll be obliged to put out?'

Lainey laughed. 'Sophie, what century do you think we're living in? Of course you don't have to put out.'

'I suppose,' Sophie said. She wanted to be convinced. A ball sounded so glamorous. A thought occurred to her. 'Maybe I'll meet someone there.'

'Or you could always get it together with Olly. He's got a lot going for him and he obviously adores you.'

'Oh Lainey, don't be silly. He's about half my age.'

'Sure you're not interested?'

'Lainey, you haven't seen him. When you do you'll understand.'

But Natasha, who rang five minutes later to check up on her, could not have been less encouraging. 'Are you sure about this? You'll be giving poor Olly totally the wrong idea. If I were you, there's no way I would go, Sophie.'

'I'm sure you're right.'

She hung up and texted him. *Can I let you know? Only Mum might be in town that weekend. Waiting to hear back from her. Otherwise would be great.*

Satisfied she'd kept her options open, Sophie went to run a bath. Shame Veronica had absolutely no goodies to nick, not even a miniature tub of Vermont Gardens bubble bath. She filled the tub high with her own Space NK stuff. She had a date on Thursday. Single life was beginning. Apart from the diarrhoea food, life was going to get so much better. Sophie was a great believer in mind over matter.

25

Since the drunken curry with Alastair a week had passed and Natasha hadn't heard a word from him. Every time she thought about him, her heart burned with misery. Initially she blamed the situation on Sophie but she knew that was unreasonable. And actually, in every other respect, having her to stay had been an unexpected treat, rekindling their friendship by giving them both the chance to be totally honest with each other for the first time in years.

It had been so good to confide in her about Alastair and her advice to leave him to do the running was right, Natasha knew that really. But could it hurt to remind him how good they were together? Perhaps she should just leave him a polite message with some suggestions she had for his book. After all, he *had* said he valued her opinion and the fact they'd slept together shouldn't come into it.

She was chewing her lips, working out exactly what to say, when the phone rang. Emilia was out, so she answered it.

'Rollercoaster?'

'Oh, hello. Is Dominic Noyes there please?' A female voice. Hesitant. Posh.

He was, reading the sports section of *The Times* and idly picking his teeth. 'I'll just see if he's around. Who's calling?'

She knew it. 'It's India.'

'I'll have a look.' She put the phone on hold. 'Dom,' she hissed. 'India for you.'

'I'm not here!' Natasha gave him an old-fashioned look. 'I'm not! Tash, give me a break. I don't want to speak to her.'

'Why not?'

'Look, just get rid of her.'

'I'm really sorry,' Natasha said, 'but he must be in a meeting. Can I take a message?'

'No,' India said sadly. 'No. No message.' She hung up and immediately Dom's mobile started to ring.

'No thank you!' he said, switching it off.

'Dom!'

'*What?* Look, I just think it's time we had a bit of breathing space. It's been quite intense, you know.'

'I know.' After the sweaty gig date Dom and India had seen each other the following night, and the night after Dom had got her into bed. They had spent the whole weekend at his place, making the beast with two backs, as Dom so charmingly put it. Same on Monday, Tuesday and Wednesday – in fact just before Dom rushed out of the office last night he'd been raving about how he knew he'd found the woman he wanted to spend the rest of his life with.

But Natasha had seen it all before. 'So what happened?' she asked.

He sighed. 'Well, yesterday she said she wouldn't be able to see me tonight because she really needed to get back to Finsbury Park and do some washing.'

'And . . . ?'

'Well, *Finsbury Park. Washing.* I mean, it kind of killed the moment. And you know . . . I had a think about it all and, well, I don't know . . .'

'Dom. Everyone has to do washing.' Natasha looked at him in despair, mingled with relief that India's call had stopped her picking up the phone. She wouldn't call Alastair after all. Imagine him discussing her like this.

Barney's assistant Antoinette stuck her head around the door. 'Natasha, could you pop into Barney's office for a moment? There's someone he wants you to meet.'

'Who?' asked Dom competitively.

'Not telling you.' Antoinette stuck her tongue out at him. Natasha suddenly realized they must have slept together.

'Who?' she said.

'Surprise. Good one, though.'

Natasha got up and hurried down the corridor behind Antoinette. Probably some dull American executive whom Barney would want her to take out and schmooze. But walking into Barney's office, her heart nearly stopped. There, sitting in front of the desk, laughing, was Alastair.

'Hello,' she said. Her voice sounded tinny in her ears.

He turned and jumped to his feet. 'Natasha!' He kissed her on both cheeks. 'Great to see you. How are you?'

'Fine thanks.' Her heart started to beat so hard, she was sure he must hear it. 'And you?'

'Great, really well. Just been having a chat with Barney. We met at a drinks party a couple of nights ago and he kindly asked me to come in. I've been telling him you and I have had a couple of preliminary meetings but we haven't settled on a definite project.'

'I want you to get moving on this,' said Barney. 'I'm a big fan of Alastair's. We need him writing for us before one of our rivals snaps him up.'

'What rivals, Barney? You guys are head and shoulders above the rest of the British television industry, as I've told Natasha until she passes out with boredom.'

Barney threw his head back, laughing. 'Well, tell her again. Because I want you two to go off and have a drink and start making some definite plans.'

'Alastair might be busy,' Natasha said as charmingly as she could in the circumstances.

'I'm not busy,' Alastair said. 'And a drink seems like a great idea. I mean, if you're free.'

'You're free, aren't you, Natasha?' Barney sounded relaxed, but she knew when her boss meant business. He got up and held out his hand to Alastair. 'I'd love to join you guys, but Dane and I are having dinner with Melissa and Tchaik at Mirabelle.'

'Hard life, eh, Barney?' Alastair grinned.

'It is actually. But there are compensations. See you, children. Have fun together.'

'I'll just go and get my bag,' Natasha said frostily. 'I'll see you down in the lobby, Alastair.'

'Fine,' he smiled. He was looking particularly devastating in a rumpled green linen suit.

She went back into her office.

'Who was it? Who did Barney want you to meet?'

'Oh, only Alastair Costello.' She wondered if there was time to redo her make-up, brush her hair and have liposuction on her bum. Why, why was she wearing her most hideous shit-brown skirt suit that she'd bought in a sale because it was Donna Karan and had a hundred pounds off, and now had to force herself to wear once a month despite its utter hideousness, because it was Donna Karan and had still cost six hundred pounds? Still, too bad. No way was she going to flatter Alastair she'd made an effort.

In the lobby, he was reading a copy of the *Sun* and whistling softly to himself.

'So where would you like to go?' she said briskly.

'Are you OK? Have you had a bad day?'

'Not at all. Where would you like to go?'

He looked confused. 'Well, that pub we went to last time seemed fine.'

Last time. So he did remember that evening. 'Fine,' she said coolly.

They set off down the street, her nose in the air. He walked beside her silently.

'I get the feeling you're pissed off with me,' he said as they turned into the pub.

'Why should I be pissed off with you?' she said shortly, opening her purse. 'What would you like to drink?'

'Er, a pint of bitter. But I'll get them. You sit down.'

She sat on a curry-stained banquette, gazing fixedly in front of her. This was going to be a work discussion. She wouldn't get emotional. Act breezy, happy, like she didn't care.

He joined her. 'I've missed you,' he said straight away.

'Alastair, we're here to talk about business,' she said in her best bored voice.

'Oh, don't be like that.' He laughed and reached out to stroke her face. 'I know I haven't been in touch for a few days, but things have been . . . difficult. But I've been thinking of you.'

'Right. Well, I hope you've been thinking of things to write for us as well.'

He laughed. 'You are such a tough woman. You know I only wangled that meeting with Barney today as a way of getting in touch with you.'

Natasha's nervous system launched into the 'Ode to Joy'. Drums and cymbals clashed in her solar plexus; a choir boomed in her heart. But she let no expression pass over her face.

'Wouldn't it have been simpler just to call me?'

'Maybe, but I had a feeling you'd be pissed off with me.' He bent towards her and smiled. 'Don't, Natasha, please. I want us to be friends.' He touched her face again. 'Well, actually I want us to be more than friends.'

'What do you mean by that, exactly?'

'I want us to go back to your place. It's just round the corner, isn't it? And your friend's not staying any more, is she?'

'No,' Natasha said slowly. 'She's not. But I think it's better we have a work discussion in the pub. Although the office would be even better.'

'Well, why don't we go back to your office then?' he said, draining his pint. 'We can talk there if it makes you feel happy. I aim to please.'

'OK,' she said. She glanced at her Georg Jensen. Nearly eight. Almost everyone would have left for the night and in the office she would certainly feel more in control.

They got up and walked round the corner again, into the office and up the stairs to Natasha's floor.

'This is my cubby hole,' she said, pushing open the door. 'I share with Dom.'

'Whoever he is I feel jealous of him.' Alastair held up his hands as Natasha shot him a look. 'OK, OK, sorry! I won't say any more.'

She sat down behind her desk, gesturing him to the leather chair for guests. 'Right, let's start again now. So, first of all, Alastair, have you got any ideas for us?'

'I have actually,' he said smugly.

'Well, then. Let's hear them.'

He began to outline them. To Natasha's annoyance, they were rather good. Not that she intended to show that too much, but at the same time she couldn't alienate a potential talent.

'Yes, that could work,' she said as he came to the end of a summary for a cop thriller. 'But does it have to be set in Scotland? That just makes it sound regional and worthy.'

'Hey! Are you saying I'm regional and worthy?'

'You're regional, certainly.' She bit her pen. 'It would work just as well set in London, though.'

'Actually, I had another idea where it could be set.'

'Where?'

'It's on my notes in front of me. But you'll have to come and look.'

'No, you can tell me.'

'I'd rather you came and looked.'

Natasha felt like her breathing had stopped. She knew what he was doing; she knew she should say no. But she felt herself drawn towards him like a pin to a magnet. *Other girls have casual flings. Why can't you? Maybe it would help you loosen up a bit, separating sex from love.* 'I don't see why I should look, Alastair.'

He got up and turned towards the Venetian blind of the glass box, tugging at the cord so the slats shut tight.

'Will you look now?'

Heart thudding, she stood up and walked round the desk until she was standing behind him.

'This is the page,' he said. She leaned forward. She could feel the warmth of his body through his shirt; smell his muskiness. Then she felt Alastair's hand on her thigh. 'This is what you should be looking at.' He nodded at the page.

'I see.' The hand inched upwards under her skirt. 'And what other points would you direct me to?'

People were talking loudly on the street below. She felt ripples of excitement all the way down to her toes.

'Well, I think I drew up a plot outline on the next page.'

'You'd better show me.' The fingers moved up. Thank you, God, for making sure I wore a skirt today even if it is shit brown. For not wearing tights and having shaved my legs. Oh God – her knickers weren't the best La Perla but a manky pair of black cotton M&S ones. Which he was tugging at now.

'Alastair, anyone could come in.'

'And do what? Disturb us having a business meeting?'

'We can't. We . . .'

His fingers were inside her now. She moaned and her legs spread a little bit further apart. 'There's always an excuse, isn't there, Natasha? Like your friend staying with you.'

'She's gone now,' she yelped as a bolt ran through her. 'I've got my place to myself.'

'Well, that's great,' he said. 'But I don't think we need your place any more. Not when we have a perfectly good office.' He was still stroking. She was dissolving for him. She glanced at him, still sitting in his chair, an obvious bulge beneath his trousers.

'I could sue you for sexual harassment,' she said.

'And I could sue you.' He stood up and pushed her forward so she leaned against the desk. She could hear him fiddling with his zip. He pulled up her skirt and then he was pushing inside her.

It was, without doubt, the sexiest thing that had ever happened to Natasha Green. And the naughtiest. Definitely the naughtiest. That turned her on. Natasha had been all over the world and eaten in the best restaurants and met many big stars, but she'd never done something dangerously bad. She wiggled, gasped and came.

So did Alastair. Just then there was a knock on the door.

'Fuck.' Breathing hard, he zipped up his trousers. She darted to the other side of the desk and sat down again.

'Yes?' She called out.

'It's Jenna.'

'Come in.' The door opened and a cleaner appeared: about twenty, Kosovan, in tight jeans and a tiny T-shirt.

'Sorry to bother you,' she said with a knowing smile. 'Do you want me to clean in here?'

'Um, in a minute, Jenna.' Natasha tried to smile. 'Just give us five.' Jenna shut the door.

'So back to work,' he said. 'What other changes do you think I need to make?'

She grinned. So this was how they were going to play it. 'I think we should have another meeting to discuss this.'

He looked up. 'You're very sexy, do you know that?'

She could hardly breathe. 'Er, well, I . . .'

'I'd like us to go back to your place now. Would that be possible?'

'Well . . .'

He smiled at her. 'There's just one thing I think I need to tell you, though.'

Doom crept over her. There was a catch. Of course. There had to be.

'I can't stay the night.'

She felt like she'd fallen from a great height.

'I can't be your boyfriend, Natasha. I want us to be clear about that from the start. I'd love to be, but right now, I . . . Well, it's not possible.'

'I thought you and Aurelia had split up,' she said in a small voice.

'We had. Temporarily. And we will again. Soon. I've told you: Aurelia and I are more like brother and sister than boyfriend and girlfriend, but she's at a tough place in her life right now. If I left her now it would destroy her.'

This was her test. She had to respond the right way.

'Sure.' Her voice was breezy, upbeat. 'I understand, Alastair. And I'm cool about it. I'm not looking for a boyfriend.'

He looked at her, admiration and relief struggling on his face. 'You're not?'

'God no. I'm not into all that – commitment, marriage,

babies.' She laughed. 'You know me, Alastair. All I want is to have fun.'

Now he was smiling. 'You're a female version of me, Natasha. I think that's why I like you so much.'

He likes me so much. 'God, I hope not. I think I'm a whole lot better than you.'

He stood up, laughing. 'Come on, Natasha. We're going back to your place for filthy no-strings sex.'

She should really have said no, said I don't want no-strings; if I'm as fabulous as I'm pretending to be I wouldn't want to share you with another woman. But she couldn't. She wouldn't. Alastair wanted to come back with her. She had to seize this moment.

'OK,' she said. 'Let's go.'

26

Tonight I'm going to get laid. A mile up the road from Natasha, Sophie woke filled with hope. She had so done the right thing splitting up with Andy. There were hundreds, thousands, millions of men out there who would make fantastic husbands. She thought of all the what ifs – the men she'd turned down in the past. What about the handsome, although admittedly wasted, gatecrasher at the office party who'd told her she was gorgeous? She'd told him primly she had a boyfriend and walked away. Damn, if she'd pursued that she could be married with a baby by now.

Or what about the tuba player she'd met at Caroline's garden party with whom she'd flirted wildly because she was pissed off with Andy who was away in Bosnia? He'd given her a lift home and asked if she'd like to go to a concert some time. She'd said yes but when he'd phoned her a week later, she'd been overcome with guilt and said she was off tonight on holiday and could they take a rain check? She should have gone. At the very least she'd have enjoyed the concert – well, actually she'd probably have been bored silly, but she could have asked a few subtle questions about commitment and children before deciding whether to groom him as a potential successor to Andy. Though there couldn't be much money in tuba playing.

But never mind, she thought as she dressed with huge care. Waiting in the wings there'd always been Julian. The electricity between them had been crackling since they first met. She put on the Agent Provocateur knickers Mum had given her for Christmas; a floaty, silk (well, polyester but it looked like silk) dress with buttons all the way down the front; strappy mules. Somehow she got through the day. He didn't call, but she kept calm. He'd be in touch. And sure enough, at about five her mobile rang.

'All right, lovely? Still on for tonight?'

'I am,' she said demurely.

'Any idea where you'd like to go?'

Sophie had thought hard about this. She wanted to start this relationship as she meant to go on. Being treated like a princess – and not Stephanie or one of those other dodgy ones who had affairs with bodyguards and ran away to the circus. She remembered Natasha saying she adored the Savoy, it was so discreet and old school.

'I'd like us to go to the Savoy,' she said.

'The Savoy?'

'Yes. I've never been. That's where I'd like us to go.'

Did he pause, or did she imagine it? 'All right, then,' he said. 'The Savoy it is. Meet you in the bar at seven-thirty?'

'Seven-thirty it is.'

When she arrived at the dark bar, fifteen minutes late, he was waiting at a corner table with a pint glass in front of him and a slightly uncomfortable expression. Sophie did a faint double take. He'd aged so much since she last saw him. There were streaks of grey in his hair and dark circles under his eyes. The jeans, leather jacket and earring which were once so hip and rebellious were now more oldest swinger in town.

'Hi,' he said, standing up and planting a kiss on her cheek. He stood back and surveyed her admiringly. 'You look fantastic.'

'Thank you,' she said graciously, taking her seat and crossing her ankles like Audrey Hepburn. *Sparkle, scintillate, entice.* She gave a little sigh. 'I do adore the Savoy. It's so old school. So discreet.'

'I thought you said you'd never been here?'

'Oh. I haven't. But . . . I mean I love what I've seen of it. So far.'

Julian smiled. 'Drink?'

'I'd love a glass of champagne.'

'Classy lady,' he said in a fruity voice. She laughed, thinking he was joking, then, realizing he wasn't, turned it into a cough.

'So how is it to be back?'

'Oh, you know. Busy. There's always so many people to catch up with. Mind you, at least this time I don't have to waste time seeing Frankie's family. They were nightmares. I should have read the signs. No reason why their daughter should be any different.'

'Mmm,' she said, looking around for a waiter. Obviously she'd never been wild about the sound of Frankie, but it did seem a little bit ungallant to start slagging off your ex before your potential new girlfriend had even had a drop of alcohol. 'So you're going to stay in Romania then?'

'Oh yeah. Living's so cheap there and the work's interesting. If I came back here I'd be commuting to an office on the eight-fifteen from Crawley. Doesn't appeal at all.'

'Yes, I can imagine.' Bugger. She really didn't fancy moving to Romania. But perhaps it would be OK. Did they have beaches? She knew they made wine there – it was always a good bet for big parties where you were just going to dump your contribution in the fridge, confident no one would ever be able to trace it back to you – so the weather must be reasonably hot.

'You should come and visit,' he said with a sudden smile, leaning forward and looking in her eyes. 'Now you're not with Andy any more.'

'Yes, that could be fun.'

'That would piss Frankie off,' he mused. 'Now she's shacked up with her new boyfriend.'

'Oh? Is that what happened? Two glasses of champagne, please.'

'Yeah. Some bastard entrepreneur wide boy. Drives a Porsche. Lives in a penthouse apartment. Wears Gucci head to toe.'

She looked at the tatty leather jacket. Hmm. Maybe Frankie had been on to something. What was that black stuff between his two front teeth? She tried to work out if it was food or dodgy Romanian dentistry. Either way, she couldn't take her eyes off it. All the same, there was still something about Julian that made her groin sit up and stand to attention.

'We were never right for each other anyway,' he continued, sighing and scratching his stubble.

'Ah, no?'

'No. She took no interest in Romanian culture what-soever. Made no effort to learn the language. Insisted we had satellite installed so she could watch British telly.'

'Really?' Excellent.

'Yeah. First thing I did when she left was have it cut off.'

'Oh.' Her glass was almost empty already and she'd somehow managed to scoff most of the peanuts from the bowl in front of them, even though Caroline always said you should never do that because each had been lovingly fondled by fourteen thousand men each of whom had recently performed an extremely large bowel movement and not washed their hands.

'Shall we eat?'

'Eat? Uh, yes. In a minute. Let's just have one more round.' He sat back in his chair and scratched his head. 'I mean, it's not that I'm bitter. I wish her well. And him. Christ, good luck to him. He'll need it.'

Luckily, more drink seemed to help him forget Frankie and the pain she had caused him and become a lot more like the Julian Sophie used to know: witty, gossipy and, most importantly, interested in her. She'd just finished telling him the story about Yvette's Brian and the hair transplant and he was laughing his head off, when suddenly a look came over his face as if he had just seen Godzilla advancing on him in the rear-view mirror.

'Are you all right?' she asked.

'Yeah. Yeah. Fine. I just . . . For a second I thought I saw Frankie. But it was just a girl that looked like her.'

'Well, maybe it's a sign we should be moving on. What do you feel like eating?' She was hoping he'd suggest they move into the restaurant.

'Oh, I don't know,' he shrugged. 'Why don't we just have a stroll and see what we find.' He picked up the tab. 'Christ! Sixty-six quid!'

'Well, we did have four glasses of champagne,' Sophie reasoned. 'And' – she leaned over to see the evidence – 'you had two lagers before I got here. And this is London.'

'God, I knew there was a reason I didn't want to live in this city.' He gave her a sly look. 'Tell you what. Why don't you get this one and I'll pick up dinner?'

Sounded OK to her, after all it was practically impossible to dine out in London without spending at least thirty pounds a head. So Sophie paid and they headed out on to the bustling streets of Covent Garden.

'How about there?' she said, nodding at Tony's Trattoria, which looked cosy and jolly inside with red raffia lampshades and checked tablecloths.

'Ah, no. Not Italian. It was Frankie's favourite. I'm not sure I want to eat another bowl of pasta as long as I live.'

On the left was Mêlée, which was a sort of French–Thai fusion place with long shared tables full of happy, chattering, cool people. 'This looks nice.'

Julian wrinkled his nose. 'Too crowded.'

True. It wouldn't have exactly been intimate. She gestured at the stone staircase leading up to Ellison's. She'd read that was where the in-crowd went. 'We could always treat ourselves?'

Julian wrinkled his nose. 'I'm not really into those fancy kind of places. Don't see the point of being ripped off just so you can tell your friends you've been there.'

It occurred to Sophie that Julian and Veronica might make a very fine match.

'Well, what do you fancy?' she said as they walked on.

'I dunno,' he shrugged, then stopped dead in front of a grubby-looking Chinese without a soul inside. 'All You Can Eat £5 A Head' read the sign in the window.

'This looks nice.'

Sophie looked at him. He had to be joking, right? But not a flicker of a smile crossed his face. 'There's no one in there,' she pointed out. More accurately, it looked like the last time someone had been in there was around the time of the invention of the postage stamp.

'So? I told you I don't like crowds.' He pushed at the door.

If it had been Andy, Sophie would have told him to get his head examined. But even though she'd known Julian for ever, she still felt she'd better be a little polite.

'I love Chinese,' he cried, sitting at the grubby table. 'There aren't any good ones in Bucharest.'

Sophie glanced at the table covered in dried-out spare ribs, technicolour chow mein, congealing rice and sunflower yellow chunks of chicken. Maybe she wasn't so hungry.

She watched him go back up to the buffet three times and then munch his way through most of what was on her plate too. How could this have happened? How come Julian wasn't anything like she remembered? Maybe she hadn't been so badly off with Andy after all?

But that physical tingle was still there. And Sophie hadn't felt that for anyone in ages.

'So how about we share a cab home?' he said finally, pushing his plate away.

'Where's home?'

'I'm staying with Mum and Dad. In Golders Green.'

'Oh, so I'm on your way,' she said sarcastically.

'Exactly,' he said with a big wink. He slapped fifteen pounds on the table. 'Shall we?'

Oh well. I don't want to marry him. It's just sex. To get me back on the horse. As it were. Veronica was at work, so there was nothing to stop them.

They got a minicab from a booth. Back at Mornington Crescent, Sophie unlocked her door in silence and he followed her silently up to the flat. As soon as she shut the door, they were all over each other. Thank God. The wait had been worth it. Julian was a good kisser: teasing and tantalizing, although she was surprised at the roll of fat she found around his waist and the hairiness of his back.

'Oh God,' he gasped, pushing her away from him. 'Do you know how long I've been waiting to do this?'

She glowed. 'What took you so long?'

'You had a boyfriend. He seemed a nice guy. But God, Sophie.' He started kissing her again and then: 'Where's the bedroom?'

'Uh, through there,' she said. It was a little too fast maybe, but what the hell?

And suddenly they were on the bed and her top was off and his hand was up her skirt, feeling inside the expensive knickers, and a few minutes and a rustle of condom foil later (Sophie had felt a bit slutty putting some by the bed this morning, but what was the alternative?) he was inside her.

And then, seconds later, before she'd begun to register anything at all, it was all over.

'Blaagh,' he cried and collapsed on top of her. Then

he rolled off, leaving Sophie fuming and frustrated. What was that supposed to be? Sex on fast forward? But she simply didn't have it in her to bawl him out.

He lay there, panting. 'You're very attractive, you know?' he muttered.

'Thank you.'

'From the moment you walked into the bar tonight I was looking forward to fucking you.'

'Oh, right.'

He pulled himself on to one elbow and smiled at her. 'It's a shame I'm not moving back to London. Because we could go out with each other.'

Arrogant tosser. Sophie suddenly knew she had no more desire to go out with Julian than she did with the Pope. Why did all men, no matter how tubby and greying, think they could have any woman on a plate? But instantly the uncomfortable thought struck her that that was how she'd offered herself to Julian tonight. A ready meal with fries and an extra-large Coke. All his for fifteen pounds and the price of a minicab.

'Mmm,' she said. Oh well. Maybe Julian had just needed to shoot his load. Now they could do it all again in slow motion.

But he was rolling off the bed and buttoning up his trousers. 'Better get back. I don't want Mum to be worried.'

'Oh, right.' She too rolled off the bed and pulled on her silky dress, which had promised so much at the start of the evening but now smelt of smoke and was stained with Chinese food.

'That was fun, Sophie,' he said, pecking her on the

cheek. 'And I meant what I said. Whenever you fancy a weekend in Bucharest . . .'

'I'll bear that in mind.' She just wanted to say as little as possible, to keep down all the anger that was bubbling up inside her.

He wandered across to the kitchen area, opened a cupboard, took out a glass and filled it with tap water.

'Or if the next time's in London, maybe you can show me a really good time. Cook me dinner.' His eye fell on *Cooking with a Microwave*, Veronica's only contribution to the communal library. 'But none of that shitty microwaved stuff. I like home-cooked food. Do you think you could do that for me?'

'I think I could chop off your genitals and fry them in boiling oil, yes,' she said with a sweet smile. Actually, she didn't. That was what she came up with talking to her shampoo the following morning, when she stood, still fuming, in the shower. Fuming at how she'd let herself be fooled by the dream of a passionate, all-consuming relationship with Julian, a dream that had thus far protected her from the reality now looming before her: that she was all on her own, with nothing to look forward to and no Julian fantasy to distract her.

As the water dribbled on her head, she shut her eyes and cringed at the memory of Julian's farewell line, on the threshold.

'By the way, Sophie, don't bother with the expensive underwear next time. I prefer those little white cotton schoolgirl jobs.'

27

At work the next morning, Caroline was sitting in front of her screen, giggling.

'What is it?' Sophie asked, desperate for some cheering up.

'I've discovered a new way to find a boyfriend. Come and have a look.'

Wearily, Sophie got up and looked over Caroline's shoulder. Her screen was full of men. Blond ones, dark ones, Asian, black, Chinese. Bald, bespectacled, unsmiling, grinning like loons.

'It's an online dating agency,' her colleague explained. 'Isn't it great? Like a shop for boyfriends.'

'Oh, right,' Sophie said. She looked at the men. They looked either psychotically eager or self-consciously nonchalant. She searched for the best looking.

'He's nice,' she said, moving the mouse on to Michael. Dark, high cheekbones, a bit Clive Owen.

'Yeah, but his shirt's tucked into his jeans,' Caroline pointed out.

'No! Yuck.' The cursor moved downwards. 'What about Franz?'

'Dodgy name.'

'Yeah, but he's gorgeous.' He was too, with blue eyes and a floppy fringe. Caroline double clicked on him, then roared with laughter.

'Read this message. I don't think so, mate.'
Sophie read.

> Hello everyone!!!!! I am intelligent, happy,
> honest, friendly, adventurus and a wicked
> sence of humour. My friends say i am
> funny, also very down 2 earth. Looking 4 a
> slim lady, who injoys life, down 2 earth,
> easygoing and outgoing. THANKS

'You're right,' she giggled. 'You can do better than that.'

'Anyone who uses the word lady is discounted right away,' Caroline proclaimed.

'The problem with you girls is you're too fussy,' Yvette interrupted, having joined them at the terminal. 'If you met this chap in a nightclub, Caroline, you wouldn't know he couldn't spell and he'd have your clothes off before he could say "lady".'

'That's not true!'

'If you say so.' Yvette shrugged. 'But you have to see that's not really what attraction's all about. That's an animal thing. When you meet the right person you just know it.'

Caroline and Sophie glanced at each other. This didn't tie in with grumpy Yvette, constantly moaning about how bloody Brian had cocked up renovating the bathroom.

'Did you know with Brian?' Caroline ventured.

'Of course I did. I was standing at a bar on a Saturday night trying to get served and we caught each other's eyes and that was it.'

'I thought I knew with Andy,' Sophie said. 'But it turned out I was just blinded with hormones. If I'd read his profile online I'd never have gone for him and I wouldn't have wasted years of my life.'

'Well, there you go, why don't you join too?' Caroline asked. 'We could have such a laugh.'

But suddenly Sophie understood why Natasha had got so ratty whenever such a scheme was suggested. Joining an agency would confirm her new clichéd status: thirty-something woman with a job, plenty of friends and a hole in her middle like a Polo mint. A hole which Julian had sensed long-distance from Romania and exploited.

'I think I'll give it a miss. I'm off dating for a while.'

A hand tapped her on the shoulder. 'Wotcha.' Olly, smiling and keen as always. If Sophie were to wet her pants in front of him that look of adoration wouldn't change. Which was a good thing, surely? So why did it make her want to hit him?

'Oh, hi!'

'Just wondering if you'd had any further thoughts about the ball. I mean I don't want to hassle you or anything, but if you can't make it, I . . .'

The ball? Oh yes, she'd told him she'd let him know. 'Sorry, Olly. I've just been a bit preoccupied recently. When is it again?'

'Not for ages yet, eleventh of June, but tickets go fast. It's at my old college. It should be pretty cool. We can stay with my friends Sean and Alice.'

Sophie still loved the sound of an Oxford ball. She wasn't so keen on the 'we can stay'. What did that mean? Together? But fuck it. Olly was a gentleman. She'd told him there was nothing going on between them. And she could wear an amazing dress and be a princess for a night. Just the treat she needed.

'I'd love to come,' she said, haughtily ignoring Fay who, while pretending to inspect faxes, was winking at her fit to dislocate her eye socket. 'Thank you so much for asking me. What should I wear?'

'Oh, something pretty,' Olly said with a smile. 'But then with you that could be an old sack, couldn't it?'

'Now don't!' she said firmly to Fay as he walked away. 'Just don't go there!' But she couldn't help feeling a lot happier. Olly certainly knew how to make a girl feel good about herself.

As she put the key in the lock of what she still felt was Veronica's flat that evening, her soul wilted again. It was all so wrong. Why was she opening and closing someone else's front door, when she had a perfectly good front door of her own just a few miles up the road? *I want my old life back. I want to be sitting in Harlesden, watching soaps and cooking something yummy for Andy's supper.*

Which would probably get burned in the oven because he'd be stuck on a job, she reminded herself tartly. Now come on.

'Hiya, Soph,' Veronica called from the living room.

Sophie's heart did another nose dive.

'Good day?' Veronica asked as she came into the living room. She was sitting with a pile of bills in front of her and was copying figures into a notebook.

'Not bad. You?'

'Yeah, not bad. Just working out the phone bill. Of

course you only owe point five three four five per cent of it for the line rental, because you've only just got here, but I'm going to have to chase down Josie for a huge whack. At least the phone's itemized. I know she used more leccy than me, she was always leaving lights on and stuff.'

'Gosh, how dreadful.' But Veronica was too involved in the maths to hear the mockery in her tone.

'Yeah, it's a shag. By the way, Sophie, I meant to mention a couple of things about your grocery bills.'

'Oh yes?'

'Well, I see you went to Sainsbury's on Tuesday.'

'I did.'

'Nothing to worry about, but just a couple of house rules I should have explained. Firstly, you bought a four-pack of bog roll. Well, we don't do that. Bog roll's always readily available to nick from work, so in future when we're running low just slip some in your bag. Otherwise you might as well be flushing money down the toilet. Ha, ha, ha.'

'Uh. Oh. OK.'

'And another thing. Some of the things on your list.' She brandished the receipt that Sophie had carefully deposited in an old jam jar. 'A ready-cooked chicken. I mean, Sophie, firstly meat is expensive, but secondly we can bloody cook our own chicken, can't we?'

'Yes, but think of the gas involved in cooking,' Sophie protested.

'Are you taking the piss?' Veronica eyed her suspiciously. 'Now, a few other things. Bonne Maman jam? Fairy Liquid? Ariel powder? In this house, Sophie, we buy own brands. And there's a lot of veggies here too, which,

I told you, you could get at the market for about a quarter of the price.'

In normal circumstances, Sophie would have told her to fuck off and get a life, but tonight she felt like a punctured beach ball.

'Sorry, Veronica, I'll bear all that in mind next time. Now, if you don't mind I've got some stuff to do.' Her voice was thickening.

'Oh, and don't forget the coupons,' Veronica continued. 'There's a jar of them on top of the fridge. Always take them to the supermarket with you, you'd be amazed how much you can save by using them.'

In her room, Sophie flung herself on the lumpy bed and hid her face in her pillow, which still, to her disgust, smelled vaguely of Julian. She didn't want to be here. She wanted to be home. With Andy. Who cared if he didn't want to marry her? Even if it hadn't been perfect at least he'd never told her to steal loo paper.

She picked up her phone and stabbed one on speed dial. She'd grovel. Surely he'd have her back. But his number went straight to voicemail. Thank God, she thought as she came to her senses. What was she doing, humiliating herself still further? But she had to speak to someone. Tash. But Tash's phone rang three times then went to voicemail too. Marcus. She'd call Marcus.

She speed-dialled number three. Marcus picked up on the fourth ring. 'Hello?'

'Marcus, hey, it's Sophie. Just calling to see how you guys are doing.'

'Soph! How are you, honey? Listen, I can't talk now, I'm afraid. We're in Gordon Ramsay's. Taking my wife out to celebrate having made it through to Friday.'

'Ah, that's lovely.' Sophie's eyes pricked with envy and loneliness. 'Well, I won't keep you.'

'I'll call you tomorrow.' She heard him say: 'It's Sophie, ducks,' and a giggly 'Hiii'. 'Lainey says "Hi". Now I must go. No phones allowed in here.'

Sophie felt clammy and cold. It was Friday night and no one wanted to be her friend. Who said being single was fabulous? Being single sucked. Sophie was going to sue the author of that book for misdirection and with the profits she was going to buy as much top-of-the-range bog roll as she could afford and get the Andrex puppy to festoon it all around Veronica's room. Plus a lifetime's supply of Bonne Maman jam.

Cheered by such thoughts, she dozed off.

Natasha, meanwhile, had spent the day in a daze. Last night with Alastair had been even more wonderful than she could have imagined. Natasha liked sex, of course she did, but she didn't always find it relaxing; she'd read so many books on how to be great in bed and it was hard work sometimes remembering it all. But Alastair seemed happy, kissing her hair and telling her she was adorable. OK, shortly after that he'd got up and left, but that was fine. He had to go home to Aurelia.

She'd gone to sleep ecstatic, but woken feeling a little more uneasy, and as the tedious day at work dragged by, her mood blackened. How could she have been such a fool? She, Natasha Green, TV executive extraordinaire, had let her guard go and had sex with an engaged man. And bit his shoulder. And muttered, 'Oh my God, don't stop.' He was probably laughing at her now, sharing stories of her abandonment with all the other Rollercoaster writers. Four times she picked up the phone to call him; four times she put it down again. She'd already made herself vulnerable enough, now she was just going to have to put her armour back on and keep fighting.

She toyed with the idea of calling Sophie. Or Marcus. Or Nikolai. But they'd tell her she shouldn't have slept with an engaged man. And she felt wobbly enough already without further tellings-off.

At home, the cleaner had been and her flat looked almost too pristine. She flung herself on her bed and sniffed her pillows, inhaling Alastair's smell of coffee and CK Be.

Just then her buzzer went. Who the hell could that be? Jehovah's Witnesses, undoubtedly. Or a pizza for Stuart downstairs. No one in London rang anyone else's bell spontaneously; you had to arrange it three weeks in advance, then cancel twice, then rearrange on the day with a seventy-five per cent chance of a last-minute blow-out.

She picked up the entryphone. 'Hello?'

'Natasha?'

It was what she'd been hoping for, but hadn't dared admit, even to herself.

'I'm afraid I didn't order a minicab,' she said, heart contracting with joy.

'No, I'm afraid you didn't. Because you're not going anywhere.'

A minute later, he was in her arms.

It was even better than last night, though once again, of course, he couldn't stay.

28

On Saturday lunchtime, Sophie got on the tube to go
down to the Caprice to meet Mum and her mystery guest.
It was a restaurant she'd always longed to go to (although
Natasha said it was overrated), yet she was still dreading
it. Rita made her go through this ordeal of meeting her
new lover approximately once every two and a half years.
Sophie was hardened to being introduced to some man
or other, with a wink and a 'Don't tell Jimmy'. As if.
They'd all make stilted conversation, with the man looking askance at Sophie, trying to work out how his lithe
lover could possibly have a daughter who was not only
so old but double her body size. Sophie made the minimum effort, not seeing why she should bother befriending
a man who at best she would never see again and at worst
would break nice Jimmy's heart.

The problem with her mother, Sophie reflected as she
came up the escalators at Green Park, was that she
couldn't reconcile her hopeless romanticism with her
fondness for the good things in life. She and Jimmy clearly
had an extraordinary physical connection, judging by the
amount of times the teenage Sophie hadn't been able to
get into the loo because the pair of them had been
giggling and splashing in the bath. But Jimmy was also
poor, and Rita, who wasn't good at holding down jobs
(she hated early mornings), resented the fact he couldn't

give her the cruises and five-star beach resorts she felt she deserved and which John – if she'd hung on in there – would have provided willingly. So for the past ten years, Rita had been actively scouting for a Jimmy replacement, but this time one with money. 'After all, darling, it's as easy to fall in love with a rich man as a poor one,' she would say, and so you would think, but thus far she'd had little luck as the rich men she uncovered were virtually always married to women who shared Rita's philosophy and had no intention of letting their catches go.

Meanwhile, she stayed with Jimmy, because – as she pointed out – he could be an utter sweetie (when he wasn't too involved in his work), and the sex was still blissful. It infuriated Sophie to see her mother living in this limbo, but she had long given up lecturing. She simply vowed not to replicate Rita's mistakes, but instead to be a sticker, a noughties version of Tammy Wynette, standing by her man through the good times and the bad times. The problem was the men, who hadn't wanted to stand by her. And she shuddered as her mind flashed back to her humiliating night with Julian.

She pushed open the restaurant door. The waiter showed her to a corner table where Rita was sitting very straight in a little chair, opposite a man with a broad back. She was wearing a tweed jacket and skirt that looked like Chanel but were probably from Zara. An imitation Hermès scarf nestled round her neck along with a string of pearls. It told Sophie all she needed to know. Rita had always been a chameleon dresser; when she'd been with John it had been all banker's wife couture, while with Jimmy it was artist's smocks and clogs. This man owned a country estate, shot, rode, fished and smelled of dogs.

Sophie took a deep breath. 'Hello, Mum, you look lovely.' She bent and kissed her perfect rouged cheek.

'So do you, darling.' Rita looked her up and down appraisingly. 'Good, you've lost weight. You're obviously one of those women who responds to break-ups by starving yourself rather than going on infantile chocolate binges. So that's something to be thankful for.'

'I guess.' Sophie didn't think she'd bother explaining her weight loss was probably more down to Veronica's cooking. She turned to the man, hand outstretched. 'Hello, I'm Sophie.'

'I'm Vernon,' he said in pukka tones. He was dapper and balding, in chestnut cords and a navy linen jacket with a colonial air that suggested long afternoons at the country club reading week-old copies of *The Times* while silent retainers topped up his Pimm's. 'How do you do?'

'Very well, thank you.' Sophie sat down.

'Darling, how many times must I tell you: the correct reply to "How do you do?" is "How do you do?"' Rita pulled a cigarette out of a silver case. 'So, Vernie, what do we think? Champagne all round?'

'If you say so, Rita.' He gave her a steamy look. Oh God, they'd obviously been at it all morning and he couldn't wait to get her back to the bedroom.

'So what are you chaps up to this weekend?' Sophie said brightly. *Chaps?* Where on earth had that word come from? But Vernon gave her the urge to brandish a hockey stick and a copy of *Horse & Hound*.

'Oh, just having fun, darling. You know. Maybe the opera tonight.'

'*Nabucco* at the ENO,' Vernon said. 'Marvellous stuff.'

'And how do you two know each other?' Sophie asked.

They glanced at one another and giggled.

'Actually,' Rita said. 'We ran into each other at Lainey's wedding.'

'Lainey's wedding?' And then a memory drifted into Sophie's head of Mum floating past on the dance floor in the arms of an old buffer.

'That's right. Vernon is an old friend of John's, although we never met when I was married to him because he was living in South Africa then. But now he lives at Cottingsmore Manor, just down the road, so we arranged to meet for lunch.'

'Oh, lovely. Cottingsmore's that Elizabethan place out near Dartington, isn't it?' *Bloody hell, Mum. Aiming high with this one.*

'That's it,' Vernon said gruffly. 'Been in the family for seven hundred years.'

'Wow.' Sophie's phone rang in her bag. 'Oh, excuse me a second,' she said as the waiter cracked open the champagne.

'Darling,' Rita frowned. 'Bad manners.'

'It might be the office,' Sophie lied. It was what Natasha always said.

Rita smiled and nodded more understandingly. 'Sophie works for the *Daily Post*,' she said to Vernon.

'Really?' Vernon said. 'Excellent newspaper. Never miss it. Would I have seen her writing?'

'She's more in an administrative capacity,' Rita whispered as Sophie picked up her phone and said: 'Hello?'

'Hi,' said a voice she couldn't quite place.

'Er, who is this?'

'It's Olly.' He sounded hurt.

'Oh, Olly, sorry! Didn't recognize your voice. It's noisy in here. How are things?'

'Fine. Just mooching. I was wondering what you were up to this weekend.'

Sophie looked at Rita, who was leaning forward and whispering something in Vernon's ear. A wave of depression washed over her. At least Mum was having fun.

'Well, I'm having lunch with my mum and a . . . er . . . friend of hers at the moment. But apart from that I'm around.'

'Who is it, darling?' Rita asked, leaning forward. Sophie waved her away.

'Well, I was thinking about perhaps going shopping,' Olly said. 'I need some new togs.'

Sophie hated shopping with boys. Jumpers, fleeces, shirts, jeans: they all looked alike, with no ribbony bits or pretty colours. 'Right,' she said non-committally.

'And maybe we could find you something to wear to the ball.'

Aha. Not that Sophie could afford anything much but an afternoon of trying on pretty dresses with an admirer like Olly in tow sounded much more like it. And, of course, there was always also the possibility that Olly might just offer to make a teensy contribution to her outfit. Not that she'd allow him to, naturally. But it would be a sweet gesture.

'That sounds like a great plan.'

'What time do you want to meet?' he asked, sounding delighted.

'I don't know.' She looked at the Georg Jensen. One-thirty. 'Maybe half past three?'

'Where?'

Sophie's mind always went blank when it came to venues. 'Um . . .'

'Why don't you get your *friend* to meet us here?' said Rita, who'd been listening with interest to the entire conversation. 'We could all have coffee and then you could go off.'

'Who was that?' Olly asked.

'No one,' Sophie said.

'Excuse me, darling! I am *not* no one.' And Rita grabbed the phone from her. 'Hello? . . . Hello, yes. I'm Sophie's mother. And I was just saying to my lovely daughter, why don't you join us at the Caprice for coffee and then you two can go off and do whatever young people do in London these days. Does that sound like fun? Us two codgers would certainly like to meet a young person. Brighten our dreary day.' Rita loved playing the old bat card when she knew she was looking exceptionally gorgeous. Sophie gritted her teeth.

'You would? Oh well then, that's marvellous. Just get along here whenever you can. Our table's reserved under the name of Coleman-Withers.' There was a little pause and then she said, 'Yes, he is that Coleman-Withers. How clever of you to spot it. Well, see you later, my dear. Goodbye.'

'Mum!' Sophie took back the phone, face blazing.

'What?' Defiantly, Rita took a sip of her champagne. 'That's what happens when you answer your mobile telephone in public, darling. But your *friend* sounds charming. I can't think why you didn't want us to meet him.'

'It's not that I didn't want you to.' Sophie wiggled unhappily in her chair. 'It's just that he really is only a friend.'

'Well, I want to get to know my daughter's friends.' She turned to Vernon, who had sat mutely throughout this whole scene, knocking back champagne. 'Anyway, he knew who *you* were, darling. Wasn't that clever of him?'

'Well, there's only one lot of Coleman-Witherses,' Vernon said smugly.

'Er, I'm terribly sorry,' said Sophie, 'but should *I* know who you are?'

Vernon looked at her pityingly. 'Of course not, of course not,' he said. 'No reason at all, if you don't take an interest in current events. Ha, ha.'

'Vernon used to be in the Cabinet,' Rita said crisply. 'First he was big in business in South Africa, then he came back to the UK, went into politics and ended up as Mrs Thatcher's Social Security Minister. Now he's in the House of Lords. He's a Whip, darling.'

'Oh.' She didn't actually know what a Whip was but it sounded worryingly kinky. 'How very interesting.'

'It is rather,' said Vernon.

'It's fascinating,' said Rita loyally and slipped her hand on top of his, smiling brightly. 'Vernon is a very, very clever man, darling.'

And very rich too, thought Sophie. Well, at least with Vernon footing the bill the champagne would keep flowing. Which was a mercy. Because they were going to need a lot of it.

Olly turned up about an hour later. He was wearing stonewashed jeans and a baggy blue sweatshirt with UCLA across it in gold letters. Sophie had never seen him out of workwear before and it gave her an uneasy feeling, like the time at school when she spotted her PE teacher Miss Derrick alone at the bus stop, obviously waiting for a lift in a black taffeta strapless dress that did her non-existent bust no favours at all.

Still, she was relieved to see him. Lunch with Vernon and Rita had been a struggle, despite the delicious food. Vernon was monosyllabic to the point of catatonia, while Rita was compensating by being so vivacious that Sophie would have suspected her of being on speed were it not for the fact her mother had firmly taught her never to touch drugs because they wrecked the complexion.

'Delighted to meet you,' Olly said. Sophie had forgotten how fruity his voice could sound. 'Olly Garcia-Mundoz. How d'ye do?'

Vernon's face brightened. 'Garcia-Mundoz? Are you the chap who writes those super articles for the *Post*? I've been reading your work for years now. Had no idea you were such a whippersnapper. Well done, my boy, first-rate opinion pieces.'

'Thank you, sir,' Olly said suavely. Sophie shuddered. *Sir?* 'I'm a great admirer of yours too, of course. In fact, I've been meaning to get my secretary in touch with yours. Arrange a little lunchy. And now here we all are.'

'Isn't that wonderful?' Rita gushed. Olly turned to her.

'But I have to say, it's simply impossible that you are Sophie's mother. You're far too young.'

'Oh, really, I . . .' Rita simpered, as if she hadn't heard it a million times before.

'Sit down, sit down, young fellow,' Vernon cried. 'I want to talk to you about that column you wrote about US foreign policy. Simply fascinating, some of those statistics you'd dragged up.'

'I'm writing a book on the subject, actually,' Olly said. 'Should be out by the end of the year. Sophie has a copy, don't you?'

'Mmm. Yes! I've been saving it up so I can really read it properly!'

Soon Olly was sitting and chattering away over their third bottle of champagne, which at some point was replaced by a bottle of port and two Baileys for the ladies. Naff, but by this time Sophie was too pissed to care.

'So what do you think, darling?' Rita hissed as the men got on to the subject of immigration restrictions.

'He's very nice,' Sophie said automatically, then lowering her voice: 'But, Mum, what about poor Jimmy?'

'Poor Jimmy nothing,' Rita said. The end of her retroussé nose had turned pink from the alcohol. She lit a cigarette. 'What he doesn't know won't hurt him.'

'But at some point he will know. And he'll be devastated.'

'No reason for him to find out. He hasn't so far. It's only if things between Vernon and me turn serious that I'll have to tell him.'

'What, if Vernon becomes husband number three?'

'Shhh.' Rita glanced at the men and lowered her voice.

246

'I think it could work this time, you know. His wife's dead. He needs someone by his side.'

'Do you love him?'

'Oh no, darling. But that's the mistake I made with Jimmy. Love simply isn't enough. What one needs in life is a provider. Someone to rely on.' She nudged Sophie. 'Which is exactly what young Olly could do.'

'Mum!' But the men were chortling away at some gag about the UN. 'I have told you twice already today, he's just a friend.'

'A friend who clearly adores you.'

'Mum, I don't fancy him.'

'So? Do you think I fancy Vernon? Fancying is a silly distraction. I fancy Jimmy and he makes me miserable. You have to start thinking long-term, darling. Strategically. Believe me, it's the only way.' Rita held out a manicured hand and stopped a waiter. 'Darling, could we have some more Baileys, please?'

29

It was nearly five when they finally left the lunch table with Olly and Vernon exchanging business cards. Sophie had to admit that since Olly's arrival the lunch had been surprisingly jolly.

'Shopping time running out,' Olly said, slurring slightly. 'So I think we'd better concentrate on you, not me.'

'Beauty before age,' Sophie giggled, then hiccupped. 'Oh no, I'm the oldest, aren't I?' She'd never have said that if she hadn't been drunk. But Olly ignored her, taking her arm.

'Since we're right next to Bond Street, shall we?'

'Oh yes! We could go to Jigsaw.' All around them chav couples were peering in windows: men in Gucci jeans and baseball caps, women clutching Louis Vuitton bags and pushing Bugaboos.

'Jigsaw?' Olly wrinkled his nose. 'I think we can do better than that.'

'What's wrong with Jigsaw?' But Sophie knew what was coming. Oh my God. Armani. Donna Karan. Calvin Klein.

'Nothing, nothing. I just thought a place like this might be a bit less run-of-the-mill.' He pushed open the door of a small boutique with a sign that read Beretskaya.

'Oh.' She tried to hide the disappointment. They'd entered a single room filled with boxy jackets in bright yellows and reds with huge mother-of-pearl buttons. It looked like the Mrs Thatcher museum. Maybe this was where Yvette got all her clothes? Sophie giggled as she thought about telling the girls on Monday.

The assistant, who looked as if she'd been put out to work by her children to supplement her pension, approached them. 'Can I help you?' she asked reedily.

'Oh, we're fine thanks,' Sophie said, just as Olly said: 'We're looking for something to wear to a ball.'

'Well, you've certainly come to the right place. And what did you have in mind for your wife?'

Sophie clenched her fists in embarrassment. Whenever someone used the 'w' word in front of Andy, he'd always make a huge deal of correcting them. But Olly just smiled.

'I was thinking of something like this,' he said, fingering a bright blue dress with a sailor collar and a drop-waisted skirt. Even by the shop's standards, it was revolting. Sophie and the woman looked at each other.

'I don't think that's quite the right outfit for a ball, sir.'

'Well, maybe not for a ball,' Olly admitted. 'But as a pretty evening dress.'

'I'm not sure it's quite me,' Sophie said hastily.

'Would you try it on? Just for me?'

'Oh, all right then.' Exchanging glances with the assistant, she went into the changing cubicle. God, even Mrs Thatcher would have thought this too frumpy. 'Olly, it really doesn't work.'

'Let's see,' he said. She stepped out. 'Hmm. I think it's really rather nice.'

'Olly!'

'Well, never mind. How about this one?'

This one was a red taffeta trouser suit. 'Oh no, I don't think so.'

'Often things look completely different off the hanger,' the assistant, seeing her first sale in eighteen years, urged. 'Try it on.'

Six more changes of horrible outfits later, Sophie was beginning to flag. This had been supposed to be fun but Olly was trying to turn her into a member of the Women's Institute.

'What about this one?' the assistant said.

She turned wearily. The woman was holding a long red dress. It was slit up the side and designed to drape over the bust. It looked delicious.

'I'll give it a try.'

Back into the changing room. The heavy silk clung to her waist and her tits, revealing the best bits of her, magically disguising the worst. Sophie stared at herself, mesmerized; entranced by a movie-star vision of the glittering, enchanting woman she could be. She stood on tiptoes trying to imagine herself in heels, her hair up, perhaps a ruby necklace round her throat.

She pulled back the curtain and Olly and the assistant gasped.

'It's perfect,' Olly breathed.

'It is,' the assistant agreed, probably for the first time in her life telling the truth about one of her garments.

'This is it,' Sophie said, wondering what the damage would be, praying Olly would offer to chip in.

Sure enough. 'Do you take Visa?' he said instantly.

'Certainly, sir.'

'Oh no, Olly,' she said hastily, but not too hastily. 'You can't, you really mustn't . . .'

He held his hand up. 'Sophie, I insist.'

'We-ell. Are you sure?'

'Of course I am. It would be my pleasure.'

'Well, then, thank you,' she said, kissing him on the cheek. 'It's the most beautiful thing I've ever seen in my life.'

'No,' Olly said. 'There are more beautiful things.'

Uh. Oh. Here we go again.

Back in the changing room, she could hear the woman putting the sale through. She glanced at the handwritten tag, still hanging from the dress.

Two thousand seven hundred pounds.

She felt dizzy. She'd been thinking a couple of hundred quid. She really couldn't let Olly spend that much. She wiggled back into her trousers and jumper and stuck her head round the curtain to hand the dress to the woman for packing.

'Ready, m'lady?' Olly said.

'Olly, I don't know. I can't – You can't . . .' But he raised a hand to silence her.

'Of course I can,' he said.

'Thank you,' she said, squeezing his sausagey fingers. 'God, it's so beautiful. I don't know if I can wait until the ball. I want to wear it tonight.'

She sort of hoped Olly would say: 'My darling, in that case I will whisk you off to the Four Seasons New York and we will dance all night.' Though of course she didn't really. Because that was the kind of thing you did with a lover. The kind of thing Mum would probably do with Vernon. Not that Mum fancied Vernon . . .

But all Olly said with a laugh was: 'Patience is a virtue. So do you need anything else? Like shoes, or . . . make-up or whatever?'

'No, Olly, really. You've been more than generous. I'm fine.'

There was a pause.

'I suppose you're busy for the rest of the day?'

'I'm not busy at all,' Sophie said.

'Good.' Olly smiled. 'Well, in that case, I was wondering if you fancied going back to my place. We could watch a DVD.'

Why not? After all, it would be rude not to when he had spent £2,700 on her. And back at his house, they enjoyed another selection of assorted goodies from the deli, played his (surprisingly cool) CDs and, at his suggestion, watched Monty Python's *The Life of Brian* on DVD. She'd never seen it and laughed uproariously, even though Olly's habit of shouting 'I love this bit' at the start of every scene and chanting the dialogue along with the characters was occasionally a little irritating.

He made no attempt to kiss her and at about midnight called her a cab to carry her and her new dress back to Mornington Crescent. It had been a lovely evening. Cosy; coupley almost. The kind of evening she'd yearned for with Andy, but almost never happened because he'd be too busy doing his VAT or refiling his negatives. As friendships went, Sophie reflected, you could do a whole lot worse.

30

A couple of weeks had passed, it was Friday night and Natasha and Nikolai were sitting at the teppanyaki bar in Roka on Charlotte Street, with a bottle of sake and the menus in front of them.

'I can't believe I've managed to get you out,' Nikolai said. 'You've been so bloody reclusive recently. Michael and Brenton have been asking me why you never return their calls, wanting to know if you hate them.'

'Of course I don't hate them,' Natasha said defensively. 'I've just been busy, that's all.'

'Darling, we're all busy but we all find time to see our friends. We have to. Otherwise we end up burned out and miserable. I'm worried about you. You never have any fun.'

'I have plenty of fun,' Natasha said shortly, her mind on Alastair who was in Norwich for a literary festival. He hadn't told her that but Natasha had checked his diary when he was in the shower and marked that evening in hers as one to catch up with friends. Who *had* been horribly neglected lately. But what could she do? It was impossible to make firm arrangements because she never knew for sure when Alastair might call and she'd have to drop everything.

Natasha had been sleeping with Alastair for exactly three weeks and the heady passion dominated her life like a golden mist, informing her every minute. He was the last thing she thought of as she set the alarm at night, the first to crash through her consciousness when it rang in the morning. Friends and family faded into insignificance, except as the source of amusing anecdotes for his entertainment. *What would Alastair think? When can I tell him? Where is he now? What would he do?*

Even if they hadn't been going to bed together, Alastair would have been permanently on her mind because she'd commissioned him to write a ninety-minute drama for Rollercoaster. That had entailed several more 'meetings', usually beginning in the office and ending up at her flat, as well as a few phone calls a day. Natasha desperately tried to make as few of these as possible, delegating as much as possible to Dom or Emilia or one of their lawyers, but often she was the only one who could make the call. She revelled in the thrill of a crisp, business-like conversation with the same man who, only a few hours earlier, she had been rubbing with baby oil (a tip from the sex goddess book), while dressed in her very prettiest underwear.

The golden haze extended to work, where everyone was thrilled to have lured Alastair on board and a press release had been issued that the boy of the moment was exclusively writing a 'hard-hitting provocative drama' for them. 'Are you going to thank your uncle Barney?' Barney exulted. 'Who's a clever sod for bringing the man of the moment on board?'

'You're a genius, Barney,' Natasha said. There was no way she was going to point out that she'd initiated things by taking Alastair out to lunch. With Barney the trick was to hand him all the credit for everything. Anyway, who cared about the script Alastair was going to write for them? All that mattered was that he wanted to go to bed with her.

Natasha had felt this craziness before, but she'd learned from her mistakes. This time she was going to make things work, by dint of steely self-control. There were lines over which she couldn't cross. She wouldn't say she loved him. She wouldn't ask anything about what happened when she wasn't there. She'd never let him know for a second how much thoughts of him consumed her, because as soon as he scented her neediness he'd get bored and move on. She had to be permanently amusing, unruffled, sunny. That way he would be too.

In a way, his 'situation', as she euphemistically referred to Aurelia, was almost a relief. Unlike with the other men, she couldn't be paranoid there was another woman, because there was. She couldn't ring Alastair at all hours, asking where he was, because she knew. He was with her. It wasn't ideal, but it brought her a strange peace.

There were other drawbacks. The fact he was writing a script for her was one. But that was in very, very early stages of development: it would be at least a year before she needed to start chasing him for it. And keeping up appearances could be exhausting. She knew Alastair liked her because she was so independent and busy, but to make their relationship work she had to be utterly depend-ent on him and his plans, which meant sacrificing her own social life. But of course she couldn't let him know this, which meant whenever he called she had to pretend to be with someone – preferably male – in some cool venue, even when more and more she was actually at home, flicking aimlessly through the TV channels, trying not to bite her nails or graze on the food in the fridge which she had ordered in from the deli round the corner so there was always a delicious snack for him, no matter when he arrived.

'So, I said to him: "I think you're really cute,"' Nikolai was saying. 'And he said to me: "Do you know what? I think you ought to meet my dad. I think you'd really get on. You're about the same age."'

She hadn't a clue what he was talking about but his tone suggested she should be outraged. 'Oh my God! I can't believe it,' she exclaimed. Nikolai nodded, satisfied. Just then she felt her phone vibrate in her pocket. She pulled it out. 'Just a sec,' she said hastily and dashed up the bar stairs to a place where she could hear him and talk privately.

'Hello?'

'Hi, noodle.'

'How's it going?'

'I'm bored. What are you up to?'

'Oh, you know. I'm in a bar in Charlotte Street. Having fun.'

'You're always having fun,' he said slightly wistfully. *Good.* 'So I guess you won't want me to come over.'

'I thought you were in Norwich?'

'Just got back. Did all my bits today and decided I couldn't face the dinner. But you're busy.' There was a coldness to his tone, which Natasha had begun to recognize.

'No, no . . . that's OK. We were just finishing up. It

was an early drink. I was going to head home in five, anyway.'

'Are you sure?' He didn't sound as pleased as Natasha would have liked.

'Of course I'm sure. Where are you now?'

'Just pulling into Liverpool Street.'

'Well, get a cab and I'll see you at mine in half an hour or so.'

She rushed back down the stairs. 'Nikolai, I'm really sorry but I'm going to have to go. It's the office. They want me back in. It's such a bugger, but we're in post-production on this three-parter and they need me.'

'But, Tash! It's Friday night. We were just about to order. Can't you stay for a quick sushi hand roll?'

'No, honey, I really can't.' She pulled a face at him. 'You know what work can be like. I'm way more pissed off than you are.'

'No you're not,' Nikolai grumbled.

'I'll make it up to you, I swear. Look, have another drink on me.' She peeled a couple of twenties from her purse and dropped them in front of him.

'This isn't about money,' he moaned, but Natasha had already dropped two kisses on his cheeks and shot back up the stairs.

An hour later, Natasha and Alastair were lying toe to toe in her bath. Glasses of champagne (she always kept a bottle in the fridge now) sat on the side, soft Brahms played in the background and two candles burned on a ledge. The only thing missing was the scented bath oil – she'd tried that once and Alastair had gently told her it wasn't on. Exotic smells might attract questions.

'I love being here,' he was saying. 'It's so restful. No one asking me questions. No one telling me what to do. It's a real haven.'

Natasha hid her smile. Alastair's home was clearly some noisy, chaotic place where Aurelia made constant demands and demanded approval. Natasha would never do anything like that. Her role was to ensure Alastair's time with her was as pleasant as possible.

'I can just feel all my troubles falling off me while I'm here.' He nudged at her soapy legs with his. 'We need more time together like this. How do you fancy a weekend away?'

She held her flute up to hide her delighted face. 'Depends where away,' she said. 'And when.'

'Where is a free weekend at Chevening House. *Smart Travel* magazine want me to write a piece for them. When is next weekend. Think you'd be up for that?'

Chevening House? It was in Somerset and, without doubt, the hippest hotel of the moment. Kate Moss and her boyfriend had just spent a week there, holed up in a suite. It had been on Natasha's list of places to check out for ages.

'Could be fun,' she said, sounding as bored as possible. Actually, next weekend wasn't ideal, she'd promised Mum she'd visit. But she could always go another time.

'I think so,' he said smiling. He looked at his diver's watch. 'Shit. Is that the time already? I need to be making a move soon.'

'OK,' Natasha said coolly. She wouldn't ask where he was going, since clearly it was back to Aurelia. Ask no questions and she'd hear no lies. She watched him climb out of the bath and dry himself on one of her Frette towels.

'I think I'll stay in here a little longer,' she said. 'Put in more bubbles. You can see yourself out, can't you?'

He was buttoning up his shirt, but now he bent over to kiss her. 'I wish I didn't have to go.'

'Well, you do,' she said lightly.

'I know. I know.' His hands twisted. 'It won't be like this for ever. And we'll have a lovely weekend. I'll call you to plan it during the week.'

'You do that,' she said. He looked at her again searchingly, then pecked her on the forehead.

'See you.'

'See you.' A moment later, she heard the door slamming. She lay back in the bath. A weekend away, she told herself, a weekend away. She didn't know why she felt so cold. Must be time to let more hot water in.

31

The past few weeks hadn't been much fun for Sophie. She'd been told off for excessive use of the washing machine, having too many baths (they used up so much more hot water than showers) and failing to get a receipt when shopping in the market. Home was such hell, she'd been spending more and more time with Olly: going to the cinema; having chilled, after-work suppers. He had made no attempt to kiss her, nor she to kiss him, and both seemed happy with the status quo. But Sophie realized that eventually they had to reach some kind of crisis point; that it couldn't go on in this cosy, sexless way for ever.

She was thinking about all this as on a Thursday evening she stood on Lainey and Marcus's doorstep. Lainey had invited her and Natasha for supper but no one was answering the bell. It was drizzling and people walked past briskly, arms wrapped around themselves to protect them from the damp.

'Soph!' It was Lainey, emerging from a cab in faded Puma sweatpants, a Bonds T-shirt and no bra. She ran up the steps. 'Sorry! Gyrotonics overran and then finding a cab in the rain was just impossible.'

'Never mind, you're here now.' Grinning at the knowledge gyrotonics was only five minutes' walk away, Sophie followed her inside, looking around. Little had changed since her last visit, the dull yellow hallway which Lainey had promised was going to be transformed was still dull yellow. A corner of the hall was still occupied by a pile of cardboard boxes.

'Lainey, have you still not unpacked the wedding presents?'

'What? Oh, yeah. Not all of them. We keep meaning to, but Marcus is never around and when he is we just want to chill. And opening wedding presents means writing thank you letters and frankly I just don't have the time.'

'But, Lainey,' Sophie pointed out, 'you don't even have a job.'

Lainey shot her a look. 'Er, excuse me. Yes, I bloody do. What do you call my painting?'

'Oh yeah, sorry.' Sophie thought it would be tactless to mention she'd seen no trace of artistic activity. 'How's that going?'

'Well, slowly. Waiting for the muse to strike, you know. That's why Uruguay will be so good. Give me some inspiration.'

'So you're going?'

'Yup, early August. I cannot wait. Marcus is still a bit pissed off about it, but I don't see why. Just because we're married doesn't make us joined at the hip. It's good for couples to have separate interests. In the meantime I've got Glastonbury to look forward to. Two weeks to go. Now, listen. Come upstairs and let's have a look for some accessories for the ball.' Lainey had been very excited when she heard about the £2,700 dress and insisted on lending some jewellery like Cartier might to a starlet on Oscar night.

They went upstairs to the bedroom. Sophie sat on the bed, lustfully noting the carved Balinese headboard and the Cath Kidston duvet cover. Lainey opened the wardrobe. 'Now, we need a wrap for you for when it gets chilly. Bollocks. Where has the cleaner put them all? She comes in every day and tidies everything so perfectly I can never find a thing. It's a total pain in the arse.'

'Great to have a cleaner, though,' Sophie observed.

'I guess. Best thing is she comes at eleven, which means I have to get up. Otherwise I could easily snooze until lunchtime. I've never been a morning person.' She pulled out a white and red beaded shawl. 'How about this? I bought it in Santorini a few years ago. Pretty, huh?'

'Beautiful,' Sophie said, stroking it reverently. 'And it would be perfect with the dress.' She glanced at the label. Chloé. Bloody hell. 'Are you sure you don't mind?'

'Course not.' Lainey pulled out a white silk camisole. 'Do you want this? Doesn't work on a size eight. It needs someone curvy, like you, Sophie, to carry it off.'

'But you can't just give it to me!' Sophie said, ignoring what she was sure was an unintended insult.

'Course I can. It doesn't suit me. Now, jewellery.' She picked up an elaborately painted Indian box and began rootling through it. 'I'm sure I had a ruby necklace somewhere that Dad gave me. And underwear. Do you need any sexy undies?'

'Lainey, I cannot wear your underwear. And anyway, what's the point? I mean, Olly's not going to see it.'

'Someone else might. You've always got to be prepared. Olly could be your path to a whole new group of men. You know, when I broke up with my last boyfriend Jezza,

I was devastated. But then a few months later along came Marcus. I bet it'll be the same for you. Someone perfect'll be waiting just round the corner.'

How do you know? Sophie wanted to protest. How do you know it'll be someone perfect? How do you know it won't be someone horrible who'll want a quick shag and tell me to cook for him and wear schoolgirl knickers?

'How's Marcus?' she asked instead.

'Working too bloody hard.' Lainey's animated face stiffened. 'I don't know, Sophie, I never see him. I'm beginning to wonder why I married him.'

'You hardly ever saw him before the wedding,' Sophie pointed out, a tightness in her throat. She didn't like any criticism of Marcus.

'I know, but I was so busy organizing it all, I didn't really care then. And somehow afterwards I thought things would all be different, but instead they're all the same. I've just got lots more kitchenware.'

'That's better than nothing.'

'Mmm.' She fingered a sparkly blue choker. 'Maybe I should book some beauty treatments. Cheer myself up.' She chewed on her lip. 'I think I'm suffering from postnuptial depression. I read about it in a magazine.'

'Maybe you should have a baby?' Marcus, unlike every other man in the world, was desperate to breed. Sophie knew it was inevitable but she was still dreading the day they announced the pregnancy. When she'd been with Andy it had been bad enough learning about other people's, but at least then she'd had a chance of getting up the duff. Now the news would be near intolerable.

'Oh God, not yet,' Lainey said. 'Marcus and I want at

least a couple of years for just the two of us before a baby comes and messes everything up. No rush. I mean, I'm still twenty-eight. It's only over thirty that your eggs start drying up.' She saw Sophie's face. 'Oh, sorry, Soph. I didn't mean that. It's over thirty-five, isn't it? Look at Emma Thompson, she was well over forty when she spawned.'

'She was.' Madonna, Julianne Moore, Helena Bonham Carter, Julia Roberts, the sixty-six-year-old Romanian. Sophie's radar for geriatric mothers was acute and whenever she read about a new one in the papers it made her day.

'Oh Soph, you've still got plenty of time for all that. I think this ball's going to be great. It'll be like a new beginning. I feel jealous of you, you know. You've got it all ahead of you. I feel like my story's over. By the way, have you seen the wedding in *Tatler*? *So* embarrassing.'

'You're in *Tatler*?' Sophie felt slightly choked. She'd always dreamed of having her wedding in a glossy magazine.

'Yeah.' Lainey pulled a copy of the magazine from under her bed. 'Everyone's taking the piss. It was my mother who insisted on inviting them. So humiliating.'

Sophie gazed at the pictures, irked that she was in none of them. 'Why are you complaining, Lainey? You look gorgeous.'

'Hmm.' She waved a chunky ruby necklace under Sophie's nose. 'Try this. I think it'll be fantastic.'

Sophie draped it around her neck. 'Do it up for me?' She gazed in the mirror. 'Oh my God. It's perfect.'

'It is nice. I should wear it more often.' Lainey smiled

at Sophie in the mirror. 'Maybe Olly will buy one like it for you.'

'Don't be bad.' Sophie unclasped the necklace and stroked it lovingly. 'Do you think I'm leading Olly up the garden path? We are good friends, I just don't want to snog him.'

'Well, good friends is what it's all about in the end.' The doorbell rang. 'Oh, that's probably Tash.'

'Who else might it be?' Sophie said, following her down the stairs.

'Well, it might be Adrian, my dealer.' She opened the door. 'Hey, Tash, it *is* you!'

'Hey!' There was a flurry of kisses and hugs. Natasha was looking very chic and even thinner than usual, Sophie thought, not sure if she should be envious or concerned. 'Been having fun?' Natasha asked a little distractedly.

'Oh yes, I've been kitting Sophie out for the ball tomorrow,' Lainey cried.

Sophie avoided Natasha's eye. She'd been keeping quiet on the ball front.

'What, lending her a dress?' Natasha asked. Sophie realized she'd completely omitted this bit.

'She doesn't need a dress. Olly bought her one,' Lainey said excitedly. 'For two thousand seven hundred pounds.'

There was a surprised silence, then: 'Two thousand seven hundred pounds? Sophie, bloody hell. And you accepted?'

'I tried not to,' Sophie mumbled. 'But he insisted.'

Natasha raised an elegantly threaded eyebrow. 'Right,' she said. 'And you're not having sex with him?'

'Tashie, I'm not a hooker.'

'Of course not. I wasn't saying that. But—'

'I don't see what the problem is,' Lainey interrupted. 'Sophie's made it clear to Olly where she stands. They're good friends and if he wants to buy her a present that's his lookout. And if she should decide she wants to *thank* him for his present, then that's hers.'

'And if she doesn't want to *thank* him?'

'She doesn't have to. But do you, Sophie?'

'No. I keep telling you. He's not attractive.'

'Looks aren't everything,' Lainey said firmly. She led them into the kitchen. 'So! Time to crack open the bubbly, I think.'

Prickling, Sophie decided it was time to strike back at Natasha. 'So no more word from Alastair Costello?' she said turning to her.

'Er, no, no. I'd forgotten all about him, actually.'

'Like hell you have. Look at her, Laines. She's blushing!'

'Well, OK,' Natasha said. It was actually a relief to unburden herself. 'We have seen each other a couple of times.'

'And is he still with his fiancée? The actress with the big head?'

'Well, sort of. It's complicated.'

'Complicated? How exactly? He's still engaged.'

'Yes, but he's planning to leave her. It's just difficult. She's in the middle of this play and it would be a bad time.'

Sophie gave a huge snort. 'Tash! I don't believe this. What else is he telling you? That they never have sex any more? That she doesn't understand him?'

'Oh, piss off,' Natasha said. 'It's not like that. He and

I are just having fun. It's nothing to get excited about.'
She lowered her voice, as if Aurelia might be watching
on a Webcam. 'Though this weekend, he *is* taking me to
Chevening.'

Lainey clapped her hands exultantly. 'Chevening! Oh
my God, Tash. How dreamy. You have to try the hot
stone massage, it's meant to be incredible.'

Sophie felt sour with envy. Suddenly the ball seemed
a little pathetic. She'd always wanted to go to Chevening.
'Well, be careful, Tash,' she said crossly. 'I don't want you
getting hurt.'

'I think it sounds incredibly exciting,' Lainey said unexpectedly. 'Good for you, Tash. Having a fling.'

'Lainey! How would you feel if she was having a fling
with Marcus?'

Lainey shrugged. 'Marcus could be flinging away for
all I know.'

'I doubt it,' Sophie said. 'He's the most solid man I've
ever met.'

'I know. That's why I married him. He's my rudder.'
The doorbell rang again. 'Oh, that'll be Adrian.'

She disappeared for a moment, then reappeared with
a thickset man in a grey Polo shirt. He looked like an off-
duty vicar.

'All right?' they all said, shaking hands with him. Lainey
offered him a glass of champagne and he said no, he
was driving, but he'd love a cuppa, so Lainey made him
one and they had an awkward conversation about the
weather.

The front door slammed. 'Duckie,' Marcus yelled. 'I'm
home. Earlier than I expected.' He marched into the

room, flinging his briefcase on the floor, then stopped dead as he saw Adrian. 'Oh, hi.'

'Marcus, mate, how are you?' Adrian raised a lazy hand in salutation.

'Er, fine, thank you.' He turned to the others. 'Hey, girls, it's great to see you. How are we both?'

'Great,' they chorused. 'And you?'

'Oh, working too hard.' He kissed Lainey, but a little gingerly, Sophie thought. 'How has your day been, duckie?'

'All right,' she said. 'Suppose I should be getting some food on. I got a ready meal from the Grocer on Elgin. I can heat it in the microwave.'

'I'd better be going,' said Adrian with a little stretch.

'Oh, no, stay!' said Lainey. 'The more the merrier.'

Sophie glanced at Marcus. His face was tight and dis-approving.

'Nah,' Adrian said. 'Gotta be on my way. Errands to run.'

'Are you sure?' Lainey looked genuinely disappointed.

'Positive. Your uncle Adrian's a busy man.'

He stood up and shook everyone's hands. 'I'll see you out,' Lainey said. Sophie realized she'd seen neither drugs nor money exchanging hands yet. Presumably that would happen out of sight.

'Thank God he's gone,' said Marcus as soon as they were out of the room.

'Markie! You're not one to say no to the ganja.'

'Yes, but it's not just ganja. It's class A he's dealing in. And I hate all that shit. And Lainey shouldn't be doing it either. We're trying for a baby, you know.'

'But I . . .' Sophie began, then stopped herself. If Lainey and Marcus's accounts of babymaking didn't match, she didn't really want to get involved. 'Lainey's not doing class As,' she tried instead. 'Just a bit of weed every now and then. She renounced all the chemicals around the time she met you.'

'I know.' Marcus smiled and loosened his tie. 'It just makes me uneasy having that guy in the house. He's pretty unsavoury.'

'I don't know,' Natasha said. 'He must have the private numbers for the crème of Notting Hill.' Time to move on. 'So, no holiday for you right now?'

'No. It's full on with this German telecoms merger we're doing.' He looked miserably at the bottle in front of him.

'At least you've got Glastonbury to look forward to.' Sophie thought the idea of sleeping in a tent and not washing for three days sounded abominable, but each to his own.

'Oh, Marcus isn't going to Glastonbury,' said Lainey, coming back into the room. 'That's just for me and the old gang. Hells, Will, Emerson, Cassa, Cloons. We do it every year. It's traditional.' She ruffled his hair. 'You're not too upset though, are you? He's going on a lads' weekend. They've hired a cottage in Wales.'

'Well, it's not exactly a lads' weekend . . .' Marcus began, but then seemed to give up.

'You're so mature. All these separate friendships and interests,' Natasha said approvingly. Sophie too looked at them in wonder. She should have been off with a gang of cool mates every weekend when Andy was working, rather than dusting the house waiting for him to return.

'It's what keeps things fresh,' said Lainey, kissing Marcus on top of his head. He smiled up at her. They were a vision of married bliss. And the evening, which had kicked off a little scratchily, went on to be a lot of fun.

32

'You know,' Marcus said to Lainey when the girls had finally left (after midnight, which meant yet again he'd only be getting five hours' sleep max), 'I've been thinking about this Glastonbury business and wondering if maybe I should come too.'

Lainey looked up from rubbing her organic moisturizer into her arms (and they were lovely arms, but that stuff cost sixty pounds, Marcus had noticed on their new joint credit card account).

'Why would you want to do that?' she asked.

Marcus took a deep breath as if he were in one of his wife's yoga classes. 'Well, you know. We're married. Most couples want to do things together. And I know how much Glastonbury means to you. I'd like to experience it too.'

Lainey pulled a flimsy camisole over her head. 'Honey, that's really sweet of you,' she said through the lacy fabric. 'But you've got your boys' weekend. You can't sacrifice that for me.'

'I wouldn't mind. Anyway, it's not a boys' weekend – everyone's bringing their wives apart from me. To be honest, I think I'll feel like a bit of a lemon.'

She smiled indulgently. 'Markie, it's a lovely idea but tickets all sold out months ago.'

'No,' he said proudly. 'You can get them on e-Bay for two hundred pounds. It wouldn't be a problem.'

Lainey sighed and climbed into the sleigh bed – which despite her assurances had got no more comfortable – beside him. 'OK,' she said, a new, firmer tone in her voice. 'Don't take this the wrong way, honey. But I don't really want you to come to Glastonbury. It was sort of going to be my time with my mates and I've been looking forward to it for months. I mean, not that I don't love spending time with you but I think it's really important that we maintain individual interests. Otherwise things get stale. You heard what Natasha and Sophie were saying. They thought we were really mature.'

Often Marcus thought Lainey should have been a lawyer for the Mafia. She could argue her way around anything. 'But couples need to do things together too,' he demurred. 'And sometimes I feel . . . I mean, take Archie and Maura. They're always inviting us to dinner but every time you find a reason to turn them down. They're really nice people, duckie. I'd love you to get to know them better.'

Lainey crawled on top of him, pulling a face. 'Archie and Maura *are* very nice, Markie, but we just don't have that much in common. Last time we saw them Maura just went on and on about how excited she was about the new Boden shop and then she got on to school fees. It's just not really me. And you wouldn't like it if it was.'

'I wouldn't,' agreed Marcus. He'd been so proud to hook Lainey precisely because she was a bit out of the traditional banker's wife mould – even though she seemed to enjoy spending his money just like the rest of them. 'But I simply want us to work out a way of seeing more of each other.'

'We would see more of each other if you were ever here,' she pointed out, nuzzling his stomach with her nose.

'I know. And I've been thinking about that some more. Making some life changes. Getting out of the bank before it's too late. A lot of people are being offered voluntary redundancies at the moment. Maybe I should take one. Retrain as a . . . teacher or a farmer or something.'

The nuzzling stopped. 'Babe,' Lainey said, pulling herself on to one elbow and looking in his eyes. 'I think that's a fantastic idea. Though we've just got to think things through a little bit. I mean, you said we couldn't afford the house if you jacked in your job. So maybe we should just wait until your next bonus and pay off the mortgage before we make any crazy decisions.'

'I'm not sure there's going to be a next bonus,' Marcus said. 'They're really cutting back right now. If you keep your job you're considered lucky. And that's why I hate banking so much. It's so bloody brutal. I really can't help thinking I'd be better off doing . . . Aaah.' He stopped as Lainey's head, which had been moving slowly down the bed throughout this speech stopped at exactly the right place.

'You were saying?' she mumbled, her mouth full.

'Aaah.' Marcus groaned. 'That's good. Don't stop.'

'No,' she teased. 'I want to know what you have to say.'

'I'll tell you later,' Marcus moaned. And once again, the thorny issue of his future and how much time he spent with his wife was forgotten.

33

The following afternoon, Sophie met Olly to take the train to Oxford. Yesterday's rain had cleared and it was a perfect English summer's day, meaning a tube full of tense, sweating people and an unexplained fifteen minutes' wait outside Paddington. But Sophie was too excited to let any of it get to her.

He was waiting, early as always, in his jeans and a red and white stripy shirt, at the entrance to WH Smith.

'I bought you these,' he said as soon as he saw her, handing over a bag. Inside were the latest editions of *Heat*, *Vogue* and *Elle*. 'It's platform eleven,' he added. 'I've already bought the tickets.'

They were in first class. 'Olly!' she exclaimed, looking round at the seats, which were only marginally wider and cleaner than in second. 'Why did you bother? The journey's only an hour.'

'Yes, but we want to do it in style,' he retorted.

If Andy had ever made a gesture like that, even just once, Sophie thought she would have died of delighted shock. But now she simply felt vague irritation at Olly's eagerness and at herself for being so ungrateful.

The carriage was empty. The train jerked slowly out of London, then picked up pace as it headed west. 'So who are we staying with tonight?' Sophie asked.

'Alice and Sean. We were all at Oxford together; they

married as soon as we graduated and bought a lovely house in north Oxford with some cash they inherited. He's an up-and-coming don at Trinity and she's a primary-school teacher.'

Hmmm. Sean sounded a bit brainy, but primary-school teacher she could cope with. 'They married young.'

'They did,' said Olly. 'They knew what they wanted and they decided to go for it.' He looked at her meaningfully. Uncomfortable, Sophie stared out of the window at the red-brick terraces of Ealing.

But apart from that moment of heaviness, the journey was a great laugh. They played a silly game of I Spy and gossiped about various people in the office (disloyally Sophie told Olly about Fay and Mr Cheesy Dick, which made him roar with laughter).

'So how's your book going?' she asked when his laughter subsided.

'Oh, coming along,' he said. He looked around as if for eavesdroppers in a way that made her laugh and then dropped his voice. 'Should be finished in plenty of time. For now I'm focusing longer term. Politics. In talks right now with the Party, actually.'

'The Party?'

He gave her a funny look. 'Yes, the Tories.'

'Oh.' Dimly she remembered Natasha mentioning him as a potential Tory Prime Minister. But Sophie was still thrown. Not that she was at all political, but everyone knew the Tories were an even worse bunch of losers than Labour. 'Right.'

'They need young blood to turn themselves around, and I'm confident I have the ideas to help them do that,'

Olly said. 'Who knows, if they find me a safe seat I could even be in the House in a couple of years' time. Vernon's actually being very helpful about it, pulled a few strings.'

'Vernon? What, as in my mum's Vernon?'

'Yes. We've had lunch once or twice.' He cleared his throat. 'So. Have you ever been to Oxford?'

'Yes, I visited Natasha a few times. Gorgeous place.'

'It's very beautiful,' he said. 'I adored my time there. Did you enjoy being a student?'

'Well . . . I wasn't a student student. I was just learning word-processing and stuff.' And keeping house for Joel, her then boyfriend: making elaborate cakes and poring over recipes for real mayonnaise. Why the hell hadn't she been having wild sex and getting her stomach pumped like a normal twenty-year-old? Why had she been in such a hurry to grow up?

The train was pulling into Oxford station. Out of the right-hand window, Sophie saw a medley of pointy, round and rectangular stone spires stretching up into the sky. Alice and Sean lived in a huge Victorian house on a tree-lined road about a ten-minute drive from the centre. Exactly what Sophie dreamed of for her four children.

A woman with a round, friendly face, curly hair and opera bosoms under a purple sweatshirt opened the door. 'Wa-hey! You made it,' she cried. She ran down the steps and kissed Olly enthusiastically, then turned to Sophie. 'Hello! I'm Alice. We've heard so much about you.'

Had she? 'Ha, ha. All good, I hope.'

'Oh, yes.' Alice sounded very meaningful. She squeezed Sophie's arm. 'Let me show you your room. Ols, you know where you are, up in the attic.'

So they wouldn't be sharing after all. Relief flooded her.

'How lovely,' she said enthusiastically, looking around as she followed Alice up the stairs. First Lainey, now this. When did everyone start living in such grown-up houses?

'Thank you,' Alice smiled, opening a door off the landing. 'This is your room. Now, do you want a cup of tea before you start getting ready?'

'That would be great. What a gorgeous house.'

'Thank you.' Alice stepped forward and lowered her voice. 'I hope you don't mind that I've put you and Olly separately. We just weren't . . . quite sure what the situation was. But you're welcome to move into his, if you want to.'

'Oh, there's nothing going on between Olly and me,' Sophie said hastily. 'We're just good friends.'

'That's nice. You work together, don't you? What do you do?'

'Oh, I work . . . in the features section.'

'How marvellous,' said Alice, who clearly hadn't a clue what the features section was. 'Well, like I say, Olly's told us so much about you, what friends you are, what fun you have.'

'Oh, we do,' said Sophie.

'Have you read his book? It sounds fascinating.'

'Er, not yet. I'm waiting until he's put the finishing touches to it.'

'Good idea.' Alice smiled. 'Well, see you in a minute. Take your time.'

It didn't take Sophie long to get ready. She put on her Beretskaya with its slit right up the side and fastened Lainey's ruby necklace round her throat. Then she slipped on her high, strappy diamante sandals from Faith and screwed matching earrings from Accessorize into her ears. Just like the magazines said: a few high-street pieces 'lifted' by some designer. Really, she decided, she couldn't look better.

There was a knock at the door. 'Come in,' she shouted.

Olly was standing there, wearing a dinner jacket. Sophie almost gasped. He looked so, so much better than usual. Black tie made him look serious and strong and by contrast she suddenly felt delicate and feminine. 'You should wear that all the time, Olly,' she said.

Olly was staring at her. 'You look stunning,' he said in a slightly choked voice. 'Absolutely stunning.'

'Thank you.' She giggled, embarrassed, even though she agreed with him. He held out his arm and she took it although there wasn't actually room for them to descend the narrow staircase together, so she went first, holding her skirt up in her hand while he followed.

Alice was on the lawn wearing an unfortunate pink dress which clashed horribly with her healthy complexion. Next to her stood a man with an equally round, pink face and cherubic golden curls. 'Pimm's, anyone?' he shouted. 'You must be Sophie. I'm Sean. Gosh, you do look super. Far too good for our Chunky.'

'Chunky?'

Olly looked embarrassed. 'It used to be my nickname.'

'Owing to his fondness for chunky chips,' Sean brayed. 'Which by the look of things still play a major role in your life, don't they, Ols?'

'Sean,' Alice nudged him. 'Like you can talk.' Olly had gone tomato red. Sophie felt an unexpected flare of protectiveness towards him.

278

Drinks were poured and they all chatted as the evening sun slanted across the garden. Sophie realized she was having a really nice time. Alice and Sean weren't the kind of people she'd normally hang out with: both way too square with all their talk about choir practice and book groups, but they were very nice and they obviously adored Olly. Maybe if Sophie had gone to university she could have had a gang of friends like this, she thought wistfully. Why had she thrown away so much time on one stupid man after another?

She heard a car honking. 'That'll be our taxi,' said Sean, looking at his watch. 'Yup, it's eight. We should be off. No point turning up fashionably late to a ball. You want to get your money's worth.'

The ball was at Magdalen, their old college. When she stepped through the narrow door, Sophie felt like Alice going into Wonderland. The courtyard (or 'quad' as Olly told her it was called) glowed with thousands of fairy lights, a jazz band was playing, beautiful women wafted around in beautiful dresses, there were food stalls serving burgers and hot dogs and sushi and popcorn and candyfloss and everywhere there were smiling waiters and waitresses bearing trays of champagne glasses. Sophie took one. She drank it in moments and then her second and then her third. Meanwhile, they strolled round all the different courtyards – sorry, quads – as well as various rooms inside the college, admiring the dodgems, the bouncy castle, the casino.

'Sister Sledge are playing later!' she yelped, studying her programme.

Olly smiled at her rather nervously. 'Are you having a good time?'

'It's *amazing*.'

'Are you sure?'

Oh, for heaven's sake, Olly. 'Of course I'm sure.' She peered at the programme. 'Look, there's a reggae band about to start. Let's go and check them out.'

The band was superb. Sophie started tapping her feet and wiggling to the beat.

'You dance,' Olly said. 'I'll watch.'

'I thought you loved dancing.' That's what he'd said when she'd told him about Lainey's wedding.

'I do, it's just right now I'm not in the mood.'

Whatever. Sophie danced by herself for long enough to get sweaty. Then they had a pork sandwich from the spit roast, then they went on the dodgems, where Olly let Sophie drive and crash into all the other cars with yelps of glee. They did some karaoke (Olly sang 'The Wonder of You' rather well and looked right at her throughout which was a bit cringey but never mind, and Sophie did 'Fame' and got a big round of applause, although more for her enthusiasm than her talent). They ate a burger and had some ice cream in the Italian café.

'Isn't this great?' said Alice, who had ordered a knicker-bocker glory. She leaned in close. 'You know, it's so nice to see Olly with someone. I mean, I know you said you're not actually together, but . . . we had been worrying about him rather and he seems so happy with you.'

'I think he's happy being with his old friends,' Sophie said, flustered, but Alice laughed and shook her head.

They did some Scottish reeling (this time Olly joined in enthusiastically; like lots of blokes he had no problem dancing when told precisely what to do) and then they all piled into a marquee on the lawn to watch a rousing set from Sister Sledge. Olly swayed a bit in an uncoordinated way and clapped his hands at all the wrong times.

'That was wicked,' Sophie gasped, after the second encore. 'All the oldies.'

'They were excellent,' Olly agreed. 'I'd never heard of them.'

Never heard of Sister Sledge? 'Oh Olly, you must have.'

He shook his head. 'Not really. I'm not a great pop music fan.' You could almost hear the quotation marks around pop music.

'But what about all those CDs you have?'

'Oh, yeah.' He looked a bit panicked. 'Well, I wouldn't exactly call that stuff pop.' He gestured down to the riverbank. 'Shall we go out on a punt?'

Normally it would have been a lovely idea, but now it made Sophie tense. Punts were super-romantic things. You might as well go on a gondola and have a man with a handlebar moustache sing 'Just One Cornetto' to you.

'Mmm, I think I might have drunk a bit too much for that,' she said. 'Why don't we have a go at the bouncy castle?'

Olly stifled another huge yawn. His face looked all doughy and creased. 'Actually, if you don't mind terribly, maybe we should think about calling it a night.'

Calling it a night? But it was still early. Sophie looked at her Georg Jensen. Only just after one. And the ball went on until dawn, didn't it? 'But there's still loads more stuff to do. It won't be long before they start serving breakfast.'

Olly looked at her and, for a horrible second, Sophie

had a flicker of déjà vu: Andy and his 'Let's leave on a high'. But then he rallied.

'You're right. There's still loads to do.'

And so the night continued in a dreamy round of more dancing, more eating, more drinking, more sitting in the cabaret tent laughing drunkenly at probably not very funny comedians. Sophie couldn't remember having such fun in years. And the more she laughed, and the more she drank, the more she thought, yes, tonight has to be the night. Olly loves me and if we just do it, we'll get the worry out of the way, and it's bound to be better than I expect.

Sean and Alice left around four. And by five even Sophie admitted defeat.

'Don't you want to stay for the survivors' photo?' Olly teased.

'I don't think I want myself immortalized on camera, the way I look right now.'

'You look beautiful,' he said softly. 'As ever.'

Her heart began to thud. She followed him through the porters' lodge on to the street where a line of cabs was waiting. In the taxi, he shut his eyes contentedly. 'Thanks so much for being my guest tonight, Sophie.'

He wasn't expecting sex. She could get away with a peck on the cheek. But she was all geared up for it now and anyway, she felt she had to thank him somehow for showing her such a great time.

'Sssh,' he whispered as they crept into the house, using the spare key Sean had given him. 'Don't want to wake them.'

'No.'

They stopped at her doorway. 'Thanks again, Sophie,' Olly said. His face glowed white like a maggot and there were stains on his shirt. 'I was the proudest man at the ball tonight. I was so honoured you came with me.'

The way he said it made her heart dissolve. Hands shaking slightly, she stepped forward and pulled his face towards her. 'Would you like to stay with me tonight?' she asked.

'Stay with . . . ? Oh, I, Sophie . . . I didn't mean . . .'

God, maybe he thought she was a total slut. 'You don't have to . . .' she said hastily.

'But I . . . no, Sophie. I'd love to.'

'Good,' she said and, taking his hand, she pushed open her door and led him to the bed.

34

It was late the following afternoon. Sophie was lying on her bed in Camden, in sleepless limbo. The sun coming through the blinds made her feel as if a hedgehog was rolling on her eyeballs. But when she closed her eyes, images from last night danced across her mind like some horror film. Her dancing, her eating bacon and eggs, her drinking champagne, and then her bloody saying to Olly: 'Would you like to stay with me tonight?'

And then the next bit. Them going into the bedroom and standing there kissing, and her instantly remembering how bad Olly was at this as he nibbled tentatively at her mouth like a mouse with a huge chunk of Cheddar. The whole thing was about as erotic as unblocking a U-bend. But Olly clearly felt differently, judging by the rising in his trousers. Steeling herself, she pressed her hands against his shirt, then began undoing the buttons. She slipped her hands inside and felt the thing she had been dreading.

Man boobs.

Just a 40AA, but definitely breasts.

'Shall we, ahem, get undressed?' he asked.

Sophie was taken aback. Everyone knew you didn't 'get undressed', you tore each other's clothes off and took each other on the floor.

'Um, OK.'

'I might just turn the light off,' Olly said, walking over

to the door. He clicked the switch. Then he closed the curtains. It was midsummer and dawn, so the room wasn't completely dark, but he was a hazy form now, rather than a sharp outline. Sophie could see him unbuttoning his shirt, unzipping his trousers and folding each item of clothing neatly on the chair in front of him.

Hang on. This wasn't the way you did it. But Sophie didn't feel she could tell him that. So she kicked off her shoes, took out her earrings, and putting her hands behind her back unzipped her dress. She turned round, wearing just her knickers – plain white M&S – and black bra and saw that Olly had burrowed under the covers.

Her instinct was to climb into the armchair by the window, pull her dress over her and go to sleep. But Sophie was a woman with a mission, so she treated that instinct as she would one of those annoying people in the street hassling you to support their charity: by walking past, head high, as if it simply wasn't there.

She climbed in beside him. For an awkward moment they both just lay there, then he rolled on top of her but, to her amazement, rather than kissing her again, wiggled downwards, slowly pulling off her knickers (they got caught around her foot but she kicked them off) and began to lick her out.

Where the hell did he learn to do this? Sophie lay there, feeling him lap at her like a cat with a bowl of milk. It was pleasant enough, even though most of the time he was nowhere near the right spot. Still, full marks for trying. And meanwhile she could simply lie back and relax. Lap, lap, lap: on he went. About ten minutes must have passed and she was no closer to orgasm than she was to becoming the

Queen of Norway. She opened her eyes and to her embarrassment saw Olly looking straight at her, with his trademark imploring expression. Oh Christ, he was expecting her to come. She'd better respond in some way because she was shattered.

'Mmm,' she moaned. 'Mmm, oh yeah.'

Encouraged, he started licking harder. His aim was even worse now, but whatever.

'Oh yes, Olly, that's good.'

Suddenly, an image of Andy's intense, slightly worried face flashed into her mind. Tears stung at her eyes. Why wasn't he here, doing this to her?

'Oooh, Olly,' she yelped, wiggling a bit. 'Oh yeah, yeah. I'm coming. Oh yeah.' And then for good measure: 'You're the best.'

It was obvious why Sophie had never got into drama school. But Olly seemed convinced. With a satisfied sigh, he pulled himself up and fiddled with his boxer shorts. 'Hang on a second,' he said, rolling off the bed and rustling about in his dinner jacket pocket. A condom emerged, was unwrapped and presumably put on. *So he was hoping this would happen.*

He climbed back under the sheets, fiddled around a bit and suddenly he was inside her. Sophie felt absolutely nothing except mild discomfort. He moved around a bit, then some more, then some more and some more. Had he been studying Sting's guide to tantric sex?

'Is that good?' he whispered in her ear. 'My darling? Do you like that?'

Sophie didn't know what to say. It wasn't actively horrible, just tedious.

'Yeah, it's great. Oh God, I'm coming,' she lied. If he didn't get the message soon she was going to get blisters.

Eventually after half an hour of pounding in and out, she could take no more. She wheedled her hand through their conjoined legs and squeezed his balls.

Ding, ding, ding, jackpot!

'Oooh! Aagh! Yeah. Oh!' And he collapsed on top of her. 'God, I'm sorry,' he whispered in her ear. 'I just couldn't control myself any longer. You're so beautiful, Sophie.'

'Mmm,' she muttered.

'Thank you,' he whispered. 'Thank you.'

What did she say to that? 'It's a pleasure?' 'You're welcome?' She settled for 'Mmm' again. Then she yawned. 'Gosh, Olly, I'm exhausted.'

'Oh?' He sounded a little disappointed.

'Yes.' She rolled on her side, her back to him. 'Goodnight, Olly.' With an effort, she added, 'Thanks for a lovely evening.'

She started breathing heavily, rhythmically. And after a while, she heard him follow her. Only then did she open her eyes, roll on to her back and lie there for a very long time looking at the ceiling, cursing herself for having raised Olly's hopes and wondering how she was going to extricate herself from this situation.

She fell asleep around eight. About two hours later Olly got up and showered and dressed in the bathroom so she was spared the sight of his pink, plump body. She lay in bed another half-hour, spent a further twenty minutes dressing and went downstairs. She half expected to push open the kitchen door to be greeted by the others shouting: 'Slaaag!', but instead they were sitting round the table, drinking coffee and reading the Saturday *Telegraph*.

'Morning, Sophie,' bellowed Sean. 'Or should I say afternoon?'

Sophie hated people who said that even more than she hated people who said, 'Cheer up, love.' 'Why should I when I've just found out I've got three months to live?' was what she always wanted to reply, but of course she never had the nerve.

'Fancy a croissant?' asked Alice who was wearing a tatty red dressing gown and looked like a fatter version of Munch's scream.

Only once or twice did she catch Olly staring at her as she devoured two croissants and three slices of toast and Marmite.

'So, Sophie,' he said as she drained her third cup of coffee. 'How do you feel about a tour of Oxford?' She knew what he was imagining: them walking hand in hand through cobbled streets, stopping for tea and cakes in a quaint café, larking on a riverbank.

'Oh. Right. Well, that could be great, but . . . I think I've got to get back to London. You know. Chores to do.' She laughed feebly.

'God, poor you,' Alice said. 'I just want to lie in a deckchair all afternoon barfing.'

'Well, I'll come back with you,' Olly said hastily.

'No! You don't have to do that. I mean, you want to hang out a bit with your friends, don't you? Enjoy the lovely weather.'

Olly looked uncertain. 'I'm happy to go back.'

'No, Olly, honestly.'

He shrugged. 'Fair enough.'

She called a cab to take her to the station. 'See you again soon, I hope,' Alice whispered as she hugged her goodbye.

'Oh, for sure.' Sophie felt sad. They were nice and she would like to keep in touch, but it was hard to see how. She turned to Olly, who was standing there looking mournful. 'See you at work on Monday.'

'Yes,' he said. 'See you at work.'

The London train was broiling, the air-con was broken and the windows opened only quarter of an inch. Sophie's stomach was churning and her brain rattling around in her skull like a pebble in an empty bowl. A gang of Italian language students hooted and catcalled in the surrounding seats. She wished she was in cool, empty first class.

Although she had been desperate to leave, doubts now started assailing her like spears raining down on a Viking battlefield. Why hadn't Olly put up more of a fight to stop her going? Perhaps he'd hated the sex? He'd gone off her, she knew it. Oh God. Now no one was ever going to love her.

Miserably, she trekked back across a scorched London. At least Veronica was out. But she'd left a note on the table. *Sophie, UO me £17.50 for electricity. PS Rescued that jar of Marmite from the bin. There was still tons in it! (Vegemite girl myself)* x

Miserly old ratbag. She felt a familiar prickling in her tear ducts. Miserably, she opened the cupboards. Oh, thank God, a pack of Jaffa Cakes. And there by the telly was a DVD of a Cameron Diaz film. She made for her bedroom, flung herself on the hard mattress and reached in her bag for her phone. Speed-dial three.

'Hey, Soph.'

'Marcus. How are you?'

'Great. We're sitting on the terrace of the River Café. London at its most glorious.'

And London at its most bloody expensive. Even Natasha had complained how her last meal there had cost a hundred pounds for just two courses and a bottle of sparkling. Sophie remembered Olly ate at the River Café all the time.

'Oh well, I won't disturb you.'

'No, that's cool, we're between courses. Here, hang on, I think Lainey wants a word.'

The phone was handed over. 'So how was it? Tell! Tell!'

'Well, the *ball* was amazing.' For a moment, Sophie was transported back to last night. The setting, the music, the food, the champagne. She described it all, up to the point when they returned to Sean and Alice's.

'And then . . . ? You did it, didn't you?'

'Maybe.'

'And . . . No, wait a minute, honey, I'll tell you in a sec. So?'

'It was vile, Lainey. The worst ever.' And she told Lainey the salient details. When she finished there was a pause. 'So. What do you think?'

'I'm not sure.'

'It's bad, isn't it?' Sophie realized she wanted Lainey to say that actually it was all cool, that Marcus had been a lousy lay when they first got it on, that all this was going to work out just fine.

'It doesn't sound good,' Lainey said slowly.

'Lust can grow,' Sophie pointed out.

'It can. But . . . Sophie, this bloke isn't your boyfriend. You've just had a one-night stand. A crap one. Happens to us all.' Sophie heard Marcus squeak indignantly. 'Oh shush, babes. Chill out. You didn't think I was a virgin when I met you, did you?'

'It's just going to be so embarrassing seeing him at work,' Sophie said lamely.

'I know. But you'll live. Soph, you're on the rebound. It's classic. So don't convince yourself Olly is a handy replacement for Andy. Because now, more than ever, you know that he's not.'

As Lainey spoke, Sophie saw the life she'd secretly imagined for herself vanishing. No more balls. No more first-class travel. No more adoring men who were going to rule the country buying her *Heat* and *Vogue*. No more lovely house in Kensington, for which Sophie had great redecoration plans. But Lainey was right. Lainey was always bloody right, which was why she had the perfect life and . . .

'Sophie!' There was a banging on the door. Damn. She hadn't heard Veronica get back.

'Hi, Veronica, I'm on the phone.'

'Sophie, have you eaten those Jaffa Cakes?' The door opened and Veronica's head poked round it. 'Because they weren't mine, they were my mate Jake's.'

'Hang on a sec, Lainey.' Shamefacedly, Sophie handed over the packet. 'I only had a couple.'

'You owe Jake two Jaffa Cakes,' Veronica said. 'Jakey! I've got them.' She slammed the door.

'Christ!' Sophie fulminated. 'I don't believe this. It's like living with bloody Ebenezer Scrooge.' She heard the buzzer go. Well, it wasn't going to be for her.

'Honey, I have to go,' Lainey said. 'Our main courses are here. Listen, do you want to come over later and tell us more?'

'No thanks,' Sophie said miserably. 'I need a night in alone with my hangover. Will it all be OK, Lainey?'

'It'll all be OK. But Natasha was right, you've just got to stop giving this Olly guy the wrong idea. It's not fair on him. You're gorgeous, Sophie. Plenty of other men will love you.'

'If you say so.' Sophie doubted this sincerely.

'All right, all right, I'll hang up. Soph, I've got to go, Marcus is getting arsey. But call me later. Lots of love.'

Click.

With a sigh, Sophie slipped the DVD in her laptop and shoved a Jaffa Cake in her mouth. The picture was shit. Oh, for heaven's sake. Veronica had clearly been buying bootlegs in the market.

'Sophie!' Christ. What had she done now? Not re-used the inner roll of toilet paper to make all her family's Christmas presents?

Veronica pushed open the door. She was carrying a gigantic bunch of flowers. White lilies and roses.

'Wow,' Sophie said, forgetting her vow never to speak to Veronica again. 'Who sent you those?'

'They're for you, you lucky moo.' Veronica handed them over. 'Must have cost about a hundred and fifty quid. Insane, when they'll be dead in a couple of days.'

Sophie read the note: *I had a great time, hope you did too. Thanks again, O x*

Once again, she felt herself melting. She had to call him. He picked up on the first ring.

'Olly, thanks so much for the flowers. They're beautiful. Just what I need to cheer this miserable dump up.'

'Glad you liked them. So have you had a good day?'

'It's been OK. My flatmate's being a bit of a cow.'

'Oh, right. Because . . . I mean, you probably want a night in tonight, don't you?'

That was exactly what Sophie wanted. But she found herself saying: 'Why? What were you thinking of?'

'Well, I've got back and my place seems a bit miserable too. So I was just wondering if you fancied coming over. Having a takeaway. But if you're tired or . . . if you have other plans, I completely understand.'

Sophie, you have to stop encouraging him.

But I don't want to stay in with miserable Veronica or locked in this horrible bedroom. I want space. I want to be eating a nice meal and chilling out.

'Why don't I cook for you?' Sophie suggested. 'I'll be over in about an hour.'

35

Alastair and Natasha left for Chevening House late on Friday night. They agreed Alastair would pick her up at about eight in his beaten-up Mini and he did, although he was an agonizing forty-five minutes late, during which Natasha hovered obsessively by her window, peeking through the Venetian blinds, convinced he wouldn't appear. Which he did, of course, although he greeted her with just an abrupt kiss, a 'Hi' and, for the first hour of the drive, silence. Sometimes Alastair could be like this. He was very highly strung.

'Good day?' she tried, glancing at him as they passed the Hogarth roundabout.

'Huh? No. Not really. The paperback of *The Silent D.*'s just out and I'm pissed off with the publishers. Don't think they've done nearly enough to flog it. I went into Waterstone's today and I couldn't find a copy.'

'Oh.' What to say? 'Maybe it had sold out?'

He ignored her. 'And your bloody script is proving a total bugger. I'm really stuck on one of the scenes. I've written it about fifteen times from every conceivable angle, but it's just not working.'

The way he phrased it made it sound like it was all Natasha's fault for having commissioned him. 'Oh dear,' she said. 'Would you like me to take a look at it?'

'Mmm. Maybe.' Natasha noticed he was checking his

hair in the wing mirror. Her stomach spasmed with anxiety. Shouldn't they be bantering like characters in a Noël Coward play, sexual tension brewing like a pot of English Breakfast? But then the fact that he wanted to talk to her about work was surely a good thing. It showed how much he trusted and respected her.

Gradually he cheered up a bit, though he was clearly in no mood for chat. Still, it was good that they could be together and not have to talk. They continued down the darkening motorway.

Alastair frowned. 'I can't remember how one actually gets to Chevening after the M4. Can you look at the map, noodle?'

A slug of dread crawled down her spine. She'd always been a terrible map-reader. 'OK.' She picked up his tattered road map, covered in coffee stains and footprints, from the floor and peered. 'Well, you come off at junction eighteen.'

'Not nineteen?'

'No, definitely eighteen. Oh.' She looked again. 'Well, actually maybe nineteen would be better.'

'Make up your mind,' he sighed.

Her hands started to shake. Natasha hated being put under this kind of pressure. 'You're right, definitely nineteen. Or . . . oh no, I think eighteen.'

'Well, the exit for eighteen is coming up. Do I take it or not?'

'Yes! I mean . . . yes! I think so. I'm pretty sure.'

'Pretty sure or absolutely sure,' he bellowed.

'Just bloody take it,' she snapped back as he swung into the left-hand lane and was hooted by a Mondeo. Her hand flew over her mouth. She'd just lost control. Wasn't she meant to be Alastair's oasis of calm?

An hour later, they were crawling down a B road behind a tractor.

'I'm sure this isn't right,' Alastair growled, revving to overtake but then dropping back as the road narrowed still further.

'No, it is,' she lied. Actually, they should have gone right at the last roundabout. Her legs felt wobbly with fear. Alastair would leave her and she would never, ever have sex again.

'There's a crossroads coming up, which way do I go?'

'Em, take the way signposted Chevening.'

'There is no signpost.'

'Then go left! No right! No, no, left. Honestly, left.'

'For Christ's sake,' Alastair bawled. 'I used to think you were clever. Now just let me see the map.'

With a screech, they pulled into a layby. He snatched the map off her, muttering to himself. 'We've come completely the wrong way. We should have taken exit nineteen. Christ, Natasha!'

'I'm sorry,' she said softly.

He said nothing, just snapped the gearstick into first and pulled off again.

It was eleven when they finally arrived. They had the attic suite.

'Very *Elle Deco*,' Alastair yawned, staring around at the huge white bed, the dun-coloured walls, the plasma screen TV. Natasha felt crushed – it was almost exactly the same design as her flat. She opened the minibar and took out a bottle of champagne.

'Shall we?' she said with her best seductress smile.

He smiled back at her. 'I think we should do something else first.' Her grabbed her, pushed her back on the bed, hands all over her, shoving his tongue in her mouth. He tugged at her dress – black with buttons all the way down the front – and within seconds, she was in her matching red bra and pants, suspenders and stockings. Then he ripped off his jeans, his T-shirt, his boxers and climbed on top of her. Natasha shut her eyes. This was heaven. But then she opened them again.

'Wait a second. What about . . .' Even though they were naked together she was too embarrassed to say 'condom'.

Alastair sighed: 'Oh, noodle. You know how I hate being unspontaneous. Relax. We'll be OK.'

It wasn't the first time they'd had this exchange. Natasha was sure the withdrawal method worked perfectly well. Afterwards, he fell asleep straight away. It took her a while longer, because she was just so happy, lying in this bed with the Somerset moon shining in through the slatted wood blinds, designer cows mooing in the field outside and the man she loved beside her snuffling as he dreamed.

When she woke up eight and a half hours later, the space next to her was empty. She hauled herself up to see Alastair, in boxer shorts, bending over the desk. 'Oh fuck,' he was muttering. 'Oh fucking fuck fuck.'

'What is it?' she asked, instantly convinced it must be all her fault.

'I've forgotten the fucking charger for my laptop. I don't *believe* this.' He banged his fist down on the table.

'How am I going to be able to work now? I've only got about twenty minutes of battery.'

Work? But hadn't he come all this way to make love to her? Of course, he had the commission from *Smart Travel*, but Alastair had already said several times all that would involve was scribbling a few notes on the back of an envelope and then knocking out the piece in an odd half-hour. Still, better not question him.

'Oh dear,' she said. 'Have you tried reception? They've probably got a spare charger.'

'For this laptop? I very much doubt it. I bought it in Tokyo. Incredibly obscure model.'

'Well, it's worth a try.'

'Nah. They won't have it.' He slammed his fist down again so violently Natasha jumped. 'Buggeration.'

Tears stung at her eyes. This wasn't quite the morning she'd hoped for. She looked out through the window. The weather had broken; rain was falling on the lawns outside. She glanced at the bedside clock: only 9 a.m. A whole day ahead of them. The thought made her a little panicked.

'Shall we order some breakfast?' she tried.

'Mmm. Maybe in a minute. I want to sort this out first.' He peered at the laptop as if he could conjure up a lead by telepathy.

'Why don't I just ring downstairs and see if they've got one?'

'They won't.'

'Well, why don't I see,' she said patiently.

They had exactly the right model. It was with them in five minutes. Alastair relaxed, apologized for the outburst, they ordered breakfast and then they made love again, more slowly than last night but just as blissfully.

'Shall we go for a walk?' she asked afterwards.

'In this weather? I don't think so.' It was true, the rain was still descending in sheets, but what else could they do?

'We could check out the spa?' *Have a couple's massage.*

'Ugh. No. Spas are for poofs.' He picked up the laptop. 'Anyway, I really need to take a look at the script. It's bugging me. Why don't you watch TV or something?'

She watched the weather on Sky, which informed her that the whole country was enjoying a heat wave, apart from the West Country, which would see torrential rain all weekend. Then she watched an old movie on TNT. Eventually, Alastair came and joined her and they ended up watching a cricket match.

It was still raining at lunchtime. Breakfast had been so huge, Natasha didn't really feel like eating more but she couldn't face another second of cricket. Nor, fortunately, could Alastair.

'Enough of that,' he said, switching off the TV.

'We could go for a drive,' she said hopefully. 'The country round here's beautiful. We could go to Wells Cathedral.'

'God, what a suggestion.' He shuddered. 'I hate doing touristy things. Why don't we just hit the bar?'

So they got dressed, Natasha in her casual weekend outfit of a white vest top and black trousers, chosen after much poring over her Trinny and Susannah book, Alastair in jeans and a holey jumper.

Downstairs, they sat in the bar, overlooking the sodden

croquet lawn, reading the *Guardian* until they were interrupted by a cry. 'Ally! What are *you* doing here?' A tall woman with a mane of golden hair and the sleek look of a perfectly groomed racehorse was waving from across the room. She had an American accent. Natasha hated her instantly. Alastair didn't look too pleased either.

'Hi, Callandria. God, is there no escape?' He sounded as if he was joking, but the steeliness in his eyes showed he wasn't.

'If you wanted to escape, why did you come to Chevening?' Callandria turned to Natasha, holding out a long hand. Her nails scratched Natasha's palm. 'And you must be the famous Aurelia. I've heard so much about you.'

There was a silence. Natasha looked at Alastair. 'Actually, this is Natasha,' he said.

'Oh, OK. Sorry.'

'*De rien,*' Alastair said briskly. He turned to Natasha. 'Better get back to the grindstone.' He smiled at Callandria. 'Natasha and I are working on a script together. Came down here to get some writing peace. Naïve or what? Anyway, it's great to see you, Cally, but . . . got to keep our noses to the grindstone. Still, maybe see you in the bar later.'

'Yeah, cool, whatever,' Callandria said with a knowing look. Alastair got up and hurried to the door. Natasha followed, hollow inside. It was so humiliating the way Alastair couldn't acknowledge their real relationship. She should say something. But if she did she might upset him and if she upset him he might end it.

You knew what you were getting into. Either put up or shut up.

'Sorry about that,' Alastair said over his shoulder as he opened the door to their room. 'I know it wasn't very gallant to disown you like that.'

'I understand,' she said, making an almost physical effort to keep her voice light and bright. 'You can't have news of us getting back to Aurelia.'

Alastair shut the door behind him, stepped towards her and took her face in his hands. 'Noodle, unlike the others, you've never asked me about Aurelia and that's one of the reasons I adore you. And now I've got a piece of fantastic news for you. She and I have split up again. And for good this time.'

Natasha had not been expecting this. 'When did this happen?'

'A few days ago. I've been back on my mate Ant's sofa again.' He ran his hands through his hair. 'Not that his girlfriend Karen's too happy about that. Thinks I'm a bad influence. But where else can I go?'

You could come to me. Why don't you ask? But Natasha said, 'Poor you. Must have been tough.'

'It's been pretty nasty, though long overdue. She kept putting the screws on about the wedding date and I just couldn't go through with it. But you and I still need to keep our relationship a bit hush hush. You know – when we're seen out together, say it's a work thing. Stuff like that. As I've told you before, Aurelia's pretty sensitive and knowing about us could send her seriously over the edge.'

'But we *are* together now?' Natasha asked slowly.

He laughed. 'In a manner of speaking, noodle, yes. But you know. Nothing heavy for now. Not that you're into heaviness, thank God.'

Her throat constricted with happiness; her eyes grew swimmy. She swallowed hard. 'So you're not going to be wanting to move in or anything like that?' she asked in as brisk a tone as she could muster.

Alastair threw back his head and laughed. 'I've said it before: you are the female version of me. You're fantastic, noodle.' He started unbuttoning her trousers. 'I tell you what. Let's stay in this room for the rest of the weekend. Not come out for anyone or anything. Let's make this a special time. One all to ourselves that we'll remember for ever.'

Natasha couldn't think of a witty comeback to that, so instead she leaned forward and kissed him.

Much later, as they lay watching a DVD, she remembered something. 'Alastair, what did you mean: "unlike the others"?'

'What, noodle?'

'You said unlike the others I never asked you about Aurelia.'

His eyes remained on the plasma screen. 'Noodle, you know what I meant. All those annoying people wanting to know what was going on. Irritating journalists in interviews. Now, shush, this is the best bit.'

Mollified, Natasha moved closer to him. Of course that was what he'd meant. She didn't know why she'd suddenly thought he was referring to other women. She kissed him hard.

'Noodle, do you mind? You're distracting me. This is giving me ideas for where I'm stuck in the screenplay.'

A couple of weeks had passed; London remained uncom-
fortably hot. Sophie supposed she and Olly were a couple
now, although she wasn't sure she wanted the world to
know about it yet.

'I don't think we should tell anyone at work,' she warned
him.

'Why not?' he asked, looking hurt.

'Well, it's just not very professional. Dating co-workers.
You might get in trouble for sexual harassment or something.'

'More likely at the *Daily Post* I'd get a rise and a promo-
tion for dating the most gorgeous girl in the office,' he
said with a grin. 'And don't forget as soon as the Party
find me a safe seat I'll be leaving.'

'Well, when that happens we'll tell everyone.' They'd
worry about that when they got there.

In the meantime, she could certainly get used to life
with Olly. For a start, there was the house in Kensington, which, apart from being even bigger than Marcus
and Lainey's place, just made life so damn easy. No more
squeezing on to the tube and enduring hour-long waits
in tunnels, instead just a brisk walk (and window shop)
along Kensington High Street to the office. It saved
Sophie two hours a day, which gave her extra time and
money to go to the gym, or have a manicure, or all the

other treats she had always longed for. Not that they were officially living together, but staying there four nights or so out of seven did make things so much simpler.

Then there were the surprises. Almost every morning, Olly would leave a little present on the breakfast table: perhaps a cake of luxurious soap, or a huge bunch of flowers. Or she'd open an email at work saying they had reservations at some hip new restaurant or for a hot band's gig. Mind you, she always found that kind of thing a bit embarrassing: neither she nor Olly really fitted in at venues like the Shepherd's Bush Empire and she was never a hundred per cent convinced he actually enjoyed himself as much as he claimed, but she forgot about that in the buzz of telling people she'd seen the Crayfish or whoever.

'He sounds perfection,' Lainey said dubiously down the phone. 'But has the sex got better?'

'Yeah, it has.' And it had, if Sophie just lay on her back like a beetle and let her mind slip into neutral. There was nothing wrong with Olly's technique, after all, it was just her emotions which refused to come out to play.

'So when are we going to meet him?'

'Em, I'm not sure. He's quite busy. Out every night. It's hard enough for me to get him on my own.'

'Well, he has to meet me and Tashie or he doesn't count.'

'And Marcus.'

'Oh yeah, and Marcus too. If he ever leaves the office. Look, it's Glastonbury this weekend, but how about Tuesday? Give me a day to recover. We can go out somewhere fun.'

'All right,' Sophie said hesitantly. 'Though I just don't

know if Olly will be free.' In fact, Sophie knew that Olly would happily turn down an interview with the Prime Minister in which he confessed to having a love affair with a horse if it meant meeting her friends. But she wasn't quite sure she was ready for it herself. But that was cool. In the past she'd rushed into relationships too quickly. Now she was learning from those mistakes.

'Well, let me know. I'll book somewhere. We'll have a laugh. And I'll insist Marcus makes it.'

Olly couldn't decide whether to wear a tie or not. 'I mean, I want to look smart, but I don't want to look stuffy,' he said, gazing helplessly at the selection laid out on his bed.

'Oh, for God's sake,' said Sophie, who had been ready half an hour ago. 'Don't bother. It's only the girls. And Marcus. And we're going to the Rah Bar and I don't think it's a very tie sort of place.'

'Yes, but I want to make a good impression. I *shall* wear a tie. What do you think: the red or the blue?'

'Em, the blue,' she said, not taking her eyes off *Big Brother* on the screen across from his bed.

Of course Olly had been free on Tuesday night and of course there was nothing he'd like more than to meet Natasha again – and Lainey and Marcus. Sophie couldn't quite stifle her unease, but as the taxi took them up Kensington Church Street, then over the dip of Notting Hill down into Notting Dale she began to look forward to the evening. A night out in the land of the beautiful people.

'Lainey and Marcus live just down there,' she said, pointing to their street. 'It's lovely, isn't it?'

'God yeah. This is where I plan to move to next.' He gave her a shy, sideways glance. 'I mean . . . Would you like to live round here?'

What was Sophie meant to say to that? Best to ignore him. 'Oh!' she squawked. 'Just here on the right please! Thank you!' And the moment was lost.

The Rah Bar was in a basement just off Westbourne Grove, all squashy Moroccan sofas and pouffes, lit only by tea lights. Lainey and Natasha were sitting round a low table inlaid with mother-of-pearl. Tash was in immaculately cut black trousers and a white suede jacket, looking even thinner than ever. Lainey was in a scarlet top with mirrors around the neck and baggy blue silk pants.

'Heeey!' she shouted, hugging Sophie and then kissing a delighted Olly. 'I'm Lainey. And you must be Sophie's man.'

'That's me,' Olly agreed. Sophie looked around the room anxiously. Everywhere beautiful, skinny people lounged on cushions. Not one was wearing a tie. Olly looked like someone's dad.

'Is Marcus here?' she asked.

'No, no, not yet. You know what he's like.'

Sophie leaned over to hug Natasha. 'I've missed you,' she said. 'Have you been avoiding me?'

'Don't be silly. I've just been busy. I've missed you too.' But she avoided eye contact, instead turning to Olly. 'Hi, I'm Natasha. We did meet before in that bar that time.'

'Of course,' Olly said, all charm. 'How could I forget? How's Rollercoaster? I do adore the stuff you produce. Real quality.'

Olly never watched TV dramas. Oh well. Sophie turned to Lainey. 'How was Glastonbury?'

'Wicked,' Lainey said. 'Didn't sleep for four nights, I was so wired.'

'Laines! I thought you'd given up on all that stuff. Only the herbal weed for you.'

'Well, I have really.' Lainey shrugged. 'But once a year at Glastonbury, that's different. With the old crowd. Helps me forget I'm now a wife. Relive my youth.'

'You're only twenty-eight.' It didn't seem fair that Lainey could have achieved Sophie's Holy Grail of marriage so young and be so unappreciative of it. But Lainey wasn't listening to her, waving instead at a man in the corner in cut-off denims and a crewcut.

'Hey! Si! What are you doing at this end of town?' She turned to the others. 'I'm just going to say hello. Won't be a sec.'

'I must find the loo,' Olly said, clearing his throat.

'He's really sweet,' hissed Natasha as soon as he stood up.

'Really? Do you think so?'

'Oh, yeah. And his book sounds fascinating. I can't wait to read it.'

'Mmm.' Sophie smiled, relieved to have Natasha's approval. 'He's OK, isn't he? I wasn't a hundred per cent sure at first, but he's growing on me.' She touched Natasha's arm. 'Anyway, what about you? How's it going with Alastair? On or off?'

'Oh, you know,' said Natasha, avoiding her eye, but then she looked up and smiled. 'He's split up with Aurelia,' she hissed. 'It's all on course.'

'Tash, that's great! So why didn't you invite him this evening?'

The familiar evasive look came into Natasha's eyes. 'He's busy tonight. And anyway, we're still keeping it all a bit under wraps. Aurelia was shattered by the break-up and he doesn't want her to find out about us for a while.'

Doesn't he want to meet your friends? But then Sophie hadn't particularly wanted Olly to meet hers. And Lainey, by the way she was talking to Si, back turned to them, seemed to have no desire to make introductions either.

'Hello, hello!' boomed a voice above them. Marcus, also in a tie.

'Here already? Must have been a slow day on the markets.'

'It was, thank God.' He looked around. 'Where's my wife?'

'Over there. Talking to one of her mates.'

Marcus frowned. 'Hmm. I'll go and say hello. Won't be a tick.'

He walked up behind Lainey and slipped his arms round her waist. She spun round looking first surprised, then faintly defensive. Marcus shook hands with Si, then gestured to Lainey to come back and join them. She shook her head with a 'just a second' gesture. He said something and that closed look, more commonly seen on men who are getting a telling off, came over her face. She shook her head again and he returned to the table.

'She's just catching up with a friend,' he said, looking put out. He turned to Olly, just back from the loo. 'So you must be the famous Olly. Very pleased to meet you.'

'You too, you too,' Olly said, shaking hands. 'Dresden, Meissen, Scheldon, I hear. I'm a bit of a mate of old Chris Pereiera's. How's he getting on?'

'He was sacked last night,' Marcus said with a grimace. 'Hard times in the City right now. Shall we get the drinks in?'

'Actually, I just took the liberty of ordering a bottle of Moët at the bar,' Olly said.

The bottle arrived and they all toasted each other. Marcus, who was looking particularly floppy-haired and square-jawed tonight, kept staring at Lainey who, head tipped back and laughing, was still talking to Si.

Natasha's phone, which she'd placed on the table in front of her, started to ring. At the sight of the caller ID, her face went white. 'Oh, sorry,' she said. 'I have to get this.' She snatched it up. 'Hello?' Holding up a hand and mouthing 'Sorry' again, she edged towards the stairwell.

'So I gather you're in talks with MKW,' Olly said to Marcus.

'Ah, yes, yes, we are. Hang on just two ticks, could you? I don't mean to be rude but . . .' He got up and headed back across the room towards Lainey.

'Is everything OK with those two?' Olly asked.

'I think so,' Sophie said. 'But she is being a bit rude.' She watched Lainey's pretty face turn thunderous as Marcus tapped her on the shoulder again. Reluctantly, she removed her eyes from the drama as a pink-faced Natasha returned to the table.

'Guys,' she said awkwardly. 'I'm really, really, really sorry, but I'm going to have to go.'

'But we've just got here.'

'It's work. There's a crisis. They need me there. Sorry, Soph.' She turned to Olly. 'I do apologize.'

'Work?' said Sophie, looking her in the eye.

'Yeah, work.' Natasha looked away.

'If it's Alastair, why don't you get him to meet us here?'

'It's not Alastair,' Natasha said over-shrilly. 'Look, I'm really sorry.' Just then Marcus, followed by Lainey looking like a teenager who'd just had her mobile confiscated, appeared before them. 'Guys, guys, I'm sorry but I have to go. Work calls.'

'Oh, for God's sake,' Lainey exclaimed. 'All you people and your work. Don't you ever get time off for good behaviour?'

'Well, at least some of us *do* work,' Marcus said softly.

'What did you say?' Lainey asked.

'Nothing.'

'Marcus, you know I work. I work very hard. But being a painter isn't nine to five, you know. I have to wait for the muse to strike. I'm not confined to little boxes like the rest of you.' The last three words came out unexpectedly venomously. Sophie flinched.

'Sorry, duckie, sorry,' Marcus said instantly. 'I really didn't mean it. Now sit down and have a drink.'

'Look,' said Natasha, who had a miserable expression on her face. 'I won't go yet. Just hang on while I make a call.' She hurried out of the room again. Sophie looked after her curiously. She recognized the signs of a woman obsessed. She wondered if Olly could ever have that hypnotic effect on her.

'Shall we order?' she said brightly. 'I'm starving.'

They picked up the menus. Lainey was ramrod stiff with suppressed fury; Natasha, on her return, looked wretched; Marcus was a zombie. Olly and Sophie desperately tried to make an effort, chattering away and swilling back the Moët.

'God, it was weird to see Si,' Lainey said, relaxing a little after they ordered mezze and a communal pot of couscous and tagine. 'I never expect to run into the old Hoxton crowd on this side of town. Made me nostalgic. I think I'm gonna go over there on Saturday. A new bar's opened on Old Street. Should be a laugh.'

Marcus heard the end of this. 'Oh duckie, not on Saturday. Tom and Marianne have invited us to dinner.'

Lainey made a face. 'Oh, no! Do we have to?'

'Yes, we do. I did tell you about it three weeks ago. They're longing to meet you properly.'

'And talk about property prices and private schools,' Lainey muttered to Sophie. Sophie looked at her, rattled. Where was all this sullenness coming from? 'Thank God, I'm off to Uruguay soon,' she said loudly. Either Marcus didn't hear, or he pretended to ignore her.

'Now, I really have to go,' Natasha said, almost as soon as the plates were removed. Sophie looked at her in irritation. Couldn't she see how rude she was being? The sex must be sensational. Suddenly she was filled with envy.

'Go on, then,' Lainey said. 'Get back to your desk.'

'It'll be very boring,' Natasha said. 'Just conferencing LA. But it has to be done.'

After that, Sophie and Olly didn't stay very long. Lainey's black mood dominated the room like an elephant. Marcus slumped on the banquette, eyes half shut, clearly longing for nothing more than his bed.

Having made their excuses and got out on the street, Sophie and Olly turned to look at each other. Both exhaled loudly. 'Well,' said Sophie. 'What can I say? Did you enjoy meeting my friends?'

Olly rolled his eyes, then stuck out a hand for a taxi. 'It was a bit *Who's Afraid of Virginia Woolf*, wasn't it? Are Lainey and Marcus always like that?'

'No,' Sophie said as they climbed in the taxi. 'Not at all. Normally, they're perfect together. Lainey used to be a bit of a wild child, but she's reformed now. I think she's just upset with Marcus for working so hard.'

'Oh dear,' said Olly, wrinkling his nose. Sophie, shaken by what she had just witnessed, suddenly felt a rush of affection for him. He took her hand. 'Sophie, I hope it's not too forward of me. But there's something I really must tell you and that's that I love you.'

It was as if all the wind had been knocked out of her. Bloody hell, Andy hadn't told her he loved her until they'd been together about two years and even then he was drunk. What was she going to say? Fortunately, the dilemma was solved by their cab turning into Olly's road.

'Just here on the left, please,' Sophie said loudly. 'Thank you.'

But later, after sex, he said it to her again.

'I mean it, Sophie. I really mean it. I've never felt this way about anyone before. And don't worry about saying it back because I know you don't feel the same. But I hope with time one day . . .'

He sounded so sincere, she was deeply moved. 'It's OK, Olly,' she whispered. 'It's OK. I understand. And . . . I love you too.'

37

On a Friday, a couple of weeks after Olly had first told her he loved her, Sophie looked in her pigeonhole at work and found a Eurostar envelope. She had a good idea what it would contain, but her heart still did a little skip as two tickets to Paris for that evening fell out.

She picked up her phone and, as she did more and more often these days, dialled his extension. 'Oh my God, I can't believe this. Thank you.'

'I thought it could be fun,' he said, smugly. 'Now, listen, I know you won't have your passport, but you can nip back to Camden for it at lunchtime. I'll pay for your taxi.'

'Oh no, you don't have to do that.' Sophie had to stop Olly paying for everything. Though, on the other hand, why not? He could afford it. She'd looked at his payslip the other day, when he'd left it lying on his kitchen table, and been amazed at how much he earned each month.

On the Eurostar, they drank champagne with their dinner. 'It's always been my dream to take a beautiful woman to Paris,' Olly said, lifting his glass to hers in a toast. 'And now it's coming true.'

For a moment Sophie felt uneasy. Did Olly mean her? Or did he mean any old beautiful woman would have done?

'I love you, Sophie.'

'I love you too.' It got easier every time she said it. And

in a way she did love Olly – well, she was very fond of him and he treated her so well and wasn't that what really mattered?

They were staying at the Georges V.

'I can't believe this,' Sophie gasped, looking at the bed the size of an ocean liner, the choice of bathrobes – towelling or quilted – the Bulgari toiletries in the marble bathroom, which she made a mental note to shove in her bag. Forget Chevening, this was the real deal.

'Only the best for you,' Olly said, smiling.

It was late, so they decided not to go out that night but to have a cocktail in the bar.

'What will we do tomorrow?' Sophie asked. *Shopping. And an amazing meal somewhere.*

'Well, I would like to check out the Musée d'Orsay,' Olly said.

'OK,' Sophie said unenthusiastically. Andy always used to drag her round museums and she'd pretend to be interested, but she'd hoped she wouldn't have to make such sacrifices for Olly.

'We don't have to if you don't want to,' he said, as always hyper-attentive to her moods.

Oh God. She'd better give Olly *something* he wanted. 'Of course I want to. It'll be fun.'

Fun wasn't exactly the word for it. Olly spent so long in front of each picture, frowning, reading the blurb beside it. Standing near it. Standing far away. Sophie had made her way through the whole museum, checked out every inch of the gift shop and still he was lingering behind her. So she went and sat in the café with a cup of tea and a pastry (well, she was in Paris and cakes were part of the culture) and watched a very pretty and oddly familiar woman, with a cute snub nose and blonde curls, sit down at the table next to her. She was joined by a tall man whose dark hair was streaked with white, like a badger's, carrying a tray bearing a pot of tea. They made a stunning couple: she so fine-featured and angelic, he dark, slightly mean-looking and burly.

'Oh, thanks,' said the girl. She had a high, carrying voice, which Sophie was sure she recognized as well.

'Are you sure you don't want any of those cakes?' the man asked. He had a Scottish accent. 'I know you and your sugar fetishes.'

'Honey, how can you say that? You know I've got to lose those extra ten pounds before the audition.'

Suddenly Sophie got it. She was the actress who'd been so good in *Free Time*. Amelia, or Azalea or . . . what was her name? But he couldn't be Natasha's Alastair. She'd said they'd split up. Well, Araminta had obviously had no problems replacing him.

She had to find out more. 'Excuse me,' she said, leaning over. 'I'm terribly sorry, but were you in *Free Time*? Because if you were, I saw you and I thought you were fantastic.'

The girl, who'd initially looked a bit suspicious, as if Sophie was going to try to sell her a timeshare, smiled. 'Yes, yes, I was, actually. I'm so glad you enjoyed it.'

'Well, I didn't really. I thought it was a bit dull. But you were great. Really good. So what are you in now? Or are you . . . resting?' Sophie had heard actors using that word and was impressed by herself for remembering it.

'Actually I'm off to the States for a few auditions. So fingers crossed.'

'Ooh, yes! Oh, good luck.' Sophie was wondering how to continue the conversation when she felt a hand on her shoulder.

'Sorry, darling. Have you been waiting long?' Olly bent down and gave her a proprietorial kiss on the cheek.

As so often with Olly, Sophie felt embarrassed. Embarrassed because this glamorous couple was so obviously in another league to them, because the actress's man was so beautifully dressed in a grey patterned shirt – probably Paul Smith – and jeans, while Olly was in chinos which made him look fatter than he was already and a pink Lacoste shirt that emphasized his ruddy face. *We look like such squares. They must feel sorry for us.*

'Olly, do you remember this beautiful lady from *Free Time*?' she said.

'Of course I do,' Olly said, instantly all affability. 'Goodness. We thought you were fantastic. It's Aurelia Farmer, isn't it?' He stuck out a hand. 'Oliver Garcia-Mundoz. How do you do?'

'Hi,' said Aurelia, still smiling charmingly.

'I'm Sophie,' she said, then added hastily, wanting Olly to seem more important: 'Olly and I both work for the *Daily Post*. We'd love to give you some publicity.'

'Really?' Aurelia did look a shade more interested now. She turned to the man. 'This is my boyfriend, Alastair Costello.'

Sophie went cold.

'Hi,' Alastair muttered, lifting a palm.

'Alastair Costello!' Olly exclaimed. 'I've just finished *The*

Silent D. Excellent stuff.' Sophie looked at him annoyed. Why did he always have to be such an arse-licker?

'Thanks,' Alastair said, not looking particularly thrilled. He took Aurelia's arm. 'Darling, we need to be getting on. We have that lunch reservation.'

'Ally! Let me have my tea first, darling!' She smiled at them. 'Do join us.'

But the get-lost vibes coming off Alastair were too strong. 'No, we must be on our way,' they both mumbled, and with lots of goodbyes and good lucks and we'll be watching out for yous, they headed out on to the hot Parisian streets.

'The bastard,' Sophie said for the fortieth time that day.

'What's that, my darling?'

'What am I going to tell Natasha? She thinks Alastair and Aurelia are all over. Shit, what should I do?'

'I would leave well alone,' said Olly, then laughed. 'You do look so serious, my love.'

'If I were her, would I want to know? I can't decide . . .' A waiter placed a little dish of scallops in front of her. 'Oh, don't these look pretty?'

They were sitting in the restaurant on top of the Eiffel Tower, watching the dancing lights of Paris spread out across the horizon. Sophie was dressed in an astonishingly tight and sexy Sonia Rykiel dress, which Olly had insisted on buying for her that afternoon from her boutique. He'd tried to keep the price from her but when he was in the shower she'd peeked in his wallet. She'd felt quite dizzy and guilty, but now she was dressed up in it she felt like a movie star. She thought of Julia Roberts at

317

the opera in *Pretty Woman*. Or no, maybe that wasn't a good comparison as Julia had been a prostitute. And she was Olly's girlfriend. She could admit to that now. Olly was looking much better dressed up in suit and tie. Casual stuff just didn't suit him.

'Here's to us,' he said, raising his glass of champagne.

'Yes.' They clinked. 'I'm sure that guy knew I was a friend of Natasha's. That would explain why he was so keen to get out of there.'

'Could be,' said Olly. 'Listen, Sophie, there was something I wanted to tell you.'

'Mmm.' She took a bite of her scallops. Oh yum. She'd have to remember this and recreate it at home.

'It's good news.'

'Mmm. Hmm?'

'The Party's definitely going to find a safe seat for me.'

'Oh my God, Olly! Congratulations!'

Wouldn't this mean a cut in salary? she thought, then guiltily slapped the thought down. But another bad thought popped up: if Olly became an MP, she wouldn't have to see him at work every day. And, quite honestly, she'd welcome the breathing space.

'You'll be one of the youngest MPs ever, won't you?'

'Pretty much.'

'Well then, cheers.' More clinking. She caught the eye of a sad-looking, middle-aged woman on the other side of the room, who was watching them wistfully. Young. In love. Celebrating.

'And then . . . there was another thing I wanted to ask you.' Olly's face was even redder than ever. 'And you may think it's too sudden and you may think we haven't known each other long enough, but they always say that when you know it's right, you know it's right and so I wanted to ask . . . and I'll completely understand if you say no, but . . . will you marry me?'

It was the question Sophie had waited her whole life to hear and now she was hearing it in the most romantic spot in the world. But she couldn't say yes. She didn't feel that way about Olly. Perhaps one day she might, but not yet. But what if she said no and Olly started to cry or something? That would be so embarrassing. Plus, they'd ordered those fantastically expensive main courses of foie gras and lobster and God knows what else. It wouldn't be much fun sitting through all of that if she refused him, would it? And she could always change her mind later.

'Yes,' she said and watched Olly's expression transform from agonized to rapturous.

'You're saying yes?'

'I'm saying yes.'

'You'll be my wife?'

'I'll be your wife.'

She'd never forget the look of relief on his face.

'In that case, may I give you this?'

He slid a black box across the table. Suddenly, Sophie remembered the night of her birthday, Andy giving her his present and that mad, false hope. But this was for real.

She opened it. A diamond, of course. Much clunkier than Sophie would have chosen and she would have gone for a platinum band not gold. But hey, it was a diamond. Which, if it had cost even a quarter of Olly's monthly salary, was the most expensive thing she'd ever been given.

Olly turned to a waiter. '*Encore du champagne, s'il vous plaît.*' He smiled and lowered his voice. '*Nous venons de nous fiancer.*'

The waiter looked utterly unimpressed. 'You have just got engaged,' he repeated. 'Congratulations.'

At the table next door an elderly woman in a white polo neck heard. 'You've just got engaged? Oh Lord, Jack, did you hear that? They've just got engaged.'

'Well, congratulations,' said the man, jumping to his feet and pumping both their hands. 'I'm Jack Belton from Norfolk, Virginia, and this is my wife Marie and we're here celebrating our fortieth wedding anniversary.'

'Oh, congratulations,' they muttered politely.

'You'll have to come here for yours,' said Marie fondly.

'I'll book it now,' Olly smiled and they all laughed. Including Sophie. Though she couldn't quite imagine that far ahead. If truth be told she couldn't even imagine waking up tomorrow and telling the world she was getting married. Couldn't imagine the shrieking and the excitement and the fuss. She'd always dreamed of making that call, but right now she just didn't fancy it. Because although Sophie had said yes, she'd actually meant maybe. She'd get through dinner first, then work out what her feelings really were.

38

Marcus couldn't help it: however little sleep he'd had in the week, however late he went to bed the night before, come the weekend he was always wide awake at 7 a.m., adrenalin coursing through his veins, pumping him for another day making millions. Then he'd remember with a start that today there was no need to kick ass – except, of course, if there turned out to be some crisis, in which case he would end up on the phone all day, to his boss in his country pile in Wiltshire or to colleagues in Hamburg or Tokyo or New York.

Today was no exception: sun poured through the windows of their bedroom – Lainey had removed the previous owner's hideous blinds but so far failed to replace them – and his eyes opened. For a second, he couldn't quite place where he was. In the past week he'd spent a night in Madrid, a night in Istanbul and a night in Copenhagen, holed up in his room, eating club sandwiches and watching CNN. Then he remembered. This was home, but one crucial thing was missing – and that was his wife, who should have been asleep beside him.

'Lainey,' he mumbled, just as he heard a crashing downstairs and a loud: 'Oh shit!'

He jumped out of bed and stumbled to the top of the stairs. 'Duckie!' he called. 'Are you OK?'

From the basement, he heard a pulsating hip-hop beat.

Of course. Lainey had gone clubbing last night, leaving him surrounded by the remains of their take-out Malay in front of a DVD. He had half-heartedly suggested he went too, but was so shattered he'd been relieved when she turned him down.

'You wouldn't enjoy it,' she'd said as ever – and as ever there was no denying it.

'I'll miss you though,' he'd tried.

'No, you won't – before you know it'll be morning and I'll be back. And I need these trips out, Markie. They provide me with inspiration.' She bent over and kissed him. She was wearing a denim miniskirt, a blue crop top and smelt of Patchouli, although Marcus knew this was no ordinary oil from the market but special designer stuff from Space NK that cost £120 a bottle. 'I'm sorry but you're at work all day and I need to go out at night. We'll spend some quality time together tomorrow.'

'We could go for lunch somewhere nice,' he said hopefully.

She wrinkled her nose. 'We could but I'll probably be too shagged. Maybe we could go for a quiet curry in the evening.'

Marcus went downstairs, into the kitchen. Lainey, with pink plastic rabbit ears on her head, was dancing around the table to some formless tune coming out of the iPod. Her friend Ninon, whom Marcus particularly disliked because she was fat and spotty and giggled every time he turned his back on her, was popping bread into the Dualit toaster. Two men he thought he vaguely recognized from the wedding, one with white dreads and one with a shaven head, sat at the table sharing a spliff.

'Hello,' said Marcus.

'Markie!' yelled Lainey, running over to him and showering him with kisses. 'Good morning, darling. Hey, everyone, this is my adorable husband. Marcus, you know Ninon, don't you? And this is Emerson and Will.'

'Hey,' said Emerson and Will.

Ninon gave her habitual sneer. 'Your ball and chain is it, Laines? I keep forgetting you're an old married woman.'

Lainey ignored her and smiled sunnily at her husband. 'We're just having a bit of a come-down session. Do you want to join us? Or you could go back to bed and I'll join you in – oooh – an hour or so.'

'I'm awake now,' Marcus said. He felt as stiff as cardboard. 'I – er – I think I'll go and get the papers.'

'Have some breakfast,' said either Emerson or Will hospitably. 'Ninon was going to do us a fry-up.'

'I'm not sure there's enough to go round,' Ninon said.

'Don't worry about me,' Marcus said, trying to keep all emotion out of his voice. Twenty minutes later he was sitting in a faux workman's caff just off Portobello, with an unread copy of the *Sunday Times* in front of him, trying to work out whether it was unreasonable to be so utterly furious with his wife for making him feel like a stranger in his home.

He read his way slowly through every section in the *Sunday Times* – even the children's pages – then turned his attention to the *Observer*. He had a fry-up and a cup of tea. Still only 9 a.m. He had another cup of tea. He couldn't quite say why, but he really objected to going back to the house while those *people* were in it.

Suddenly Marcus felt very lonely.

He was obviously a very boring man, he decided. Well, everyone knew the City was dull as fuck; that the only reason you did it was to make as much money as possible. But why did he and Lainey need so much money anyway? Half the rooms in their house never even got used. Flicking through the pages of the paper, he gazed at pictures of sportsmen, actors, directors, tree surgeons – all the things he could be if he left the hated bank, all things which Lainey's crowd would surely approve of.

He needed to talk to someone, he realized, to be reassured that Lainey could be a little wayward but that she obviously adored him, that the late nights and hosts of friends he'd never properly met were unimportant. But confiding in people came about as naturally to Marcus as playing the bagpipes. On the very rare occasions when he'd had to open his heart it was always to one of two contenders – either Sophie or Natasha. He debated which one to call. Sophie he was a bit closer to, by virtue of teenage years spent under the same roof, but Natasha often spoke more sense. He'd call them alphabetically, he decided, but if he got voicemail he'd leave no message and try the other one. Then he looked at his watch. Still only 9.30 a.m. Bollocks. Far too early to be disturbing anyone. He'd have to wait until at least noon. But fuck it, there was no way he was going to sit until then in a café reading about autumn fashions and the euro. He would go home and reclaim his turf.

As he pushed open the front door, he realized the loud music had stopped. Tiptoeing, as if around a sleeping lion, he made his way down to the basement, which reeked of marijuana and fetid bodies. Emerson was asleep on the chaise longue. He went upstairs. Through the spare-room door on the first floor, he could see Will in stripy green boxer shorts supine on the bed. Suddenly filled with new hope, he carried on to the next floor. Lainey would be in their bed, he could slip in beside her and . . . surprise her. That would bring the day back on course; assuage all his doubts.

He pushed open the door, already fumbling at the buttons on his jeans.

'Oh, what . . . ?' mumbled Lainey, rolling over.

'Wha' . . . ?' repeated Ninon from Marcus's side of the bed.

Marcus had always had a thing about two girls in bed together, but not his wife and this ugly, sulky sidekick of hers. And anyway, there was clearly nothing porno about this coupling: these were just two tired girls trying to come down from God knows what.

'Markie, I'd just dropped off,' Lainey moaned.

'Sorry, duckie,' he said, backing out of the door.

As he shut it, he heard Ninon cackle and say: '*Duckie?*' and Lainey reply, 'I know, it's what he calls me. Cute, isn't it?'

Marcus felt as if someone had slipped a knife under his ribs and was twisting it hard. 'Duckie' was what they called each other; they had done so ever since that weekend in Cornwall when they'd just been together a month. They'd stopped hand in hand by the village pond and watched a mother duck and her chicks and Lainey had said: 'I wonder if ducks ever call each other "my duck"?'

Looking back, they were hardly the words of Simone de Beauvoir, but at the time it had seemed so cute and later that day Marcus had bought her a china duck from an arts and crafts counter in the corner of the village tea room, and the whole thing had just escalated from there, with the duck becoming their motif, to the point where Marcus now avoided ordering it in restaurants because of the emotions it evoked.

Although, on reflection, Lainey hadn't called him duckie for weeks.

Sighing, Marcus glanced at his watch. He'd call Natasha at noon and if she didn't pick up he'd try Sophie in the evening. For now, he'd go down to his study and in the absence of company he might as well get on with some work.

39

Sophie didn't sleep well on Saturday night. Back at the hotel she and Olly made obligatory celebratory 'lurve' and, as usual, it was fine, even though she had to resort to the usual wiggling and groaning and finally 'You're incredible' to get Olly to come.

After that, he was asleep within moments and for hours Sophie lay there in the huge, luxurious bed, trying to come to terms with the situation. She'd just accepted a proposal of marriage. Which meant that this man sleeping beside her would be the only man to sleep beside her for the rest of her life. Except she'd only accepted because the proposal had been so public and she hadn't wanted to spoil a beautiful evening and because she was wearing a gorgeous dress Olly had bought her. So in the morning she'd have to say she'd changed her mind.

But then she looked at Olly's happy sleeping face. She imagined his anguished expression, and then the silent journey home. It was more than she could bear. She couldn't do this. And besides, why shouldn't she marry Olly? He adored her. He was her friend. With him she felt so safe. In control. She could have babies and bring them up in style, live in a proper house, have dinner parties. The life she'd always dreamed of. Finally, she felt that missing tingle of excitement. She looked around the dim room. Oh my God, if she did marry

Olly the rest of her life would be spent in places like this. Where would they go on their honeymoon? Tomorrow she'd buy *Condé Nast Traveller* and start compiling a shortlist. Lainey would have plenty of tips. She couldn't wait to tell her. And Marcus. Maybe they'd buy a house on their street? She'd have to call them tomorrow. And Mum. And Fay and Caroline. God, they didn't even know she was going out with Olly, let alone now engaged to him. And she'd better let Andy know. She hoped he would be happy for her, but of course she also hoped he'd be jealous. And so he should be. She, Sophie Matthewson, was a catch, the fiancée of up-and-coming media star Olly Garcia-Mundoz. Sophie Garcia-Mundoz. Uncharacteristically, she'd never practised the name before, but she liked the sound of it: it could be one of the women in the pages of *Tatler*, attending some charity bash.

Smiling now, Sophie drifted off to sleep.

'Mum?'

'Hello, darling. How are you?'

'Fine. I'm in Paris.' Sophie looked around the room. The breakfast table by the window was laden with croissants, a silver coffee pot, a jug of fresh orange juice and the remains of two omelettes (which had been a bit dry, actually; frankly Sophie could have made them better). This was the life.

'Paris? Gosh, lucky old you. I wish I could go somewhere nice like Paris. But Jimmy says we can't afford a holiday this year. Honestly, darling, I'm so fed up. It's been pouring with rain for days. Have you been shopping? I'd love a shopping trip, only what's the point when there's no one to dress up for?'

'Oh Mum, it's not that bad . . . Anyway, listen—'

'It *is* that bad. I don't know. Moira's on holiday in Greece and she's the only amusement one gets in this godforsaken dump. Are you going to come and visit soon?'

'I'll try. Anyway, *listen*, Mum, I have something to tell you. Olly and I are engaged.'

For the first time during the conversation, there was a pause.

'Engaged?' Rita said eventually. 'You and Olly?'

'Yes, Mum. Me and Olly. We got engaged last night. On top of the Eiffel Tower. Isn't that romantic?' Sophie caught a glimpse of herself in the mirror, swaddled in her fluffy robe, like J-Lo in the 'Jenny from the Block' video.

'Engaged? But that's terribly quick.'

'Well, not really. We've known each other for ages. We just haven't . . . been a couple for very long. So, anyway . . .'

'Well, congratulations, darling. I'm very pleased for you.'

'Are you?' She didn't sound it. Mum was a pain in the arse, but Sophie still wanted her endorsement.

'Of course I am, sweetie. I'm just a bit . . . surprised, that's all. You know, so soon after Andy and everything. But it's great news. Really great. So when will the big day be?'

'Oh God, Mum, I don't know. We only got engaged last night. No rush.'

'I think that's very sensible, darling.' There was a loud noise in the background. 'Oh darling, Jimmy's just dropped something. I've got to go. But congratulations to you and to Andy.'

'Olly, Mum!'

'Sorry, sorry, Olly. I'll call you later. Have a lovely time in Paris.'

Sophie felt hugely dissatisfied. This was *not* how the conversation was meant to have gone. Mum was obviously jealous, because her daughter had an engagement ring from a rich man, while she (judging by the lack of mentionitis) was quite obviously not with Vernon any more.

Olly, who had tactfully disappeared into the shower (she couldn't have quite stomached him standing over her smiling cornily), now reappeared, a towel wrapped round his waist. Hmm. Perhaps it was time to cut down on the breakfast omelettes.

'What did she say?'

'She was thrilled. Sent you all her love.'

'So are you going to call your dad?'

Sophie couldn't face the thought of hard-faced Belinda picking up the phone. 'No, I'll wait until he's at work tomorrow. Aren't you going to call your parents?'

'I'll do that right now.'

Olly's parents were delighted, although a little surprised. They couldn't wait to meet Sophie, they said, although it wouldn't be for a few months as Olly's dad was having a heart operation and was under strict instructions not to travel or have any excitement at all.

'We'll visit them when he's on the mend,' Olly said.

'I can't wait.'

He glanced at her suitcase on the floor, which, as usual, was a jumble of knickers, tops and assorted shoes. 'Do you never bother unpacking when you go away?' he said, but more indulgently than disapprovingly.

'Oh, shut up, Olly. You sound just like . . . Oh, never mind.'

She decided to wait until she got back to London to call the girls. She'd do it alone. From Veronica's place. Where, she decided, as they wandered around Versailles, she wanted to spend tonight: mad, stingy Australian or no mad, stingy Australian.

'Do you mind?' she said to Olly as the Eurostar whisked them back under the Channel. 'Only it's been such an overwhelming couple of days I feel I need some time alone. You know, to reflect.'

'I understand completely,' he smiled. 'Which isn't to say I won't miss you.'

'I'll miss you too.'

But actually it was an odd relief to open the door to the tatty flat (it was double-locked which meant Veronica wasn't there, hooray!) and finally be alone. Being with Olly was great, but the way he constantly watched her to see how happy she was and flinched if she so much as frowned could be a bit oppressive. Sophie had been planning to make all her calls but suddenly she didn't really feel like it. She fancied a solitary potter in the kitchen, making a salad as an antidote to all that rich French food and then flopping on her bed and enjoying an orgy of crap TV.

But just then the phone rang. 'Hello?'

'Hi, it's me.' Marcus, sounding a little sad.

'Hi, babe. How are you?'

'Oh, well, you know, I . . .'

'Well, listen. I've got some big news. I'm getting married!'

Again, there was that pause. 'Getting married? To . . . to that guy I met in the Rah Bar?'

'To who else?'

'Oh my God. I . . . Sorry, Soph, I've forgotten his name.'

'Don't worry. It's Olly. Anyway, isn't it amazing? He proposed on top of the Eiffel Tower.'

'But . . . I mean, this is great. But it's very quick.'

Oh for God's sake. Not this again. 'Well, you and Lainey got engaged after three months.'

'I know. And in retrospect maybe it was a bit too hasty. There's no need to rush things, Sophie.'

Was anyone going to give her the response she wanted? A bit of squealing would be nice, but then Marcus *was* a man. 'Aren't you happy for me?' she asked petulantly.

'Of course I am. I'm just . . . surprised. So when's the big day?'

'I don't know. But don't worry, it won't be as quick as yours. Not for a year at least, I think.'

'Good.' There was some noise in the background. 'Just talking to Sophie,' she heard. 'Guess what, she's got engaged,' and then there was the most almighty shrieking.

'Engaged! Engaged! Oh God, put her on now!'

This was more like it. 'Hey, Laines.'

'Sophie, you're engaged. How romantic is this?'

332

'Merely following your and Marcus's example. You're going to have to be my wedding mentor.'

'Oh, absolutely. You'll have to come round and check out all those silly books and magazines I've got stashed in the third bedroom.'

Sophie laughed. 'You mean you've kept them?'

'Of course. Could be useful for my second marriage.' Lainey yawned hugely. 'Sorry, babes. Big night last night. I've only just got up. So have you told Natasha?'

'No, not yet. I've just got in.' Suddenly Sophie remembered. Alastair and Aurelia at the Musée d'Orsay. All this kerfuffle had sent it straight out of her head. How was she going to tell her? But Marcus was back on the line.

'Sophie, congratulations. It's terrific news. Sorry if I didn't quite respond properly, it was such a surprise.'

'That's all right. Listen, are you OK? Only, you know, you're not a great one for ringing up for a chat.'

'Oh, just bushed,' Marcus said. 'Don't worry about me. Your news has really perked me up. You'll both have to come round sometime next week and we'll have a celebratory drink.'

They said their goodbyes and Sophie sat holding the handset debating what to do about Natasha. It wasn't as if she'd been relishing telling her she was engaged and now she had to decide what to say about Alastair. In the end, she decided to leave it to fate by calling the landline. If she got the machine she'd say nothing, if Natasha picked up she'd come out with it.

It was the machine. 'This is Natasha Green. Leave a message or send a fax . . .'

'Hi, Tash, it's me, Sophie. I wanted to let you know

I've got engaged. To Olly. So . . . well, yes, I just wanted to let you know. Hope you're well. Bye.'

She hung up, feeling hollow. She hated keeping something from her friend but she also had no desire to be the bearer of bad news. Time to think of other, more cheerful things. Like her new life. A life as Mrs Oliver Garcia-Mundoz, glittering society hostess, who had an amazing villa in Provence, a town house in Notting Hill and maybe . . . a lodge in Bali? But first there was the wedding to organize. Oh God. Sophie couldn't wait to get together with Lainey. She was so stylish she was bound to have tons of good ideas. But in the meantime, she should compile some of her own. The newsagents on the corner was still open. Ten minutes later, Sophie was curled up on her bed, engrossed in *Wedding and Home*.

It was the highlight of the whole weekend.

40

That same weekend, Natasha spent alone. Alastair was away in France, in some borrowed cottage, trying to get to grips with his novel, which he had been neglecting recently in favour of the screenplay. To be honest she was relieved, as for the last few days she had been feeling horribly nauseous.

On Saturday she cancelled a drink with Nikolai, impervious to his moaning, and spent the evening slumped in front of the TV nursing a glass of very good Chardonnay, which – frustratingly – she had no desire to touch at all. On Sunday she didn't wake until ten and immediately pulled her head back under the duvet. She must have food poisoning. Oh no, she really needed to pee. Which was infuriating, since she'd already gone about three times in the night. Hauling herself out of bed, she was struck by a wave of giddiness. Bloody hell. She remembered some travel-sickness pills she kept in the medicine cabinet. Maybe they'd help. In the bathroom, she woozily pulled out the packet. Better check the sell-by date; she'd bought them years ago for a cross-Channel ferry. Ah. 'Best Before May, 2004.' But did that really matter? She'd just skim through the leaflet and see what it said. Blah, blah . . . 'Not to be taken in combination with any other medicines, when pregnant . . .'

Natasha stopped reading. Pregnant. Feeling sick in the

morning. Needing the loo all night. But no, that was impossible. When did she last have her period? She staggered into the living room and delved into her bag for her Psion. Right. Last period was on June 7. Which means the next one should have been July 5. And today was the eighteenth. Could she have had a period on July 5 and forgotten to mark it down? It seemed unlikely. And anyway, no, that was the night she and Alastair had gone to the theatre and she'd have remembered.

Did it come the next day? 'Drinks with LA executives at Savoy, dinner with A.' She remembered that week clearly and there had been no period. And Natasha was a totally regular twenty-eight-day girl. There couldn't have been a mistake: it was impossible. But then Natasha thought some more. Alastair complaining about loss of spontaneity. The withdrawal method. Which, as the magazines always warned, was not a hundred per cent safe.

Natasha looked at the clock as foreboding settled over her. Eleven a.m. Sunday, so the chemists wouldn't be opening for another hour. She'd slowly eat a piece of toast to curb the queasiness, get dressed and then she was going to have to go to Boot's.

Three hours later, she was sitting on the side of the bath, two plastic sticks beside her. What the hell was going on? According to the diagram, the news she was dreading should mean a blue cross in the first box and a blue horizontal line in the second. Well, she had a blue horizontal line in the second, but in the first box there was just a blue vertical line. So that was good, wasn't it? Except a negative result should be horizontal. The whole thing gave her a headache. Why couldn't she, Natasha Green, executive extraordinaire, get her head round a system designed for frightened fourteen-year-olds?

She'd initially cocked up by failing to see you had to remove the stick's lid and peeing on that, so nothing came up at all. For a minute she'd been overjoyed, thinking she was off the hook, then she'd read the instructions, tried again and got this confusing result. And so then she'd had to go back to Boot's and buy another test from the same assistant, who she was sure wasn't fooled by her sunglasses disguise – especially as it was raining. She did the test again and got the same confusing result, so eventually she'd had to ring the seven-day helpline to learn from a bored-sounding woman with a nasal voice that a vertical line definitely meant she was pregnant.

At which point she retched into the basin, sat down on the edge of her bed and cried and cried and cried. She cried all afternoon and into the evening, only dimly aware of the phone ringing and Mum leaving a message and Sophie later waffling on about something else. Someone hung up a couple of times and in hope she dialled 1471 but it was only Marcus. Not that she'd have picked up for Alastair – she might have lost control; but it would have been wonderful to hear that Scottish voice.

This couldn't be happening. Not to her, Natasha Green, who was so in control of her life. She remembered the conversation with Lainey and Sophie that night after Lainey was back from honeymoon. 'Women don't get pregnant unless they really want to. There's no excuse for an unplanned pregnancy.'

She felt such a fool.

At about seven, she switched on her laptop and went online. Apparently, you calculated how pregnant you were from the first day of your last period. Which made her six weeks up the duff.

'Your baby is about the size of a pea but is developing tiny buds that will become arms and legs.' Like she needed to know that. Panic-stricken, she poured a huge glass of whisky, then ran the hottest bath possible, and undressed. The water scalded her toes. Breathing deeply, she lowered herself down. Ow. Ow. Her legs were turning scarlet. Come on. Come on.

'It's either this or childbirth,' she hissed.

She stayed in for an hour, sipping the whisky and gradually growing drowsier and cheerier. This had to work. Mad that she'd had to resort to such an old-fashioned method, but then it was equally mad that she'd found herself in such an old-fashioned situation. She remembered everything she had ever even vaguely heard about miscarriages. Weren't they incredibly common? Like one in every six pregnancies? Surely she'd fall in that category, if she just kept on going like this.

By the time she hauled herself out, all wrinkled, she felt positively upbeat. That had to work. In the morning, she'd have a period and the whole thing would be like a bad dream. But to prevent any nightmares tonight, she took two Valium. They couldn't exactly be good for the baby either.

But in the morning, as she sat on the loo, again weak and dizzy with nausea, there was no blood.

'Damn,' she breathed. She'd have to buy another kit

on the way into work. Another wave of sickness picked her up. She staggered through to the bedroom and collapsed on the white duvet. This couldn't be happening. A baby. She didn't want one. Well, she did one day and one with Alastair would be amazing, but of course not right now. Not while she and Alastair were still so . . . unofficial.

'Are you OK?' Dom asked as she sat at her desk, head in hands, a cup of extra-strong espresso in front of her.

'Just a bit hungover. Big night last night.'

'Oh, right. Me too. Do you know what my latest plan is for the wife hunt?'

'No. What?'

'Internet dating!'

'Oh Dom, no. Don't be such a cheesebucket.'

'Why not? It's fantastic. There are some total babes online. All desperate for love. Just waiting for me to step into their lives. Look,' he said, swivelling round his screen. 'Aren't they all gorgeous?' There did, indeed, seem to be a remarkably attractive range of women on display.

'They probably work for an escort agency or something.'

Dom ignored her. 'Now, *she* is beautiful. Marina. Hmm. Yes. Works in finance. So probably loaded. But . . . oh no. She's divorced. With children.'

'Dom!'

He continued scrolling. '*She's* a bit of all right. But she's thirty-bloody-five.' He clicked his mouse decisively. 'Sorry, honey, but I don't think so.'

'So all women with kids or over thirty-five are out of

the picture?' Natasha was so outraged she was temporarily distracted from her woes.

'Over thirty, I've stipulated.'

'So no Uma Thurman? No Nicole Kidman?'

'Uma I might make an exception for. But I've never fancied Nicole. I just can't imagine giving it to her good and hard over the kitchen sink.'

'Shame, because I've heard she really fancies you.' Natasha's bladder was tingling. Good. She'd decided to wait until it was really full before doing the next test. Because almost certainly the problem before was that she'd done it with just a trickle, which probably distorted the result.

Five minutes later, locked in a cubicle, her world was once more shrouded in black.

She'd drink coffee all day and have another go tonight. And if that didn't work she'd try the clinic.

So at 7.45 p.m. that evening, Natasha was once again staring at the evil plastic stick, trying to work out the reading, or at least find a new interpretation for it.

Buzzz.

She jumped. Who the hell could this be? Alastair back early? Her heart twanged at the thought, but then she looked around at the empty whisky glasses and the Predictor packets and started to panic.

Buzzz.

'Who is it?' she said fearfully into the entryphone.

'It's Sophie. Can I come up?'

Sophie? She hadn't been expecting this.

'Natasha?'

She looked around the room. 'Well, yes, just give me two seconds.'

By the time Sophie was in the flat, the glasses were in the dishwasher, the Predictor in the bathroom cabinet and Irene Cara was playing on the stereo.

'Sophie. How nice to see you. Were you just passing?' God, she sounded like Mum when she had visitors in Betterton, not like someone welcoming in her oldest friend.

'Yeah,' Sophie said, an odd look on her face, half excited, half nervous. 'I'm meeting Olly at Bam-Bou at nine, so I had time to kill and I saw your light was on, so . . .' No need to say that after a day of agonizing, Sophie had decided she would tell her friend what she'd seen, but face to face, rather than on the phone. Although it was very odd Natasha hadn't called to congratulate her. She must *really* disapprove.

'So my news must have come as a bit of a shocker,' she said tentatively.

'What news?'

'About me and Olly? I left you a message yesterday.'

'Oh.' Natasha struggled to recall. 'Sorry, Soph, you did. I accidentally wiped it. I was . . . having a bit of a day yesterday.' Her grey eyes filled with tears.

'Were you, honey? What happened?' Sophie said coaxingly. She obviously knew Alastair was back with Aurelia. Well, that was a relief. As was the fact that Tash was probably too upset to have a go at her about the engagement.

'I think I need a drink,' Natasha said. She got up and went into the kitchen area, where the whisky bottle was sitting open on the counter. 'Like one?'

'Absolutely.' Poor Tash. It wasn't like her to hit the bottle.

She came back with two glasses.

'So,' Sophie said, sitting down beside her. 'It can't be that bad.'

'It is. It's as bad as can be.'

'Tell me . . .'

Natasha started to sob. 'I'm pregnant.'

'*What?*'

'You heard me. I'm pregnant. Six weeks gone.'

'Right.' Sophie's mind was a kaleidoscope. Now was not the time to tell Tash what she'd seen in Paris. 'With Alastair's baby?'

'Of course with Alastair's baby.'

'Oh my God. Have you told him yet?'

Natasha shook her head forcefully. 'And I'm not going to,' she added, taking a gulp of the whisky.

'What do you mean you're not going to? You have to. You're having his baby.'

'Well, actually I'm not.' Natasha's eyes were fixed straight ahead. 'I'm going to get rid of it.'

'Get rid of it? Tash, you can't do that. Well, not just like that anyway. You've got to talk to Alastair about all this first.'

'I can't,' she shouted. 'That's the whole point. Alastair and I don't have talks like that. We're about having a good time.'

'But this is his baby too.'

'Not if he doesn't know about it.' Natasha's mouth was set and firm.

Sophie shook her head. 'Tash, I don't know. From what

you're telling me, this guy is a selfish tosser. Would you really have an abortion just to keep him happy? Why can't you keep the baby? We're living in London in the twenty-first century. It'd work out fine.'

'But if I kept the baby, I'd lose Alastair.'

'Yes. And which is more important?'

'Well, Alastair, obviously,' Natasha said. Her voice broke. 'You must see, Sophie. I'm so in love with him. If I can't have him I'll die. I've never wanted anyone or anything so much in my life.'

'Right,' said Sophie slowly, trying not to show how shaken she was by her friend's vehemence. 'Well, fine. But who's to say if you have the baby you won't have Alastair? Lots of guys say they don't want kids and then when they're presented with one they're thrilled.' Sophie thought back wryly to her Andy trick and his positive response. And now here was Tash properly in the club and refusing to confess to it. It was all wrong.

Natasha was shaking her head. 'Not Alastair. He hates that kind of thing. I just know. What we have is a casual thing. We see each other when we see each other. Make no demands on each other. That's just the way it works.'

'Fine.' Sophie felt like she was walking in a spacesuit on Mars, so unreal was this conversation. 'But still, Tash, before you do anything, I think you should wait at least a week. It's not going to make any difference and you need some time to calm down. And remember, whatever you do, I'll help you. I'm your friend.'

Her words were aftersun on scorched skin. Natasha exhaled. 'You don't have to help me.'

'Yes I bloody well do. You've always tried to pretend

343

you don't need anyone, Tash, but you do. We all do. So just let me be there for you.' Her mobile started ringing in her bag. She glanced at her watch. 'Oh, bollocks, that'll be Olly wondering where I am.' She grabbed the phone. 'Hello . . . Yeah, hi. Hi . . . Yes, I'm just round the corner. I just dropped in to see Natasha. I'll be five minutes, darling . . . Yes, can't wait to see you. Bye.'

'You won't tell Olly any of this?' Natasha asked fearfully. Her eyes were red; her face streaked. Sophie had never seen her so vulnerable, not even during the Steven episode.

'Of course not, don't be absurd.' Sophie looked at her sorrowfully. 'I'm really sorry I have to go, babe. If I'd known about any of this I would have cancelled Olly. I still can if you want me to. Stay here with you tonight.'

Natasha shook her head. 'Don't worry. I'll be fine. You go and have fun. By the way, what was your message about? I should have got back to you.'

'No you shouldn't. You really were having a bad day. It was just to say that I went to Paris with Olly at the weekend and we got engaged.' She held out her knuckles and flashed her rock under Tash's nose.

'Engaged?' Natasha gawped. 'Oh, Sophie.'

'It's been quick, I know,' Sophie said defensively. 'But it felt right.'

She could see Natasha struggling with what to say. 'But that's fantastic,' she came out with after what seemed like aeons. 'Congratulations. I feel so selfish going on and on about myself.'

'Natasha Green, for such a mover and a shaker, you are actually insane.' Sophie stood up and hugged her hard.

'Now, I really do have to go. I have a fiancé waiting. But I'm going to call you tomorrow and the next day and the next day and whatever happens you will not be alone. We are going through this together.'

41

Alastair called the following morning. It was only just after eight and Natasha was lying in bed fighting morning sickness combined with a hangover from three huge whiskies and no dinner, all exacerbated by having to get up four times in the night to pee.

'Hello?' she croaked.

'Crikey, you sound rough.' He sounded particularly jovial.

'I'm fine,' she said, pulling herself up on her elbow and forcing herself to smile, so she sounded warm and inviting. 'Just half asleep, that's all. Big night last night.' Always play the party-girl card.

'Well, I hope you're on for another big night tonight. I've missed you.'

He missed me! 'Not like you to call so early,' she said offhandedly.

'I'm on my way to the library, so my phone'll be off all day. But how does Hakkasan sound for tonight?'

'Great,' she said.

'Cool. Listen, can you make the reservation? Say nine? I'll see you later.'

Her heart sank. Nine. Ideally she'd be tucked up in bed by then. She'd have to try to sneak home first and get a nap. But then she really ought to go to the gym and try to get her roots touched up as well. Hang on, though, hadn't she read somewhere you couldn't dye your hair when you were pregnant? She stopped herself. Why the hell was she worrying about details like that? She was carrying a bundle of cells and in a week or so's time they'd be gone. No. Much more important to make herself perfect for Alastair.

For once he had got there first and was waiting at the bar for her, with a faint tan and a big smile. 'God, it's good to see you,' he said, pulling her to him. 'You look gorgeous.'

'Thanks. So how was France?'

'Dull. Just worked. But whatever. Let's get some champagne.'

Natasha really didn't feel like drinking. For a start, she'd had a lot of booze the last couple of nights. And then there was the baby, as she couldn't help calling it however hard she tried. She didn't want it, of course not, but . . . Alastair was so gorgeous and just imagine the three of them sitting on a sundrenched lawn, as the little bundle tottered towards them, holding out chubby arms and cooing: 'Mama . . .'

Stop it! It wasn't going to happen. But just in case it did . . .

'Madam,' said the waiter, filling up her glass.

'Thank you.' She smiled, then turned the beam on to Alastair. 'Cheers.' She'd just pretend to drink, have the odd little sip, but better safe than sorry. Because maybe Sophie was right. Maybe he'd be thrilled. He seemed pleased to see her right now.

'So how's the novel? Did you make much progress?'

'Not as much as I would've liked. Actually, I was kind of hoping you'd have a look at what I've done. Sometime. When you have a moment.'

'I'd love to. You know I would.'

Various dishes were set before them. Her stomach growled. She was starving. In a most un-Natasha-like moment she'd wolfed down three pittas and a tub of taramasalata before she came out, but it hadn't been enough.

Alastair smiled. 'You've gotta try the pigs' trotters.'

'Mmm.' Nausea slapped her round the face. 'Yeah. I will. In just a sec. So how are paperback sales going?'

A cloud passed over his face. 'It's too early to tell.' Then he brightened. 'Still, I got a great email today from a guy I vaguely know on the *Telegraph*. He said he'd just read it and loved it.' Deftly, he picked up some pigs' trotters with his chopsticks. 'Come on, have a mouthful. You'll love this.'

'I don't really feel like it. I'm not that hungry.'

He shrugged and took the wine bottle and poured himself another glass, then – as an afterthought – turned his attention to hers. 'Not drinking?'

'Of course I am! Just slowly. A bit hungover. I told you last night was a big one.'

'Ally!' An American accent. Natasha looked up. It was glamorous Callandria from Chevening. 'How are you?'

'Oh, Cally.' Alastair didn't look thrilled. 'I'm good. Just back from a few days' writing in France. How are you?'

'Fine, really good.' Callandria ran a manicured hand over the waistband of her Evisu jeans. 'Actually, I couldn't tell you last time we met, but number three's on the way. I just had my twelve-week scan.'

'Congratulations.' Alastair sounded as if he were reading the label on a jar of instant coffee. Natasha smiled enthusiastically as her mind raced ahead. Twelve weeks – that would be her in six weeks, only of course it wouldn't. So it still didn't show at that stage. How long before you started to pant and waddle?

Callandria turned towards her. 'It's Natalia, isn't it? Working on that script again, are we?' She looked around the dark, humming room with its phosphorescent bar gleaming at the back. 'You do choose glamorous venues.'

'Oh, it's all about glamour these days,' Natasha assured her with a frosty smile. Her heart was sore. Would she and Alastair ever be able to admit they were together? Not that she was going to tackle him about it.

'So I see. Well, got to run. We must catch up *à deux* sometime, Ally.' She bent down and kissed him on both cheeks.

'God, what a bitch,' Alastair said immediately she'd moved on. 'Why didn't she mention *The Silent D.*? She must know it's out in paperback. The posters are bloody everywhere. It means she must hate it.'

'Of course not! How could she possibly?' As always when Alastair got like this, Natasha fished around for something to distract him. 'How do you know her?'

The furtive flicker which she knew so well passed over his face. 'Oh, I just do. A crowd of us went to Marrakesh a few years ago. She's got the two most revolting kids. God knows why she feels she can inflict a third one on the world.'

'What was wrong with the kids?'

'Nothing, they were just kids. Well, one was a baby. It

349

cried and the toddler kept climbing on me and leaving dirty hand prints. No different from any others, I suppose. I just can't stand them as a breed.'

'You were a kid once,' Natasha said, keeping her tone as light as possible.

'So? I didn't ask to be born.' He deftly pronged a ball of rice.

'And you've never wanted any yourself?'

'Christ, no. Can you imagine? The expense. The mess. The demands. How could I do my job?' He shuddered, then eyed her suspiciously. 'It's not as if you've ever struck me as the broody type.'

'Oh God, no. I love children but I couldn't eat a whole one.' She expected him to laugh approvingly, but to her confusion his lips pursed in faint disapproval.

'I don't know if a woman can be whole if she doesn't have children.'

'Oh, nonsense,' Natasha cried. 'Where did you get that idea from? Hello? I didn't know I was having dinner with some retired colonel from Tunbridge Wells.'

He laughed a little. 'Whatever. It's just what women always tell me. They're all the same: "Oh no, I don't want kids," and then six months down the line they're bleating about being incomplete.'

The bill arrived. 'I'll get it,' Natasha said, as she always did. Sometimes it occurred to her it would be nice if Alastair offered. He wasn't exactly broke, especially after the advance Rollercoaster had given him for the still-untitled script. But, on the other hand, she could put all their meals down as expenses. And Alastair knew that.

'Shall we have a nightcap at Black's?'

'Why not?' Natasha said, trying to ignore the sick feeling in her stomach. Which might be the baby – correction, the ball of cells – or might be the effect of this conversation. Alastair didn't want children. Not with her, or anyone. And she wanted Alastair more than she had ever wanted anything in the whole world.

She'd make that appointment in the morning.

42

Natasha thought she'd never get any peace. It was Wednesday morning in the office, the phone rang incessantly and bloody Dom never seemed to leave the room. She tried to distract herself from scary thoughts by flicking through the early edition of the *Standard*, which had just been placed on her desk. Her eyes stopped on the books pages near the back and a brief review of the paperback edition of *The Silent D*.

A feeling of sickness that was entirely pregnancy unrelated crept over her. 'Pretentious', 'vapid', 'over-slick', she read. 'The most over-rated book of the year. Save your money.' Oh God. Furtively, as if Alastair might suddenly jump out of the stationery cupboard, she slipped the copy in the bin. Out of sight, out of mind.

She flicked through a few more magazines and eventually found what she'd been hoping for in *FHM*. 'Acute psychology', 'devastatingly funny', 'heartbreaking in its searing portrayal'. She'd make sure he saw this one.

When Dom finally got up to go to lunch with some castings director she steeled herself to make the call.

'The Pall Clinic.'

The phone was answered so quickly, it took her by surprise. 'Oh, er, hello, yes. I'd like to make an appointment.'

'Certainly. For a test?'

'Er . . .' She looked around nervously. 'For a termination.'

'I see. How many weeks pregnant are you?'

'Six weeks.'

'That's absolutely fine. Could you come in on Friday at eleven-fifteen?'

'Sure.' But then Natasha looked in her diary. A big meeting with Barney that morning. 'Oh no, sorry, I can't!'

'How about Monday then? At five-forty-five?'

Bugger. That was when she was meeting a commercials director they were desperate to get on board. 'No, sorry, that's no good either.'

Eventually, after three more time slots were suggested and rejected by an increasingly despairing Natasha, they agreed on Monday August 2 at 10 a.m.

'That's nearly two weeks away,' she said anxiously.

'Well, I did offer you plenty of alternatives. I could call you if any other slots come up.' The woman sounded almost spookily kind.

'You won't tell anyone where you're calling from?'

'Of course not. Now, if you don't hear from us, you've still got plenty of time at eight weeks, so don't worry. Do you know how to find us?'

'I'll find you,' Natasha assured her.

Her evenings were developing a pattern. Slip into Boot's on the way home, praying she'd get a different assistant, buy another pregnancy test. Hurry home and pee on the stick.

Positive again.

She'd spent fifty pounds so far on tests. Oh well, at

least the points were adding up on her Advantage Card. She let out a little gurgly giggle, and pulled her trousers up. At least she was smiling. It must be because at last she was taking some positive action.

Alastair had come back with her last night, but although she had climbed acrobatically all over him and rubbed him with baby oil, her heart hadn't been in it and she'd actually been relieved when he said he couldn't stay as he had a five o'clock start to Manchester to sign books. But then of course as soon as the door slammed she'd started panicking that he'd sensed something and that she'd lost him for good.

Sophie's words floated into her head. 'From what you're telling me, this guy is a selfish tosser.' But then what did Sophie know? She'd just got engaged to a man who was only twenty-six and looked like a bulldog's arse. Natasha had grave doubts about what Sophie was doing, but right now she didn't have the strength to worry about anyone except herself. Maybe after the . . . procedure, she'd have a serious word with her.

The phone rang and her heart swooped like a bird. She wouldn't pick up; she'd make him think she was out there enjoying herself. But suddenly Natasha felt shattered. Being with Alastair was like playing some endless tennis match where you could never take your eye off the ball. But then again, imagine the exhilaration when you finally clinched match point and got to hold the trophy above your head. Sophie couldn't be feeling any of that.

The machine clicked on. 'Hi, Natasha. It's Sophie. I'm just down the road, thought I might pop in . . .'

At the sound of her friend's voice, Natasha's throat contracted. 'Hi,' she whispered, picking up.

'Oh hi. You're there.'

'Just walked in.' Another lie. Would she spend the rest of her life lying to everyone? 'How are you?'

'I'm fine. But I've been thinking about you. I'm on the corner of your street. I want to see you.'

'Why not?' Better than running a hot bath and sitting in her nightie crying at a repeat of *Animal Hospital*, which so far had been the plan.

But as soon as she saw Sophie on her threshold, she felt a pinching at the bridge of her nose and a scratchiness in her throat.

'Hey!' Sophie exclaimed. 'Hey, don't cry, don't cry. I'm here.'

But it was like someone had opened a tap. 'Oh Soph, what have I dooone? I've ruined my life.'

'Hey. Hey.' Sophie stroked her hair. 'What's this crap? How have you ruined your life?'

'Things like this don't happen to people like meee.'

Sophie laughed. 'Tash. Tash. Bad things happen to everyone. No one's immune. But this isn't the worst thing that will happen to you. You'll get over it. In time you'll realize finishing with Alastair was the best thing that could ever have happened to you.'

Natasha stared at her, puzzled. 'But I'm not going to finish with Alastair. That's why I'm going through all this.'

'Oh. Right. Sorry. My mistake.'

Gradually, Natasha calmed down. 'So I'm going to the clinic a week on Monday,' she said, with just a faint wobble of the lower lip.

'Well, I'll come with you.'

It was a very sweet and very tempting offer. But she couldn't have anyone there dissuading her. 'Oh, no thanks, Sophie. I'd rather do it alone, I think.'

'Well, maybe I should pick you up afterwards.'

'Would you?' Another tear ran down her face. 'God, that would be nice.' The phone rang again. 'I'd better get it,' Natasha snivelled. ''Lo.'

'Noodle?'

'Oh, Alastair!'

'How are you, sweetie?'

'Er, fine! Just got a friend here at the moment.'

'Oh. Right.'

It was his cold tone. Natasha felt as if a bucket of iced water was dripping down her spine. 'What were you thinking of?' she said hastily.

'Well, I was hoping to come over. I've had the day from hell in Manchester and I'm worried sick about how the book's going. It'd be great to show you some of the stuff I've written.'

'Oh. Well. That shouldn't be a problem. My friend's just going.' She made an apologetic face at Sophie, who raised a disapproving eyebrow back.

'No, no. I don't want to trouble you.'

'It's no trouble. I'll be here.'

'OK. Well. Actually I'm just five minutes away.'

'Sorry. Do you mind?' she said, hanging up.

'No worries,' Sophie said calmly. 'But call me about the clinic. I'll pick you up. Although I don't think you should be going alone.'

They both jumped as the buzzer went. 'That was quick.'

Natasha buzzed Alastair up. 'See you, Soph. You've been a really good friend.'

He was through the door before she even had time to brush her hair, let alone redo her make-up and cover up the blotchy puffiness.

'Who was that I passed in the hall?' he said, giving her a careless kiss on the cheek. 'She seemed familiar.'

'She was familiar. She's my friend Sophie. You met her for about a millisecond at Lainey's wedding?'

'Did I?' Alastair said, an odd look passing over his face. He walked straight to the mirror over the fireplace. He ran his fingers through his hair, then slumped back into the sofa. 'Could I have a drink?'

'Of course. Some wine? Red or white? I've got a lovely claret.'

'Whatever,' he snapped. Oh God, he was in one of those moods. His mouth was compressed, his brow furrowed. Clearly someone today had failed to appreciate the genius that was *The Silent D*.

Gratefully, she remembered the magazine. She pulled it out of her bag. 'Have you seen this? Page one hundred and sixty-five.'

He picked it up, lip curling. 'Hmm. *FHM*. I think the publishers might already have faxed this over. But let's have a look.' He flicked through the pages, his lips twitching nervously, then relaxing into a complacent smile.

'Well, I've had worse.'

'It's fantastic,' Natasha cried, handing him his large glass of wine. 'Would you like anything to eat? I was going to have the remains of some beef bourguignon I made at the weekend.' Actually someone at the deli had made it and it had been sitting happily in the freezer for a couple of weeks, waiting for a night like this.

'Maybe later,' he said irritably. 'First of all I'd like you to read these chapters.' He handed over a manuscript. 'Tell me what you think. I really need a steer.'

'Right now?'

'Yeah. Go and read it in the bedroom, maybe. I might watch some telly. I need to unwind.'

So Natasha found herself sprawled across her bed, clutching a glass of wine, reading Alastair's work, while he chortled at a repeat of *Frasier* in the other room. It was impossible to concentrate. She was so tired and images of a week on Monday kept floating through her head. She had no idea what was going to happen. Did they just give her a pill or would there be an operation? She'd been planning on a bit of a surf tonight to inform herself – she didn't dare do it at work, Barney might monitor their internet usage – but now she'd have to wait until tomorrow.

'How are you doing?' Alastair's head was peeking round the door.

'Fine, fine. I'll need another twenty minutes or so.'

'I love the fact that you get the Comedy Channel. It really chills me out.' He disappeared again.

She struggled to read on, making the odd note here and there. She was starving. The sooner they got the work over the sooner they could eat. That gave her a focus.

'Finished,' she said, coming back into the living room.

He looked at her suspiciously. 'That was very quick. Are you sure you read it properly?'

'Of course I did,' she protested. She went over to him

and stroked his hair. 'Come on. You know I'm a fast reader.'

'You are,' he agreed. 'So . . . ?'

'I love it,' Natasha said sincerely. 'Bits of it really remind me of *Showpiece* and that's my favourite.'

His expression didn't alter, but too late she knew she'd said the wrong thing. Recently, Alastair had told her he hated it when people praised his second, breakthrough novel too much, that he was much prouder of the following two, which, in the words of one of his favourite critics, 'marked a definite advance in creativity and power'.

'What did you think of the scene in the mall?' he asked. 'Did the dialogue ring true?'

Natasha was starting to dread these questions. If she said 'yes' he would tell her she was just humouring him, if she said 'no' he would sulk all evening.

'I did,' she said. There was a pause. 'But I wasn't sure what he was doing there in the first place. I mean surely if he's as angry with his girlfriend as you say, at this point he would have just left.'

'No he wouldn't,' Alastair retorted immediately. 'He'd want to stay and sort things out.'

'I'm not sure he would. I think the kind of character he is would just want to cut his losses.'

'Well, I disagree,' he suddenly roared, slamming his glass down.

'Oh Alastair, I'm sure you're right. I mean you definitely are. It's your book not mine.'

'No. No,' he sighed. 'You're probably right. Which means the whole book is based on a false premise. So I'll just have to start again from scratch and rewrite the whole fucking thing.' He slammed down his fist. 'Fuck.'

'Please don't say that. The book's brilliant. It was just a . . . just a thought. But you're right. I can see that now.'

'Fuck,' he muttered again.

'Have another glass of wine.'

'I don't want another fucking glass of wine.' He was almost screaming. 'I want to get this book right. Fuck, Natasha. Can't you see this is my whole career at stake here?'

Oh, don't be such a prima donna, she wanted to scream. Instead, to her shame, she let out a little sob. 'I was wrong to say that. I'm sorry.'

The mood suddenly defused. He reached out and touched her arm. 'No, I'm sorry, noodle. I can be a bit of an ogre sometimes. I just get . . . so tense.'

'That's OK,' she said, love flooding through her.

They ended up in bed again, of course. But once again, she was almost relieved when Alastair said he couldn't stay tonight and, after a shower, left.

43

Sophie sat at her desk, staring at the newspaper page in front of her.

MR O. O. GARCIA-MUNDOZ AND
MISS S. J. MATTHEWSON

The engagement is announced between Oliver
Oberon, younger son of Mr and Mrs Anthony Garcia-
Mundoz, of Ollioules, France, and Sophie Jane, only
daughter of Mr David Matthewson, of Newcastle, and
Mrs James Billingham, of Totnes, Devon.

Oberon? Olly had kept that quiet. Still, there it was in the *Daily Telegraph*. And *The Times*. Her eye kept going back to it. This was her. Official. In the paper. Like Lainey and Marcus. She'd finally arrived.

In the office they'd been outed. From being just one of many secretaries, Sophie had suddenly achieved celebrity status. Excited girls kept stopping by her desk and asking to see the ring and Sophie would regally hold out her hand and twist it this way and that to catch the light, while they oohed and ahhed over the size, the cut, the obvious cost.

'Congratulations, Sophie,' said that mealy-mouthed old bat Andrea Bussell, stopping by her desk with a suddenly friendly smile. 'How exciting. Have you named the day yet?'

'No, no, not yet.' *And don't think you're getting an invite, after all those years treating me like a piece of poo for being just a secretary.*

'Congratulations, Sophie,' said Keith Livingston with a wry smile about his lips. 'I suppose I have no chance now.'

'You never did, Keith.' Sophie blushed slightly as she remembered that dream about him, her and a hot-air balloon. But he was married and had four kids or something and anyway that whole book was closed now. This was it.

'It's the beeest news ever!' Fay had shouted. 'You two are just made for each other. I've always known it. Oh my God, it's soooo exciting. Can I be a bridesmaid?'

'Maybe,' Sophie smiled. She glanced over at Caroline, who'd been very gracious about the news, but then unusually absorbed in work all day.

Yvette was a bit more sniffy. 'So hope's triumphed over experience, Sophie. Well, good luck is all I can say. Every marriage needs it.'

Cow. Just because she and Brian were so miserable. Sophie smiled and resolved to hide this week's edition of *Heat* from her.

'So, you've seen it?' Olly said, leaning over her shoulder and breathing hard in her ear. Sophie flinched slightly. Olly always seemed to be around these days and when he wasn't he was sending her little love emails and texts. But wasn't that great? Wasn't that what she had always wanted? 'You look so beautiful, darling. And listen, my phone's been ringing off the hook all afternoon. Friends who've seen the announcement. They want to know why

I've kept you hidden for so long. Dying to meet you. So I was thinking, maybe we should have a dinner party for a few of them. Saturday night? I know some jolly good caterers.'

'Caterers? Don't insult me. You know I'll cook.'

'You are the perfect woman.'

On Saturday morning, Sophie wrote out a list of ingredients before setting out to Waitrose (Waitrose! No more Poundstretcher for her). She'd give Olly's friends the most delectable meal they would ever have tasted.

'Do you want to come with me?' she'd asked Olly, who had got up an hour or so before her and was sitting tapping into his computer in his (hideous) study with its hefty mahogany desk, maroon leather chair and a portrait of some constipated-looking Victorian bloke above the fireplace.

'Er, I won't if you don't mind. I loathe supermarkets. And I really need to do the final revise of this chapter. My publishers are on my case.'

'But it's Saturday.'

'When else am I going to get a chance to work at it? And remember, my darling, if I become an MP, which is seeming very likely, I'm going to have to work lots of Saturdays. Constituents' surgeries and all that.'

Lots of Saturdays? Well, obviously he was, but Sophie hadn't thought about it until now. But what about the weekends away, the shopping trips she'd planned? It would be just like being with bloody Andy, mooching around the house waiting for him to come home.

He saw her stricken expression and looked pleased.

'Darling, it's all right. I'll snatch time for us during the week.'

'But in the week I'll be at work.'

His chuffed smile was dropped, to be replaced by confusion. 'But you're going to be giving up your job, aren't you?'

'Olly! Of course I'm not. What on earth would I do all day?'

He shrugged. 'I don't know. Look after the house. Perhaps do a bit of my secretarial work. I thought you hated your job. You've always said how much you envy ... what's your friend called? ... Lainey, for not having to go to work.'

'Well, I do ... but no. Work's not that bad.' Sophie thought of her and Fay gossiping in the smoking room, her giggling down the phone with the contributors, the lunches in the caff with the secretaries from the different departments, the whole buzz and hum of office life. Of course it could be a drag, and she must look for something more challenging soon, but what on earth would she do without it? After all, Lainey seemed a little bit lost. Talking of which, she must call her before she left for Uruguay and arrange an evening browsing wedding mags. Sophie was so busy being engaged and keeping up to date with Tash, who was still determined to go ahead with this abortion, that recently she hadn't had time for anyone else.

'You'll have to give up work when we have children,' Olly said.

'Well, I ... yes, then, of course. For a while anyway. But until then I think I'd like to carry on.'

'But you have a nothing job. Why does it matter?'

Sophie felt as if she'd been punched in the stomach. 'It may seem like nothing to you. But it's my everything. And it has been for a very long time. Now, if you don't mind I'm off to the supermarket. To buy dinner for *your* friends.'

It was, she realized, as she stormed shaking up the road, their first row.

She'd expected Olly to be distraught, but when she announced her return with a loud slamming of the front door, he didn't even come out of his study. She stomped into the kitchen and with much clanging and banging started to put the shopping away.

Eventually, he appeared in the doorway. 'Darling, do you mind? I'm working on a really difficult bit.'

Sophie couldn't believe it. 'Hello, darling,' she snapped. 'How are you? How was packed Waitrose on a Saturday morning? Did you enjoy shopping for a bunch of people you don't even know?'

'Are you about to get your – er – monthlies?' Olly asked.

'No, I am bloody not!' she snapped, even though she was. 'I'm just finding all this a bit of a thankless task.'

'But I thought you loved cooking?'

'I do. But . . .' It occurred to her that the tasty nibbles which he once used to ply her with no longer made an appearance. Now it was her job to shop for them. And the CDs he used to play her now stayed in their cases. It was like how in the early days with Andy she'd always worn stockings but once she'd moved in she'd reverted to holey tights. Olly just didn't have to try any more.

Olly came over and put his arm around her. She shrugged him off. 'Look, darling. We're a team now. I'm working hard upstairs to get us the life we both deserve. You are making this a beautiful home. I don't expect you to help write my books, and I suppose I thought you wouldn't expect me to help with the domestic stuff.'

'Olly, I like the domestic stuff. But I am not giving up my job to become your servant.'

'Oh, right. You're still upset about *that*?' He patted her on the head like some cute Shetland pony. 'You can keep your little job if it means so much to you.' He glanced at his watch. 'Now, if you don't mind I really do need to get back to work.'

Everyone has rows, Sophie told herself as she made stock for the pea and lettuce soup. *It's normal. Olly's right. He's working bloody hard and he's going to be rich. Unlike Andy who worked bloody hard and had nothing.*

By seven, the lamb was roasting in the oven, the cous-cous salad was sitting under a muslin cloth and the pistachio crescents were cooling on a tray. Sophie had a long bath soaking in her Origins salts, which she'd bought with a twenty-pound note Olly had slipped to her the other day with instructions to treat herself. She dressed in her Sonia Rykiel and did her make-up. Look at her. She was just like those women you saw in *Vogue*. Just like Lainey, but a better cook.

'You will make the most perfect wife,' Olly said from the doorway behind her. He approached her and slipped his arms round her waist. 'Darling, I'm sorry. I don't want us to fight. I want us to have fun.'

'Me too,' she said.

She thought he was going to slip his hands under her dress and braced herself for the inevitable grope, but instead he said, 'Right, I think we need to do a seating plan, so you can get to grips with who all these people are.'

These people, it transpired, were all quite a bit older than Olly, in their late thirties or early forties. There were Vanessa and Philip Braxton-Smythe, both columnists on different newspapers, who were all over Olly, but who, although polite to Sophie, seemed bemused to discover she was a PA.

'I did wonder why I didn't know your byline,' Vanessa said. 'Olly said you worked for the paper, so I assumed you must be a section editor or something. How long have you been on the *Post*?'

'Uh. Five years.'

'And you were never tempted to write or anything?' Vanessa asked with incredulity.

'I don't think any organization can function without support staff,' Sophie said, smiling, as a new couple entered the room. Immediately, Vanessa turned away from her.

'Horace! Miranda!'

Horace was an economist, whatever that meant, and Miranda had the even more obscure job of working for a think-tank. Immediately, the two couples plus Olly fell into intense conversation about the NHS. 'I mean the proposals are totally unworkable. Absurd.' 'I did the number-crunching and . . .' 'It's another blatant vote-winner, though.' 'I know. Did you see *Question Time*?'

'What do you think of Olly's book?' Horace asked, suddenly turning to her. 'Brilliant concept, isn't it?'

'Mmm, er, excuse me a second. I must just go check on the lamb.'

When she came back the last guests had arrived. Liv, who was standing as a Tory MP at the next election (you discovered what these people did before you discovered anything else), and Peter, who was a TV producer. Both blinked politely when she said she was a PA and then turned to their old friends and began bitching about some politician they all knew.

At least they all sat down for dinner making noises of excitement and appreciation. 'Pea and lettuce soup, oh yum,' said Miranda, who had a beaky face like a cross hen. 'Now, don't tell me. Nigella, right?'

'Er, yes, it is actually. With a couple of twists of my own.'

'Don't tell me.' Miranda lifted up a hand. 'Lamb and couscous to follow. Pudding: Turkish delight figs with pistachio crescents.'

'Er, yes, actually.'

All the women started laughing. 'The Nigella Indian-summer dinner. We must have had it – what – about three times already this month?'

Tears stung in Sophie's eyes. To her fury, Olly started to laugh with them. 'I did think when Soph mentioned it, it sounded a little familiar.'

Peter smiled at her. 'Well, from this mouthful it's by far the best version. So well done, Sophie.'

'Oh God,' Miranda said. 'I wasn't belittling you, Sophie. No, what you've done is fab. Well done, you.'

The Shetland pony had been given a carrot.

For the rest of the dinner, Sophie was bored witless. They tried to include her but they were talking about education, the next election, foreign policy in Sudan, a bunch of people she'd never heard of. She felt like asking what they'd thought of the pictures in *Heat* of Geri radically slimmed down again, but she decided she'd better not.

Peter, who was to the right of her, was the only one to make an effort. 'That truly was delicious,' he said as he finished his second helping of Turkish delight figs. 'Have you always been into cooking?'

'As long as I can remember. My mum was a rubbish cook, so I felt I had to step in.' Sophie remembered how she'd always longed for a mum who smelt of baking powder and flour like Natasha's, rather than one who reeked of Opium and fag smoke; how she'd longed – still did – to be neat and nuclear, to be married to the father of her children until death did her part. Which now, of course, was going to happen. 'And we moved around a bit and cooking always seemed the best way to get settled in a new place.'

'And you've never thought of doing anything with it? Professionally, I mean.'

OK. More covert ways of saying why are you just a PA? 'The idea of being a caterer used to appeal but the hours are too anti-social and I . . .' She glanced at Olly but he was animatedly discussing the European Union. 'I was with a guy for a long time who also worked anti-social hours and I thought if I cooked, we'd never see each other. Although in retrospect I should have because we never saw each other anyway and the whole time he was off working I was at home, bored and lonely watching shit telly and wasting my life away.'

'You must have watched some cookery programmes. What did you think of them?'

Now Sophie was on a subject she felt confident about. She started gabbling about Jamie versus Gordon Ramsay versus Rick Stein. Peter listened and nodded and occasionally asked questions, apparently fascinated.

'I must be boring you,' she said, suddenly shamefaced.

'Not at all. Remember, I work in telly.'

She realized the rest of the table had fallen silent too.

'Darling,' Olly said gently. 'I think people would like some coffee.'

So why don't you bloody get it for them? 'Of course,' she smiled. 'Or tea. There's lots of different kinds.'

Everyone wanted something different. In the kitchen, Sophie tried to remember the various orders. Liv had wanted soya milk in her decaff, 'If that's not too annoying.' She could have ordinary, Sophie thought, suddenly vengeful. See if she noticed.

Of course she didn't. They stayed for what seemed like for bloody ever. It was one before they got up to leave, suddenly squawking about babysitters.

'Such fun to meet you, Sophie,' the women all said insincerely. 'You must come over soon.'

'Good effort,' Olly said as soon as the door was closed. 'I think they really enjoyed that. I've owed so many of them dinner for months now.' He didn't notice Sophie's look as he kissed her on the head. 'Shall we go to Bedfordshire? I'm absolutely done in. You can clear up in the morning.'

44

'Is that Sophie?'

Sophie was sitting at her desk and was grateful for the interruption. Caroline was upset Friday's internet date hadn't called. Questioning had revealed that he'd said one day he wanted marriage and babies and Caroline had responded: 'Well, why don't we make babies together?' Five minutes later he'd asked for the bill.

'Do you think I was wrong to be so upfront?' Caroline was asking. 'I just don't see the point in playing games.'

'Who's speaking?' Sophie said to the caller, silencing her friend with an apologetic hand.

'Sophie, this is Peter. Peter Stern. I was a guest at your marvellous dinner on Saturday. Do you remember?'

Nice Peter, the only one who was kind to her. Insanely, for a moment Sophie thought he was calling to ask her out. Even more madly she thought she might accept.

'Of course I remember. How are you?'

'Really well. Look, I'll get straight to the point. Remember I work in TV? Well, we're scouting around for someone to present a new cookery show for us. And I have a feeling you could be perfect. We're looking for a girl, but not a pro. We want an enthusiastic amateur to team up with a big chef – possibly Gordon Ramsay – to learn the tricks from. I just think you might have what it takes.'

Sophie was silent. This had to be a joke.

'Hello? Hello? Are you still there?'

'Yes. Yes. I am. I just . . . I can't believe it.'

'Well, look,' Peter said, 'I'm not making any promises. Just saying we'd like to give you a test. It may not lead to anything, but it could be a bit of fun. So what do you say?'

'I say why not?' Sophie said casually, trying to make out she got calls like this all the time.

The test was a week on Friday. Frothing with excitement, Sophie picked up the phone to Olly. 'You'll never guess!'

'What, darling?' he said indulgently.

She told him about Peter's call. At the end of her burble there was a silence. 'So? What do you think? Isn't it great?'

'I'm not sure about this.'

'Olly! What do you mean not sure? It's the kind of thing I've always dreamed of.'

'I don't think it sounds like a suitable job for my wife.'

He sounded so Victorian that Sophie thought he was joking. 'You're quite right. I should be at home, chained to the sink, wearing skirts that cover my ankles. In fact I should be busy covering all the table legs in case they offend anybody.'

'Sophie. This isn't funny. Can you imagine the kind of attention I'd attract if my wife was on some tacky TV show?'

'Olly! It won't be tacky. I thought Peter was your friend, anyway.'

'He is my friend, but that doesn't stop me from thinking he makes the most ridiculous garbage. It's people like him who are responsible for our nation's moral decline.' He sounded like he was reading from one of his leaders. If they had been face to face, Sophie would have wanted to shake him.

'Olly, it's the chance I've always wanted. To do something with my life. Be more than just a PA.'

'Look, Sophie, I haven't got time to discuss this now. But you know there's no need for you to do anything with your life now. You're going to be my wife. Talking of which, we must sit down and fix a wedding date. I'll talk to you later, darling.'

Sophie stared at the phone in amazement. 'You arse,' she muttered. 'You bloody arsehole.' And the first of the many shapeless fears, which so far she'd shoved to the back of a mental drawer like unopened bank statements, now took on an unavoidable form.

'Would you mind reading something for me, Alastair?' Natasha said, her heart beating a little bit louder than usual.

He was sprawled across her sofa, reading a magazine. 'Have you been writing a book too, noodle?' he asked.

'Just read this,' she said, putting the letter under his nose.

'A letter. God, how lovely. No one writes letters any more, do they?'

'It's from Amanda, my parents' neighbour. She hasn't quite got to grips with email.'

Dear Natasha,

 As you may have heard Steve is getting married!!! His bride-to-be is a lovely girl called Eve, who's a phlebotomist at the local hospital. I hope the news doesn't upset you too much but we'd love you to come to the wedding. It's at our place, breaking with tradition, because Eve's parents are dead. A little birdie (called Lesley!!!) tells me there may be a certain young gentleman you'd love to bring. So happy there's someone special in your life too, you have been a worry to your mum, you know.

Let us know if you can make the wedding, it's on August 21 at two in the Betterton church followed by a reception in the arboretum and of course all the rest of the Green clan will be there!!!

Hugs and kisses,

Amanda xxxooo

'What do you think?' Natasha said emotionlessly.

'So who's this Steve?'

'He was my boyfriend when I was seventeen. Broke my heart.' She laughed. 'Anyway, what do you think? Could you come?' It was absurd that it mattered so much to her, but she did not want to turn up to the former love of her life's wedding alone.

'Aw, no, noodle. A family wedding. I'd be intruding.'

'Hardly. Half the village will be there.'

'I don't know. I'm not much good at these formal things. I hate going home and having to meet Mum's friends. People asking me dumb questions about being a writer. "I'm sure I could write a book if I just had the time."' He put on a silly, high voice. Natasha laughed dutifully. 'I'm sorry but it's just not for me, noodle.'

'But you were so lovely when you met Mum and Lesley.'

'That was a surprise thing. It was different.' He picked up his magazine.

Natasha inhaled. 'Please, Alastair,' she said, keeping her voice level.

'No, noodle. I don't want to.'

'Do you never do things you don't want to do?'

He looked faintly surprised. 'Not if I can help it, no.' He turned a page. 'You've got so many admirers, noodle, there must be dozens of them who'd love to accompany you.'

He wasn't coming. He shared her bed almost every night, but he wouldn't do her this one favour. Natasha had to make a choice. Either accept this or demand more. But the door had been closed to more. If she pushed it any further, she might lose what little she had and end up with nothing.

And that would be unbearable.

'True,' she said cheerfully. 'Maybe I'll ask my friend Dom. Your loss. It should be a fantastic knees-up. Great material for your next book.' She forced herself to sound uncaring. There was no way she was going to let Alastair know she was hurt. She picked up a script, a smile on her face. She could feel him watching her.

'Come here, noodle,' he said, patting the sofa. 'You're far too sexy to waste your time reading.'

Afterwards, he lay beside her sleeping, while she watched him, breathless at her good luck in having netted him. She was doing the right thing. She could have cried, she could have sulked, but then that blank expression would have come over his face and he would have just left. She'd passed the test, and for another day she had her reward. Alastair Costello wanted her. That was worth any compromise, including next Monday's trip to the clinic.

45

Alastair was being lovely tonight. It was Wednesday and he'd taken Natasha out to a quirky little Moroccan restaurant, where he'd ordered all sorts of dishes containing things like sheeps' eyeballs and told her funny stories about a radio programme he'd recorded yesterday. Afterwards, they went back to hers and Natasha put on a fine sex-goddess performance, even though she didn't enjoy being touched at the moment, her breasts were so tender and she was worried she might have to stop mid-act to vomit.

And anyway, her mind was far away. She was so frightened about Monday. She'd found out that they weren't actually going to do anything to her then, but there would be an 'interview' to 'assess' her situation. Which Natasha didn't want at all, because she had a horrible feeling that the slightest probing question was going to start the tears flowing; tears she was determined to suppress. For that reason, she'd been avoiding Sophie, who'd left several concerned messages on various machines. Concern was lovely, but right now Natasha didn't think she could cope with it. Concern suggested what she was doing was wrong. And looking at Alastair as he lay, eyes closed, she knew she was doing the right thing.

'Do you want a glass of wine?' she asked, sitting up.

Alastair peered at her in the half-light. 'Noodle, is that a bit of a belly I'm seeing on you?'

Horrified, Natasha whipped the sheets round her. 'Probably,' she said, making an almost physical effort to keep her voice light. 'After the amount you fed me tonight.'

'It looks like you're having a baby,' he said, disgustedly.

She wanted to scream. 'It's just all that food inside me. It's a food baby.'

'Mmm.' He settled back on his pillows, but she was sure he was eyeing her critically. She grabbed her silk dressing gown from the back of her door and wrapped it round her. She surely couldn't be showing yet, but her body did feel all bloated and her appetite was out of control. It was a disaster.

'So, tomorrow,' she said, going for the well-tried distraction tactic. 'I've got tickets for a screening of the new Al Pacino. Wanna come?'

He didn't look at her. 'I'm busy tomorrow. Maybe we'll do something Saturday.'

'Cool,' Natasha said, automatically breezy. Oh God, he was turning against her because she was getting fat. But surely the spare tyre would disappear when . . . But the callousness of the thought appalled her. She shut her eyes and tried to block it out.

But on Saturday, he didn't call. This wasn't unusual. Natasha knew Alastair's style was to leave arrangements as late as possible, or – better – just to turn up. She followed her usual routine: put on her best outfit (right now featuring a tummy-disguising top), full make-up and lit the candles. She wished she didn't have such a stomach-ache. There was a pain in her shoulder too. She assumed it was baby-related in some way and that made her feel guilty – it was as if it was telling her it knew it was unwanted. Normally, she'd take a painkiller, but was that allowed in pregnancy? But why was she thinking like this? This pregnancy wasn't carrying on. The pain was so bad, eventually she gave in and swallowed two Ibuprofen. 'Sorry, baby,' she whispered, then wanted to slap herself. It was not a baby. Not yet, anyway.

She lay on her bed trying to read the next few pages of Alastair's novel, but she kept picking up her guide to pregnancy, which had joined all the other tomes under the bed. 'Eight weeks: Your baby is about the size of an olive.' Well, that wasn't worth getting too fussed about. She kept flicking through the book, greedily inhaling words like lanugo and episiotomy. If she had been going to have this baby it would have been born in March. 'When you go to hospital you should pack a hat and mittens if the weather's cold. Babies like to be kept wrapped tight.' Oh God, stop it. This was ridiculous.

She felt so sleepy. She'd just close her eyes for a minute.

When she woke it was nearly dark. The bedside clock said just after seven. She peered at her mobile, at the answering machine. He hadn't called. Dullness overcame her. They had entered one of these phases again. She thought of calling him but immediately dismissed it. That was not the way the game worked.

She felt a stab in her tummy. Like a period pain. Only sharper.

'Ay-ah!' The things this baby – no, group of cells – was doing to her.

Buzzz.

She jumped six inches in the air. Bloody Alastair. Typical to pitch up with no warning. Not that she'd show she was put out.

'Hello?' she breathed into the entryphone.

'T-Tash?' A male voice, but she couldn't immediately place it. Not Alastair, anyway.

'Yes?'

'It's Andy. Can I come up?'

Andy? What the hell was he doing here? 'I . . . OK.'

He was carrying his bike helmet, looking tanned and dishevelled.

'Andy, what a surprise. What can I do for you? Were you just passing?'

He had a pained look on his face. 'Er, yeah. Yeah . . . Well no, actually. I just wanted to see you.'

'Me? Why?' She was already in the kitchen pouring herself a large whisky, although this time not for its abortifacient effects but to numb the pain in her stomach.

'Have you heard about Sophie?'

'Sophie?'

'She's got engaged. To Olly G-M. I just got back this morning from Sudan. Shacky called me while I was away. Said he'd seen it in the paper. But I've heard nothing from her. I can't believe she didn't tell me.'

'God, Andy. I'm sorry. You must be really upset.' Natasha felt the twinge again and winced.

He breathed deeply. 'I don't know. Upset isn't the right word. I mean, it's not as if Sophie and I were going anywhere. But she's moved on so fast, it's as if all our years together meant nothing.'

'I think she moved so fast because it was the only way she knew to get over you,' Natasha said gently.

'So all she wanted was to get married? It didn't matter who to?'

'I'm sure she doesn't see it that way,' Natasha said wearily. 'But she did want to get married a lot and you didn't, so . . .'

'Sophie and I wouldn't have worked. She's lovely, but we weren't right for each other, Tash. But she could have told me.'

'She was probably embarrassed. Didn't know how to tell you. Have you talked to her?'

'No. Not yet. I don't know what to say to her.' He snorted. 'I guess that was always our problem. We were never any good at communicating.'

'Maybe you should call her. Try and talk.' Natasha breathed in sharply. Christ. What was going on?

'I just can't believe she wants to be with geeky Olly, though.' Andy looked at her. 'Tash? Are you OK?'

'I'm fine,' she said, but then she let out a squeak.

'Are you sure? I'm sorry. Christ, I'm so selfish. I come round here to vent and I don't even ask how you are.'

'I'm fine. I'm just a bit tired.' But her voice was shaking She exhaled hard. 'Oh, fuck.' It really hurt now.

Andy was next to her. 'Tash? What is it? What's wrong?'

Tears started pouring down her face. 'Andy, I'm pregnant. But I think there's a problem.'

And then Natasha passed out.

When she woke she was in a dimly lit room. Lights were flashing on a screen. She opened her mouth to say something, then pain cuffed her around the head. She fell back on to a pillow.

'Tash? Tash? Are you OK?'

Who was speaking? She struggled to focus. 'Andy?'

'Hey, Tash. How are you doing?'

'What's happening?'

'You're in hospital, Tash. You've been very sick.' He paused. 'You had an ectopic pregnancy. The baby was growing outside your womb. And it r-ruptured. They had to operate or you'd have died. But you lost the baby. I'm sorry.'

'Oh.' Natasha felt too groggy to react further.

'You've been in here twenty-four hours. How are you feeling? Can I get you anything?'

'You've been here all this time?'

'Yeah.' He did look even more unshaven than usual. 'I didn't know who to call. I wondered about your mum, but . . . I could be totally wrong but I didn't know if you wanted her to know. And I thought about Marcus but I just got his machine. And of course I tried Sophie but her phone just rang and rang. I left about a hundred messages but she didn't reply.'

'Thanks, Andy.'

'I . . . er . . . Well, the obvious person to get in touch with was the dad. But I didn't know who that was. I'll call him now?'

Natasha shut her eyes. 'No. No need to do that. We'll leave the dad alone.'

46

This week Sophie and Olly had been out every night. Functions which he'd once attended alone now had an '& fiancée' scribbled in the corner. Sophie would rather they'd used her name, but nobody had learned it yet. After work, they were always off to the Travellers' Club or the Reform, or – with luck – somewhere a bit cooler like the Groucho for a book launch or a lobby group's annual party or a politician's birthday do. Sophie would stand by Olly's side, face frozen in an animated smile, while old bores yelled at her over the party clamour and checked out her legs.

To be honest, it was rapidly becoming a bit tedious. Sophie yearned for a night on the sofa eating Pringles and watching a programme about the property market, but even when they stayed in the telly didn't go on as much as it used to. When he got the chance Olly'd slip in a Monty Python DVD, but he would eject it as soon as it was time for the headlines or *Newsnight*.

Strangely, she still wasn't a hundred per cent officially living with him. Much as she loathed Veronica and had no desire to pour rent money down the drain, she just hadn't got round to giving her the required month's notice. Besides, lots of her stuff was still in that flat and she couldn't seem to find the time to move it out. That was what she told anyone who asked, anyway. Deep down,

Sophie knew there was another reason she hadn't quite said goodbye to Mornington Crescent. Even though her time there had been brief and grim, it still symbolized a period of independence, an era when doors were open to her and her future path was a blur. She knew she'd have to make the break soon – she could hardly get married and still keep renting a manky flat – but somehow she couldn't quite face the thought of the doors all slammed shut and the rest of her life mapped out like the *A–Z*.

Yet in so many ways, being engaged was fantastic. Olly's snootier friends aside, almost everyone wanted to talk to her: to discuss dresses, flowers, honeymoon venues. The ladies in the canteen, the sub-editors, the men in the postroom: they all knew and her news seemed to bring so many of them a disproportionate amount of joy. Everywhere she went people seemed to be smiling at her, eager to share tips, anecdotes, memories of their own wedding days. Sophie liked it; she liked it a lot.

She also liked moments like Thursday's, when Fay waved the *Evening Standard* under her nose. 'Page thirty-one! Have a look.'

Sophie leafed through. *Londoner's Diary*. And, oh my God, a huge great picture of her at last night's party: smiling into the camera, holding a glass of champagne, in her new MaxMara suit, which Olly had bought her at the weekend saying she needed more clothes for functions. Behind her, Olly beamed like a baby with a rusk.

Some guys really have all the luck [she read]. *Take Olly Garcia-Mundoz, rising* Daily Post *and Tory Party superstar, with – insiders*

predict – every chance of a shadow minister's post by his thirtieth
birthday. Then there's his publishing deal with Webber rumoured
to be worth a cool £600,000 for two political tomes. And last, but
not at all least, there's his recent engagement to the gorgeous
Sophie Matthewson (above). 'I proposed in Paris and we couldn't
be happier,' Olly told me at Donald McKay MP's summer party at
the Reform.

'I have a famous friend,' Caroline cooed.

'*You've* met thousands of famous people,' Sophie said quickly. She was acutely aware of having to play down her happiness in front of her single friend.

'Only to interview. It's not the same. God, you know you and Olly are soon going to be appearing in those lists of power couples, like Jay Jopling and Sam Taylor-Wood.'

'Except Sophie's not powerful,' Yvette chipped in. Nobody argued with her.

But having your picture in the paper was an amazing feeling. Sophie remembered how when Mum was married to John she'd study pictures of them in *Tatler* and *Harpers & Queen* at a ball or some race meeting: Mum radiant and smiling in red or black with her sleek black hair hanging over one eye. Mrs John Brandon, the caption would read.

'Why don't they say Rita Brandon?'

'Because when you're a wife you lose your identity,' Mum had snapped. Funny, until right now Sophie had forgotten her saying that. Her marriage must have been on the rocks by then. But who cared what they called you in some silly picture caption? The point was you were in the glossies, looking gorgeous. You were *somebody*.

*

Sophie and Olly spent the weekend with John and Constance Somers-Seton in their damp and cold second home in the Yorkshire moors. John and Constance, who were both very high-up people in the Tory Party, wanted to talk about election strategies all weekend and although Sophie kept looking longingly at the ancient telly in the corner, there was no way she dared turn it on. And she'd bloody forgotten her mobile so she couldn't even text her mates for a bit of light relief.

Their only breaks were for long, muddy walks which ruined Sophie's Adidas trainers. 'Didn't you think to bring wellies?' Constance asked in exasperation.

Sophie had longed to cook Saturday dinner and Sunday lunch, but Constance had shooed her out of the kitchen, only to produce two meals of horribly overdone meat and underdone vegetables. Then they had had to squeeze into the back of John and Constance's Audi and endure a never-ending journey back down the M1, listening to a Monty Python tape, which Olly had bought specially for the journey. The others all howled with laughter, but Sophie, who was beginning to know the lines off by heart, found it about as funny as a spider in the bath-tub.

When they walked into the Kensington house just after 11 p.m. on Sunday, Sophie immediately heard her phone ringing.

'It's very late for someone to call,' Olly said, looking put out.

The phone was charging in his study. Forty-eight missed calls. Nearly all of them voicemail, but the rest from . . . Andy. Sophie's heart started to beat in a very unacceptable rhythm. He must be back. Must have heard her news. What was he going to say?

She held the phone to her ear.

'S-Sophie, I don't know where you are, but Tash is in hospital. She's . . . lost her baby. So could you call me when you get this? It doesn't matter when.'

Sophie called him immediately. 'Andy? I'd forgotten my bloody mobile. What the hell has happened to her?'

'She collapsed. Something called an ectopic pregnancy where the baby isn't properly growing inside the womb. Luckily I was there when it happened or she could have died.'

'But she'll be all right?'

'Yes, she'll be all right. But she's pretty shaken, as you can imagine.'

'Poor thing. Poor thing. Thank God you were there. When can I go and see her?'

'Tomorrow. I'll give you the ward number, shall I?'

Only long after Sophie put the phone down did it occur to her that it hadn't been at all weird to hear Andy's voice and that the conversation had conjured up nothing more than desperate worry for Natasha.

She lay pale in her hospital bed. Sophie reached out and stroked her hair. 'My poor, poor lamb. I can't believe I wasn't there for you. I'm so sorry.'

Natasha smiled weakly. 'It's not your fault.'

'Yeah, but . . . How long are you going to be in here for?'

'Probably two more nights. And then I have to take at least a week off work, maybe two. I've told them I've got appendicitis.' She smiled again. 'It'll be sod's law when I do actually get it a month or so down the line.'

'And what has Alastair said?'

'Nothing. I haven't told him.'

'You haven't . . . ? Tashie! But you must. You could have died.'

'He hasn't called me for the past few days anyway. When he does, if he does, I'll say I've got flu.' The determined look that Sophie despaired of passed over her face.

'Tashie! You can't do that. He has to know!'

'Why? He hasn't been in touch anyway. It may all be over. Why upset him by telling him about something that was never meant to be?'

'Surely, he'd want to know . . . I mean . . .'

'Alastair won't want to know. Believe me.'

'So,' Olly said on Monday over a rare supper of roast chicken at home, 'tomorrow it's the Fenton-Coopers' drinks party and then we're going out to dinner with Helen and Ross Birchstanley. Do you remember them? We met them at that party at the Hurlingham.'

'Oh. Olly, I'll try to make the dinner, but I can't come to the drinks. I've got to see Tashie. I promised I'd go round after work. Make her comfortable.'

Olly's brow furrowed in that all-too-familiar way. 'But, darling, I promised the Fenton-Coopers you'd be there.'

'You didn't ask me if I would,' Sophie pointed out as reasonably as she could. 'Tash has been very ill, Olly. I need to look after her.'

'Can't her boyfriend or whoever he is do that?'

'No he can't.' Sophie hadn't fully filled Olly in on the horrors of Natasha and Alastair, although reflecting on her friend's situation certainly made her appreciate Olly more. Or think she *ought* to appreciate Olly more.

'Well, if you must go, darling, you must. But please be in time for dinner. The Birchstanleys are very important contacts of mine.'

'I will be, I promise.'

He cleared his throat as he always did when he was about to make a pronouncement. Sophie used to find that sweet; now it was starting to annoy her. 'So, this weekend,' he began. 'I was thinking of taking a trip to the country. To look at houses.'

'Houses? What for?'

'Well, you know. It looks like I'll be selected for a country seat, so naturally we'll want somewhere in the constituency. So we might as well get rid of this place and buy a pied à terre somewhere round Westminster, for my work and of course for when you want to come up shopping or whatever.'

'But, Olly, how would I work?'

'I thought we'd been through this,' he said with faint exasperation. 'You won't be working for much longer. And wouldn't a lovely country house be nice? Somewhere we could entertain at weekends?'

A vision flashed into Sophie's head of Vanessa and Miranda *et al.* sitting in a long dining room blabbing on about tax cuts while she served them their dinner, silver-service style.

'Olly, I love the country, but I'm not sure I want to live there just yet. All my friends are in London. And . . . I thought we'd agreed I was going to carry on working. I mean there's this screen test . . .'

Olly raised a majestic hand. 'We'd agreed that was out of the question.' He forked a mouthful of stuffing into his mouth. Some gravy ran down his chin. 'God, this is good. Now, darling, more importantly we need to settle on a date and choose a venue. I was thinking maybe Easter. And how about St Margaret's, Westminster? It's such a lovely church and so convenient for all my friends. It's difficult but I'm pretty sure I could pull strings and get us in there.'

Sophie stared at him, appalled. 'But, Olly, I want a summer wedding. And we can't get married in London. We have to get married in Betterton.'

There was the shortest pause, then: 'I don't see why, darling. Neither of your parents live there any more. London would be so much more convenient for all our guests.'

'But it's where I'm *from*. And there's this lovely country house with an arboretum and a lake. Wouldn't it be nicer to be married there than in some musty old church which means nothing to either of us?'

'Sophie, we're not getting married by a lake. We're getting married in church. The proper way.'

'Why? You never go to church.' Sophie declined to mention she had always planned a wedding in Betterton church until a few years ago when they'd relaxed the rules on where you could marry and she'd decided a lakeside ceremony would be more romantic.

'That's not the point,' Olly retorted. 'Church is where people get married. It's how it's always been done.'

'Not any more, Olly. You can get married wherever you like. I think getting married in church is hypocritical. I don't believe in God. And I didn't know you did either.'

Olly put down his wine glass. 'Darling, it's the right thing.'

Sophie was too tired for this. 'Well, we'll see,' she said mildly. She simply felt too confused to argue. Anything for a quiet life. And a London wedding could be fine, it was just she'd always dreamed of the Betterton arboretum.

Funny, she thought, that when all her plans for her wedding day had been so clear, the face of the actual man she'd marry had been so hazy. But Olly was it. Olly was the missing piece of the jigsaw. For better or for worse.

She got up, went to the stereo and put on his Keane CD. A bit of music. That always calmed her down. A pained look came over Olly's face. 'Darling, do we have to listen to this rubbish?'

'What do you mean, rubbish? It's your CD.'

'I know. It's just . . . I'm not in the mood for it now.'

'Whatever.' She turned it off again.

He glanced at his watch. 'Anyway, it's *Newsnight* in five minutes.'

'I think I'll have a bath,' Sophie said. She was spending a lot of time in the bath these days.

Natasha was lying in her hospital bed, a pile of books and magazines beside her and roses in a vase on the bedside table.

'I've brought you soup. I made it myself,' Sophie fussed.

'Actually I'm OK. I've eaten.'

'Are you sure?' All Sophie's maternal instincts were kicking in. 'You have to keep your strength up, you know. When are you going home?'

'Tomorrow, unless there's some disaster.' Natasha paused and then said all in a rush: 'Andy says he'll take me. You don't mind, do you?'

'Of course I don't.' Sophie considered this. She'd been expecting some sort of delayed reaction to Andy's reappearance, but still she could only summon up profound relief that he had been there to help Natasha. *There you are. I'm over him. It's so right to be with Olly.* Talking of whom . . . 'Honey, I'm sorry but I'm going to have to go in a sec. I've got to meet Olly for this fuck-boring dinner. I wish I could stay with you.'

'Don't worry. I'll be OK. I've got my books to read.'

'Have you heard from Alastair?'

'No, but that doesn't mean anything either way. He often goes quiet for a chunk when he's working.' She forced a smile. 'How's Olly?'

'Fine. Being a bit tricky about the wedding. He wants something much more stuffy and traditional than I'd like. And . . .'

'And what?'

'Nothing.'

'And what?'

'And he doesn't want me to try out for this amazing job.' Sophie told her about Peter's offer.

When she finished speaking Natasha was silent.

'What do you think I should do?' Sophie asked.

Natasha sighed. 'Oh Soph, I don't know. If I were you, I think I'd forget about the job. Olly really doesn't want you to do it. And these pilots usually don't come to anything anyway. Ask yourself: is it worth the grief?'

'Mmm.' Sophie surveyed her friend who'd decided her man should come before everything. It wasn't an inspiring example. 'I'm sure you're right. You usually are.'

'Hello? Is that Peter?'

'Speaking. Who's this?'

'It's Sophie Matthewson. From the dinner party. You called me about the screen test.'

'Hi, Sophie. You're still up for it, aren't you?'

'I am. Yes. Definitely. But there's just one thing. You haven't told Olly I'm coming, have you?'

'Olly? No. He's much more a friend of my wife's than he is of mine.'

'Good.' She paused for a second before launching into her well-rehearsed excuse. 'Well, if you do bump into him or whatever would you mind not saying anything? You see, I want it to be a surprise for him. If I get it.'

'Sure,' Peter said, sounding as if he knew exactly what was going on. 'Let's hope we can make it a nice surprise for him. But I've got high hopes for you, Sophie. Look forward to seeing you on Friday.'

'Me too.' Sophie put the phone down, giving Norris Wharton, who happened to be passing, a huge smile that made his day.

47

In the end Natasha came home on the Thursday evening. Sophie came round straight after work. Andy had just left, apparently. 'You're to rest all weekend,' she warned her friend as she fussed around her bed rearranging cushions. 'And no going back to work on Monday either.'

'Not on Monday. But soon. I have to. We've a big pitch coming up.'

'If you go back to work before you're ready, I will personally shoot you.'

Natasha knew that warning tone. It wasn't to be messed with. 'OK! I won't. I promise.'

Sophie had wandered into the kitchen. 'God, it's a good thing I'm here,' she yelled over her shoulder. 'What is your fridge like? All you've got in there is tinned foie gras, smoked salmon and champagne.'

'The food of love,' Natasha muttered to herself.

'What?'

'Nothing.'

'Well, it's not good enough,' Sophie said, reappearing in the doorway. 'I'm popping out to Tesco's. Going to feed you up, girl. I know if I leave you alone, you'll go straight on to some grapes and water diet.'

'Get me a copy of *Broadcast*,' Natasha begged.

'Only if you promise to eat everything I put in front of you.'

'Oh, bugger off.'

As Sophie shut the front door, Natasha fell back on the bed. There was a mountain of post to deal with, but she couldn't face it right now. She was still so tired. She'd just close her eyes and doze for a moment.

Buzzz.

Oh, for God's sake. Sophie must have gone out without a key. All the same, she was back quickly. Grumpily, Natasha rolled off the bed and walked gingerly towards the entryphone.

'Yeah?'

'Hey, noodle.'

'Alastair!' Bollocks. She was wearing no make-up and she was dressed in an old T-shirt, which said Microsoft on it, and a pair of baggy running shorts.

'Can I come up? Or do you already have a man up there?'

'I've been a bit ill. I'm in my pyjamas.'

'How sexy. Can I come up?'

'Sure.' She pressed the buzzer, then raced into the bedroom, pulling on an old blue and white striped number dragged from the bottom of a drawer. She ran her hands through her hair, then, wincing slightly at the pain in her tummy, ran to the front door.

'Well, don't you look gorgeous. Why have I never seen you in those before?'

'Probably because you've never seen me on my death bed,' she said, turning round and heading back into the bedroom.

'What's wrong with you, noodle?' A thought crossed Alastair's mind. He took a step back. 'It's not contagious, is it?'

'No, no. I've just had horrible flu. Real killer. I haven't been at work all week.'

'Poor baby. You should have told me. I could have come round. We could have played doctors and nurses.' He was sitting on the bed by now. He reached forward and stroked her hair. Which she hadn't washed since yesterday in the manky hospital shower. Natasha flinched.

The door slammed. 'Yoo hoo. It's your home from hospital service. Helping the crippled and weak.'

'Hi, Sophie!' Natasha yelled as loudly as she could. 'Guess what? Alastair's just popped in.'

'Oh. Hi.' Sophie appeared in the bedroom doorway, laden down with carrier bags.

'Hospital?' Alastair asked.

'Yeah. I had to go in for a quick check-up today. Make sure everything was all right. After my *flu*. Which it was,' she added hastily.

'Right,' he said, edging away from her.

'Hello, Alastair,' Sophie said sharply. 'I'm Sophie, Natasha's oldest *friend*.'

'Hi,' he said. He clearly recognized her from Paris. Their eyes met and locked, like two pit bulls preparing for a fight.

'So I hear you haven't been around for a while,' Sophie said. Natasha shot her an anxious glance.

'Oh, you know how it is. I've been busy. Holed away working.' He flashed his Tom Cruise grin. 'And then I find poor Natasha sickening with love for me.'

'Hardly,' Sophie said dryly. She turned to her friend. 'Sweetie, would you like some soup? I've got broccoli and sweetcorn, ham and pea or chunky tomato?'

To her fury, Natasha looked straight at Alastair. 'Which would you like?'

'Oh, I don't care.' He yawned and stretched lazily. 'Ham and pea could be good.' Catching Sophie's eye, he added hastily, 'If there's enough to go round.'

'I'm sure there is.'

In the kitchen she could barely stop herself from seizing the bread knife. But she wasn't sure whom she wanted to stab – Alastair for being such an arrogant idiot or Natasha for allowing him to be. Flu, her bloody arse. Alastair had no idea that her friend had nearly died because of him.

She warmed up the soup – she hated using supermarket stuff but there'd been no time today to prepare any herself – made six slices of toast, buttered them thickly and knocked together a salad. 'The perfect invalid supper,' she said under her breath and with a little smile, envisaging her TV debut. Then she stopped smiling as she heard whispering and giggling and a sudden shrill 'Ally!' coming from the bedroom.

Not wanting to look at him, she marched in with a tray. 'Shall I leave you two dinner while I eat next door?' she asked. She knew she sounded like a sulky bitch, but she couldn't help it. Again, she ignored Natasha's look.

'Don't be silly,' Alastair said, getting to his feet and taking the tray from her. 'I'm the gooseberry tonight, not you. I know you girls were going to have a pyjama party.'

'In your dreams.' She glared at him. He smiled back.

'Sit down,' Alastair said, gesturing towards the chair in the corner. 'I want to hear all about you, Sophie. Natasha says you're getting married. That you're the next-but-one

Prime Minister's wife. Like Jackie Kennedy. Hey, Tash, she looks a bit like Jackie, doesn't she?'

'Jackie was the President's wife,' Natasha said with a fond smile. 'But yes, she does.'

Sophie still glared. Flattery was going to get him absolutely nowhere.

'So are you hanging out with loads of lascivious Tories? Is it true that they're all into wife-swapping?'

'I wouldn't know,' Sophie said, but she sounded so ridiculously prim that a little giggle escaped her.

'I heard the most fantastic piece of gossip the other day about Prince Charles,' Alastair said. He carried on chatting and soon they were all laughing. To her annoyance Sophie understood what Natasha saw in him. He was very charming and very sexy. Perhaps that Aurelia weekend had been an aberration. She glanced at Natasha. Her face had illuminated like a watch dial. Do I ever look at Olly like that? she wondered, but she knew the answer.

'Well, it's great to see you both,' Alastair said looking from one to the other. 'I'm sorry you're so poorly, Natasha. Pity I have to go away so soon.'

'Go away?' Natasha's face turned even whiter than it was already.

'Yeah. Ant's got a couple of weeks off and we found some super-cheap deal on the internet. Two weeks in a villa in Thailand. We only sorted it today.'

'And you . . .' Natasha looked upset. So upset that Sophie knew she had to help out.

'What a laugh,' she said hurriedly. 'And is it going to be a proper holiday for you or are you going to be writing?'

'Oh, a proper holiday, I think. I've been working pretty

hard recently. Dreaming up ideas for my slavemaster here. I think I need a break. Sun and sand. Good food and beer. Nightclubs.'

'When are you going?' Natasha said in a pained little voice.

'Sunday. The flight's in the evening.'

'How fantastic.' Sophie was as animated as she could be to draw attention from Natasha's stony expression. 'And where's the villa exactly?'

'It's in Pattaya. Where all the girlie bars are apparently, but Ant's girlfriend Karen says there are some really nice tranquil bits too.'

'Is she going too?' Sophie asked, before Natasha did in a whisper.

'No. Actually, that's one of the reasons we're going. Karen's really putting the pressure on about commitment and babies. Ant needs a break. Has to show her he's still his own man.'

'Oh, well, that makes sense,' Sophie says. 'Sometimes you need a bit of a breather in these situations. In fact . . .' She glanced at Natasha. 'In fact Tash and I were thinking of having a bit of a girls' holiday to help me get my head round the whole settling-down thing.' She glanced at Natasha, praying she wouldn't say: 'What girls' holiday?' But to her delight, the sickened expression of a moment ago had been replaced by a broad smile.

'Yeah. Maybe we should get Karen along too,' she said slyly. 'What do you think, Soph?'

'God, the three of you on holiday,' Alastair said wistfully. 'Do you think I could come? As your love slave?'

'Certainly not,' Natasha said.

'When do you think you might go?' he asked.

'Oh, whenever we can get a good deal. Who knows?' She said it so coolly, Alastair looked at her in admiration. So did Sophie. But at the same time, she realized what her friend was up against. If she wanted Alastair this was going to be a long haul. There could be no natural behaviour, no true emotions, no chance ever to relax. This was about being forever vigilant, never showing your hand, like some wily old Samurai warrior. Sophie knew she would never have the energy, but then Natasha had always been the harder worker.

She left about nine. Alastair and Tash were growing giggly, exchanging more and more looks.

'You're not going to have sex with him,' Sophie hissed in her ear as she kissed her goodbye. 'It could be bad for you.'

'Of course not,' Natasha said. 'Do you think I'm crazy?'

'I'm not sure what I think about your mental state.' She stood up, turned round and nodded curtly at Alastair. 'Goodbye.'

'Bye.' He bent down and kissed her on the cheek. To her annoyance she noticed he smelled of crisp, clean linen. 'Good to see you.'

As she closed the front door, the giggling started again.

48

The following morning, the day of her screen test, Sophie threw a sickie.

'I think I'm getting a migraine,' she moaned, lying in bed as Olly knotted his tie in the mirror.

'Oh my poor darling. Is there anything I can do?'

'No, no, I'll be fine,' she growled hoarsely, then remembered sore throats weren't a sign of a sore head. 'I'll be fine,' she moaned again. 'I'll just stay here and sleep.'

He frowned. 'We're going to the Benthocks tonight.'

Sophie saw an opportunity for a night curled up in front of *Top of the Pops*, followed by *'Enders*. 'Oh Olly, there's no way I'll be able to make that, I'm afraid. You'll have to go on your own.'

'I could miss it,' he said dubiously.

'No, no. You go, you go. I'll be fine. I'll just be sleeping.

She'd already left a whispery message for Yvette on her voicemail, telling her she'd got food poisoning and would be unplugging the phone and trying to sleep. It was the twelfth time she'd used that excuse this year, but she didn't care. Soon she'd have another job to go to.

As soon as Olly shut the front door, she gave a little whoop at the thought of a whole day ahead of her without Yvette nagging, Fay giggling, Caroline whining, finished off by braying voices asking her what she did for a living. She had a screen test and she was going to spend the whole morning doing her hair and make-up to knock 'em dead.

She was just plugging in her curling tongs when the doorbell rang. Bugger. Could it be Yvette checking up on her? she thought paranoiacally. She hurried downstairs.

A courier was standing on the doorstep. 'Parcel for Mr . . .' He peered at the label. 'Garcy-Munder?'

'Yes, I can sign for that.' Probably some boring political biography that Olly had been sent to review. 'Who's it from?'

The man yawned. 'Keepuptodate.com.'

'What's that?'

'I dunno. Have a look inside.'

It was naughty but she couldn't resist. *I can always say I thought it was a get-well present from the office,* she told herself, tugging at the fastenings on the Jiffy bag. She held it upside down and three CDs fell out, all from very cool-looking bands Sophie had very vaguely heard of. There was a paperback book with a picture of a skinhead on the front brandishing a razor blade and a thick envelope. She opened it and a pile of tickets to gigs and films fell out.

Hi Olly [she read in the accompanying letter],

How are you doing? To keep you up to date in September our team here has compiled the usual list of the grooviest new releases. Plus our tickets to the latest events in London and a copy of the hippest book of the moment, Skin Trade *by Geirson O'Flannery. Your mates will take you for the coolest dude . . .*

She should have been shocked, outraged, but instead a huge balloon of laughter welled up inside her. 'Oh my God.' It explained everything. The CDs that never came out of their packets, the pristine paperbacks in the bedroom, the tickets for events which bored him. They'd all been organized by a company that specialized in making square people cool. 'Oh my God,' she bleated again. 'Oh Olly. You poor, poor thing.'

She knew this was something she was going to have to think about later. But not now. Now she had to go out and get herself a glittering new job.

The production company was in Notting Hill and when Sophie came out just after three, she was so buoyed up she had to share with somebody. And there was Lainey and Marcus's road, just here on the right.

Fizzing like a Vitamin C tablet, she ran up the steps and rang the doorbell. No answer. Lainey was probably at yoga or something. She rang again, waited a moment and was turning back down the steps, about to dial Tash, when the door opened.

Marcus stood there, looking quite unlike himself in a white towelling dressing gown with a coffee stain down the front, hair in the air like a mad professor. He stared at Sophie a little wildly. 'What are you doing here?'

'Bunking off. I thought I'd see how Lainey was doing. But if it's a bad time . . .'

'No!' Marcus sounded a bit dazed. 'No, no, it's fine. I was just having a sleep. Come in.'

Sophie followed him in and down the stairs to the basement kitchen. An overflowing rubbish bin sat in the corner and there were empty wine and beer bottles all over the place. 'Marcus, are you ill? Is everything OK?'

'Oh yeah, fine. Lainey went to Uruguay this morning and we had a bit of a night last night, so I called in sick.'

'Me too . . .' But then Sophie registered his expression. 'Markie, are you OK? This isn't just a hangover, is it?'

'No,' he said and, to her horror, sat down at the kitchen table and started to cry. Sophie had only seen him weep once before, when Englebert, his spaniel, got run over by the butcher's van.

'Marcus! What's wrong?'

'Ah, it's nothing.' He shrugged, wiping a tear away from his handsome face. 'Just feeling rough.'

'Are you sure?' She'd give it another stab. 'Is it Lainey?'

'No, Lainey's cool,' he faltered, but the tears started to flow again.

'Marcus! Tell me!'

'We had a big row last night. I didn't want her to go to Uruguay. She said I couldn't stop her. I said I'd miss her and why didn't I fly out and join her just for the weekend and she laughed at me and said hardly, I'd be cramping her style.'

'Wooh.' Sophie felt a flicker of hatred towards lovely Lainey. 'Not very kind.'

'I mean, I know I'm not exactly Gilles Peterson or whoever, but I could have tagged along at least for a bit and then buggered off. And we could have spent the days together. I just feel . . . she's my wife, Sophie, and I never see her. Either I'm at work or she's out and our two lives don't seem to overlap at all. We're . . . we're like Mrs Sun and Mr Rain on a barometer. When one of us is out, the other stays in.'

'Oh Marcus.' She put her arm around her stepbrother.

'You and Tash are the only friends of mine she'll even tolerate. And I've tried to have some nights out with her friends, but I can tell they find me boring, although that didn't stop them coming along to the wedding and drinking all the free champagne . . .'

'But you always seem to be taking her to the River Café or whatever.'

'Well, I've tried that kind of thing, but she doesn't really like it very much. Says she goes out plenty with her friends and that when I'm around she likes to stay in, have a takeaway and watch TV. It makes me feel like I'm a cat or something. I want us to *do* things, like a couple.'

'But it wasn't like this before the wedding.'

Marcus smiled bitterly. 'I think it was a little, it's just she was so caught up in planning this perfect day she didn't want to go out and take Es and dance on podiums all night. But even on honeymoon it was all getting a bit dodgy.'

'But your honeymoon was fab, wasn't it?'

'Not really. It rained almost every day and when the sun did come out, Lainey was straight out in it and so I went and sat with her and then I got burned. And she insisted on us going to these awful clubs but I was driving so I had to sit with a glass of water that cost fifty euros and watch everyone else mashed out of their heads and when I suggested dinners *à deux*, she just yawned and said that was boring. And now we're back, it's just getting worse and worse. Before the wedding, she was still working so she had to keep a vague grip. But now that's over, she's got nothing to focus on. She hasn't completed a single painting, you know. As far as I can see she just sleeps late and then wanders around the house in her underwear, until she can go out again. But I can't blame her. I'm out of the house at six and I don't get back until ten, so how else is she supposed to entertain herself?' He sighed and rubbed his forehead with his fist. 'But I love her, Soph. I really do. I want this to work so badly.'

'I know you do.' She rubbed his back. 'Hey, hey. It'll be OK. Everyone says the first year of a marriage is the hardest. You'll get through this.' She didn't know if she meant a word of it.

'And I hate bloody work,' he continued. 'I keep dreaming of handing in my notice. Becoming a carpenter. Doing something meaningful. But then we'd have to move to a semi in zone five.'

'But if that's what you want to do you should do it,' Sophie cried. 'Lainey loves you for who you are. She'll understand.'

'Maybe,' Marcus said dubiously. He swallowed hard. 'Soph. You're a trooper. Now, you won't breathe a word about this little scene to anyone, will you?'

'Of course not!'

'Anyway, tell me.' He sat back in his chair, visibly relieved to let his smooth public-school manners take over. 'Why aren't you at work today? What are you doing here?'

'I just had a screen test . . .' Sophie started fizzing again as she told him all about it. She'd had to pretend to make a salad in a little kitchen, while chatting to a video camera and then she'd met the celebrity chef and they'd made soup together while chatting some more and there'd been a bit of banter and she thought they'd got on really well and . . .

'Well, that sounds great. Have you told – sorry, what's his name? – Olly about it?'

'No, I'll only tell him if I get it. Not worth the aggro otherwise. He doesn't think I need a job, thinks I should be having babies in the country. But I reckon he'll be chuffed really. He has to be. Don't you think?'

'Well, of course. It's a fabulous opportunity.' Marcus rubbed his hand across his bloodshot eyes. 'So how are the wedding plans?'

Sophie grimaced. 'A bit of a nightmare. Olly's so fussy about what he wants. But I think we're getting there. Church in London, then a reception at the Travellers' Club. At Easter.'

Marcus sat up in his chair. 'But, Soph, that's not what you want at all. You wanted the Betterton arboretum at midsummer. And for it to be all simple and pretty. You've been going on about it since you were fifteen.'

'Yeah, I know I have,' Sophie said a little grumpily. 'But sometimes you have to compromise.'

'Yes, but you've given up on everything you wanted. Don't do that, Soph. It's your day, you know.'

'Yeah, but . . . Olly's paying. And it will be amazing. There's going to be a photographer from *Tatler* at the reception.'

Marcus frowned. 'Do you really want to be in *Tatler*? I mean, I know it was part of your dream wedding, but . . .'

'*Your* wedding was.'

'Only because Lainey's mother insisted. I felt like a complete prat and Lainey was mortified.'

'Oh, I think she quite liked it really.'

'No, she didn't.' Marcus reflected for a moment. 'Well, maybe she did. But listen, Sophie. Are you sure you want to go through with this?'

'Of course I am,' Sophie retorted indignantly.

'Are you *really* sure? I just wonder if you're more in love with the idea of a wedding than you are with Olly.'

'That's not true!' Sophie's face burned. She'd come round to celebrate her successful screen test, not to have Marcus have a go at her.

'Do you really love Olly?'

'Why? What's wrong with him?'

'Nothing. I think he's a good bloke. But I'm just not entirely sure you're crazy about him.'

'Marcus, you only met him that one time, when you and Lainey were having a row. And being crazy about someone doesn't get you anywhere. I was crazy about Andy in the beginning, but by the end we were just making each other miserable. I'm looking for something longer term. Olly and I are good friends.'

'And he's rich,' Marcus said softly.

'Excuse me?'

'You heard me.'

'What, and you're not? God, Marcus, I can't believe you of all people are going on about how much money Olly has.'

'My situation is irrelevant. But I know how you feel about money, Soph. It's not a crime. We all want more than we have. But I don't think you should marry someone just

407

for that reason.' He sat back in his chair. 'I mean, like I said, I don't think Lainey married me for my salary, but it has created certain expectations.'

'This is not about money. I told you it's about being very . . . fond of someone and having a good friendship and knowing we can build on that.'

'And if Olly jacked in his job and you had to live in a shack in the French countryside, that would be cool?'

'Of course, it would!' Sophie exclaimed. Or would it? She decided to revisit that question later. 'Anyway, how can I answer that when it's totally hypothetical? Marcus, you're depressing me. I've thought all this through.'

'Sorry,' Marcus said. 'I just want you to get this right. Because being married is bloody tough.' He laughed ruefully. 'As you can see.'

'I know! And I will get it right. Now please, no more lecturing on the day of my screen test. I'm all excited about my new career.'

'A new career that Olly doesn't want you to have.'

'Hey,' said Sophie, patting Marcus's hand. 'Hey, hey, it's really not that drastic. Olly will come round. Honestly. And Lainey will too. She'll get a load out of her system in Uruguay and when she gets back you need to sit down and talk about how you both need to make more of an effort to have a bit more one-on-one time.'

'I'm sure you're right.' Marcus's phone started ringing. 'Blast. It's the office. I told them I'd be available in case of emergency. I'm going to have to take it. Do you mind?'

'No, no. Go ahead. I'll see myself out.'

They blew each other kisses, but Marcus was already distracted, shouting orders down the phone. Sophie let herself out of the front door and headed up the road towards Kensington Church Street. She tried to recapture the afternoon's early sparkle, but it had vanished. Marcus and Lainey in trouble already. Perhaps they could work it out, but somehow she knew in the pit of her stomach that it was always going to be a struggle for her dependable, kind stepbrother to keep the attention of his sexy, thrill-seeking wife. Would Lainey really want more one-on-one time?

And then she thought of herself and Olly. She couldn't swear to exactly loving the evenings spent with his friends. And her friends – who were a much more disparate bunch – didn't seem to impinge on them as a couple. Could she really face a life of Tory Party dinners? But then what was the alternative? Gruesome one-night stands with other Julians? Nights in Soho House pretending to be fascinated by your girlfriends' company while eyeing up some man in the corner? Online dating? All Bar One? Not to mention no money, and the money *was* nice. Was it so wrong to admit that? It wasn't as if Olly was like Marcus, tied to a job he hated to keep his woman happy. Olly loved his work.

No, Sophie was doing the right thing. The lesson that she'd learned from Marcus and Lainey was that no relationship worked without making adjustments. Both she and Olly would just have to give a little. Reassured, she pushed open the door to the fishmonger's at Kensington Place to treat herself to something lovely for tonight's solo dinner, which she was so looking forward to.

49

It was Wednesday evening, Natasha, with four more days until she had to get back to work, was curled up in a dressing gown, a plate of takeaway Thai in front of her, talking to Andy who'd dropped in to see how she was getting on.

'I feel fine,' she was assuring him. 'Still a little tired, but hey.' She wasn't going to confide her biggest worry, that the doctor had said she might have difficulties conceiving from now on and if she wanted children she should get on with it 'sooner rather than later'. The pregnancy had made her realize she did want them, far, far more than she had ever known, but still not as much as she wanted Alastair, who was in Thailand with the mysterious Ant.

But the phone was ringing now. Maybe he was thinking of her. 'Excuse me a second,' she said and picked it up. 'Hello?'

'Natasha?' A reedy, cross voice.

'Oh, hi, Lesley. How are you?'

'Not bad, I suppose. Kids driving me mad, but then I wouldn't be without them. They're worth more in the end than designer clothes and fancy cars. Anyway, just calling on Amanda's behalf. You've been a naughty girl and you haven't got back to her about the wedding. I told her you could be ditsy but she's a bit hurt. You could have been more thoughtful, you know.'

'God, Lesley. I'm sorry. I've been ill. It completely slipped my mind.'

'Typical,' sniffed Lesley, without enquiring after her welfare. 'Well, it's the weekend after this, so is it a yes or a no?'

The prospect of witnessing the first of the many men who'd broken her heart getting married was not an appealing one, but what was the alternative? Hurt Amanda's feelings? Have everyone talking about how Natasha still hadn't got over Steven?

'It's a yes, of course.'

'Hmmm. And what about that Alastair, then? Is he going to come?'

Natasha remembered that conversation they'd had. It seemed like months ago. 'Um, no. No, he can't, unfortunately. He's away right now.'

'Right,' Lesley said knowingly, then over her shoulder: 'He's not coming, Mum. Too busy for *us*.'

'Lesley, it's not like that,' Natasha cried, but Lesley said, 'Mum wants a word.'

'Hello, angel. So you are coming to the wedding. But not with that Alastair. What a shame.'

'He's away, Mum.'

'I heard that Sophie's getting married, to some chap with a terribly exotic-sounding name. You'll have to give me her address so I can send her a congratulations card. Will the wedding be in Betterton?'

'I don't think they've decided yet. And I don't know her new address. Send the card to the *Daily Post*.'

'I'll do that.' Mum sighed wistfully. 'By the way, I've been reading such a good book. By Jeanette Winterson.

Oranges Are Not the Only Fruit. Have you read it?'

'Years ago,' said Natasha. 'Look, Mum, I have to go now. I have someone here. But I'll see you at the wedding. Love to Dad.' She hung up and turned to Andy. 'Bugger.'

'What's that all about?'

'My first love's getting married a week on Saturday. And they expected me to bring Alastair, but he wouldn't come, so I'm going to have to go alone like Miss Havisham. Everyone's going to be expecting me to jump out and shout: "Don't do it, he's mine."' Once Natasha would never have confided such a dilemma, but somehow the last week or so had made her care less about losing face.

'W-well, you'd never do that.'

'Perhaps I should. Might liven things up.'

Andy cleared his throat. 'Well, if you n-need a date, I could always come with you.'

She stared at him. 'Andy, I wasn't hinting. You'd absolutely hate it. I mean, thanks for the offer, but don't worry. I can cope.'

'A week on Saturday. I'm not working then. If it helps you I'll come.'

'But you're not my boyfriend, Andy.' It was obvious, but she had to say it.

Their eyes met for an unusually long time. 'I k-know,' he said finally. 'We're just friends. But I'd like to help you out. Seeing as Alastair won't.'

'Alastair's in Thailand. On a lads' holiday.'

'Is he? And he didn't think you might want a break somewhere?'

'Andy, he only thinks I've had flu. He doesn't know what really happened.'

'No. I guess he doesn't.'

Ever since the screen test, Sophie's nerves had felt like they were being strummed by a heavy-metal guitarist. Her initial confidence had long gone, as five days had passed and Peter hadn't got back to her.

At work, she stared at her phone, willing it to ring. It stared back obstinately like Clint Eastwood. Strong and silent. Not giving a damn about her pain. Laughing at her behind its red plastic casing. She never thought she'd feel like this about a job. This was how you felt in the early days of a love affair. Not that she'd ever felt like this about Olly. But then he always called when he said he would.

'Ring me, you motherfucker,' she muttered under her breath. It made her feel better, but the silence persisted. A moment later, she prayed, 'Please ring, please. If it happens in the next five minutes, I promise I'll start going to church. I'll give ten per cent of my salary to Oxfam. I'll start caring about the environment.' She glanced at Yvette, who was filling their corner with the pungent smell of orange nail varnish. 'I'll even be nice to Yvette. No, I will, I'll have lunch with her tomorrow. Or sometime this week. That's a one-time offer, God. Act now.'

She got up. She'd go and have a ciggie; that would teach it. 'Coming to the smoking room, Fay?'

'Too right I am!' Fay bounded to her feet. 'We'll just be a sec, Yvette.'

They were walking away from the desk when she heard it. Dring, dring. Dring, dring. 'Oh! I just have to get that!'

413

'Why? It'll just be some TV press officer. Yvette'll pick it up.'

'No, no, it could be important.' Sophie dashed back across the room to see Yvette press the hash key to pick up her line remotely.

'She's not at her desk at the moment.'

'No, no, I am! I'm back! It's cool!'

'Oh. Well then, she is. And she seems very keen to talk to you.' She tapped at the dial with a pencil, transferring the call back. 'It's Olly.'

'Oh. Hello.'

'I hear you're very keen to talk to me,' Olly said happily.

'I'm always keen to talk to you. You know that.'

'Just calling with the weekend's arrangements. The Jarvises have invited us to Saturday lunch. And then on Sunday it's down to the country to see the Patersons.'

'OK, OK, fine,' she said breathlessly as Yvette picked up her phone again.

'Hello? Hello, yes, she's on the other line. Can I help?'

'I'll get it,' Sophie almost screamed.

'Darling! What is it?' Olly said.

'Sorry, sorry. I have to go. It's urgent. Tape we desperately need biked over. See you later.' She slammed the phone down. 'You can transfer it, Yvette!'

'Oh sorry,' Yvette said. 'He's gone now. He said he'd call back though.' She went back to painting her nails, while Sophie stared at her in fury.

But actually Peter called back two minutes later. It was good news and it was bad news.

'The good news is we absolutely loved you, the bad news is at the moment it's looking very unlikely the programme will ever get commissioned at all. We'll have to keep you posted. But the other thing you might think of as good news is we were all very impressed by how much you obviously know about food and we were wondering if you might be interested in a researcher's post that's coming up for our cookery shows.'

'Oh my God, that sounds amazing.'

'The pay's not great but it does mean that if and when another presenter's job comes up you'd already be in the building, which would make life easier for everyone. Of course you'd have to have an interview, but it would be a bit of a formality. I'll let you know when we have a date for that, but in the meantime you might want to watch as many cookery programmes as possible. You had some good ideas already, but you want to get them perfect.'

'I'll do that,' she said and then slowly hung up, her heart hammering with excitement. For a millisecond, she considered calling Olly, but then dismissed it. After all, couples couldn't share everything.

50

'You really don't have to do this, you know,' Natasha said as a week on Saturday she and Andy sat in traffic on the M25 four junctions from the Betterton turn-off. 'I can let you out at the next service station and you can get a taxi back to London.'

'Natasha,' said Andy, who was looking unusually smart in the suit he'd worn to Lainey and Marcus's wedding, 'it's OK. I want to come.'

'*Want* to come?'

'Well, you know. I'm happy to. It's getting you out of a hole. And it could be a laugh.'

'Ooh, I so sincerely doubt that. Maybe if you don't laugh you'll cry.' The traffic, having passed the Mini that had rammed into the back of a lorry, suddenly started to move. 'Uh-oh,' Natasha said. 'Half an hour and we'll be there.'

Her parents' house was in chaos. Paige was running around in a vest and knickers, her face covered in chocolate mousse. Vienna, in a mint-green dress, was slouched in the hallway like a beggar, playing on a Gameboy. Mum was in the kitchen in a dressing gown, her hair in curlers, buttering sandwiches. Lesley, in a petticoat, was ironing a dress.

'Hi, everyone!'

'Darling,' Mum whirled round, then her hand flew to her head as she spotted Andy. 'Oh!'

'Mum, this is Andy Walters. Andy, this is my mum Helen and my sister Lesley.'

Natasha spotted the lightning look that flashed between them.

'Oh. Hello,' said Lesley. 'Sorry about the state of undress.' She stuck out a hand, looking Andy up and down like a customs man surveying passengers at Bogotá airport. 'At least you're in good time. We were placing bets on whether you would or not.' She smiled conspiratorially at Andy. 'My little sister. Can be a bit scatty, you know.'

'Sure.' Andy smiled.

'Tashie,' cried a booming voice. Natasha turned round. Amanda in cyclamen pink, bearing a glass of white wine. 'You made it, love. Well done.'

'How are you, Amanda?' Natasha said, kissing her. 'You must be so excited.'

'Oh, so excited. I've come over here to take a bit of time out, Eve's friends are running around all over the place. Of course, I'm sad too. This is my little boy I'm losing. You must feel it too, of course . . .'

'Um, well, Steven and I went out quite a while ago.' Natasha glanced at Andy, who looked as if he was desperately trying not to laugh. 'I'm just happy for him. And the bride, of course. Anyway, Amanda, this is my . . . friend, Andy Walters.'

'L-lovely to meet you, Amanda. It's an honour to be here.'

'Oh.' Amanda touched her hat, astonishment all over her face. 'Oh, lovely to meet you too, Andy. We weren't sure if you were going to make it or not.'

'It can be very difficult with my job. I'm often away at short notice.'

'Natasha said. You're a writer, aren't you?'

'No, a photographer.'

'Oh, I knew it was something arty-farty. Well, how lovely. Maybe you can take some piccies today. Wouldn't that be fun?' She touched Natasha on the arm. 'I know Steven's dying to see you. He and Eve have bought a lovely house in Sutton now, you know. Anyway, I'll see you all later, just wanted to check in.'

'See you later,' they chorused as Amanda headed out of the door.

'God, I bet she's relieved,' said Lesley with a significant look at Andy.

'Lesley!' Mum sighed. She turned to Natasha. 'Darling, you do look lovely. Where's that dress from? It's so beautiful. You're going to upstage Eve if you don't watch out.'

'Um, Top Shop,' Natasha lied, feeling Lesley's beady eye upon her.

'Really? And it's pure silk. Amazing the quality there these days. We must check it out sometime soon, Lesley.'

'Yes, well, I think a lot more's available in the *London* branches than out here in the sticks,' Lesley snapped.

'Is Dad around somewhere?' Natasha asked hastily.

'In the den. Watching golf.'

'I'd better say hello,' Natasha said. 'You don't have to come, Andy. Stay here and have a cup of tea.'

But just then Dad appeared in the doorway. 'Tashie!' he yelled, opening his arms wide. 'How are you, darling? Why haven't you been to see your old dad in so long? Don't you love me any more?'

Natasha hugged him, feeling a tightening in her throat. Her parents were so lovely. Why didn't she see more of them? But she knew. It was because she was ashamed that her personal life couldn't meet their ridiculously high standards, especially after recent events. God, if Mum and Dad knew what she had been through recently they would die – well, actually they wouldn't die, they would suffocate her in love and understanding – and once again Natasha didn't think she could bear that.

'And who's this?' Dad asked, turning to Andy.

'Andy Walters, Dad. My *friend*.' Ought she to say Sophie's ex? No, that would only complicate things. And Dad was pumping Andy's hand, exclaiming how nice it was to meet him and had Andy been watching the golf and, somewhat to her surprise, Andy was responding with a big smile and none of the customary awkwardness.

Again to her surprise, the wedding turned out to be not an ordeal but a giggle. To her delight, Steven had changed immeasurably in the seven years or so since Natasha had last seen him, developing a noticeable paunch and blood-hound bags under his eyes. At a party, she wouldn't have glanced at him twice.

'And you broke your heart over him?' whispered Andy as they watched him standing awkwardly at the altar.

'It was a long time ago,' Natasha hissed back.

'But these things take years to heal. Are you sure you can cope?'

'Well, I may start to get a bit emotional during the "Do you know any reason why this wedding should not take place . . ." bit. So have the chloroform handy.'

They giggled and Lesley shot them a suspicious look. Natasha thought of Alastair. He would have laughed at all this too, but he was in Thailand and even if he hadn't been, he wouldn't have come so that was that. Thank God for Andy, stepping in when he did.

She looked sideways at him, and he looked back. As she caught his eye, she felt a little shiver in her tummy. Obviously gratitude. For pulling her out of a sticky situation. Nothing more. How could it possibly be? This was *Andy*, her best friend's ex and as untouchable as a leper.

The reception was a laugh too. The speeches were interminable, the food forgettable and the band was dire.

'At least you're not going to make me dance,' Andy said as the lovely lady singer's version of 'Black Velvet' shook the room. 'Sophie was always on and on at me.'

'No, you're safe there. I'd rather gnaw through my own elbow than make a fool of myself on the dance floor. I have no natural rhythm.' Natasha smiled at the sight of Mum getting on down with Amanda, waving their hands in the air like windscreen wipers. Dad was nowhere to be seen, no doubt having slipped home to watch more golf.

'Hey, Natasha.' It was Steven, very pink in the face and a little sweaty. 'Good to see you.'

'Steven. Congratulations. Your bride is beautiful. I know you're going to be very happy.'

'I think she's the right girl for me,' he said. He glanced at Andy. 'And you are . . . ?'

'Oh, this is my friend Andy Walters.'

They shook hands cagily, sizing each other up. 'Congratulations,' Andy said. 'It's been a fantastic day.'

'Well, you never know,' Steven said. 'Might be you two next. Eh, Natasha?'

'Y-you never know,' Andy agreed charmingly.

'You'll have to come down to Sutton sometime for a barbecue. We've bagged ourselves a bit of a bargain. Course the loft needs ripping out and the garden's just wasteland at the moment, but it's nice to have a project.'

'Oh, it is,' Andy agreed, while Natasha stood there, trying not to laugh, wondering what had become of Steven's Che Guevara posters and his Sisters of Mercy albums.

They managed to get out just after 6 p.m. 'Thank God it isn't one of those all-night bashes. I really couldn't have subjected you to that,' Natasha said. 'Mum! Mum! We're off now. See you soon.'

'Oh angel, are you leaving so early? We were all going to go back to ours for a nice cuppa and a post-mortem.'

'No, we have to go. I've got work in the morning.'

'On a Sunday? Angel, you never stop. Andy, you tell her to take it easy. She can be a bit of a workaholic, you know.'

'Bad idea,' Andy said solemnly. 'She should calm down.' He bent down and kissed her. 'Lovely to meet you, Mrs Green. I hope I'll be seeing you again.'

Mum looked as if she'd just been asked out by George Clooney. 'Oh yes, I certainly do hope so. It's been very, very nice to meet you too, Andrew.' She lowered her voice, but in her inebriated state it was still quite audible. 'We have been so worried about Natasha, we even thought she might be a . . . *you know*. I mean, not that we would have minded at all as I've always tried to make clear to her, but even in this day and age I think it just makes life easier if you're . . . you know . . . *normal*.'

'N-Natasha's normal,' Andy said, patting her on the shoulder while her daughter looked on mortified. 'I can promise you that.'

'I can't believe she said that!' Natasha cried as they crawled in the other direction round the M25.

'Oh, y-you know what mums are like. Full of silly ideas.'

'Thinking I was a lesbian. All those remarks about k. d. lang make sense now. God, it shows what kind of place Betterton is! If you have a job and you're not married by twenty-five, you're obviously gay.' She should have been furious, but instead she started to laugh. So did Andy.

'I l-liked your mum,' he said. 'She was very cosy. In fact, I liked your whole set-up. It was much more ordinary than I'd have expected.'

'What do you mean "ordinary"?'

'Well, you know, Natasha. You can come across as superwoman. But you come from an ordinary house and your family bicker at each other, and your mum gets pissed and in a flap. It just makes you more human, somehow.'

'Do I not seem human?'

'You do. Of course you do. Just a little too perfect, sometimes. Although I've seen another side to you in the past few weeks. But anyway, your family's lovely. Really lovely. And it's so sweet the way your mum boasts about you.'

'Does she boast about me?' Natasha asked, surprised, again thinking Andy was saying a lot of things which needed to be filed away and then looked at again later.

'God, yes. I could hear her talking to Eve's mum. "My daughter's a very important executive, you know. Jets all over the world. Lives in a wonderful designer apartment in central London." She was loving it.'

Natasha took this in. 'Still, you shouldn't have told her you'd love to come back and see her. You'll have got her hopes up.'

'W-well, maybe I will.'

An odd silence fell.

It was time to say what had been crouching on her mind. 'You know, I didn't tell Sophie you were coming today.'

'Oh yeah? Why not?'

'Well, I thought she might find it a bit weird. You know, being her ex and all that.'

'You and I were friends first,' Andy said casually.

'I know. But . . .'

'And she's marrying Olly G-M.'

'Are you sure you're not just hanging out with me to get back at her?' Natasha had meant to say this in a casual way but it came out in a rush. She stared straight ahead at the road, thanking the Lord it was getting dark.

'God, no!' Andy laughed. 'Tash, I know this is going to sound callous but I now realize Sophie leaving was the best thing that ever happened to me. I was upset she got engaged to someone else so quickly, but talking to her on the phone, thinking it through, I feel like a cloud that had been following me around has vanished.'

Natasha frowned. It didn't seem right to refer to her friend as a cloud. Andy saw her face. 'It wasn't Sophie's fault, it was both of ours,' he said rapidly. 'We weren't happy and we weren't right for each other any more. Probably not ever. Then she lied to me about the baby, which was such a Sophie thing to do, and from then I just knew we'd grown so far apart, we were never going to find a way back.'

'And you're not jealous about her and Olly?'

'No, not jealous. I wonder if she's making a mistake, but that's her lookout. How's it going with you and Alastair by the way?'

She noticed the way he linked making a mistake with Alastair. 'It's going fine,' she said firmly. 'How's work?'

'Interesting,' he said slowly. 'I've been talking to *News Magazine*. They've got a staff job coming up in Cairo and they've offered it to me. Dodgy part of the world right now, but some fascinating opportunities. I need to think it through a bit more, but I think I'll take it.'

'Oh, right,' Natasha said after only the briefest pause. 'Yes, yes, I can see that would be an amazing opportunity. Well, well done you.'

'You'd have to come and v-visit me,' Andy said with a sideways glance.

'I'd love to. I've never been to Egypt.' And the rest of the way home, they avoided any more awkward conversations in favour of an animated discussion about Middle-Eastern politics.

51

Having tentatively agreed on Easter and St Margaret's, Olly wanted to talk about the wedding list. 'People keep asking me where we have ours,' he explained to Sophie over Sunday dinner at home, after a weekend whirl of drinks parties, lunches and a visit to the opera. 'I know the invitations haven't gone out yet, but it's the done thing to send presents months in advance these days, you know. So I say Harrods. I mean, you can't go wrong with that, can you?'

Harrods. Once Sophie's dream. But Olly saying it made her feel perversely mutinous. 'Oh no, not Harrods. It's far too posh. None of my friends could afford it.'

'Darling, I'm sure they could. Natasha is doing very well for herself. And Marcus and Lainey. And not everything on the list has to be expensive.'

'It's just . . . Harrods. It sounds so snobby. Can't we go for something a bit more down-to-earth like John Lewis? Or groovy, like the Conran Shop? That's where Marcus and Lainey had their list.'

'Darling, I hardly think that would be giving out the right impression. I really think it should be Harrods. The Ravenswoods had their list there.'

'We don't have to do what all your friends do,' Sophie snapped. She decided to broach another subject, one which she'd been putting off for days. 'Olly, what would you think if I got a new job? *Not* television presenting, but maybe doing something in television, like researching?'

'What would you want to do that for?'

'Well, for a change. It's got to be more fun than organizing couriers to deliver video tapes.'

'But that would be a job in London,' he protested. 'And you know how I feel about moving to the country.'

'And you know I think I'm not quite ready for that,' she said mildly. She glanced at her watch. It was nearly ten. There was a new cookery show on Living. She picked up the remote.

'Oh, is it news time already?'

'Well, actually, I really want to check out this cookery programme.'

'Cookery programme?' He sounded like Lady Bracknell shouting '*A handbag!*' 'But it's the news.'

'But you can watch the twenty-four-hour news. I'd really like to see this.'

'You know it has to be the ten o'clock news. BBC.' He picked up the remote and turned on the television, then sat there glowering.

'OK. I'll go and watch TV in the bedroom.'

'Oh, don't do that,' he whined. 'You know I like you here. Next to me.' He patted the sofa invitingly. 'Come.'

Sophie came. After all, relationships were about give and take. She wasn't going to be like Mum, walking out every time there was a hitch, or Marcus and Lainey with their power struggles. She *had* to stay and let the rough times be cancelled out by the smooth.

*

But the next night she was still relieved to be granted a chink of freedom.

'I've got a dinner with some people from the Party. No wives I'm afraid, darling. Do you mind terribly? You'll probably enjoy a night at home with your wedding magazines.'

'Yes, I probably would,' she said, simultaneously tapping out an email to Fay that read: *What u doing tonight?*

They started in the Dog and Duck at 6.17 p.m. 'A double vodka and slimline,' Sophie told the barman. 'And the same for my friend.'

Gradually, the pub filled up with colleagues. Norris from news, Liam from foreign, even Keith Livingston, who Sophie couldn't help noticing had a rather nice, tight bum.

'Have to buy you two ladies a drink,' he said. As they stood propped at the bar, he said to Sophie: 'Surprised you aren't embarrassed to be seen mixing with the hoi polloi any more.'

'What are you talking about?' Sophie laughed, although she knew.

'The future Mrs Oliver Garcia-Mundoz. You can't slum it in the local with the rest of us hacks. You're a future Prime Minister's wife. Plus the fiancée of an about-to-be best-selling author. Have you read his book? It sounds really interesting.'

'Of course I've read it,' she lied, lighting her eighth cigarette of the evening.

By closing time, she'd had fifteen more, as well as five vodkas and a packet of cheese and onion crisps.

'How about we all go for a Chinese?' said Norris, who

couldn't believe he was getting to spend a whole evening with Sophie Matthewson.

'Yeah, a Chinese!' Fay cried.

'I might slip off now,' said Liam. 'Gotta meet Amy.'

'Amy?'

'My girlfriend.'

'Ah, don't do that,' Fay yelled. 'Sophie's giving her fiancé the slip tonight. It's like an unofficial stag and hen night. Come on!'

'OK, then.' Liam smiled the satisfied look of someone who knew they were certainly going to pull.

So Sophie, Fay, Norris, Liam and Keith ended up having a very nasty Chinese on the Bayswater Road, where Sophie ate about twenty prawn crackers and then had no room for the chow mein and lemon chicken. Instead, she had a couple of beers. She hadn't been this drunk in ages and couldn't take in much of the silly work banter. Her head felt like a disco ball, full of flashing lights.

'Isn't young Olly worried about where you are?' Keith said.

Shit. Olly. She'd completely forgotten about him.

'He's cool,' she said, as she pulled her mobile out from the bottom of her bag. Oh bollocks. Nineteen missed calls drowned out by the muzak.

She put the phone to her ear. Most of them were her voicemail calling her back but there were five messages wanting to know where she had got to.

'Darling,' said the last one. 'This is really most unlike you. I'm home now. It's eleven-thirty and you still haven't called. I'm starting to get worried.' He did sound very anxious. Guilt tugged at her heart. ''Scuse me.'

In the loo, she called him. He picked up on the first ring. 'Darling, where have you been?'

'Just having a Chinese with some of the gang from work.' She tried to enunciate slowly and clearly.

'You're drunk.'

'Don't be silly. I've just had a couple.'

'So when will you be back? It's late you know and I've got a big day tomorrow.'

'You don't need to wait up for me.' Sophie felt like someone was building a brick wall all around her.

'But I worry. I can't get to sleep until I know you're safe.'

'Olly, don't worry. Listen, I'll go back to Veronica's tonight. I won't disturb you.' She fished around for an excuse. 'I'm just trying to cheer Caroline up, you see. She had a nightmare date last night and she's all upset, banging on about why can't she meet a lovely man.' Her voice softened. 'Like I have.'

It did the trick. 'OK darling. Go back to Veronica's. I'll miss you though.'

'Me too. But I'll make it up to you tomorrow.' Why was it that when Sophie said things like that she felt as if she was reading from a play script? Her battery bleeped. It was almost gone. Good thing she'd got that call in on time.

'So where to now?' Fay said when she got back to the table.

She smiled. 'Oh, home, I think.'

'Bollocks. The night is young. We need a boogie.'

Sophie noted a weary look pass over Norris's face, quickly to be replaced with one of grim determination.

Norris hadn't been dancing in seven years, not since his youngest was born, although even in the old days he'd never been much of a mover. But he wasn't going to pass up a chance like this. 'How about Funky Buddha?' he said. He'd read about it in the 3 a.m. column.

'Funky Buddha it is!' Fay cried.

'I've gotta go,' said Liam, who'd been looking increasingly uncomfortable. 'Otherwise my missus is going to be waiting for me with a rolling pin.'

So he disappeared, but the rest of them piled in another cab and half an hour later found themselves in a basement just off Piccadilly where dozens of girls with bright orange skin in miniskirts were gyrating to the Black Eyed Peas.

'We're the oldest people here by about twenty years,' Sophie giggled.

'It's great, isn't it?' Keith agreed. He'd had a word with some mean-looking guy in black who had picked up a red velvet rope and ushered them behind it, to a little table where they sat surrounded by what looked like arms dealers and their teenage concubines.

'Bottle of Moët,' Norris shouted to the waiter.

'Norris! Do you know what that'll cost?'

'I'll expense it. Put it down as researching a story about the London club scene.'

They all danced – with varying degrees of skill – until the magic 3 a.m.

'What school do you go to?' various Prince Harry clones asked Sophie. It turned out they were all on holiday from Stowe or Eton.

'I'm at Cheltenham Ladies' College,' she told them all

before giving out several made-up phone numbers. *I should have done more of this,* she thought regretfully. *I should have spent every night in my twenties out on the town. Why did I throw away my youth baking apple crumbles and trying to be a wife? And now I will be a wife and there's no way Olly will let me do this kind of thing.*

Suddenly there was a tap on her shoulder. She looked round to see a tall, skinny man with a roundish face and a thick mop of brown hair. He looked vaguely familiar. And very attractive.

'Excuse me, but are you Sophie?'

'That's right. And . . . I'm sorry?'

'Dom. I work with Natasha.'

'Oh, that's right!' she exclaimed. She'd met him a couple of times when she'd passed by Tash's office. Lechy Dom, as they always referred to him. But luckily she wasn't quite drunk enough to forget her manners entirely. 'How are you?'

'Fine. I was just out with some friends and I saw you. I hear you're getting married.'

Automatically, Sophie slipped her left hand behind her back. 'Yes, well, that's the plan,' she said.

'I'm sorry to hear that,' Dom said with a smile. And a warm feeling spread all over Sophie, as if she had just downed a tumbler of Amaretto.

'Oh, well,' she managed to say. 'It hasn't happened yet. In fact, this is sort of my unofficial hen night. Me and a few mates from the office.'

'Well, in that case I'd better get you a drink,' he said. Was it her imagination or did he seem to be talking a little dreamily too?

431

'I'd love a glass of white wine.'

'Who's that?' Fay asked, slipping her arm around Sophie's waist as Dom headed towards the bar.

'Someone who works with my friend Natasha.' Sophie could feel herself flushing.

'Well, he's got the hots for you, girl. Hubba hubba!'

'Don't be silly. Have a drink with us.'

'I don't think so. I'm going to leave you two lovebirds alone.'

'Fay! I'm an engaged woman.'

'So you say,' she said, with a smile. 'Later!'

Dom returned carrying two glasses of wine and they found themselves a table to sit at. Over the music, they laughed at the footballers out on the pull and the girls whose handkerchief tops strained over their fake boobs. It was as if they'd known each other for ages. *Like how it used to be with me and Olly*, Sophie thought with a pang. Except she had never felt the faintest urge to stroke Olly's face, to wrap herself around him.

The conversation moved on to more personal topics. Sophie found out that Dom was brought up in the wilds of Northumberland, that he had two sisters and he'd been a slow starter, who hadn't lost his virginity until he was nineteen. She told him about Betterton and Mum's three husbands and infinite lovers and Floyd, the pony John had given her for her thirteenth birthday, whom she'd had to abandon when Mum ran off with Jimmy. It was the kind of conversation you would never have with a passing acquaintance, but only with someone you wanted to know a lot, lot better.

Someone you wanted to snog.

No, she thought. I'm engaged. To Olly. Nice Olly. Rich Olly. Doting Olly. Future Prime Minister Olly. I can't get off with Dom serial shagger. Dom who is turning out to be so funny and interesting and whom I'd have shot my pony for the chance of kissing.

'I think I'm a bit drunk,' she said, hoping the banality of the comment would kill the moment.

'Me too,' Dom replied.

'But you're used to nights like this.'

'What do you mean?'

'Tash told me. You're out every night on the pull. A toxic bachelor.'

'Tash said that, did she?' Dom seemed amused rather than pissed off. 'Well, she's hardly one to talk about toxic bachelors.'

'Alastair?'

'Who else? He's left emotional bombsites all over London and beyond. And Tash is obsessed with him although she won't admit it. I hate to see what's become of her. She used to be such a feisty girl but now she's a shadow of what she was. Everyone's talking about it at work. It's horrible. Natasha thinks their affair's a secret but she's becoming a laughing stock.'

Sophie felt queasy and not just from the booze. Just then the lights came on, revealing a roomful of mascara-streaked faces and sweaty bodies.

Fay and Norris bounded over. 'Where to now?' he asked. He had had such a good time, he was never going back to Blackheath; he was getting a divorce and buying a little flat in Soho that would be his love nest.

'Turnmills,' yelled Fay, who had mysteriously developed

a faint white moustache after one of her trips to the loo.

'No,' Sophie said with an enormous effort of will. 'I'm going home.'

'Which direction is that?' Dom asked.

'Kensington. Er, no. Camden.'

'I'm in Gospel Oak. We can share a cab.'

'Oh, very fortunate,' Fay yelled, then sniggered as Sophie glared at her.

Fay and Norris climbed in a minicab going to Turnmills. Keith took another to Chiswick. Dom and Sophie took a third, going north.

'God, that was fun,' Sophie breathed, glowing with the freedom of dancing, booze – having fun.

'We'll feel terrible in the morning,' Dom said happily.

She edged across the cab so their knees were brushing. 'Funny I never got to know you before,' she breathed.

'I think Natasha wanted to keep us apart,' Dom said.

Sophie jerked backwards. 'Why? She's not interested in you, is she?'

He laughed. 'Oh God, no. Hardly. But she knew how much I fancied you and you were always attached.'

'I still am,' she said. She looked at her rock. Dom looked at it too.

'Whereabouts in Camden?' said the driver.

'Second set of lights, turn right.' She turned back to Dom and smiled in what she hoped was a seductive way. 'Would you like to come up for a coffee?'

'Um, no thanks, Sophie. It's very late.'

'Oh. Just here on the right, please. Are you sure?' She leaned over and kissed him lingeringly on the cheek.

'Another time,' Dom said, pushing her away. 'You're drunk. And you're engaged.'

Humiliated, she stumbled out of the cab, fumbling in her bag for the keys she hadn't used in weeks. Then she saw him standing on the doorstep.

'What time do you call this?'

She stumbled slightly, peering at her Georg Jensen. 'It's ten to four. But Olly—'

'I kept calling you. You lied to me about whom you were with. You said you were with Caroline. But I rang her when you didn't answer and she said she was having an early night.'

'Olly!' She leaned against the railings. 'Oof.'

'You can't do this to me, Sophie. You're my fiancée.' His face was taut. She'd never seen him like this before.

'I was just . . . out with Fay. Having fun.' She glanced guiltily over her shoulder, but Dom's taxi had gone.

'Well, the fun's over now.' Sophie realized with a start that a car was waiting, its engine purring. 'You're coming home with me.' He took her by the elbow and led her to the car. Sophie was too drunk and too tired to argue. She felt oddly calm, as if she were sitting on a planet high above, watching this happen to someone else.

'I'm sorry,' she said.

'Yes,' said Olly gravely as the car drove off. 'So am I.'

52

The wedding had given Natasha plenty to think about. Taking Andy home had made everything fall into a different pattern. Her mum may have thought she was a lesbian, but she still boasted about her – it didn't matter that she wasn't happily married and making jam in a cottage somewhere. And the perfection she'd worked so hard for hadn't drawn people to her, it had frightened them away. And her time with Andy had been so easy and relaxed with none of the fear that permeated her every exchange with Alastair. Before, of course, she'd always been nervous around Andy because she was so besotted by him, but now they were just friends she could be herself and it felt good.

And funnily, the fact that Alastair was in Thailand and she'd not heard a word from him bothered her far less than it should have done. Of course, his existence still dominated her life like an electronic billboard in Piccadilly Circus, but now she could co-exist with it, rather than being dazzled. She knew he would be just back from Thailand, but the realization left her oddly untroubled. When he wanted to ring, he'd ring. That was the way their relationship worked; she'd encouraged it to go that way, so why worry? Sitting in the office she felt an odd benevolence, a feeling that everything in the universe was in its proper place. It helped, of course, that she was physically feeling much stronger than she had in weeks, probably – she admitted ruefully to herself – because she was forcing herself to eat proper meals rather than subsisting on lettuce leaves and sushi.

Dom, on the other hand, was in the strangest mood this morning: weirdly subdued and unusually snappy.

'You all right?' Natasha asked after he had bitten her head off when she asked if he had a document she needed.

'I'm fine,' he growled, picking up a pile of magazines that had just been delivered and starting to flick through a copy of *Hello!* Natasha looked at him and shrugged.

'Anything in there?' she tried. 'What's the latest on Beckham?'

'He says everything's great and denies all the rumours.' Dom carried on flicking, then suddenly his face changed.

'What is it?' Natasha asked, only mildly curious.

'Nothing.' He turned another page, but he was frowning. She shrugged and pressed *send* on an email.

'Can I see that after you?'

'I wouldn't bother, there's really nothing in it.' He picked up *Heat* and chucked it over. 'Why don't you read this?' He stood up, holding *Hello!* to his chest like a cache of uranium. 'I've got a lunch now. See you around three.'

'Leave the magazine.'

'No, I want to read it in the cab.'

Why was he being so weird? Natasha's curiosity was piqued now. She picked up her phone. 'Antoinette? Is there a spare copy of *Hello!* in Barney's office? Could I possibly borrow it for a minute? Thanks.'

Antoinette brought it down. There was no clue on the

cover as to what Dom was getting all weirdy about. She began flicking. J-Lo; some minor European royal who was getting married; Anastacia. Claudia Schiffer and her babies; Ben Affleck; Zara Phillips modelling some dresses that made her look like a drag queen and . . .

Oh. 'Gorgeous Aurelia Farmer, star of *Free Time*, and her boyfriend, fêted novelist Alastair Costello, tell us why it's time to make their mark on Hollywood.'

OK.

He had his arm wrapped around her shoulder, a goofy smile on his face; she, in a blue chiffon top, was staring back at him. She was so beautiful, with curly blonde hair and bright blue eyes. Nothing like Natasha with her highlights and starved body. If Natasha were a man she knew which one she'd choose. It would be no contest.

'We've been together four years now and we think it's time to try our luck on the other side of the pond [she read]. I've had a few meetings in New York and LA recently and everyone tells me I could really make a go of it. I figure you only get one shot. I don't want to be tortured for the rest of my life with what-ifs.'

'**What about you, Alastair? How do you feel about leaving Britain?**'

'I'll miss HP sauce. And Marmite, too. But I'm an artist. I can work anywhere. I suspect the US will provide me with a lot of inspiration. And it's really important for Aurelia to show the world what she's made of.'

'**So when are you off?**'

'In the next month. At first we're going to rent in New York, until we've decided which coast we like best. I've always been a bit

438

wary of Hollywood, but now I've started work on a TV script I've been thinking the film business could be where it's at.'

She read it again, through misting eyes. Her phone started ringing. 'Hello?'

'Tash, it's Sophie. Listen, I just wanted to warn you. In *Hello!* this week—'

'It's all right. I've seen it.'

'Oh.' Sophie sounded scared. 'And what are you going to do?'

'I'm going to go ballistic,' Natasha said.

Of course, his mobile was switched off.

'Alastair, I believe you're back from Thailand. I would very much like to talk to you. You know what about. As soon as you get this message please call me.'

Once she would have worried about the frost in her voice. But no longer.

And once she would have fretted when he didn't call back and steeled herself not to call him again. But today she simply waited until six, then tried again.

'Alastair, it's Natasha. If I don't hear from you within the hour, I'm going to have no choice but to go round to Aurelia's place and ask her where I can find you. So please call back.'

She had no idea where Aurelia's place was. But the call came in minutes.

'Hi.' He sounded nervous.

'Hello, Alastair.'

'So you saw that stupid article?' he said resignedly.

'I hope you were paid well for it.' Oddly, she felt giggly, light-headed almost.

'Aurelia insisted on it. Said it would be good for her career. It didn't seem like too much to do for her.'

'Does it seem like too much to do to move to New York without telling me?'

There was a pause. 'I think we'd better talk,' said Alastair Costello.

He arrived at hers, tanned and glowing, just before eight. Of course she'd spent the past half-hour brushing her hair, checking her make-up and changing her outfit. But for once it wasn't so he'd rip them off her in a fit of passion. It was so he'd see what he was losing.

'Hi,' she said as he walked in the door.

'Hi.' He didn't make eye contact.

It was the moment to offer wine, beer, Belgian chocolates, oral sex. But no more. 'So were you going to tell me you were moving to America?' she said. Pleasant but cool.

'Of course I was,' he snapped, sitting on the sofa. 'I wasn't expecting that article to go in so quickly. We gave the interview before I went to Thailand.'

'Were you going to tell me you were still with Aurelia?'

'We weren't still together. I swear. We split up and it's just recently we started talking again and we decided to give it another try. I went to Thailand to try and get my head round it all.'

'But you forgot to tell me that?'

'Noodle,' he said, looking pained. 'I didn't forget. I was going to tell you. Talk to you. But it's been so difficult for me.' He looked at her mournfully. 'I've been torn.'

'Yes. It must have been very hard.'

'I want to be with you,' he said.

'Really?' Her tone remained icy, but to her annoyance her heart gave a little leap.

'But it's impossible,' he said. 'You see, Aurelia's pregnant.'

She felt like she was falling from a great height.

'Right,' she said. 'Well then, congratulations. Although I thought you said you never wanted children.'

'I did. And I meant it. But . . . I've been thinking about it and I've come round to the thought that a mini-me could be rather nice. Someone to look after me when I'm old, you know . . . And anyway, I couldn't abandon Aurelia. She's so fragile. Not like you. You're a tough cookie. An independent woman. You can look after yourself.'

'Yes,' Natasha said. 'Yes I can. So could you please go now?'

'Oh Tash.' He reached out to her. He looked as handsome as he always had. 'Don't be like this. Come on. We're friends, aren't we?'

'Yeah,' she said. 'We're friends. Which is why you'll listen to me when I say I want you to go.'

He looked at her nervously, judging whether she'd cry or make a scene. She should, she knew, because that was what he really hated. But she just couldn't bring herself to show so late in the game that she cared.

'I think you should go,' she said. 'I've got someone coming round in a minute.'

'OK,' he shrugged. 'But . . . I mean, I'll keep in touch. I'd love still to see you.' He gave her a sly glance. 'It worked before. Is there any reason it couldn't now?'

So this was what it came down to. She was being offered

a time-share in Alastair Costello. 'Sorry he's fully booked for the summer months, but honestly he can still be very pleasant in October, although you will need a cardigan at night.' But then what else had they ever had?

'I don't think so, Alastair. I think we've seen enough of each other. Of course, we'll still have to work on that script together, but don't worry. Since you'll be in the States it'll be mainly conference calls. Now goodbye.'

Of course she cried after he'd gone. But she didn't cry for losing Alastair, she cried for the baby she'd been unable to hold on to, maybe because it sensed her life was in too much of a mess to cope with it. For the baby she now knew she wanted and needed to start trying for sooner rather than later. For her old, glittery life which had been such a blast and which now would never completely satisfy her again.

And then, after an hour, she picked up the phone and called Sophie. Voicemail.

'It's finished,' she said. 'But don't worry. I'm going to be OK.'

She put down the phone, picked it up again and called Andy.

53

Sophie had woken that morning after only two hours' sleep, a tornado whirling in her stomach. She dashed to the en-suite bathroom and watched last night's prawn crackers mingled with bucketloads of beer, champagne and vodka disappear down the pan. Crawling back into bed, sweaty and weak, she heard Olly sighing. Bastard, she thought furiously. How dare he turn up on her doorstep like some kind of gaoler and drag her off? But her fury was mixed with guilt. Oh God, she had tried to kiss Dom. Suppose he had kissed her back. Olly would have caught them at it in the back of a taxi. And how would she ever face Natasha again, knowing she'd jumped on her colleague? And what if Fay and Keith and everyone talked and it got back to Olly and . . . ?

She fell back asleep and next thing she knew she heard a clinking beside her. It was Olly carrying a tray and bending over her. 'Darling?'

'Hello,' she said warily.

'I've brought you breakfast. Darling, I'm sorry about last night. I was a bit OTT, but I was just so worried about you. I care about you so much and I thought you might have been kidnapped or—'

'Oh Olly.' Wretchedness engulfed her again. 'What time is it?'

'Nine. So we really should be off to work quite soon.

443

But I knew you'd want something to eat and . . . I know I'm not a cook, but . . .'

The tray contained a glass of OJ (good), a cup of tea (ridiculous, she always drank coffee in the mornings, hadn't Olly noticed?) and two slices of burned toast with butter scraped across them and a pot of marmalade. Sophie hated marmalade.

All the same . . . Andy had never done such a thing for her in her life.

'Oh sweetie, that's so thoughtful.' She took a sip of juice. 'You couldn't just run down and get the Marmite pot, could you?'

'Oh. I just finished the Marmite. Threw it out.'

Never mind. It was still a very sweet gesture.

She was at her desk by 10.30 a.m. Half an hour later, the flowers arrived.

Dom, she thought instantly, flushing deeply. But then she read the note. 'Sorry for being such an ogre. It's just because I love you so much. Your Olly x'.

She got up and dashed to the loo to dry retch. She examined her greenish face and red eyes in the mirror and shuddered. Back at her desk she called Olly to thank him.

'Let's have dinner, just the two of us. I know you're hungover, so we'll go somewhere quiet,' he said.

God, he was good to her. Sophie felt so spoilt. How could she even feel the tiniest hint of dissatisfaction?

The early morning throw-up seemed to have dulled the hangover and the bacon sarnie she had at 11.15 with a Diet Coke more or less put paid to it.

Fay, on the other hand, was in a terrible state. 'Never

again,' she kept groaning. 'Never, ever, ever. Why did you let me go off with Norris, Soph? Why?'

'What time did you get in?'

'Seven. I've had no sleep at all.' Being twenty-five, she still looked infuriatingly rosy-cheeked and dewy.

'But, Fay . . . you didn't . . . ?'

'Course not,' Fay snapped, quite obviously lying. 'He's old enough to be my father.'

Normally Sophie would have seized on this fine opportunity to take the piss, but today she knew that she was living in a glass house and that Fay had a boulder aimed straight at it. So she cast her eyes back downwards, while the video in her mind played and replayed last night's events. The way she'd felt when Dom had looked at her, the warmth of his thigh next to hers in the cab, the singe in her loins when she'd leaned forward to kiss him. But then he'd pushed her away. When she'd been so sure he felt it too. Damn. What was happening to her? Why didn't any man want her except Olly?

You can't marry someone just because he wants you.

'Oh, bog off,' she muttered to her conscience.

But she couldn't stop thinking about him. Dom, Dom, Dom – it banged in her head like the chimes of Big Ben. He wasn't classically good looking, just like Tash had always said, but he had that big chest and wide shoulders and that smile and . . .

She thought she might just ring Tash. It couldn't hurt, could it? Of course sometimes Dom did pick up her phone when she was out, but that wasn't the reason she was trying, she just wanted to see how she was doing. As any good friend would.

It rang and it rang, then: 'Rollercoaster.' Bollocks. It was that annoying Emilia.

'Hi, is Natasha there, please?'

'I'm afraid she's in a meeting. May I take a message?'

'Yeah, tell her Sophie called, please.'

'Sophie who? And may I have your number?'

'It's Sophie who calls her every day and she knows my number.'

'Yes, but just in case . . .'

Sophie really wasn't in the mood for this. As she dictated her number, which bloody Emilia must know off by heart by now, she glanced down at this week's copy of *Hello!* keen for some distraction. J-Lo on one page. She turned to the next . . .

Oh shit!

'Never mind the message, Emilia. I'll call her on the mobile.'

Natasha's troubles threw Sophie's into a completely new perspective. Damn that bastard Alastair. How dare he do that to her friend? How could he choose that actress bimbo with the too-big head over her? Sophie's mind sizzled with revenge fantasies. She'd reveal him to the *Sun* as a supercad, like John Leslie or James Hewitt. His book sales would stop abruptly and Aurelia would leave him. Except it probably wouldn't work that way, he might end up even more famous than he was already, making appearances on *Celebrity Big Brother* and with a column in *Hello!*

Once again she reappraised her own situation. It was time she pulled herself together and appreciated Olly for what he was: a kind, devoted man who would never pull a stunt like this on her. Not that Aurelia Farmer would have Olly. The very thought made her giggle.

That night they sat in J. Sheeky, Sophie sipping orange juice and devouring a plate of chips to soak up the hangover. People stopped continually at their table. *Olly's the man to know. Without him at my side, there's no way I'd be sitting in here.*

'So, I was thinking,' he said, polishing off the last of the bottle of claret. 'Honeymoons. Never too early to organize one. What would you like, my darling? I want it to be the holiday of your dreams.'

This was more like it. 'Oh, I don't know. I haven't really thought about it.' Actually her middle drawer at work was full of Kuoni brochures and *Condé Nast Traveller*s but she couldn't really admit that.

'I was thinking somewhere like the Shetlands. Get away from it all. Nothing but the sound of seagulls crying and the waves breaking on the shore.'

'Oh. Right.' Sophie popped another fat chip in her mouth. 'It might be a bit chilly, don't you think, at Easter?'

'I suppose. I'm not wild about the heat though, darling, you know. Brings me out in a rash.'

All Sophie wanted was a five-star hotel. With a private plunge pool. And maybe a private beach as well. And a pile of paperbacks. And a waiter bringing her cocktails. And Dom on the lounger beside her, undoing her bikini top and . . .

Where the hell had that come from?

'There's such a thing as air-conditioning,' she told her fiancé. 'And shade. I do want a break from the British weather.'

'I understand, darling.' He reached across and took her hand. 'How about India? I'd love to explore the history of the Raj. Stay in some old Maharajahs' palaces.'

'India might be possible,' she said dubiously. 'Maybe with a week in Goa.'

'I'm sure that could be arranged.'

Sophie should have felt happier about this. But she still felt weirdly flat, like a pair of JP Tods. It must have been the hangover. Nothing, of course, to do with the fact that every time her eyes flickered shut, even for a second, she could feel the warmth of Dom's hand on the small of her back as he'd steered her towards an empty table.

'What are you smiling at?' Olly asked fondly.

It was like being jerked awake by the alarm. 'Nothing,' she said hastily. She held out her hand. 'Just thinking how lovely it is to be here with you.'

At that same moment, Natasha and Andy were lying next to each other on the big, white bed. 'I can't believe we just did that,' said Natasha.

'I can't believe you're talking like you're in some made-for-TV movie.'

She giggled. Then: 'It's not funny. You're Sophie's boyfriend.'

'Not any more I'm not.'

'But what would she say?'

'Good luck to you. Sophie's with someone else now, Tasha.'

'But she doesn't love him.'

'She doesn't love me.' He reached out and stroked her

448

cheek. 'And I certainly don't love her. It's OK. I promise you, it's OK.'

Natasha lay staring at the ceiling. Guilt about Sophie was mingling with a lumpy certainty in the pit of her stomach that if her prettier friend just snapped her fingers Andy would come running back. Of course she wouldn't say anything. That was how she worked. She'd play it cool.

'Are you OK?' Andy asked.

'I'm fine.' But then she heard herself saying. 'I don't want to be your second best.'

There was a silence. *Oh fuck, I've blown it. I've blown it.* Then Andy rolled over on to his elbow and looked her in the eye.

'And I don't want to be yours.'

'What do you mean?'

'Well, Alastair. You're still hung up on him, aren't you?'

It was like a light had gone on within her head. She hadn't thought about Alastair from the moment Andy walked through the door. 'No. No, I'm not.' She'd never been so clear about anything. 'I promise, Andy. Alastair was like . . . measles or something. I had it badly, but you can't catch it twice.'

They both laughed softly, then another thought came to Natasha. 'But you think I'm Switzerland.'

He turned to look at her, puzzled. 'I what?'

'You think I'm Switzerland. You said so. When we played that game all those years ago.'

'Oh, so I did,' Andy said with a laugh, as he pulled her very close to him. 'My favourite country. Do you know how beautiful it is up in the mountains? Or down by the lake. And the skiing.' He whistled softly to himself. 'We'll have to go some time.'

'But you're off to Cairo soon,' she said, overcome by a sudden bleakness.

'I haven't decided about Cairo yet,' he said gently. 'So for now, why don't we just live for the moment?'

54

Going to bed with Andy had seemed so natural, so perfect, that it wasn't until the following morning when he'd got up at six for a job in Leeds, kissed her gently on the eyelids and disappeared out of the door, that the full realization of what Natasha had done set in.

Oh my God, she'd been naked with Andy and muttered passionately and gazed gooily in his eyes without it even occurring to her to burst out laughing. There'd even been some very rude squelching sounds when she'd been on top of him. What must he have thought of her stretch marks? Her pancake boobs?

It had all started so suddenly. One minute she'd been telling him about Alastair, but laughing about it, rather than crying, the next he'd reached out to touch her and for a moment she'd frozen. Then suddenly, like the reflex action when your knee is tapped, her arms had shot out and coiled around his neck. Her hands were moving about all over his body and then she was brazenly taking him by the hand and leading him to the bedroom.

Oh, he must think she was such a slut.

Though in the bedroom, the sluttiness had evaporated spectacularly. She knew she ought to rip off her clothes, grab the Agent Provocateur riding crop from under the bed and beg him to spank her, but suddenly all she wanted

451

to do was sit on the edge of the bed and hide her face in her hands.

'I'm so nervous,' she confessed.

'I'm so nervous too,' he said, sitting down beside her.

But then they had started kissing again, and quickly, indecently so, the nerves were rushed away in a flood of desire. Before she knew it they were naked and not laughing at each other's wobbly bits at all, but licking them, sucking them, stroking them. The pressure she had always felt with Alastair to perform like a porn star had disappeared; she had just done what she wanted to do.

Which means he had probably *hated* it. He'd probably been thinking about Sophie throughout. Sophie had always been prettier than her, sexier, more vital. She was a nicer person too. Look at how she'd taken care of her over the past few weeks. And this was how Natasha had repaid her: by sleeping with her ex, her ex with whom – she was pretty sure – Sophie was still in love.

But Sophie's mind was very far from Andy. Instead, it was focused fully upon Dom. When she went to Pret in her lunch break he was standing beside her telling her to treat herself and have an almond croissant. At the gym he was on the next Stairmaster, pointing out the absurdities of the MTV video. Every time the phone rang, she jumped, then grew twitchy when it was Olly, Mum, Olly again. Never Tasha. Tasha was oddly silent. Oh God. Maybe because she knew about her and Dom? That had to be it. And Tash was in love with him too. She must be. Who wouldn't? And Tash would win him because Tash was so sophisticated and glamorous with her amazing career and Sophie was just a secretary/future Tory wife.

At work the following morning it took her an hour to crack. She picked up the phone and dialled Tash's mobile.

'Natasha Green.'

She slammed the phone down, heart thudding. What could she say: 'Is Dom there? Does he look lovestruck? Will you tell him I fancy him?' But she had to find out something. Try again.

'Natasha Green.' This time she sounded a bit annoyed.

'Hey, it's me.'

'Oh! Hi!' It wasn't Sophie's imagination, Natasha sounded wary. She knew! Dom had probably had their entire office in hysterics at her tarty behaviour.

'How are you?'

'Fine!' There was definitely a nervous sharpness to Natasha's voice. 'You?'

'Fine.' There was a nasty pause. Oh God, they never spoke to each other like this. It was so obvious what was going on. 'So, what are you up to today?'

'Me? Oh! Well, it's meetings, meetings, meetings, basically. We're putting together this new police series and there's tons to do. It's amazing you caught me actually.'

'But it sounds like it's not a good time. Shall I call you back later? Then we can chat properly.'

Natasha sounded relieved. 'Yes, yes. Why don't you do that?'

So Natasha was going to be in meetings all day. This was the information she wanted. Mind you, Dom might be in meetings too. Or he might be on a Caribbean cruise with his long-term lover. But she had to keep trying.

Five times in a row, she got sodding Emilia. 'Hello, Rollercoaster?' Click. Dial tone. 'Hello, Roller—' 'Hello, Ro—' 'Hello—?'

Bollocks. The girl was doing her job way too efficiently. She'd have to wait until lunchtime to get a chance.

'Coming to the canteen?' Fay asked. Norris had come back to her house after work again last night and she radiated a no-sleep, lots-of-sex glow.

'No, I'm waiting for the Channel Four press office to call. They've got some info we desperately need.'

'What, Michael Hevers?' interrupted Yvette. 'No, he called me half an hour ago. That's all sorted. You can go.'

'No, there's some other stuff I have to do.' Sophie fished around. 'I have to ring Natasha. Her life's full of dramas right now and she can only chat properly at lunchtime.'

'Fair enough,' Fay shrugged.

'I'm free,' Yvette said hopefully as Fay's face creased in horror.

'C'mon then. We'll leave Sophie in *peace*.' She grimaced at Sophie. 'I'll get you for this,' she mouthed as Yvette eagerly grabbed her bag. Sophie smiled back sweetly.

The minute they'd gone, heart thudding, Sophie picked up the phone.

'Rollercoaster.'

At the sound of his voice her bones felt weak. She thought she would atomize into a million different pieces.

'Rollercoaster?'

'Oh. Uh. Is Natasha there, please?'

'No, she's gone to lunch.' A different tone came into his voice. 'Is that Sophie?'

'Yes, yes it is.'

'Hi, this is Dom.'

'Oh, hello. How are you?' Her voice sounded squeaky and as if it was coming from far away.

'I'm very well. I've been wanting to talk to you.'

'Oh. Really?' *Breathe, Sophie, breathe.*

'Yes. I wanted to say . . . I was sorry about the other night. I didn't want to push you away like that. I wanted to kiss you. So much. But I know you're engaged to someone else and . . . I can't do that. I can't be second best. But I just wanted you to know that you're the most perfect woman I've ever seen.' The last bit came out all in a rush.

'Oh.'

'I know you were drunk. I'm sure you're regretting what you did. But, as you know, nothing happened, so don't feel guilty. And I hope you're very happy with your fiancé. I hear he's quite a big shot.'

'He is.' Sophie felt like her heart was being wrapped in barbed wire.

'Then the best of luck.' There was a beat, then he said, 'I'll tell Natasha you called.'

'No, no! Don't do that! I'll ring her on her mobile.'

'Goodbye, Sophie. Like I say, I'm glad I got the chance to talk to you.'

'Goodbye.'

That night Sophie and Olly had dinner with the Braxton-Smythes at Claridge's.

'We're getting so excited about the wedding,' said Vanessa. 'And then of course there's your book launch.'

Her voice was so penetrating, it made the cutlery clink. 'Have you set a date for that?'

'Well, publication's the first of December, so we were thinking that day, weren't we, darling?' Olly said.

Were they? Nothing Olly had said in the past couple of days had even vaguely penetrated her lovestruck brain. 'Yes, that's right.'

'And then the wedding at Easter? Although what will happen if they call an early election?'

'Well, that's why we still haven't one hundred per cent settled on a date,' Olly said, taking a swig of claret. 'Assuming I get selected, I'll be pretty busy canvassing and Sophie will be helping me, of course, so she won't have any time for the wedding arrangements and I know they're terribly important to you, aren't they, darling?' He patted her hand gently.

'How will I be helping you?' Sophie asked uneasily.

'Well, you'll be canvassing with me, won't you? Leafleting. Knocking on people's doors. Hosting drinks parties. With Sophie at my side I think I'll have a bit of an advantage over those Lib Dems, don't you, Philip?'

'Absolutely,' Philip barked.

'I should keep an eye on Olly if I were you,' Vanessa whispered in Sophie's ear. 'He's starting to look a bit chubby round the old tum-tum. That's your job as his wife, to keep him in shape.'

'I'm not his wife yet,' Sophie snapped.

Vanessa gave her a long, hard look. 'Are you suffering from pre-wedding nerves? I'd be more than happy to help you out.' She turned to Olly. 'Now, darling, you are giving Sophie all the support she needs, aren't you? Weddings can be scary things. Even worse than elections.' She patted Sophie's hand. 'I do hope he gets selected for Devonshire South. The schools in the area are excellent. It would just be glorious to be living down there, far away from everything. Don't you think?'

'Mmm,' Sophie said, thinking of her mother imploding from boredom. They might end up as neighbours. Could you imagine?

Back home, Olly made straight for the TV. 'We'll just catch *Newsnight*. Could you bring me a glass of whisky, darling?'

Sophie obliged. She sat beside him and watched him loosen his tie. A bit of white, hairless belly was escaping through his shirt. 'You need to keep an eye on how much you drink,' she said.

'How much I drink?' He turned to her, an outraged expression on his face. 'I'm just relaxing, darling. You know I have a stressful job.'

She tried a gentler approach. 'I know, but there are so many calories in alcohol. I should watch it too. We should cut down together.'

He looked at her, utterly wounded. God. Maybe she'd pushed this one too far. 'I'm sorry,' she continued, leaning forward and kissing him. 'It's just Vanessa's right. You've got to be looking your best for the voters. It's all about image these days.'

'My Sophie will give me the right image,' he said smugly. Then he put down his glass. 'But you're right. I should keep an eye on things. Maybe my Sophie could find out about a personal trainer for me. For us. We could work out together.'

Sophie had always longed for a personal trainer, but the thought of jogging round the park with Olly made her feel faintly hysterical. 'I'll see what I can do,' she said, trying to force a smile.

Olly leaned over and kissed her. 'That's what I like to see. A happy Sophie.' He kissed her neck. Then he stroked her hair. *Here we go.* Yes. Sure enough, the next move was a hand on the thigh. 'Mmm. You smell lovely, darling.' Move three. Hand up skirt to fumble with tights. How come when he mauled her she felt absolutely nothing, but when Dom had touched her a thousand volts had gone through her?

'Shall we go upstairs?' he asked.

'Why?' Sophie snapped. 'What's wrong with the sofa? Or the floor?'

'Oh darling.' A look of pain crossed his face. 'I don't know. I think bed would be more comfy, don't you?'

'OK. We'll go to bed.'

Upstairs, Olly began neatly removing his clothes.

'Don't do that!' Sophie suddenly screamed as he turned to the wardrobe to hang up his jacket. 'Show some passion! Chuck your things on the floor.'

Olly turned to her. 'But, darling, they'll only have to be picked up later.'

'Can't you be at all spontaneous?'

He looked as if she was about to hit him. 'OK,' he said meekly and began dropping his clothes one by one on to the floor. Sophie did the same thing, then turned to see him climbing under the duvet.

'Today we're going to try something different,' she said, climbing on top of him.

Olly looked terrified. 'Are you sure, darling?'

'Yes,' she snapped. 'It's time for a change.'

But being on top was a bad idea. He was soon whispering and groaning, but Sophie found herself having to work much harder than normal, rather than just lying there and thinking about the reception and her dress and the *Tatler* photographs.

'We should do it again like that,' he whispered, when – after what seemed like for ever – she climbed off him.

'Mmm. Yes.'

Luckily, quickly, he was snoring. Meanwhile Sophie lay there and thought. Thought about how Dom had said she was the most perfect woman he'd ever seen. But then Dom was a Lothario, like Julian, just in it for a quickie. Cold feet were normal, she told herself. Getting crushes on other men was probably normal too.

But somehow Sophie knew that even if this was just a crush, there would be another one and another after that. That there was no way she could stay with Olly for the rest of her life. That if she did marry him, at some point she would end up just like Mum embarking on one affair after another, in an attempt to be true to her real self, whom she'd lost sight of from the second she'd accepted Olly's proposal.

And Sophie knew what she had to do. She just needed to summon up the courage.

55

'Oh my God,' said Natasha. 'How hilarious is this?' She shoved the copy of *Harpers & Queen* under Dom's nose. 'Recognize anyone?'

'Yeah,' said Dom, frowning at the page of posh people at a party. 'It's your friend Sophie.'

'She'll be in her element.' Natasha giggled as she read the caption. 'The Kensington and Chelsea annual summer drinks party. Well, I guess it's what she always wanted.'

'Is it?' Dom sounded very serious. Natasha looked at him, surprised.

'Well, I think it is. When we were at school, she always used to moan about what a dump it was and why did we have to hang out with boys from the comprehensive rather than the boys from Eton where Marcus went. She's always wanted to be posh and now she is.'

'Sounds like a weird ambition to me.'

'Are you OK?'

'Of course I am, why shouldn't I be?'

'I dunno. You just sound sort of . . . scratchy.' But before she could probe further, her phone rang. 'Hello? . . . Oh, hello.' Her voice dropped. 'I'm fine. You? . . . Mmm, hmm . . . Mmm.'

Recently, Natasha had been having a lot of these conversations. She knew Dom eavesdropped on them, but she didn't care, she was so happy. She might have carried on cooing all morning, but Antoinette stuck her head round the door and waved vigorously.

'Natasha, Barney needs to see you now.'

She sounded odd. Natasha looked up. 'Andy, I'm going to have to go. Some work thing. Yeah, OK. I'll see you later. Yes, I can't wait.'

Barney was sitting at his desk, filling in a Sudoku puzzle.

'Wow, are you sure your intellect's up to that?' Natasha joked. She didn't often cheek Barney but she was in such a good mood.

He didn't smile though. 'Sit down, Natasha,' he said.

A few hours later, Natasha and Andy were lying draped round each other. 'I can't believe it,' she was breathing. She should have felt angrier, but somehow Andy's presence blocked those kinds of emotions.

'And you really didn't see this coming?'

'Of course not. I've been working for Barney for nearly nine years now. And this is how he rewarded me.'

She thought back to the scene. Barney, not even looking embarrassed, explaining that cuts were being made, the drama department needed freshening up, so with great regret he was going to have to let her go. On a fantastic pay-off, of course. And of course they'd tell the world that she'd resigned. And no hard feelings, he had the fondest regard for her, blah, blah, blah.

'But I've worked so hard for you, Barney,' she said, her face bleached with shock.

'I know, darling, and I love you and appreciate it. But we think you and the company would respond better to fresh challenges.'

'But I've won you all these awards. Brought so many amazing writers on to the team . . .' She stopped. She knew what this was about. 'Has Alastair Costello said something?' she asked slowly.

Barney's face was a picture of innocence. 'Alastair Costello? Well, he might have mentioned that he didn't find you that easy to work with. And he is a big, big name. And the draft of the script he emailed me yesterday looks amazing. And his acting contacts mean I think he might be able to persuade some serious names to come on board.'

Barney knew. Had Alastair told him? Or had he known anyway? Whichever. In the end, Natasha was the grafter and Alastair was the star. And the star's needs would always come first.

'You're great, Natasha, but to be honest, you haven't really been yourself recently. You've been so dreamy. Forgetful. Like I say, I think you need a new challenge. So, no hard feelings, darling. You and I will still be best friends.'

'You'll walk into another job,' Andy assured her now.

'I don't know if I will. Everyone will know I got the boot. Anyway, I don't know if I want to. No one makes quality stuff like Rollercoaster. And why devote all those years to a company when on a whim they can just hang you up to dry?'

'Then maybe you should do something different,' Andy said, tracing his finger along her arm. Despite herself, she shivered and the events of the day seemed suddenly un-important.

'Hey,' she tried feebly. 'Enough of that. We need to get

dressed if we're going to make the film.' Natasha had insisted that despite her sacking, she and Andy would carry on as before with their plans to go to the cinema.

'I'm not sure you should get dressed,' Andy said seriously. 'You've had a shock. In fact, as your doctor I would advise serious bed rest.'

'Would you now?' she said, laughing, flicking her bra at him. 'Funny, because I feel perfectly healthy.'

'Excuse me, but you are in no position to judge.' He stood up, cleared his throat and put on his most pompous voice. 'I think a thorough medical examination would be in order before you can be permitted to leave the house. Which I do not think will happen this evening.'

'Andy! What about the film?'

'Fuck the film,' he said in his normal voice and pushed her back on the bed.

At Olly's they were having a night in too.

'God, that was good,' he said, pushing away Sophie's pork casserole. He glanced at the grandfather clock in the corner. 'Couple of hours until *Newsnight*. Shall we watch a DVD?'

'That could be fun,' Sophie said.

He started flicking through his pile. 'Something jolly tonight, I think. End of a long week and all that. And my Sophie still seems a bit down in the dumpsters.'

She smiled weakly.

'I know,' he said triumphantly, fishing through the pile. 'How about this one?' *Monty Python and the Holy Grail.*

Sophie groaned inwardly.

'It's bloody funny.'

'OK, then,' she said.

They sat on the sofa. Olly pressed *play*. John Cleese, Terry Jones and co. crowded on to the screen, dressed in silly costumes, talking in silly voices. Olly chuckled. Sophie looked at him so innocently sitting there and was overwhelmed with the desire to scream the place down. This was going to be her life.

'"Where'd you get the coconuts?"' He was speaking along with the screen. '"Found them? In Mercia? The coconut's tropical!"' He gurgled with laughter. He turned to Sophie. 'Lord, this is a classic.'

'Olly,' she said. 'Maybe we could watch something else?'

'"The house martin or the plover may seek warmer climes in winter, yet these are not strangers to our land?" Ah, ha, ha. Mmm. What's that, darling?'

'I said: "Maybe we could watch something else?" I'm not really in the mood for Monty Python.'

'Oh, nonsense. Who could not be in the mood for the Pythons?' His eyes stayed fixed on the screen. 'I saw my old housemaster from Charterhouse today,' he suddenly said. 'Was saying it's never too early to get a nipper's name down. Even if it is still unborn.' He looked at her slyly.

'Olly, it may not be born for years. If at all. And anyway, I don't know I'd want to send a child to a school like Charterhouse.' Actually, Sophie had always dreamed of sending her children to a public school, and worried how she and Andy would be able to afford it. But if going to Charterhouse meant the baby would turn out like Olly she might have to think again.

'I was just saying,' he said huffily.

Something in Sophie's brain snapped like a twig. 'Olly, I'm going out.'

'Going out?' He peered at her, bewildered. 'But wherever to?'

'I'd forgotten. I said I'd meet Natasha for a late-night drink.' If Tash wasn't around, she'd call Caroline, or Fay, or Marcus, or someone. She just couldn't be in this house any more, sharing it with these looming, unpalatable truths.

'*A late-night drink?* Whatever for?'

'To talk. She's been through a lot lately.'

'Mmm. She's been a very silly girl.'

Something frighteningly close to hatred surged through Sophie's veins. 'She was madly in love,' she snapped. 'It makes you do funny things.' And grabbing her bag and keys, she stormed off into the hot night.

'I always fancied you,' Andy was saying. 'But I never got that vibe back. You always seemed so busy, to have so many friends. I was just another one of them. And anyway, you were . . . out of my league.'

'Out of your league?' Natasha laughed. 'Don't be silly.'

'So after a while I kind of gave up on you and then you had that dinner when you seemed to be almost pushing me towards Sophie and I thought: OK, time to cash in my chips. Natasha and I are clearly not meant to be and here's another pretty girl making a play for me.'

At the words 'pretty girl' Natasha felt that familiar coldness inside. Sophie was prettier than her. She was a fraud. 'Are you sure you don't want Sophie really?' She would never have asked Alastair such a question, but somehow with Andy the old rules no longer applied.

'Oh, change the record, Tash.' He laughed. 'It's all so silly, you banging on and on about Sophie. You know she never shuts up about you either. How chic you always look. How wonderful your life is. How inferior she feels when you talk about your job. She'd love to be you.'

'Sophie would? No. Don't be silly.'

'I heard it all for years. Drove me crazy.'

Natasha was still taking in this new fact when the door buzzed.

'Oh, cool. That'll be the pizza man.' Over the past fortnight, the I-cook-gourmet-meals façade had flown out of the window to be replaced by an orgy of takeaway Indians, Italians and Chinese.

A sheet wrapped round her, Natasha waddled over to the entryphone. 'Hello?'

'Tasha!'

It was like a bullet going through her heart. 'Oh! Hi!'

'Tash, I've had a row with Olly. Let me in.'

'I . . .' But then Natasha heard another voice.

'Hiya, Sophie, all right?'

'Hi, Stuart.' Her voice was louder in the intercom: 'It's all right, Stu's letting me up.'

'Oh, shit! Sophie's coming up! Shit!'

Andy leaped out of bed, pulled on his boxers, his jeans and his jumper. He ran towards the bathroom. 'Get dressed,' he hissed.

Heart sprinting, Natasha pulled on her pyjama bottoms and a T-shirt. There was banging on the door. 'Hello! Tash? Let me in.'

'Coming! Coming!' She raced to the door. 'Sorry. I was just about to get in the bath.'

'Sorry to bother you. I had to see you.' Sophie had a pale, set expression. She walked straight into the living room and sat down.

'God, what's happened?'

'I've had a fight with Olly. I'm so glad you're in. My mobile was out of juice and I had to talk to someone. Tash, I'm feeling wobbly. I think I should call off the wedding.'

Natasha hadn't been expecting this at all. 'Oh Soph, are you sure?'

'Not completely.' Sophie looked around despondently. 'But I don't see how I can go through with it. Olly gets on my nerves, Tash. I think he'll get on my nerves for the rest of my life.'

'Then you have to call it off,' Natasha said, as a cold voice whispered in her ear: *But then she might want Andy back.*

'But if I do I'll be back at square one. No man. Even more time wasted. And it'll be so embarrassing cancelling it. And Olly will be gutted.'

'He'll be much more gutted if you get divorced a few months down the line.' Natasha couldn't really concentrate. 'Listen, shall we go to the pub? I've got nothing to drink here and it looks like you need one.'

'I'd rather stay in.' Just then the buzzer buzzed again. 'Who's that? Oh God, do you think it's Olly? Did he follow me here?'

'I . . .' Fuck. The pizza man with a large Four Seasons and large Quattro Formaggi with a side order of garlic bread and four bottles of Corona. 'They must want Stu. I'll ignore it.'

Buzzzzzzzzz.

'Well, aren't you going to see who it is?'

'I . . .'

The phone started ringing. 'Hello!'

'Is that Ms Green? You have a pizza delivery man waiting outside.'

'OK. OK. I'll buzz him up. Shit,' she said to Sophie, 'I totally forgot. I ordered pizza when I got in. I was starving and . . .'

'Cool,' Sophie said as Natasha went to the door and overtipped the disgruntled pizza man. 'I know I should be grief-stricken and not wanting to eat, but I could manage an elephant.'

'Mmm.' How was she going to explain so much food? 'God, the idiots. They've sent two pizzas instead of one. I thought they'd charged me too much.'

'And a lot of beer,' Sophie observed. 'Blimey, Tash, that's spooky. Are you sure you didn't know I was coming?' She lay back on the sofa. 'I can't believe what I've done. I can stay here tonight, can't I?'

'Emm.'

Sophie picked up a beer. 'Have you got a bottle opener? Actually I'll just go to the loo first.'

'You can't!'

Sophie looked around, startled at her friend's tone. 'What do you mean?'

'It's broken. It's blocked. So . . . actually you can't stay here tonight. Not without a loo. Obviously. I mean, I wasn't going to stay here either.'

Sophie giggled. 'We could always pee in a bucket.'

'No. No. I was going to call Nikolai. See if I could stay there. You could too, I'm sure.'

'I'm sure I could fix it,' Sophie said. 'You know I've always been good at those kinds of things.' She started walking towards the bathroom. 'Maybe my new career should be as a plumber. They earn at least seventy grand apparently.'

'No! Don't go in there! It's . . . disgusting.'

Another curious look. 'I can cope. Have you got a plunger?' Her eyes darted around the room as if she expected to see a complete plumbing kit. Instead they fell on a clunky diving watch, sitting on the coffee table right next to the rug where Andy and Natasha had initially had sex.

'What is Andy's watch doing here?'

Time froze.

'It's not Andy's watch,' Natasha tried. 'It's mine. I – uh – was going to show you.'

Sophie's voice was steely. 'This is Andy's fucking watch.' She picked it up. '"AW and SM",' she read from the engraving on the back. 'It's the one I gave him the first Christmas after we started going out. What the fuck is it doing here?'

'I . . . He came round to look at the plumbing. He must have taken it off.'

'Then why did you say it was yours?' Sophie pushed past Natasha and opened the bathroom door. For a moment Natasha couldn't see him. Where had he gone? Had he found some secret doorway like Alice in Wonderland? Was he sticking to the roof like Spiderman?

'You bastard,' Sophie screamed and Natasha, coming in behind her, saw Andy standing there in the bath, one hundred per cent visible through the fibreglass shower screen.

'Hi, Sophie.'

'Why the fuck are you here?'

'I'd just popped over to visit Natasha.'

'And you didn't tell me?' Sophie's eyes narrowed. 'You hid in the bath. You two are shagging, aren't you?'

'No, no, we're not,' Natasha pleaded, just as Andy said, 'Yes, actually, we are. Do you have a problem with that?'

'I don't fucking *believe* it. How long has this been going on?' She turned to Natasha. 'I thought you were my friend.' Then her attention fell on Andy: 'You betrayed me.'

'Sophie, we were all over.'

'And it hasn't been going long,' Natasha begged. 'I was going to tell you but—'

'But what?' Sophie drew herself up to her not very impressive full height. 'I never want to see you again,' she spat at Andy. And then to Natasha: 'And you. You are dead to me.'

She stalked to the door. It slammed. And she was gone.

56

The following morning, Sophie was sobbing in one of Lainey and Marcus's spare rooms. Thank God they'd been in last night because there'd been nowhere for her to go. Even after the shock, Kensington seemed out of the question. Mobile dead, she'd rung Olly from a call box and told him she was staying at Natasha's. He'd not been pleased, but then her money had run out, so she was mercifully spared further argument.

She'd taken a taxi round to Mornington Crescent, but it was empty and – bloody cheek – the locks had been changed. But Lainey, just about to head off for a night's clubbing, opened the door, ushered her to a bed that smelled of L'Occitane lavender water and then called her friends to cancel.

'I can't believe it,' Sophie was snivelling down her borrowed Pacha T-shirt. 'My best friend and my boyfriend. Together. They betrayed me, Lainey. Betrayed me.'

'Well, you and Andy *had* split up. You *were* engaged to someone else.'

'Yes, but Tash *knew* it was rocky. She knew I might have wanted Andy back.'

'Well, Andy had a say in it as well.'

A bit more sympathy would have been nice. Sophie

wanted to cry some more, but the tears wouldn't come. Instead, she just stared bleakly into space. 'I've lost my best friend.'

'Tash is still your friend. Anyway, you've got me. And Marcus. Come on, cheer up. The Cross is having a warehouse sale today. Why don't we go to that?'

'I haven't got any money. Or a place to live if I leave Olly's.' She really hadn't thought this through. Perhaps she should just go back to him.

'You can live here,' Lainey said. 'I'd love to have some company with Marcus never around. And we've got, like, five spare rooms for the babies that are never going to happen. Well, at least not for a long time.' Her eyes flicked to the *In Style* open in front of her. 'Oh, look. "Eight body flaws and how to hide them."' She read on, frowning. 'But I don't have any of these.'

Sophie looked at Lainey, skinnier than ever, eyes sparkling bright blue, in her lace Temperley top and Puma pants. 'So how was Uruguay?'

'Oh, wicked. It's somewhere I'd never even heard of before, but it was full of the most beautiful people and the clubs . . .' For a moment, she was lost in a reverie, back dancing in a sea of foam on the other side of the world.

'I think Marcus took your going pretty hard,' Sophie tried gently.

Lainey's eyes were as hard as marbles. 'Marcus knew the kind of person I was before he married me. I don't know why he thinks a wedding ring might have changed me.'

'But you *were* a little bit different before you got

married,' Sophie replied. 'I mean, you and Marcus went on all those trips together and then you were so busy planning the wedding and you'd said you'd jacked in the class As.'

'Oh, for God's sake, I'm hardly an addict. I do class As maybe once a month. And it's hardly my fault if Marcus is never around and I have to make my own entertainment. Anyway, I like to think Marcus deserves more than a little wifey who sits at home and dreams up cordon-bleu dishes, like the women most of his mates are married to. I thought that was going to be me for about a week, but it was just so dullsville. And I have to say if you do marry Olly, I'd be seriously worried that that's what you'd become, Sophie. Another Sloaney Stepford wife, lost to the world.'

'Well, that's telling me.' Sophie laughed, although she felt as if she'd been kicked in the guts.

'Yeah, well, someone had to say it. I told Marcus he had to tell you, but he said it wasn't anyone's business except yours and no one could know what really went on in a relationship.'

'I think Marcus tried to tell me. But I didn't want to listen.'

'So you'll dump Olly,' Lainey said happily, picking at the cranberry varnish on her toes. 'Christ, I must get down to Bliss and have a pedicure.'

'I'll think about it,' Sophie said, flustered. 'But you know, he has been very kind to me.'

'Bugger "kind". He's not a nurse.'

'But that's why you're with Marcus, isn't it?' Sophie said, suddenly seeing attack as the best form of defence. 'Because he's such a good, reliable bloke?'

'Yes, it is. A lot of it's about that. But the difference between Olly and Marcus is that firstly, Marcus makes me hot and horny and whatever you say about Olly I don't think he does the same for you. And Marcus gives me my space, while Olly comes chasing after you when you have just one night out on the razz.'

'Yeah, but I had been a bit naughty,' Sophie sighed. She'd told Lainey about her night out, but omitted the encounter with Dom.

'A bit naughty, going to a club and getting rat-arsed! Sophie, what century are you living in? Girl power, sister.'

'But if I leave Olly, I'll be all alone. And . . .'

'And what?' Lainey said, looking at her with challenging blue eyes.

'And now I couldn't go back to Andy.'

'Babe, you'd lost Andy anyway. You hadn't loved each other for a long time. We could all see that. What you need, Sophie, is some time on your own to have a bit of fun, instead of love-leapfrogging.'

'Instead of *what*?'

'Love-leapfrogging. I read about it in *Elle* when I was waiting for the reflexologist. Always moving from one relationship to the next, because any man is better than none. That kind of thinking gets you nowhere fast.' Lainey yawned and looked at her watch. 'Shit, I was going to do some painting this morning. Still, it's more important to help out a mate.'

Sophie's mobile, which had been recharging overnight, beeped with a text. 'Oh help, I hope that's not Yvette.' She'd called in with a bad cold. 'Maybe it's Tash. Or Andy.

Or Olly.' So far, Olly had been completely silent. She looked. 'I don't recognize this number.' She peered at the message. 'Oh my God.'

'What?'

'It's from Peter.' In the maelstrom of the past twelve hours, she'd forgotten all about him. She peered at the screen. *Good news on researcher's job. They want you – no interview necessary! Start in two months – hope OK? Call me and we'll talk it through, Peter*

Sophie whooped so loudly they could have heard her in Uruguay. 'I've got the job, Lainey. I've got it. I don't have to be a secretary any more. I'm going to be someone! In television!'

She was so overwhelmed with excitement, it was another hour before she got back on to the subject of Natasha and Andy. And when she finally did, she realized to her great surprise that the hurt, which had been so raw last night, was already fading like a nettle sting, leaving nothing more than a faint rash. And even that would probably be gone by evening.

'No more *Daily Post*. No more Jiffy bags. I'm gonna have a real job. A career.'

'You're going to move out of that cow Veronica's place and make her pay you back all that rent,' Lainey agreed happily. 'You're going to be a cool, single girl about town. I'm so jealous.'

Pointless telling Lainey yet again that her life was perfect and Sophie would give anything to be her. And anyway, oddly, at this moment, with a broken engagement behind her and her ex in her best friend's arms, she was still suffused with a sense of well-being, a sense that there was no one in the world Sophie Matthewson would rather be than herself.

Before she could completely relax, however, there was just one more thing she had to do.

She called Olly and arranged to go to the house in Kensington after he finished work that night.

'But we have a drinks do at the Garrick,' he said.

'This is more important,' she replied and he didn't ask why.

On the way over the hill from Lainey and Marcus's, she felt like Marie-Antoinette en route to the guillotine. She walked down Kensington Church Street, mellow in the wavery evening sun, past the fish shop, past Kensington Place, past the lovely pub that did Thai food, past the pretty little boutiques and the courtyard full of ramshackle little restaurants like Maggie Jones, then on to Ken High Street with the chain stores and milling shoppers. Goodbye to all of that. She wouldn't be working here any more and she wouldn't be living here either.

He opened the door to her, his face a wooden block.

'Shall we go into the kitchen?' she asked. He nodded and she followed him in there. They sat at the table. 'Olly, I don't think we can get married,' she said straight away. 'I don't love you enough. We wouldn't make each other happy.'

Olly said nothing, just sat there looking very sad.

'So we're going to have to tell everyone the engagement is off,' she said very slowly, as if she were speaking to a child.

He nodded dumbly.

'I'm very sorry, Olly. But I don't think we're right for each other.'

'I do,' he said weakly.

'No. No. We're not. You'll see that in time. There's someone out there who'll be better for both of us. I promise.'

'But you're the most beautiful girl I've ever seen,' he said. He was trying so hard not to cry.

No, I'm not. I'm the most beautiful girl who's ever given you the time of day. 'Olly, there are many girls out there and you will meet someone wonderful. This isn't about you, it's about me.'

'There's someone else, isn't there?' he said, his face suddenly growing pinched and ugly. 'It's that Keith Livingston. I knew it.'

'There's nobody else,' she said almost truthfully. *Although I'd like there to be.*

'I bet it's fucking Keith.'

Olly never swore. 'It's not Keith,' she said. 'Now, Olly, I'm going. Here are my keys.'

'You can't give them back. You live here.'

'No I don't. I never did. Not properly.' She twisted at her finger and the ring slid off. 'You should have this back too.'

'Oh, no. No. It's yours.'

'It isn't. It never was. I had it under false pretences. It belongs to someone else, Olly. You just need to work out who she is.'

He reached out and grabbed her arm. 'But what about my interview with the selection committee?'

Was this some kind of joke? 'The selection committee?'

'Two weeks on Tuesday. I have to have you by my side,

Sophie. I'll be a laughing stock if they find out you've left me.'

Suddenly, her pity for him vanished. Instead, she just felt anger: anger at herself for having allowed this ridiculous charade to go on so long. 'Goodbye, Olly,' she said, kissing him lightly on the cheek. 'And good luck with finding another wife.'

'You never read my book,' he said suddenly.

This was when she wanted to cry. She turned around. 'No, I'm sorry. I did mean to.'

She picked up her bag and walked out of the kitchen, out of the front door and down the steps, back into her old life.

57

Three months had passed; it was a Saturday in December, one of those sublime winter days of electric blue skies and crisp air. On the steps of Marylebone register office, Lainey and Marcus stood, her resplendent in a vintage Pucci coat, him in a Paul Smith grey suit. In the crowd around them mingled Nikolai, Dom, Rita in daring orange and white and Jimmy blinking at the sight of all the London traffic roaring past.

There was Lesley in a purple dress from Next; Geoff looking weary; Paige and Vienna jumping up and down and asking if they could go to Hamleys later and choose Christmas presents; and Natasha's parents: Helen dewy-eyed in an unflattering pillbox hat and Christopher red in the face with pride.

'Here they come,' gasped Emilia as Natasha and Andy pushed their way out through the glass doors, followed by Sophie. Everyone was smiling goofily.

'Hooray!' Lainey shouted and confetti flew through the air. Natasha laughed as the crowd homed in on her. She was in a cream wide-legged trouser suit that Lainey had helped her pick out, and looked everything a bride should. Andy, also smiling in his suit, shook hands with everyone.

Sophie – in her £2,700 Beretskaya dress: she'd decided

no one would benefit if it just hung in the wardrobe – flapped around taking photos, brushing confetti off shoulders and straightening the hem of Natasha's jacket.

'She seems fine,' Marcus said softly to his wife.

'I told you she was. Her pride was shaken for about ten seconds when she discovered Andy was with Tasha but as soon as she thought about it, she realized they'd been all wrong together for years. And now she's thrown herself into being the best bridesmaid in the world.' Lainey reached out her arms to Natasha, who was approaching. 'My darling, a million congratulations.'

'Thank you,' Natasha said, pink-faced.

Marcus kissed her. 'Well done, my dear. And now it's off to darkest Africa?'

'I don't think Cairo counts as darkest. But yes, we're off as soon as we get back from honeymoon. Our stuff's already been shipped over. Then we have a couple of weeks before Mum and Dad are coming over for a month to see the Pyramids. The Nile. Promise you two will come too?'

'That'd be wicked,' Lainey said. 'Get some ideas for my jewellery.' Lainey had recently decided that being a painter was not for her and she should be a jewellery designer. She'd spent ten thousand pounds on a state-of-the-art silver press, which so far had sat unused in one of the spare rooms.

'So what are you going to do with yourself out there?' Marcus asked.

'I don't really know.' Natasha shrugged. 'I'll travel with Andy as much as I can, be his assistant. Learn the language. Then we'll see. I don't have to worry about money anyway. My Rollercoaster pay-off should see me good for at least a year.'

'But you don't have a proper plan?' Marcus threw back his handsome head and laughed. 'Natasha, that really is marvellous. It must be the first time since you were about five that you don't know exactly where you're going to be three months from now on Wednesday at 5 p.m.' He held out his broad hand. 'Andy, mate. Congratulations.'

Andy slipped his arm around Natasha and kissed her on the cheek. 'I think we ought to be making a move,' he said. 'Don't want the guests arriving at the reception without us there to greet them.'

'You're right,' Natasha said, turning to him and kissing him hard on the lips. They made their way down the steps to where the white Bentley that Andy had insisted on was waiting for them.

The reception was back at Natasha's now virtually empty flat. A small marquee had been strung over the roof terrace in case of rain, but it wasn't needed; in fact even the blow heaters were a bit redundant.

'Isn't this fun?' gushed Rita, popping a bonito sushi hand roll into her mouth. 'And doesn't Tashie make the most glorious bride?'

'She really does,' said Sophie, glancing around to see if Jimmy was anywhere in the vicinity, but he was on the other side of the room, talking to Nikolai. 'So you never really told me, Mum. What happened with Vernon?'

'Mmm. The sex simply wasn't up to snuff. I'm sure he's actually gay. You know what those Tories are like. And there's never any complaints on that score with

Jimmy.' Her black eyes rested lovingly on her husband's hairy neck. 'Was Olly a ghastly lay?'

'Mum!'

'I bet he was. You could see it in his eyes. Dead like a cod's.'

'You never said that at the time.'

'Didn't I? Well, I certainly thought it.'

Mum! You were virtually ordering me to marry Olly. There was no point in saying it. Mum would always be a flake. She glanced over at Andy's mum, who wore her usual snooty expression. She hadn't even acknowledged Sophie. Thank God she was out of that, Sophie thought, but poor Natasha.

She felt a hand on her elbow. 'Hi, Sophie.'

'Oh, hi, Dom.' She said it as casually as she could, as if she hadn't been tinglingly aware of his presence all afternoon.

'How are you?' he said, looking square at her. Sophie tried not to blush. In the past couple of months, once she and Natasha had ridden the Andy hump and – as a result – grown even closer, they had talked a lot about Dom. Tash had been honest: he had a good heart, but he did leave a string of broken hearts behind him, and the way he'd approached Sophie – first turning it on, then off – was a classic part of his repertoire. Mind you, the fact that Dom had rung Natasha up out of the blue just after she left Rollercoaster to tell her awkwardly that he really, really liked Sophie was definitely a positive sign, but Natasha thought it would still do her no harm to take it ultra-slow and keep other options open.

Once Sophie would have ignored the good advice and

blundered right in there, sure of what was best for her and – more importantly – eager to fill the hole in her bed. But recently she had changed. She still wanted a husband and babies, of course she did, but she wanted to have a bit of fun first. She wanted to get the hang of her new job, which was such a laugh and which was introducing her to dozens of new people, without feeling she had to rush home and play house for her boyfriend.

If she and Dom were meant to be, they were meant to be: that was her philosophy. He'd called her a couple of times since he'd heard about her broken engagement, but both times she'd genuinely been busy on the night he'd suggested going out so things had remained hanging promisingly, like cherry branches during a winter frost. One day they would break into blossom. Which wasn't to say she didn't feel very, very attracted to Dom as he stood there in front of her now.

'I'm really well,' she said, smiling. 'Loving my new job. And really excited about moving in here. I'm living in Dalston at the moment, but Tash says she wants me to housesit for as long as she and Andy are abroad. How about you?'

'Loving my new job too,' he said. 'I couldn't stay at Rollercoaster after the way they treated Natasha. But I walked straight into a new one. Head of drama for Cocorico Productions. Of course, Natasha could have had it if she'd wanted it.'

'But she's chosen to jack it all in and just be a wife.'

'Oh, I don't think she'll *just* be a wife. I can't exactly imagine Natasha bitching about the servants with her chums from the bridge club. She'll have probably sorted out the whole Middle East peace problem within a month of arriving.' They looked over at Natasha fondly.

'I hope she'll be safe,' Sophie said, suddenly panic-stricken.

'Course she will be. *News Mag* are providing body-guards. She'll have a ball.' He cleared his throat. 'I saw your ex-fiancé on telly last night.'

'Oh, was he on *Newsnight* again?' Olly was always being asked on telly as the voice of the young Tories. Sophie had come across him a couple of times when channel-hopping. At first she'd been racked with guilt at the sight of him but then Caroline had rung up and confessed they'd started seeing each other, so now all she felt was exasperation with herself for ever having got into such a situation.

'He was talking about his book that's just been published,' Dom was saying. 'Have to say it sounded quite interesting. I might read it sometime.'

'Good,' Sophie said. Their eyes locked.

'So . . .' they both said together and laughed.

'You first.'

'No, you,' she insisted.

'I was just wondering if we ever were going to have that drink . . .' he began, but then Sophie felt a bulky arm slide round her shoulder.

'Hello, stepsister.'

'Hello, stepbrother!' she said loudly. She did *not* want Dom thinking this was her boyfriend.

'Er, must just pop to the loo,' Dom said.

'Oh,' Marcus said. 'Did I interrupt anything?'

Sophie smiled. 'It's OK. He'll be back. So how are you, boy? How's married life?'

Marcus smiled ruefully. 'Well. Still not easy. We're still not spending nearly as much time together as we should be. And Laines is still going on her benders. But we've got a new joint project now, so I'm hoping that'll make things better.'

'Oh, yeah? What kind of project?' *Must be babies.*

'Yup.' He beckoned to Lainey, who was cackling campily with Nikolai. 'Tell Soph about our plan.'

'Oh, it's so wicked,' Lainey crowed, bounding over. 'We've bought this little cottage in Norfolk my friend Cassa told me about. It's a total wreck, but we're going to do it up and it'll be amazing. Miles from anywhere. Perfect place for me to work in peace. You can come and stay, Sophie.'

Sophie tried to ignore the vision of her being shown the attic room with the spinster's single bed. 'Sounds amazing. So how much time do you think you'll spend down there?'

'Oh God, every weekend, and I'll probably do a chunk in the week too. There's so much to be getting on with. I've got this great idea for knocking walls through to create a party space and I reckon we could build an infinity pool out the back, like my friend Hugo has at his place outside Barcelona.'

'But don't you need like a cliff for an infinity pool? And isn't Norfolk totally flat?'

'Oh, we'll get round that,' Lainey said, the familiar indomitable look in her eyes.

'And what about you, Marcus? Still planning on getting out of the bank?'

Lainey slipped her arms around him. 'He's going to.

We're just waiting for his next bonus. That should pay off a big chunk of the mortgage.'

'The mortgage on the Norfolk house needs paying too,' Marcus warned.

'Well, hopefully you'll get enough in the bonus to pay off some of that as well,' his wife retorted. 'If not it'll only take another year. And then you'll be free to follow your dreams. He's thinking of retraining to be a landscape gardener, aren't you, honey?'

'That's the plan,' Marcus said stoutly. *And Elvis will be the next King of England*, Sophie thought.

'Apparently there's a lot of money to be made out of landscape gardening,' Lainey said hopefully.

Meanwhile, Natasha and Andy had gone into her empty bedroom to enjoy a private moment.

'Imagine if we'd looked in a crystal ball at the beginning of the year and it had said that by the end of it we'd be married. Would you have believed it?'

'No,' she said. 'Of course not.'

'Well, we are. Mrs Walters.'

'Oi! Less of the Mrs Walters. It's Ms Green. Just like it always has been.'

'This time tomorrow we'll be on honeymoon.'

She grinned. 'In Switzerland.'

'In beautiful Switzerland. As the first snows start to fall.'

'I'm still not going skiing.'

'We'll see about that,' he laughed, bending over to kiss her.

'Hey! Enough of that,' bellowed Shacky, the best man,

opening the door, a child hanging from his arm. 'You've got to come out now. It's time for a toast.'

So they followed him back into the marquee, where everyone's glasses had been filled.

'Ladies and gentlemen, to the bride and groom.'

And all Natasha's friends clinked and chorused: 'To the bride and groom.'

FREE manicure or pedicure

worth up to £20 for EVERY READER

If you're always admiring your friends' ability to appear effortlessly groomed then we have the perfect pick-me-up for you.

We've selected the very best salons in the UK and organised a super-indulgent offer – guaranteed to leave you feeling sexy, glamorous and completely pampered.

Choose from either an immaculate manicure or a perfect pedicure and make sure *you're* the one turning heads on the beach this summer.

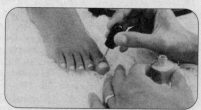

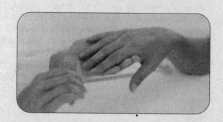

Maximum style. Minimum effort. Claiming your luxury treatment couldn't be easier – simply follow these easy steps

1. Buy this book from any Tesco store

2. Peel off the voucher from the front of the book and keep it safe

3. Call the offer hotline on 0870 444 1015 quoting the reference code on the card and your choice of treatment

4. Our concierge specialists will book your appointment at a salon near you

5. Enjoy your FREE manicure or pedicure